La Scrittore

The Lady Who Writes The Letters

A NOVEL

BY

JIM LACEY

Limited First Edition

482 / of 750

LINDEN HILL
PUBLISHING

Limited First Edition

Published in the United States

LINDEN HILL
PUBLISHING

11923 Somerset Avenue
Princess Anne, MD 21853
www.lindenhill.net

ISBN #0-9704754-3-8

Old Italian Saying:

L'amore fa passare il tempo,
Il tempo fa passare l'amore.

Love makes time pass,
Time makes love pass.

Jim Lacey

FOR

MY GRANDPARENTS,
MARIA AND ANTONIO

ACKNOWLEDGEMENTS

Bishop Library, Toms River, N.J.
Church of Jesus Christ Latter Day Saints Family Research Center,
Toms River, N.J.
Newark Public Library, Newark, N.J.
New Jersey Historical Society, Newark, N.J.
New Jersey State Archives, Trenton, N.J.
New Jersey State Library, Trenton, N.J.
Seton Hall University Library, South Orange, N.J.
United States Archives, New York, N.Y.
Youngstown Public Library, Youngstown, Ohio

A special acknowledgement to my cousin,

ANN MASUCCI

whose input and encouragement were invaluable.

Preface

It never occurred to me that I would ever write a book, let alone have it published; my experience has always been in commerce. I had a normal childhood. I was raised in Newark, New Jersey during the great depression of the 1930s. My family consisted of my parents and two siblings as well as many aunts, uncles, and cousins. I knew and loved my maternal grandparents, but that was not the case with my paternal grandparents. My father's mother died when I was less than two years old and I was told that my paternal grandfather died when my father was about two years old. So I never knew my father's parents and what little I did know about them was whatever I was told by my father and his two brothers and a sister. Still, I would, from time to time, ask about their parents. Invariably, whenever I asked about my paternal grandfather, I received only a short reply that he had been killed in a coal mining accident in New Castle, Pennsylvania. Then the subject of the conversation was always shifted to my paternal grandmother, whom my father and his siblings adored to the point of apotheosis.

When I retired in 1990, at the age of sixty-three, I purchased a computer and began to use it for normal everyday reasons, like e-mail, Internet surfing, financial management, etc. In 1995, through a very good friend, I became interested in genealogy and thought it would be a good hobby. I was fortunate enough to have had an aunt, my mother's sister, who had, over the years, become the family historian. When she passed away I inherited all of her records and using a computer program I learned how to fill in a lot of details she did not have. However, her records, for the most part, were only of my mother's family. Knowledge of my father's family was almost non-existent and by this time my father and his siblings had all passed away so there was no personal source of his family history available to me save what my mother knew, which was woefully little.

I began to think back to my formative years, trying to recall conversations I had with my father regarding his family and I realized how little he told me. Was his avoidance of the subject deliberate? Was something 'wrong' in the family? These ideas began to germinate in my mind. I also realized that I had been remiss in not having had more interest in these matters much earlier in my life. It was a mistake of omission, which I now regret. And what a mistake it was, because now that I was interested, there was no one to turn to except my mother.

So, starting from scratch, I began to trace my father's family history hoping to construct a simple family tree. I started, not surprisingly, at the public library. It was there that I discovered a set of volumes listing the ship passenger manifests of all emigrants from Italy from 1800 to 1900. I looked up my father's surname but could only find that of his older brother, immigrating into the United States in 1894, when he was just under four years old. It appeared that he was traveling alone because no one else on the ship had the same surname as his. I found it difficult to accept that a four year old was traveling alone from Naples to New York City in 1894. Then I noticed my grandmother's maiden name on the same manifest. My grandmother and uncle were on the same ship alone; there was no husband and she was registered under her maiden name.

What a find! That was it! Grandma was not married! At last I had found out the family's dark secret. Now I knew why my father and his siblings never talked about grandpa. I would later discover that on official documents it was the Italian custom to list a married woman by her maiden name, which, for the genealogist is a very helpful custom indeed. Armed with this newly discovered skeleton in the family's closet, I went to my mother and confronted her with my 'discovery'. At the time my mother was a very young ninety years old having been born in 1905. She knew I was working on the family tree. How she must have fretted over the possibility that I would uncover the truth. I am sorry for that.

The next time we spoke I got straight to the point. "They were not married," I exclaimed. I'll never forget the look on her face.

"Who told you!" she said to me with a look of shock and horror. I knew I had opened a Pandora's Box, but to my surprise, it was not the one I thought. Thinking she would tell me the truth about grandma and grandpa not being married, I pleaded with her to tell me the full story. Reluctantly, she agreed. I expected one story but she told me another, and because of this misunderstanding between us the hidden truth started to unravel. She began, not about grandma and grandpa not being married, but about grandma and her here-to-fore unknown lover who, in reality, was my father's father and therefore my biological grandfather! What a shock! Unfortunately, she did not know too much more except that my father was the son of this mystery man. She knew the man's surname but not his first name. I had literally stumbled onto the 'secret' and what a secret it was. I was stunned and incredulous. An insatiable desire for the details took hold of me and I became obsessed with the need to know more.

I started my search through the official documents available to me, and later on with people I located who knew part of the story, but this was only second hand and in some cases third hand information. As I plodded along, very slowly, a story began to unfold as I gathered data from many sources, even from as far away as Italy. It was a story that rivaled any

Hollywood movie ever made. There was tragedy, romance, murder, illicit love, adventure, and another here-to-fore unknown family, all documented by a paper trail that required detective work of the first order.

Still, I found it hard to accept what the data seemed to indicate until the day I found my father's birth certificate. It was not easy. It seemed like there was no record of his birth anywhere. However, in my research I became aware that on birth certificates that did not have a father's name, the document was filed alphabetically under the mother's maiden name. As the cynics are wont to say, "One always knows who the mother is." As incredible as it seems to be, the first letter of grandma's maiden name is also the first letter of her lover's surname. So I began to search the first letter of my grandmother's maiden name. Then, all of a sudden, there on the viewing screen, was my father's birth certificate, filed under his biological father's surname and listing my grandmother as his mother. The certificate had my father's first name. The birth date matched and the birthplace was the address where my grandmother lived with her legal husband! The find boggled my mind. I still shake my head in disbelief when I think about it. I remember sitting there for a long time looking at the screen, numbed by the realization that it was true. *Nonna* had a lover and he was my grandfather. Subsequently, I was able to determine that the affair went on for over thirty years, from 1897 until her death in 1929 at the age of sixty-four.

I began to compile the data in a chronological journal that I distributed to my cousins, all of whom were unaware of the surprising history. Some were upset but most accepted it and some were even grateful as they too had doubts regarding the 'official' family story. The history was so complex and intriguing that a desire to write a novel about it started to grow although I feared that anyone reading it might find it contrived and unbelievable. After all, it was the America at the turn of the century and we were still living with Victorian values, or so at least it seemed.

Mostly, the idea of writing the family history grew because I was trying to understand the personalities involved. I daydreamed about their relationships, their motivations, and their conversations. I knew facts, but that was not enough. I wanted to understand their personalities, to know what the circumstances were that changed their lives, leaving a paper trail of seemingly impersonal data that was hard to believe, yet undeniable. Who were these people? What were their emotions, fears, and anxieties? People are not automatons. They are not marionettes responding to the pull of strings manipulated by some unseen force. They act because of reasons, good or bad, thought-out or impetuous – they have choices. But unless a diary is kept, we can never know what they thought or what motivated their actions. In my obsessed desire to know what made them tick I began to fictionalize their lives based on the data I had uncovered and thus the book began to take shape.

It was obvious from the start that the emotions, fears, anxieties, and dreams of the central characters would have to be creations of my imagination. Not only that, but I also had to create some unknown characters and imagine some events which fit in with documentation in order to make the story hang together in a cohesive and chronological format. This historical novel is the result. Emotions, dialogue, and motivations, as well as many characters are figments of my unbridled imagination even though the central characters are actual historical entities and most of the events are true and follow an historical chronology that can be documented.

I experienced unexpected feelings of pleasure and a strong sense of accomplishment in the effort. It was hard work but it was a lot of fun and I am sorry it is over. I found that the detective work was exhilarating. Including the research, the project has taken over eight years to complete. I hope that the reader will take some enjoyment in the story in which fact and fiction are interwoven in history.

Chapter I

MARIANTONIA 1865

Mariantonia felt no lingering regrets about leaving her country. On the contrary, she was elated. *'It is Italy that has abandoned me,'* she reasoned as she stood there on the afterdeck, holding the hand of Raffaele, her three-year-old son.

The SS Alesia was built during the era of conversion from full sail to steam. It had one stack for the coal fired engines, but it still depended on the wind for auxiliary power. She looked incongruous with a single smokestack and three square rigged masts. Nevertheless, she was called a steamship and the sails were furled in preparation for leaving port under steam power only. The tall stack, jutting up between the foremast and the mainmast, was belching black smoke. Orders were being shouted from the ship's crew to the dockhands as the lines were cast off.

"Single up aft," was followed by the command, "Single up forward." The deckhands began hauling the lines aboard and then quickly the additional orders "Let go forward," and, "Let go aft," were shouted out. The last lines were hauled aboard as the ship began to ease away from the pier. That afternoon, November 25, 1894, the Alesia was sailing to America, leaving Naples on the afternoon tide. Aboard were hundreds of passengers, all emigrating from various parts of Italy to the New World. If all went well, the ship would make the trip in fifteen days, docking in New York City on December 10. They were starting off with good weather. It was unusually clear for late fall and the visibility was unlimited.

The ship steamed parallel to the long breakwater toward the mouth of the harbor into the *Golfo di Napoli.* Steering southwest toward the *Mare Tirreno,* her course lay between Sardinia and Sicily and then a western leg would take the ship into the *Mare Meditirreno.* Passing Sardinia, which lay to the north, and Tunisia to the south, the course would be due west through the Mediterranean Sea. In a few days the ship would traverse the Pillars of Hercules, those two headlands on either side of the Strait of Gibraltar, then out into the great expanse of the Atlantic Ocean. Leaving Europe to the north and Africa to the south, the crossing to New York would take eleven more days, depending on the weather.

Mariantonia was looking eastward toward the receding horizon. In the pre-dusk light she was able to see the entire port of Naples with *Il Vesuvio* looming ominously, 4000 feet high, to the south of the city. Usually, the tip of the huge, cone shaped volcano was shrouded in a thick cloud formation and could not be seen. But with today's clear skies she was able to see its smoldering peak and a thin ribbon of smoke rising skyward. She fleetingly thought of how awful it must have been in 79 A.D. when, in a cataclysmic explosion, it erupted and destroyed Pompeii and Herculaneum, smothering and burying alive most of the fifty thousand inhabitants in its scorching ash, all within a few hours.

Jutting out into the gulf, on an islet connected to the city by a causeway, she was able to see the ramparts of the old fort, *Castello del'Ovo.* While the Alesia was increasing its speed, the setting sun behind her, low in the western sky, had turned the city ablaze in gold. Her long chestnut hair blew around to her face and she repeatedly drew it back with her hand. She was taking in the entire scene as it unfolded in front of her in a spectacular panorama.

Mariantonia stood proud knowing that she was finally starting out toward a new life, a complete turnaround from what it had been. Her high cheekbones were pink from the nip of late fall and her full, red lips were slightly parted revealing a glimmer of white teeth. The wind made her eyes tear and she appeared to be crying but she was not. She was happy, almost ecstatic, her adrenaline flowing throughout her body from the feeling of renewal and anticipation.

She had never traveled more than a few miles from the small, mountaintop village of Pietramelara, where she had been born and raised. Now she was going to travel thousands of miles away from her hometown. It was more than a trip; it was going to be an adventure.

She and her young son had left Pietramelara at first light the day before. They arrived in Naples by train early in the afternoon. They were exhausted from the trip and her first concern was to find a room so that Raffaele could get a full night's rest. As much as she wanted to see the city at night there wasn't enough time. Sightseeing would have to wait until morning.

*****

"Get up Raffaele," she said, as she poked at his ribs to tickle him awake. The sun was beginning to rise and she wanted to see something of the city before they set sail in the afternoon, especially the section of the city called *Santa Lucia,* famous for its melodic song. She also needed to make arrangements for her trunk and suitcase to be sent to the docks. Arrival in America would be hectic and she also wanted to buy a Christmas present for Raffaele before they left Italy. She decided to wait until they were in America to buy a present for his fourth birthday in January.

2

Naples was abuzz with activity, even this early in the morning. She was forced to be very selective in choosing places to see. Time was not on her side. She had made a list of places to visit in the order of importance to her. Her first visit was to Piazza Dante, a wide semicircular area. Dante, the great Florentine poet, was her favorite. Whenever she thought of him she always fantasized herself in the role of his beloved Beatrice. At home, in the privacy of her bedroom, she would often stand in front of the mirror and imagine Beatrice looking exactly as she did. She would take a deep breath to accentuate her firm breasts and wish that Dante had been tall and could hold her tightly in his arms, her head barely resting on his shoulder.

The square is also called Piazza Mercatello after the large marketplace that has taken place there since 1588 A.D. The piazza was crowded and noisy, especially the market place. Local farmers were selling their produce, each one announcing louder than the other the different types of juicy, vine ripened fruits and vegetables they had to offer. Garment makers were all trying to get her to buy the latest cloth they had woven or the scarves they had brought from overseas, some all the way from India.

'*I can't believe all that I have missed out on,*' she thought to herself. '*But never mind, I shall never want for the excitement of a city again.*'

She found a small toy train, hand carved by a local woodworker, and paid for it while the gentlemanly vendor distracted Raffaele for her. She wanted it to be a surprise for him on Christmas morning.

Raffaele, clutching her skirt, let her know it was time to eat. She was hungry too so she located a small trattoria and they had their usual large noontime meal. '*It's better that we eat now. Who knows what kind of food we'll get aboard the ship?*'

After eating she once more read her list of places to visit. Frustrated that strolling through the marketplace had taken up too much of their time, she discarded the list. She thought it best to head toward the docks to be closer to the ship. They walked through the *Port'Alba*, the gate from the piazza into the most densely populated area of *Napoli*, on their way to the port area.

'*At least I'll be able to savor some of the daily life of the city.*' They had to rush now, there was no time left to squander in idle sightseeing.

The afternoon came upon them all too soon and by three o'clock they were through customs and aboard the ship. By four o'clock they were finally on their way. She and Raffaele were standing at the stern as they slowly left the port. Mariantonia was leaving Italy to join her husband in America.

As the ship steamed westward she had an unobstructed view of the harbor. To the north, on her left, the island of Ischia was fading into the horizon, and on her right, on the southern horizon, she could see the island

3

of Capri with its famous *Grotto Azzurro* and its towering mount called Anacapri. On the very top of Anacapri stood the palatial ruins of the Roman Emperor, Tiberius. The city itself sank into the *Mare Tirreno* and with it her former life.

'All these places that I've read about are gone from my sight within minutes and I will never see them again. But, che c'entra, never mind, they are all insignificant and useless to me now.'

She thought of the old Neapolitan saying, *'Vede Napoli; puoi mori!'* 'See Naples and then you can die'. It means that once you see Naples you will never be able to match its beauty anywhere else in the world.

But that was not true for her. She was Maria Antonia and was on her way to America to live with Giovanni, and for her that would be the most beautiful experience for which she could ever hope. Little Raffaele clutched her tightly, his arm wrapped around her leg. She looked down at him and wondered, *'What could the child be thinking? He has no concept of what brought him to this point in his life that had barely begun. Will he remember any of this?'* Her thoughts drifted back to the earliest memory she could recall. She could not remember being four. For her, the earliest memory was of her sixth birthday on July 15, 1871.

*****

Her mother, Lucretia, was a seamstress and had spent the last several weeks making a new dress for her. She remembered the hours that seemed like an eternity as she was forced to stand still, her mother using her to make the pattern for the dress. And now she was making the final fitting.

"Maria Antonia! Stop fidgeting," her mother scolded, "Stand still." Mama always called her Maria Antonia when she was cross with her but usually it was just Mariantonia.

"But Mama, I'm tired of standing still."

"Well, if I don't finish it now your dress will not be ready when Papa comes home and you won't have a party." That was all the feisty Mariantonia needed to hear. She stood still as stone. She was able, even then, to discipline herself against immediate gratification if it ultimately meant getting what she wanted.

*****

Politically, Italy is divided into regions, which in turn are divided into provinces. Pietramelara is an old mountaintop commune in the province of Caserta, in the region of Campania. The capital of Caserta is also called Caserta and it is located about fifty miles due north of *Napoli*, the regional capital. At the turn of the century the population of Pietramelara was

4

about three thousand. It is basically a farming community. Mariantonia was born in the commune in 1865 and baptized in the main church, *Chiesa di San Rocco*. Her family lived in a small stucco house on a very narrow street called Via San Giovanni. The house was attached to the two houses on either side but it possessed a rather long rectangular back yard. The yard was fenced, which afforded privacy for the privy and also protected Papa's prized fig tree from the young boys in the neighborhood.

Papa had a small farm in the valley near their home. It was along a steep, winding, dirt road on the way to another nearby mountaintop town called Riardo, to the west. Papa was born in Riardo but moved to Pietramelara when he was very young. He worked his farm alone except for harvest time when he employed a few local boys to help gather the crop. He always came home tired and sweaty from the fields. But no matter, he would always hold out his arms to her. "*Vieni qui*," he would shout. "Come here my little Mariantonia," he would say, as he bent down to pick her up and swing her legs up in the air until they almost touched the ceiling. Then he ended the ritual with a big kiss as her feet landed back on the floor.

"*Ciao*, Papa," she squealed with delight. But tonight would be different. It was her birthday, and after supper her aunts and uncles and cousins were coming over for a party. Cakes and pastries and *caffelatte* would be a part of the celebration. There would be presents too!

It seemed odd that these memories should flood back into her thoughts after these many years. Now she was twenty-nine, it was December 1894, she was married and a mother. Mama and Papa were dead. The events of the past few years, since Raffaele was born, happened so quickly that the memory of them was almost a blur.

*****

They were good parents, Lucretia and Michele. She thought of how they doted on and spoiled her, their only child. She never quite understood why she was an only child. All of the other families in Pietramelara were large and some of them were veritable tribes in their own right. Her family consisted of only the three of them. Sometimes it was lonely, but there were compensations. Theirs was a small house but she had a bedroom all to herself, an unheard of luxury for a girl her age, and why not? Papa was a landowner and Mama was an excellent seamstress whose services were very much sought after. They were not rich but they were very comfortable. Staunch Catholics, her parents saw to it that she practiced all the teachings of the church. She was educated in the small church school run by a few nuns in a nearby convent.

5

While not a rebel, as she grew older she took all the liberties she could get away with. As an only child she did not have to share. It was easy for her to learn how to manipulate a situation or people to her benefit. She also resented the confinement imposed upon her by the 'rules', even from an early age. "Do this, don't do that," were the constant admonitions hurled at her and her classmates. She developed an ability to appear attentive while she would daydream about far away places and adventures. Still, she enjoyed the academics, especially the classes in reading, writing, and history. It was at these that she excelled. She endured the constant discipline from her teachers in order to learn what pleased her. It was a trade off.

Her interest in history went beyond the academics. She wanted to understand her father's hatred of the 'new' Italian government. Papa was an ardent supporter of the church and Pope Pius IX and the Papal States.

In 1870 the unification of Italy changed all that when the Papal territories were incorporated into the new Italian government, and the Pope lost all of his temporal authority. The French were also to blame for removing their forces from Rome, leaving the Vatican defenseless against the northern government. As a result, the south was united to the north and the new Italy was formed.

Stripped of his territorial domain, the Pope was a virtual prisoner in the Papal Palace located on one of Rome's seven hills, called the Vatican Hill. The situation was an abomination to Michele.

Michele was born and raised in the Kingdom Of The Two Sicilies, and he did what he could to resist the revolution, *Il Risorgimento* it was called, 'the revival', which united Italy when Mariantonia was only five years old.

"What revival?" he would argue with some of his friends, "This is heresy! The true governor of this land is God and His representative on earth." Garibaldi, King Vittorio Emmanuele II, and Count Cavour were not heroes to him. They were interlopers. Michele's views were not popular with all of his neighbors and would one day prove fatal for him.

While Mariantonia's interest in her surroundings was keen, her father's feelings against the new government never quite rubbed off on her. All she had ever known was a united Italy and she was happy with Mama and Papa and her simple life in Pietramelara. Her attitude was to let them do whatever they wanted as long as they left her alone. She had family and friends. She did not have time to hate.

Chapter II

MARIANTONIA AND GIOVANNI 1880

At an early age it was evident that Mariantonia would grow into a beautiful woman. She had long, flowing, chestnut hair and large, round, brown eyes that sparkled, revealing a personality that found life exciting. Her eyes were accentuated by long, black, eyelashes with perfectly formed eyebrows in a natural arc. She grew tall and slender with long, delicate fingers that helped her to learn her mother's sewing skills. Her mother taught her well and she made all of her own clothes that kept her apace with the fashions of the time.

One of her favorite dresses that she helped her mother make was a dinner dress for a wealthy politician's wife from Caserta. It had frills with lace everywhere. The woman had come to the house several times with her custom-made corset in order that Lucretia could get the measurements just right. It was important that the bodice clung to the corset perfectly. Mariantonia liked everything about the dress, especially the plunging neckline, a bit risqué for the time, but filled in beautifully with satin buttons. She liked the way the jacket of the dress was gathered around the waist with a long train at the back. The whole dress simply bespoke class and every time she remembered it she thought of how one day she would wear one like it.

Because of her beauty, style, and clothes, Mariantonia stood out in a crowd. If her parents and convention had allowed it she could have had many suitors and would have been able to pick whomever she wanted. However, that was not allowed and reluctantly, she agreed to decorum mainly because her interest in boys was yet minimal. That was, until she met Giovanni. School, family, and social gatherings were her prime concerns through her formative years, and she loved the farm.

As expected she grew into a handsome woman with high cheekbones and full, red lips which precluded the need for cosmetics. Impeccable posture and firm breasts rounded out her other features. She had that poise and grace that seemed reserved for girls of the upper class. These qualities cast her apart from the other local girls and earned her both respect and resentment from her contemporaries. While she had many friends, it was those very qualities that prevented her from establishing any kind of intimate friendship with other girls in the town.

That was why Mama and Papa were appalled that she would be so attracted to Giovanni. They felt she could do better. Giovanni was one of the young men that Michele hired at harvest time to work on the farm. He was from Camigliano, another mountaintop town a few miles south of Pietramelara, as the crow flies but not as a man walks. To get to Michele's farm, Giovanni had to traverse hills and valleys every day before and after working on the farm.

Giovanni was born on December 7, 1861. His father was a day laborer. His mother had passed away when he was a child. He lived with his father's sister and his father lived wherever his spirit moved him. They were poor, like most in the south, and because Giovanni was needed at home, his education was sporadic. As he grew older, he abandoned school completely in order to earn money for the family. However, he managed to learn how to read and write before he was forced to stop attending school. Still, he considered himself more fortunate than most boys his age. Other families he knew were even poorer than his own, and the children were non-literate. Unfortunately, when his formal education stopped, so did his interest in intellectual growth. He lacked the mental motivation to learn anything beyond what he needed in order to cope with life.

He was hard working and dependable. To earn money for the family he hired himself out to the highest bidder. He was a tall, strong young man, with black curly hair, thick eyebrows, and chiseled features. He looked more Greek than Italian. Even as a teenager his massive frame gave the impression of a physically powerful man, which he was, and one to be reckoned with. Yet he had a smile that lit up his face and gave him away as a gentle person whose company was a pleasurable experience.

What he learned, he learned from experience, although he had a tendency of not always thinking things through. As a result, he sometimes found himself in situations he did not expect. For him the present was enough to think about. Instinct governed his actions. But he was honest and kept his word. Walking through the towns he would see those 'Men Of Honor', as they were called, in smart clothes, with women and children kissing their hands, thanking them for this and for that. Giovanni knew who and what they were, a sub-culture to which the people related. They looked after the town's folk; they looked after their own.

'*The government doesn't seem to take care of us anymore,*' Giovanni thoughtfully reasoned. '*But, che c'entra, it doesn't matter. I will take care of myself and depend on nobody.*' And on he walked to the day's work ahead of him. He was eighteen when he went to work for Michele.

One day in the fall of 1880, during harvest time, Mariantonia decided to walk down to the farm to see how the harvest was progressing. She had just turned fifteen in July. Papa greeted her and introduced her to all the farmhands, and that is how she met Giovanni. As soon as she saw him she sensed a feeling that was entirely new to her. His smile and the touch of his hand in hers felt electric. His broad torso and strong muscular arms, tanned from working the fields, had her thinking about him the rest of that day. She wanted to meet him again, but how? She devised a plan to solve that problem.

During harvest time there was no break for the usual large noontime meal and the following siesta that was common during the rest of the year. Lunch was just a short pause in the day's labor. They were fighting the shortening daylight of autumn and the change in temperature. Soon winter would come and the harvest time would be over. Lucretia supplied food for the noontime meal and normally brought it down to the farm herself.

Mariantonia decided that this was her opportunity and the day after she met Giovanni, she volunteered to help her mother. Lucretia was delighted to be relieved of the chore. Mariantonia brought the food to the farmhands in a large, wicker basket. They all sat down on the ground and ate lunch and talked. She watched Giovanni as he talked with the other workers and Papa. Not shy, he was respectful toward Papa and also to his contemporaries. She could tell from his dialect and vocabulary that he had little education. But that infectious smile…. She did not speak with him very much during that second meeting. What little she said he seemed to listen to as though there were only the two of them there, sitting on the ground, having their own private picnic. She was so taken with him that she was determined to work in the fields until harvest time was over.

"No," shouted Papa that night. "My daughter will not work in the fields." Lucretia agreed with her husband. Mariantonia did not, and the battle of wills was joined. Michele and Lucretia should have known that their opposition would have to give way to Mariantonia's determination. It was not possible for them to win.

She ended her argument with, "Listen Papa. You have no sons. I must be both son and daughter to you. Therefore I will do the work of both son and daughter. I will help you and I will help Mama. If I don't learn the farm how will I know how to manage it when the time comes? Do you want the land to leave the family?" Michele had no answer to that argument. He agreed that the land must stay in the family.

This new government raised taxes at every turn! It was difficult to keep costs down and he had to admit, even to himself, that Mariantonia could carry a good share of the work and save him from paying additional wages for day laborers. Lucretia relented, realizing that her daughter would win out no matter what arguments they made against her. Neither of them suspected Mariantonia's ulterior motive. Mariantonia was sure that Giovanni was interested in her. She could feel the chemistry between them.

Working on the farm she was able to see Giovanni every day until the harvest was over. If working were the price she had to pay then she would do it gladly. By the end of the harvest season she felt confident that she would be able to establish a relationship strong enough for him to want to see her throughout the winter. She disliked the subterfuge she played on her parents, but she was so smitten with Giovanni that she was willing to do whatever was expedient to keep on seeing him.

Over the next few years her relationship with Giovanni blossomed into courtship. It was obvious to Michele and Lucretia that there was a potential problem brewing, but both had the common sense to remain silent. They knew their daughter. If they tried to prohibit her from seeing Giovanni they knew they would be inviting trouble into the family because of her headstrong personality. Initially they thought that when the harvests were over there would be no reason for Giovanni to return to the farm. They resolved to do nothing in the hope that the problem would go away of its own accord.

It was not as if they disliked Giovanni. On the contrary, he was a very likeable young man. He worked hard enough and he was dependable. They just thought, like most parents, that their daughter deserved and could do better. They really did not understand her. The truth was that she wanted Giovanni and that was that.

By the time she was eighteen Mariantonia had not accepted the attentions of any potential suitors. Michele was approached on numerous occasions by parents of local boys and even of one all the way from Caserta. It was a large city, the capital of the province, and they thought that, with the opportunity of living in the city, he might be an acceptable match. Mariantonia rejected all of them, especially the one from Caserta. Despite his background, Michele didn't like him either so he didn't press the issue.

All through the winters Giovanni was there, climbing up and down hills and valleys to see their daughter every weekend. Sometimes he even found a place to stay overnight and attended Sunday mass with them the next morning. Attending mass was one major point in Giovanni's favor as far as Michele was concerned. Most of the other suitors hadn't seen the inside of a church since their confirmations, the heretics!

In the spring of 1885 Michele decided to plant additional crops on some fallow land that he owned and he hired Giovanni on a full time basis. The extra labor would produce more from the farm and the additional crops could pay for his wages, the increase in taxes, and maybe a little extra left over for him and Lucretia. So he planted the entire farm. During the growing season Mariantonia continued to work on the farm part time. It was no longer necessary to play the game. It was understood that she and Giovanni were courting. She also did her full share at harvest time.

Finally, realizing that Mariantonia would have it no other way, Michele and Lucretia gave their blessings, and in February 1890 Mariantonia and Giovanni were married at mass in the *Chiesa di San Rocco*. She was twenty-four and he was twenty-eight. Giovanni moved into his father-in-law's house and they slept in Mariantonia's bedroom. Michele and Giovanni continued to plant every square foot of land they could. He might not have a son but he had a hard working son-in-law who idolized his daughter. Things were not exactly the way he had envisioned, but they were good.

*****

Mariantonia had always resented menstruation. Mostly because the period came without her permission and never deviated from its own schedule. She always referred to the unwanted event as 'it'. 'It' started when she was twelve and she had endured the onset every month for twelve years and she still detested 'it'. Not having control is what she despised most of all. But things were different now. She was still in the honeymoon stage of her marriage and she hated the control 'it' held over her lovemaking with Giovanni. 'It' took away the spontaneity of the bedroom. Three months after her marriage she woke up one morning and realized that 'it' was not on schedule. Her instinct was to tell Giovanni immediately but instead she opted to tell her mother first.

"Wait to see if you miss again next month," counseled Lucretia, "If you're pregnant there will be plenty of time to tell Giovanni. Wait until after we are sure."

So she waited, preoccupied with counting the days. June came and still there was nothing so she told Giovanni the good news. He was elated, bursting with pride. They counted the days together. Would the baby be born in December 1890 or January 1891? Would it be a New Years Eve baby, or maybe a Christmas baby, like Jesus? They played the date-guessing game over and over. As it turned out, the baby came on the Solemnity of the Epiphany, January 6, 1891. They named him Raffaele in honor of her paternal grandfather.

The baby was baptized on a Sunday afternoon, and the extended family celebrated with all their friends. That night Michele went into town to continue the festivities with some friends. Too much wine had flowed throughout the day and into the evening. They all began to talk too much about things better left unsaid. *'If only Papa had shown some restraint regarding his feelings toward this blasphemous government.'* A few close friends shared similar views with Michele and they often met in the town square and talked about the 'old times' just like they did on the night of

Raffaele's baptism. Their camaraderie served to embolden their complaints.

They continued on and on with their litany of grievances. Gone was the protection of the local officials. When the locals held authority over the town they never lost sight of the fact that they were living with their neighbors and in many cases their relatives. Problems were solved quickly and justly. Taxes were low and local expenditures were fairly well dependent on the approval of everyone.

"Where are the local officials now? They used to live among us and they understood our problems. Where is the tax money we pay every season? It doesn't come back to Pietramelara, that's for sure. It's Campania and Caserta that tell us what to do and they take our money for the privilege!" So the complaints went. It started out as innocent, drunken talk, but it began to take on a meaner tone. Unfortunately, on that night, there were some officials from Caserta in the bar. As the talk about government oppression, high taxes, and the hated military conscription laws became louder, an argument ensued which escalated into a bar brawl.

No one really knew who hit Michele on his head with the wine bottle. He just fell unconscious to the ground. His friends carried him home and tried to treat him but he never regained consciousness. He died there the next day. Lucretia was inconsolable, Giovanni was beside himself, and, for the first time in her life, Mariantonia's heart filled with anger and bitterness toward the corrupt government that her father had always complained about.

She went in to the baby and looked at him with sorrow instead of happiness. He would never know his grandfather. He began to stir and cry. She picked him up, held him in her arms, and sat on a rocking chair to quiet him. She took out her breast and began to nurse him, and as she rocked, the two of them fell asleep. Giovanni put them both to bed and went out to make arrangements for the funeral.

Lucretia, grief stricken without her Michele, died of a broken heart the next month. Now, instead of the family of three she had known since birth, Mama, Papa, and herself, it was a new family of three, Giovanni, herself, and her son. The shock of the sudden change in their lives prevented them from coming to grips with the situation. They walked around as if in a daze, but reality changed that, and quickly.

It was planting time again. Now it was Giovanni who had to work the farm alone and he was not able to plant all of the land as they had done the previous season. They could have rented out some of the land for a share of the crop but such long range planning was not his style and Mariantonia, in her mourning, never thought of it either. Hard work was Giovanni's solution to everything.

To add to their troubles, the crops were not good that year. Giovanni tried to make a go of it anyway but the farm income just about paid their expenses and the cost of two funerals earlier that year only exacerbated the problem. After harvest time and paying the taxes there was barely enough money left to get them through the winter.

To their disbelief, and despite the poor harvest, the government again raised taxes. Even Mariantonia's ability to cope, her resiliency, was put to the test. They were forced to reevaluate their situation. Giovanni's solution was to work harder, but she knew that option would lead nowhere. If they were to keep the house they would have to sell the farm, or a good portion of it. If they were to keep the farm they would have to sell the house. To sell neither would force them into debt and the eventual loss of both.

Giovanni anguished over the situation. Although he had helped out with family responsibilities before in Camigliano, even to the extent of sacrificing his education, he basically only had himself to worry about then. Now he had a wife, a son, and hardly enough money to see them through till next season. For sure he would not be able to pay the taxes on both the farm and the house next year. While they wrestled with the problem it was Mariantonia who came up with a solution.

"We will sell the farm!" she exclaimed. "Then we will go to America! There is nothing here for us anymore Giovanni, and this government will bleed us dry if we stay!"

All of a sudden it felt good to damn the government, just like Papa used to do. They were to blame for Papa's death and Mama's too, for that matter. There was some measure of relief in having someone to blame for their misfortune.

"You take what you need and go alone. The balance of the money I will keep here as our surplus. I will stay here with Raffaele. When you have become established I will sell the house and join you there, in America."

She spoke with such determination, authority, and confidence that Giovanni never even raised an objection. He silently nodded his assent. He felt reassured now that they had a plan.

That is what they planned and Mariantonia was determined to make the plan work. They sold the farm. Giovanni took what he needed and went to America. He arrived in New York City in May of 1892. She lived in their house and started to make preparations to join him in a few months time.

The separation turned out to be the biggest mistake of their marriage. The few months turned into two and a half years and still Giovanni wrote and told her that he was not ready for them to come to America. Finally, she refused to wait any longer. The money from the sale of the farm was running low and she could not earn enough from her seamstress business to support herself and her son. She sold the house for a fraction of its value, bought two tickets to America, and then wrote to Giovanni to meet her at Ellis Island. She would arrive in December 1894, and that was that.

*****

A blast from the ship's horn stopped her reminiscing and pulled her back into the present. She smiled, resigning herself to how little control she wielded over the recent events that had reshaped their lives. From misfortune she learned. If she could not make things happen her way, she would control how the unwanted events affected her. What happened could not be changed. Yesterday was yesterday and today was almost gone. She was determined to live tomorrow on her terms. Naples and Italy were gone now, out of sight, and with them her past. Ahead lay the sea that separated the old from the new.

America, 'where the streets were paved with gold' and freedom reigned, would be her new life. She would prevail. She would not allow herself to be vanquished. She could fight her way out of any unwanted situation. Her power lay in her self-discipline. She simply turned her back and walked away from problems which could not be solved and let the devil take the hindmost. She refused to live with misery and she did not waste time trying to defend the untenable. If she had to reevaluate her goals and change them frequently she found she could do it and not look back. Turning into a pillar of salt, like Lot's wife, was not in her character.

She was tired now, and Raffaele had fallen asleep in her arms. It was getting colder out on deck. She decided to go below to find as comfortable a place as possible for them to spend the night. Like most emigrants, they were traveling steerage and she knew that there would be little comfort for the next fifteen days. She hoped, for her son's sake, that the crossing would not be rough.

Steerage was only a bare steel deck and offered no comforts whatsoever. Men and women were separated into groups. The younger boys and the girls stayed with their mothers and the older boys with the men. The stale air, caused by so many people confined in a closed space, was almost unbearable but at least it was better than the cold nighttime air. It was cold even though they were still in the Mediterranean. There were no toilet facilities in steerage. They had to walk up to number 2 deck. There was constant traffic, coming and going for that purpose. Mariantonia wondered how either one of them was going to get any sleep. She looked down at her son. He was sound asleep.

14

'*Ah,*' she thought, '*God is very kind to withhold knowledge from the little ones. They can sleep in innocence, their minds not yet filled with life's troubles.*'

She smiled as she patted her left breast to feel what was left of the money surplus she had knotted in a silk handkerchief and pinned to the inside of her brassiere. Mama had shown her that trick. As she closed her eyes to sleep, she thought back over the plans they had made once she and Giovanni had decided to go to America.

Financially they were not in as good a position as she had hoped. Living expenses over two and a half years had put a strain on her resources. She still had a little money left over from the sale of the farm but the net proceeds from the sale of the house were not as much as she had expected. In order to retain as much of the surplus as possible she purchased ship tickets in steerage for herself and her son. In spite of the hardships she was still going to bring something to Giovanni and she had it tucked away in its hiding place.

Mariantonia thought back to the morning when Giovanni left her in 1892 and that first day that she was alone. She had started to make a list of what she would sell and what she would take with her. At the time she had thought that he would send for her very soon, and with great expectations she waited patiently for Giovanni's first letter to arrive from America.

Chapter III

LETTERS 1892

15 June 1892

My dearest Mariantonia;

It is almost two months since I left you. I miss you and Raffaele more than I thought I would. It is very lonely here without you. I do not like New York. There are no farms, just buildings. It is very crowded. The people who live in New York are from all over the world. It is hard to know who an American is, with so many different languages. Even most of the trees are gone, all chopped down to make room for houses and warehouses. Also it is very difficult for me because of the language problem. English is very hard to learn and many times I don't know what is going on.

There was a mix up when the ship arrived. It docked in the wrong river. The officials herded us off the ship just like sheep. I didn't like it and when they weren't looking I just walked away from them and went into the city on my own. Then I started to look for work right away. I was lucky and found a job in a large fish market on the river right near where the boat landed. I didn't want the job but I took it anyway until I could find something better. There were a lot of Italians working there and they helped me get the job. One of them told me that there were a lot of farms in a place called New Jersey, across the other river to the west. I didn't want to work with the fish again, the place smelled awful so I took my pay that night and left.

I slept in the pew of a large church on my first night in America and the next day I went to New Jersey to a town called Newark. When I got there I was walking up one of the streets looking for a place to sleep that night. I met a man who is a baker and he was looking for someone to work in his ovens. I had a job even before I had a place to live. What good luck I had! Maybe it is a good sign for us. I hid in another church that night and slept there. They locked the doors and I prayed they would open them the next day. It's not like home where the churches are always open. They opened the doors for the four thirty mass. I just pretended that I was going to mass and then walked out and went to my new job. The bakery is in the Italian section of the city on Eighth Avenue. It is not much of a job. I shovel coal into the ovens and do all of the lifting and moving. The owner's name is Luigi. He likes me because I am used to getting up early and I work hard. I think he would be upset if he knew that I slept in the church the first night I was in Newark. All of the people in the neighborhood are Italian. That makes it easy although I don't understand some of them. It's just like home, different areas speak different dialects, but even with them I can get by. The church has a German pastor but he speaks very good Italian.

I met a man named Antonio who also works in the bakery and we became friends right away. Actually, I work under him. He is from San Sossio Baronia over in the province of Avellino. He helped me get a place to live. I share a furnished room with three other men. Actually, there are four cots and a dresser with four drawers, one for each of us. I don't like it but it is the best I can do for now. I'm not sure how much it costs to live here. It's hard to understand the money system. In Italy we only have the lira. Here they have dollars, half dollars, and a coin they call a quarter and the smallest is a penny. They also call the penny a cent. It is very confusing, but you learn fast when you have to.

Newark is a big city, bigger than Pietramelara, but not as big as New York. There are some small farms in the city but they are just plots of land and the farmers work them all by themselves. The big farms are outside the city and are far from where I live. On a couple of Sundays I walked many miles to visit some of them, but so far I have not been lucky enough to find a job in any of them. Mostly I am too tired to walk all the way out to them and besides, none of the owners are Italian and they don't like us so that makes it hard. Lately I have not been spending too much time looking for farm work. Maybe at harvest time something will happen but I don't want a temporary job. The one in the bakery is permanent so I'm going to stay here for a while.

How is Raffaele? I am so afraid that he will forget who I am. There are a lot of men here who have done the same thing we did and are working hard to bring their families to America. We all want our families. Also, there are a lot of unmarried men just looking for a better life and to get away from the conscription. They are lonely too and are trying to get a bride to come over from Italy. There are *agenzie matrimonio* in the city and they make arrangements to have women come over to marry them. They charge a fee for their services. Can you imagine, buying a wife without even seeing her first!

Write to me soon, my dear wife. I miss you and Raffaele very much. Kiss him for me every day. Tell him that his Papa thinks about him all the time and prays for him every night. Stay well and happy twenty-seventh birthday. I wish I could give you a present but that will have to wait until we are together again.

Your loving husband,
Giovanni

*****

15 July 1892

My dearest love, Giovanni;

Your long awaited letter arrived today, and on my birthday too. I cannot believe I am twenty-seven, more than a quarter of a century. When I went to the post office and saw it my heart jumped for joy. I rushed right home so that I could read it in private. What a lovely present your letter is. You could not have given a better one to me.

I am well and so is Raffaele. He is beginning to talk now and he gets into everything. I talk to him about you every day so he will not forget that you are Papa. I tell him that you are working and we will see you soon.

I know that you are disappointed in not finding a farm job, and I am disappointed also. My heart goes out to you. But look at the situation in a positive way. Working in a bakery gives you the opportunity to learn a trade and maybe someday you will be able to own your own bakery. If it doesn't work out that way perhaps we can save enough money so that we can buy a small farm in New Jersey. Dear Giovanni, don't despair and don't try to accomplish everything immediately, have patience. Things will work out for us. I feel it.

I looked up New Jersey and Newark on a map so now I know where you are living in the world. I am earning enough money by making dresses to pay for living expenses so don't worry about that. Most of Mama's customers have remained loyal. The only problem that we may have is with the taxes on the house. The rumor is that the government will raise them again after the harvest. If that happens then I may have to use some of our surplus to pay them if you are not able to send some money to me.

One alternative is for me to rent out my old bedroom to a boarder. Raffaele sleeps there now, but there would be no problem in having him sleep in the big bedroom with me. I could move a cot in there for him. I think I will put the word out that I have a room available and we will see what happens. Maybe I can get one of the teachers from the school. There are several women there who sleep two or three to a room and if I don't

18

ask too much maybe one or perhaps two of them could manage. I would prefer to rent to only one person, but two will be acceptable if necessary.

Oh my dear Giovanni, how fate has changed our lives. I miss Mama and Papa so much and the life we had with them. I can cope with being alone but being lonely is hardly bearable. I miss you more than you can know. My arms ache to hold you at night. I miss your touch and your affection and the security I felt when we owned the farm. Somehow owning land makes one feel safe. But, as we now realize, that is only an illusion. We can only be secure in our love for each other and by working toward our mutual goals. These feelings and longings will only serve to make our reunion that much better, and more passionate, if 'it' is not with me when we first meet again.

Oh, my dear Giovanni, the language barrier is a subject we never discussed. How thoughtless of both of us. Of course there would be a problem. It was fortunate for you to find an Italian section in Newark in which to live and work. I have contacted the nuns at my old school. One of them speaks a little English. She is going to try to obtain an English language textbook for us and we will try to teach each other the language. Perhaps you could do the same. If your new friend, Antonio, is willing why don't the two of you try to speak only English between yourselves? That way you will not feel embarrassed whenever you make mistakes and need to correct each other. You will learn as I will learn.

Dearest John, I will now call you by your American name since we are going to be Americans. And we will call our dear Raffaele the American name Ralph. It will all work out. We will prevail in spite of what the world has thrown against us. I feel it. I know you are working very hard as you always did. I am proud of what you are doing and I'm very impressed by your progress in so short a time. Stay well my dearest. I think of you always and I constantly pray for us.

Your most loving and devoted wife,
Mariantonia

*****

19 August 1892

Dearest Mariantonia;

I send my kisses to you and our beloved son, Ralph. I am so saddened that I can't see him grow. I know I am missing something important in my life and in his. It is now almost four months since I left both of you. I don't like it but we have no choice. I don't make too much money. In order to keep expenses down I live in a room with three other men. The prices of things are very high. My friend, Antonio, lives in a room with two other men. We are all trying to save money so we can send for our families. Antonio has a wife and three children in Italy, a boy and two girls. They live in San Sossio Baronia, about thirty miles west of Pietramelara. You can look it up on your map. They live with her mother and father.

What a coincidence about you trying to rent the small bedroom. Antonio has explained an idea to me. He says that if we join up together we can rent an apartment he knows about. It has three rooms and is on the second floor of a building on Eighth Avenue here in Newark. It is very close to the bakery where we work. It is funny, but in America the first floor is on the street level and the next floor is called the second floor, not like in Italy where we call the floor above the street the first floor. There are very strange customs here. Anyway, the apartment has a front room facing the street, a kitchen, and a back bedroom. We can share the bedroom and rent the front room out to boarders. He has it worked out that we could do it and live rent free with a little money left over. Also, we will have more space for ourselves. It is terrible living in a room with three other men.

Did I tell you about the mosquitoes here in New Jersey? They are very bad, they bite and get in your ears, and when I smack them it squirts my blood all over my skin. When we go to sleep at night we hang a thin piece of cloth over the doorway to try to keep them out and still let some air in the room but they find a way in anyway. Antonio's idea sounded good to me so I said yes. I think Antonio is a very smart man. Did I do the right thing?

Living here is not easy. Some Italians don't like it here and are going back to Italy. Sometimes I think that's what I should do. Newark is a big city and you could put all the people in Pietramelara just in my small neighborhood. I think it is even bigger than Caserta. It is very crowded and noisy. The bakery does very well and now I know how to make bread and I am learning to make cakes and pastries, but I still shovel the coal. Luigi is a good teacher. I think I like baking better than farming. Antonio and I work good together. He doesn't look Italian. He has blue eyes and very fair skin. I am so dark next to him. That was a good idea to speak English together. We call everything in the bakery by English but I don't know if we say it right. If you call me John I will call you Maria and Raffaele will be Ralph. Maria, if the apartment works out I may be able to save some money. We will see. Stay well, my dear wife and kiss Ralph for me.

Your devoted husband,
John

13 September 1892

My dearest love, John;

I think being apart makes me love you more than I thought possible. Because I don't see you I think of you constantly. It is good for me to sew because I can work and think of you at the same time except when Ralph demands attention. Yes, I now call him by his American name so that he will get used to it. He must grow at night when he sleeps. I think he will become tall like you. He talks all the time now but I am the only one who can understand what he says, so he is at me all the time demanding attention. What do people do when they have large families? Will we have a large family, John? Not if I don't come to America!

The nights are getting colder now, autumn is here, and the moon, *la bella luna*, how beautiful it is this time of year. The farmers have all started harvesting the fields until dark. After the harvest season is over the taxes will be due once more. The leeches, they know when there is money around. If you are not able to send any money to me I may have to pay part of the taxes from our surplus. However, it will not be as bad as I thought as I have three wedding dresses to make and the mending is constant.

Fortunately, I was able to rent the small bedroom to one of the schoolteachers. The additional income will help. I did not get as much as I wanted because the rent had to fit what she could pay. Maybe later I will be able to find another teacher. But I don't think I want to do that at present. One extra person in the house is enough. We'll see what happens as time goes on. She almost didn't take the room when she found out I was going to America as soon as possible but the thought of being in a room all by herself, even for a little while, was enough to overcome any doubts she had, so she took it.

Antonio is certainly an industrious as well as an intelligent man. The apartment idea sounds like a very good course of action to take. Will the two of you have to purchase any furniture or is the apartment furnished? If you have to buy furniture it will probably take all the rent money you save, at least for a while. Nevertheless, it still sounds like a good investment. It's just that it is postponing my coming to America and to you, my dear, sweet, husband. Be careful as you make financial arrangements in the future. Sometimes you jump before you think things out. However, I am very proud of you for having agreed to go in with Antonio. I think you made the correct decision. I am so happy that you and Antonio have found each other.

I have decided to send to *Napoli* for my passport and apply for our visa. There are some new government regulations and it now takes about three to four months to get the paper work through Caserta and then on to *Napoli* and back. I even have to get one for Ralph, can you imagine, for a two year old! They will jump at any excuse to charge a fee! I want to be ready at a moment's notice when you send for us.

Many people are emigrating from all over Italy to the new world. A lot are going to South America, to Brazil and Argentina, and some even to Canada where the French are, but mostly they emigrate to America. That is why I am so surprised to hear that some people don't like America and are returning to *Italia*. Not many have left from Pietramelara. However, from the few that have, no one has returned yet so that must mean that whatever life is like in America it must be better than here, at least for them. For me there is nothing here for us anymore, and especially for me without you and Mama and Papa. Also, the farm is gone and a house is just a house no matter where it is. It is the family that makes it a home and we will have our family and our home in America.

In the meantime, since I cannot hear your voice or see your smile, our letters will have to suffice. Write soon. It took so long for me to receive your last letter and I can't stand the waiting. Why is the mail so slow? It must be the government. They ruin everything!

I kiss you too my dearest husband and I can't wait to hold you tightly in my arms once again.

Forever I am yours,

Maria

*****

6 November 1892

Dear Maria;

I thank God for your patience and understanding. Besides being my loving wife you are a wonderful woman. On October 1st Antonio and I rented the apartment I told you about and we moved in. Our apartment is on the second floor, the American second floor. My new address is 138 Eighth Avenue, Newark, N.J., U.S.A. You were right, there was no furniture. Not only that, we had to pay two months rent in advance as a deposit, that's another American custom. That did not leave us with enough money to buy furniture, even used furniture. We borrowed some money from our boss, Luigi. What a wonderful man. He has been a warm friend to us.

We slept on the floor for a few nights until we found furniture that we could afford. We bought four cots for the front room. Once the cots were here we got four boarders right away. Actually, Antonio got them. He sure knows how to do things. They sleep in the front room that has two windows by the street. It is very cramped for them, but at least they have the two windows. We sleep in the back bedroom where there are no windows. The kitchen is in between the two bedrooms so we have some privacy. I miss the fresh air of Pietramelara.

Now that we live rent-free, there are a few dollars left over to pay Luigi back. Also, we have a kitchen and we eat at home. It is cheaper than eating in a restaurant and we always have breakfast and lunch at the bakery. Luigi pays for it and the bread tastes so good. But we have to pay Luigi back a little each week on the loan so we don't have any money left over. Antonio says that as soon as Luigi is paid back we will each be able to save something so we are paying him back as fast as we can. Also, Antonio found jobs for us shoveling snow for some of the buildings downtown. You will be amazed at the buildings downtown in Newark. If the snow cooperates and falls during the day and then stops we will be able to work in the evening and at night, and on Sundays too. That Antonio sure is something, he is always thinking of ways to get ahead. I am so fortunate to have him as a friend. It is hard to understand, because we are not at all alike. He says property ownership is the way to success in America. I still can't make up my mind between the bakery business and a farm. I miss the open fields but I love the smell of the bread.

It makes me so sad not to be with you for the Christmas holidays. Ralph was so young last Christmas that I am sure he did not know what was going on. Now that he is almost two years old I am sure he will be able to enjoy it more and it makes me sad that I will not be there to see it. Please try to buy a Christmas gift for him and tell him it is from his Papa and also for his birthday in January. I am sure he doesn't remember me, but he will remember the presents. We will be going to midnight mass if we can get into St. Lucy's. That is the church I slept in the first night I came to Newark. Remember? St. Lucy's is a small church and it can't hold everyone in the church at the same time. But, if it snows, then we will be going to work downtown. Pray for snow because we can make extra money for working on Christmas Eve. My love is my Christmas gift to you.

Forever yours,

John

24 December 1892

My dearest love, John;

   This is our first Christmas apart. The emptiness around me is as though I were in a dark, quiet, forest except that there is no peace. I miss you and I cannot understand the events that separated us. Our married life started out so beautifully and the world was ours. As I think back I know now that it was because Mama and Papa worked so hard for us and we benefited without realizing it. I guess that's why children appear to be ungrateful, not that they are, it's just that they don't know how hard their parents work. Through no fault of our own that happy life was changed for us. I find it very hard to understand God's will in all of this. It is only my faith that He has a plan that keeps me sane. How do people get through life without believing in God? I guess that's why there are so many suicides. Do they have that problem in America too?

   All the families are getting ready to celebrate Christmas dinner tomorrow, but our family is separated. I am very sad and jealous, but our time will come, you'll see. Ralph is asleep now. I was going to take him to midnight mass but he was so tired that I did not have the heart to demand that of him. We will go tomorrow, and I will light a candle for you, no, for us. I made a new suit for him and bought new shoes as a Christmas present. I also purchased some wooden blocks with letters on them. I will tell them that they are from you. Whenever he plays with them I will call them Papa's blocks so he will remember. This New Year I will try to teach him the letters.

   I went to visit Mama and Papa's graves today. It will not be too long before I cannot do it anymore and I wanted to wish them *Buon'Natale*. I took Ralph with me, but of course he does not remember them. It was a cold day in the cemetery and lots of families were there leaving flowers on the graves. I did not have any flowers but I had lots of prayers. Do you think that they approve of what we have done, selling the farm and soon the house? I agonize over it every day even though I know there is no other option open to us. Please pray for them as I do.

   I do have some good news. I was able to pay the taxes without taking too much from the surplus. I was afraid that my left breast would get to be the same size as the right one. It is funny, we all think we have our secret hiding place. All the women do the same thing. It is common knowledge. When you think about it, it is really funny to hide money in our brassieres.

   I know it is hard for you but I spend only what I need to keep body and soul together. We are lucky to have the house and no debt or I would not be able to do it. My boarder is working out well. She spends most of her spare time going out with her friends and when she is home I hardly know she is here. Since it is working out so well I am not going to try to get another boarder.

More and more people are leaving for America and I understand they are boarding ships in *Napoli* by the thousands, whole families!

I was told that a few years back there was a famine in Ireland and that the Irish also went to America by the thousands. Is that true? America must be a huge place to be able to take in so many people. But, at least the Irish can speak English so it must be easier for them. How is the English between you and Antonio coming along? I still work with the nun, but we don't know if our pronunciation is correct. You have the advantage because you hear people speak the language. But at least I am becoming able to read and write English. It is very difficult. They put everything backwards.

Tomorrow I will make a special Christmas dinner for Ralph and me. I am going to invite the boarder. She has no family here and would be alone if I didn't. I will set a place for you and pretend you are here so it will be the four of us at the table. When you have Christmas dinner, you do the same for us. That way we will all be together.

Yours forever,

Maria

Chapter IV

LETTERS 1893

2 February 1893

Dear Maria;

Buon'anno. I hope that before 1893 is over we will be together again. It is very cold and snowy here. I never realized how much snow could fall. Even in the mountains of Pietramelara we never had so much snow as here. But it is snowing at the wrong time, mostly at night, and we don't make too much extra money shoveling, but still we earn some. I save all of it in the bank. The deep snow sometimes makes things come to a stop. The other day we almost ran out of flour at the bakery because they couldn't make delivery. It did not matter too much because many people did not come out to buy bread anyway. Antonio said that the problem is giving him an idea. You never know what he will come up with.

They tell me that there was a snowstorm here in 1888, the worst they ever had, and it stopped everything for over a week, even the banks had to close. In New York City it was so bad that they decided to build a railroad under the ground for people to get around, and in a few years the first trains will run under the city. They call it a 'subway'. Can you imagine, trains that run underground! They are taking all the dirt out of the ground and sending it over to Ellis Island by barge. So many people are coming over from Europe that they need more space so they are making the island bigger. Do you believe it! But that's America for you. After March, Luigi will be paid off and I will be able to save more money.

Let me tell you what Antonio did. He met a man who owns a pork sausage store down on High Street. He just sells sausage and Antonio talked him into selling bread also. So now Antonio delivers bread to the store every day and Luigi pays him a commission on every loaf he delivers. Antonio says he is going to try to expand the idea and sell to other stores and even some restaurants. He thinks that just selling bread instead of making it will make more money for him. I hope he is right. He sure is a smart one.

Being a landlord is not all that great. The boarders come and go and sometimes run out on us still owing us money and they are very sloppy in the way they live. That only bothers me a little, but it bothers Antonio a lot. He is so neat with everything. Antonio says from now on they must pay by the week in advance or out they go. We don't like to do it. We remember how it was with us when we first came over, but they don't care about us so we don't have a choice.

Thank you for getting a Christmas present from me for Ralph. We worked extra hard at the bakery. I could not believe how many cakes and pastries we made because of the holidays. We made almost twice the amount of bread. I wish I had been with you for Christmas dinner. I send my kisses to you and give one of them to Ralph. All my love,

Your husband forever,
John

*****

1 March 1893

My dearest love, John;

I think of you more today. The farmers are preparing to start the spring planting soon. I think of you and Papa getting everything ready on our farm. I think of Mama preparing the noon meal and how I would pack everything in the basket and bring it to you and Papa. Then we would have a little picnic. Papa would walk around the farm and leave us alone for a little while so we could talk. I used to think that he did it accidentally but now I realize he was just trying to give us some privacy, he was so thoughtful. Life was so simple and carefree then but that was because Papa did all the worrying and planning. That is all gone now. Now we have the problems, and the agony of our separation only adds to them. Now we must worry and plan and being apart like this makes it almost unbearable.

I was talking with a farmer's wife while I was shopping for some cloth for a dress I'm making. She says that her husband predicts a worse harvest this year than last year. Time is running out. If what he says turns out to be true, then my dress making will suffer, especially wedding dresses, which are my most lucrative. Mending clothes is better than nothing, but it cannot cover my expenses.

John, my love, I am thinking it would be a good time to sell the house now and take whatever I can get for it and come to America. If you and Antonio can make a go of it, so can we. We could get an apartment and take in boarders just as you and Antonio are doing in America and I am doing here in Pietramelara. Perhaps we could get a larger apartment or even a house and have more than four boarders. Surely we could live cheaper together than apart. And besides, I could still get work as a seamstress.

Also, I understand that some women write letters in America for those who cannot read or write. We have a woman here in Pietramelara who does it. They call her *La Scrittore*, the writer. I could become *La Scrittore* in America. For me it would be easy. We could do it. Please, John, I don't want to be separated any longer and your reply letters are taking longer and longer to reach me. Please don't make me suffer any more. Besides, little Ralph needs a father in the house and the truth is my body aches for yours, my love. And now it's *Pasqua,* and Easter means another holiday alone.

My passport just arrived today so I am ready, all I need to do is sell the house and the furniture and then purchase the steamship tickets. Do you believe it took over four months to get the passports? In spite of all that government interference in our lives, I am ready now. Shall I try to sell the house? I don't think it would be wise to wait any longer.

You haven't written about the church in Newark. You said it is called St. Lucy's. It must be a wonderful building, all new. Remember our church here, *Chiesa di San Rocco*? It was built in 1308. It is so old and needs a lot of repair work now, but who has the money? Tell me more about St. Lucy's in your next letter. Call me to you soon my love.

Your faithful and devoted wife,
Maria

*****

21 April 1893

Dear Maria;

My love. Your last letter caused me so much pain. What you and I want and what is possible is not the same thing at this time. Let me explain the problem. Antonio quit working in the bakery. He is trying to set up a bread delivery business. Thank God he is buying the bread from Luigi. I was afraid that when Luigi found out that Antonio was going to leave that he would be angry with both of us but he seems happy enough so my job is safe. But that is the way Antonio does things. He explained the whole idea to Luigi first, almost like he was asking for permission. Luigi gave him his blessing.

But now Antonio is earning less money than when he worked in the bakery. The truth is that his share of the little extra we make on the boarders he needs to live on and he is already talking about buying a horse and wagon. Just now he is renting them. If he is not successful then he will be out of a job and I will have a problem. He and I are such good friends and he has helped me out so much that I could not break up the partnership in the apartment just now.

Please, my love. A little longer, please. Luigi has given me a raise because I am now his assistant. He hired a young man to do the work that I used to do, so my job is now more secure than before. I don't want to see you come to America and work. I realize you are working in Italy and it would not be too different. Still, I want to be able to provide for you and little Ralph.

You are right about *La Scrittore*. There is a woman over on Garside Street who writes letters for people. Thank God I can read and write a little. So many of the Italian immigrants are peasants and don't know how to read or write.

Here in America education is very easy to get. The government provides schools and teachers for free. All the children must go to school. It is the law. But not all of the children go. Some of the parents do not force them to go to school. When you come to America, we must make sure that our children go to school. I don't want them to be like me without an education. I want them to be like you and Antonio.

Ah, did we bake for *Pasqua*, all kinds of special Easter breads and *torte*. The bakery smelled even better than at Christmas. I too want to hold you in my arms. I want to hold you in my bed. It is so lonely at night without you, so I suffer what you suffer. Just a little while longer. Kiss Ralph for me.

Your loving husband,
John

*****

16 May 1893

My dearest love, John;

Happy birthday, my love, and Ralph sends his greetings and love too. Now you are thirty-two, where does the time go? I must confess that your last letter made me cry for the first time since you left. Certainly I understand your position and your feelings and concerns for Antonio. It does you proud to be so honorable. Friendship is so important in life. I too am grateful to him for what he has done for you and therefore for us. But dear John, we have an obligation to ourselves and to our son and the life we are planning. Of course I will respect your wishes and wait for you to call me to you. However, we must all realize that whenever I come to America it will require a major adjustment for everyone. We cannot put it off continually. For now I will wait, but please, let it be soon.

My seamstress business is not doing very well at present. It goes in and out of cycle. Just now the economy is not too good and people are not buying new clothes. I can always tell when things are going to become bad because my mending work increases. I have decided to try my hand at becoming *La Scrittore*. As you know, when you left last year, not too many of the families in Pietramelara had gone to America before you did. Since you have left, quite a few more have emigrated. I understand that a lot of families from your old town of Camigliano went too and also many from my father's town of Riardo. I think the same is happening for the rest of Italy.

I will have to wait for word to get around that I am available to write and read letters. I must wait for people I don't know to come to me. People always look for strangers to write for them so no one close will know their business. So far it has not been very successful, I have only written one letter but I am sure other people will become aware of my services.

Ralph continues to grow and I thank God he is a healthy boy. He is never any problem. But he is more and more demanding of my time and he wears me out. It would be good for him to have a brother or sister to play with or he will become spoiled and not learn to share and compromise. I know what I am talking about because I was an only child and I know that I was spoiled. So, as soon as I come to America, the first thing we will do is to take care of that pleasant obligation.

We are experiencing a drought here, and so early in the season too. We haven't had any rain in over two months. It is that hot wind blowing across the Mediterranean from Africa, you know *Il Scirocco*. It should bring rain but this time it isn't. It happens from time to time. The farmers are afraid that it will not be a good year for the crops and if rain does not come soon it will be a disaster. It is all that the people are talking about, and as a result they are only spending money for the bare essentials, so no new clothes. If that happens, on top of the existing bad economy, it will be a very hard winter for me. Also, my boarder is going back to her family's house in *Napoli* for the summer, so I will lose her rent income while she is gone. She says she will be back in the autumn. I said nothing, but I hope I will not be here by then.

Write soon. I live for your letters. They are the only things that sustain me and help me to endure without you.

Your loving wife,
Maria

28 June 1893

Dear Maria;

I am very concerned about how things are in Pietramelara although I thank God you and Ralph are well. I am well, and everything was going so well here until the other night. I really felt we were making headway. Then we had a problem that was not of our doing.

One night last week, one of our boarders got drunk and brought a woman home with him to the apartment. Antonio and I were asleep when we heard shouting. He took the woman into the front room where the other three boarders were sleeping. Antonio and I don't know what happened but a fight broke out. By the time we stopped the fight the police came. I guess one of the neighbors sent for them. I think I know who it was too – that wagging tongue that lives next door. We had a very difficult time explaining the situation to the police especially since we don't know what happened. The language barrier is still a big problem. Anyway, we threw the man and the woman out of the apartment but the police issued us a summons anyway and we had to go to court. Can you imagine, we didn't do anything but they said that we were responsible?

In the old days, in Italy, we would have just thrown them out into the street and that would have been the end of it. When we got to court we were lucky because we had an understanding judge. But it was still difficult because we had to explain everything through an interpreter. But he let us off with a small fine for creating a disturbance. Then it turned out that we were supposed to have a rooming house license. We didn't know that. There was a fine for that. Then we had to buy a rooming house license and on top of that I lost a day's wages. I am not angry with Luigi for that. He had to work so hard without me and even hire some part-time help for the day. In fact, thank God for Luigi! He advanced us some of the money we needed to pay the fines and now we are indebted to him again. And, on top of that, we lost a boarder and we cannot replace him because the other men say that four men sleeping in one room is too much anyway. So, the money I was going to send to you to help pay the taxes is gone, taken by the government here. I am afraid you will have to make your left breast smaller again. I am so sorry about this.

I have some good news though. It looks as though Antonio's business is going to be successful. He is hopeful that soon he will be able to send for his family. They are worse off than we are. His wife, Joanna, works and she and her children live with her mother and father. This immigration thing is not an easy process. I guess you are correct about people coming to America from Italy, but it seems to be from all over Europe too. Every day we see new Italians in the neighborhood and Antonio says the same thing is happening all over Newark from different countries. He sees it when he makes his deliveries. I can only imagine what New York must be like and the other big cities too.

I am sorry for the setback here, and I am angry at the system. But not having a license was our fault, we will just have to be more careful in the future about obeying the laws, although some of the men in the neighborhood here don't care about any laws. They make their own rules and change them whenever they want. You know the kind I mean, we have them in *Italia* too. They must be all over the world, these *animali*.

I beg of you to understand and be patient with me a little longer. It seems that every time I write to you there is another excuse why I can't send for you. It is very upsetting for me too. It is not an excuse, but most of the men who are working to send for their families are having the same problem. It is much more difficult than any of us had imagined. And believe me when I tell you that the ones who came over with their families are the ones suffering the most. Some live two and three families in one room. And there is not enough food sometimes and the children suffer so much. Even the poor in Italy did not go without food. The way we did it is hard but it is easier. It must be awful in New York City.

Kiss Ralph for me. Happy birthday, my love. I am so sorry I cannot buy a present for your twenty-eighth birthday and be with you to celebrate it.

Your husband always,

John

*****

30 July 1893

My dearest John;

What a shock your last letter was. What a terrible experience for both of you. You and Antonio should be more careful to whom you rent the front room. You are right, thank God for Luigi. The situation is not too good in Pietramelara either. The crops are close to failure. There is so much anxiety here. More families are leaving for the western world. My heart feels for them after you described some of the living conditions in America. At least here they have some family and friends who care. When they go to the new world they are among strangers. But when things get bad people will grasp at anything that promises to be better.

I haven't made a new piece of clothing in weeks. I did write six letters though since my last letter to you. While I do not earn a lot of money writing, it is the easiest way I know of to earn something extra. I am now established as *La Scrittore*. Everyone here is feeling the strain of the economy. Some of the townspeople are going to big cities to try to earn a living, but people cannot get employment in the big cities either and I understand that living conditions are becoming very bad. I hear they are having a lot of trouble in *Napoli* and that it is not safe to walk the streets at night. I don't know what the world is coming to when even the streets are not safe.

Well, we have endured setbacks before and we will get through this one also. The greatest disappointment for me is that I am not going to be with you for a while longer. Do your best, dear John, as I know you will. Don't worry about the taxes. There is more than enough in the surplus for this year. We will let next year take care of itself. Pray that I will not be here next year.

Ralph is growing so quickly. It is fortunate that I know how to sew since he outgrows everything so fast. I try to sell the clothes he outgrows. I make them all myself so even second hand they are desirable. But there is little money available in town. If I can't sell them I give them to the church for the poor. No matter how we feel we must remember that there are people worse off than we are.

I think Ralph walked for only one day and he has been running ever since. I can never take my eyes off him; he is so quick. He speaks well now and he is good company for me. We play games and I read to him. He asks about you on his own so I have done a good job of keeping you alive in his mind. I even use some English words and he seems to be able to understand them. He likes to play with Papa's blocks and that helps him a great deal with his vocabulary.

I miss you and live only for our reunion. Dearest love, hold on, it will work out, I have faith, God will not abandon us, we will prevail. We have each other but the wait to unite again is weighing me down. In retrospect we should have gone to America together. As bad as things are there for immigrants I think we could have done it. But what is done is done. However, I will not wait much longer.

Your wife forever,

Maria

22 October 1893

Dear Maria;

Good news, our debt to Luigi is paid off and Antonio's business is doing well, but we are through with the boarding house business. They are more trouble than they are worth. Besides, I have found an extra job working on Sundays, so, on December 31st, we are putting the boarders out and starting the new year fresh. We will be carrying the rent between us. We can do it – we will do it. My total income will be a little more than I need so I will be back to saving something each week. As I told you, there is a good bank here in the neighborhood and that is where I keep my surplus although where you keep yours is much more desirable.

Antonio is going to take the front room and I will sleep in the back bedroom. It will be wonderful to have a room all to myself. I need the space. Newark has become so much more crowded in the little time since I have been here. There is a reservoir just up the street, past St. Lucy's Church, and there are small picnic groves around it with tables and benches and a playground for the children. I go there every chance I get just to have some fresh air and open space. There are many *bocce* courts and I play whenever I get a chance. Last week we celebrated a religious feast. There was a procession from the church up Eighth Avenue, around the reservoir then down Seventh Avenue for a few blocks and then around again up Eighth Avenue and back to St. Lucy's Church. There was a band leading the whole procession.

We had to work extra hard at the bakery to make enough bread and pastries for the street vendors. There were food stands everywhere lining the streets and the wine was flowing like water. The summer was hot and dry here too. It must be the same all over the world because more and more people are coming to America. The new Italian immigrants continue to pour in and people from other countries, too. But so far our neighborhood remains Italian. I don't know where they are going to put all the people who come. I understand that New York is having a severe problem with overcrowding and that the rents are going higher each day. Two and three families are living in one apartment. It is becoming more and more crowded in the streets here in Newark. Sometimes it is even hard to go across the street. We have a lot of accidents with wagons running down people and even crashing into each other. The police are becoming very strict and are giving out summonses for driving the horses too fast.

Soon, my love, I will send for you and Ralph. In the meantime I send my love to both of you.

Your loving husband,
John

34

10 December 1893

My dearest love, John;

I am so sorry for not writing to you sooner, but I think all of Pietrame-lara has become ill with the influenza. First Ralph got sick for ten days. He was very sick, and I was so worried. He had high temperatures and he ached all over. My heart ached to see him suffer so. Just as he was recovering, I became ill and I was sick for over a week. Even when the sickness left me I was weak for days afterwards.

Your last letter was here for five days before I was able to get out of the house to pick it up at the post office and read it. While I was ill I sent Ralph to a neighbor's house. I think three people in town died from the disease. It was terrible. Thank God we are all well now and Ralph is back home with me. To pay for the doctor and the medicines, I had to draw on the surplus. I also had to give something to the woman who cared for Ralph when I was ill. I am sorry to tell this to you but I had no other choice. Also, my boarder did not return to teach here and that didn't help either. However, I am making two wedding dresses for January so that will help, and, believe it or not, I am writing letters, five since I have recovered from the influenza.

The second Christmas of our separation will soon be here. We must make sure it does not happen again. I have made a vow that it will not. One way or another I come to America next year. On this I insist so start to make preparations. Trouble in America cannot be any different from trouble in Italy. At least we will be together and little Ralph will have the father that he needs and, if we work hard at it, maybe a sister or a brother. I am now thinking we made a mistake in separating. The three of us should have emigrated together as a family. Some families do it, but what is done is done.

What is your extra job on Sundays? You didn't explain the details. I am always interested in what you are doing so tell me in your next letter.

Dear John, pray for me as I pray for you. When our two loves are reunited these last two years will seem like a bad dream. My love is yours. Merry Christmas and let the new year be ours.

Your loving and lonely wife,

Maria

Chapter V

LETTERS 1894

28 January 1894

Dear Maria;

My love to you and to Ralph. I send you kisses and embraces. It pained me to hear of your illness and little Ralph's too. Many people in my neighborhood are sick also. The sickness must be all over the world but so far Antonio and I have both been very lucky; we are well. It was a good thing that we got rid of the boarders. Five people living in this small apartment would have been very risky. I pray to God that you are completely well now. Please be careful.

Antonio is doing well. He is earning as much as he was when he worked in the bakery. Luigi caught the influenza for ten days so I ran the bakery for him. I had no trouble with anything. I was able to take care of everything but I had to work hard and long hours to make up for Luigi being out sick. Thank God that Luigi's wife, Gia, did not get sick so she worked in the store as usual.

But I ran everything else, I did it and I can now say that I am a baker and it was easy. I made all the cakes and pastries and felt proud. Antonio helped as much as he could but he did not have too much time to spare. Working in the bakery is not like baking at home. The large quantity makes quality a problem. I am very lucky to have Luigi for my teacher. He is a master baker. He is well known even outside the neighborhood and people come from all over to buy from him. Even the rich people from the Forest Hill section of Newark send their servants here for cakes and bread. I have decided that some day I will own my own bakery. I like it better than working on the farm. There is work all year and we are not at the mercy of the weather except when we have a heavy snowstorm but even that does not last too long. But I miss the open fields and the clean air on the farm.

Soon we will be together again, I promise you. Again I missed little Ralph's birthday. Three years old on the 6th. It is hard to believe how time passes so quickly.

On Sundays I work for some people collecting payments on loans, like a bill collector. It is hard for people to get money from the banks so they go to rich people and borrow. Then I make collections for the lenders. The work is easy, I just knock on doors and I get to be outdoors. It takes about three or four hours on Sundays.

Sometimes Antonio has extra work to do cleaning the wagon and we are not together on Sundays like we used to be. We used to play *bocce* and argue about who was winning. It was a lot of fun. We don't do that too much no more like we did when he was working at the bakery. I miss those times we had together. Stay well and continue to tell Ralph about me, it is important to me that I am not a stranger to him when we meet again. When you come over I will teach Ralph to play *bocce* and how to argue about the score. Also, I am beginning to need some new clothes so I need you to sew for me, like you did when we were together, remember?

Your loving husband,

John

*****

28 February 1894

My dearest love, John;

My love, kisses, and fidelity to you. I am proud that you have been able to master your new trade in such a short time. A trade is an asset you will always have. No one can ever take it away from you. I believe you will have your own bakery someday. I have faith in you. When I come to you we will work to make it happen. How fortunate we are that you took your first job with Luigi. See, my love, God and His angels watch over us.

The economic situation in Italy is not good at all. Just when I think it is at its lowest point it somehow manages to become worse. I think when the time comes, it will be difficult to sell the house. We could always sell it if we ask a low price but I want to get as much as possible for you. I am going to put the house up for sale now. There is no reason to wait any longer. If we can get our price I can come to America with a nice surplus. If we wait much longer, I think I will be forced to almost give it away. We will see what happens. But, one way or another, I will sell it.

I am also going to start to sell everything in the house except for the bare necessities. It will be sad to see all of Mama's beautiful things go but it is not practical to even think of shipping anything to America. I will take only some clothing and a few precious things I cannot bear to part with.

I don't understand your Sunday job. If those rich people make loans why don't the borrowers go to them directly to make payments? Why do they need you? There are strange customs in America.

I am so glad that I started to study English. I am becoming more comfortable using it. I am starting to be able to think in English without having to translate in my mind. I will just have to be careful with my pronunciation but when I come to America I will just listen and imitate the sounds I hear.

I had a small birthday party for Ralph, nothing elaborate. I didn't invite anyone until the last minute. I didn't want them to have time to get any presents. No one has any money to spare for that. I just made a cake for him and that was all. He enjoyed himself and so did the other children. For his next birthday, and for mine also, you can make a grand cake and show us all that you have learned.

Pray that I sell the house soon. The time is getting shorter, my love, when I will hold you in my arms once again. Have you forgotten how I feel next to you? I have not. Till we are together again my love.

Your impatient wife,

Maria

*****

2 April 1894

Dear Maria;

I send you my love and my emotions. I do not forget you or how you feel, but it is hard to remember Ralph. It is now over two years since I have seen him. At his age children change every day. I hope I will recognize him when I see him. I know he will not recognize me and I am so grateful that you have kept me alive in his mind.

I understand why you have offered the house for sale but I still think it is too soon. As you say, we will wait and see what happens. Antonio and I are discussing what to do. He does not want to be a boarder again. If he moves out, we will have a hard time with expenses. He is having a problem with his oldest daughter. She refuses to come to America. She is only ten years old but is causing a problem. Joanna's mother and father are not helping any. They will be alone if all the children come so they are encouraging the older one not to leave. Antonio is very upset. When they do

38

come, it will be necessary for us to separate and get apartments for each family.

We have decided that when you sell the house you will come first. There will be only the three of us. With him there will be five with one boy and two girls. Antonio can still have the front room and we will share the rent and the expenses until his family comes. At first Antonio refused to stay here. We almost had our first argument over it, but this time I won and we are going to do it my way. In a year or two when he sends for his family we should both be able to make it on our own. It will work out.

Antonio is very quiet you won't even know he is here. Besides, he has all the extra work of running a business and he is not home very much, only on Sundays, and sometimes not even then. We will let fate handle the matter. I feel the pain of our separation in many ways. Stay well, my love.

Your loving husband,

John

*****

10 May 1894

My dearest love, John;

I deliberately waited to reply to your last letter, as I wanted to wish you a happy birthday. So, you are thirty-three! My God, I am married to an old man. But I am not worried. They say that making love is like riding a bicycle, once you learn how, you never forget how to do it. I cannot wait to feel you next to me.

Ralph has no problem with remembering you, I have seen to that. I teach him his prayers and he always asks God to protect his Papa. He knows who you are and that we are coming to see you. He is so bright, he now knows his letters, and I am beginning to teach him how to spell two-letter words. I will not let him forget you, only if we are not together soon he may stop believing me, and that would be sad. We must not let that happen.

No one has offered to purchase the house. I am very disappointed. If I do not receive an offer by the end of June I will lower the price. In the meantime I am selling some of the furniture and things.

I cry when I see them go. It makes me think of Mama and Papa. How sad they would be to see how things are. The farm gone, now their possessions are being sold off, and soon the house will go too. Oh, John, I hope we have done the right thing. I have always felt self-confident but lately I have been having frightful premonitions. It is a feeling that I do not like. So much of what we planned did not happen. Will we have the same bad luck in the future? Life is very hard. But there is no going back now. What is done is done and we must only look to the future. For us there will be no past.

I am able to put the money from the sale of our possessions into the surplus, which is not as much as it was when we sold the farm. When I sell the house, after we pay our share of the taxes, and then our traveling expenses, there will not be as much left as I had hoped. Still I will come to you with something, and with your savings we should have a good start, more than most who are emigrating, so we should not complain.

I understand the problem with Antonio and I also understand his point of view. You must not try to force him to do anything he doesn't want to do. I realize that he will feel like an intruder when I come. Please tell him that he should not feel that way. Your letters about him have made me feel like he is an old family friend. The basic plan you have both worked out seems the best practical solution. Be sure to make him understand that there is no rush for him to move. He is to move when it is convenient for him. Tell him I am his friend just as you are.

In so far as taking the full expense of the apartment on ourselves is concerned, we should not have a problem if we are careful. I am sure I can earn some money as a seamstress and as *La Scrittore*. We will manage.

Just this one time I will use your name as I ask you, dear Giovanni, to remember our love and that it will take us through this terrible period. Have faith in us.

Your faithful wife,

Maria

*****

15 July 1894

Dear Maria;

I, too, waited until today to write so I can wish you a happy birthday. Today you are twenty-nine and I am married to an old woman too. I first met you when you were only fifteen, remember, on the farm, during the harvest? How everything has changed since then, or maybe it is we who have changed.

Forgive me, but sometimes I think it would have been better if I did not come to America. Maybe if I stayed in Italy we could have found a way to save the farm. I don't know how we could have done it but maybe we could have and I would not be here alone for two years without you. But, as you say, what is done is done, and what has happened has happened.

Loneliness makes for very hard times and people forget the important things and brood over their loneliness and do foolish things. But I should count the blessings I have. I am very comfortable in my job at the bakery. Luigi leaves whenever he can and I am in charge of everything when he is gone. Besides us there are two other men working here now, so it is a great responsibility. Soon I will ask Luigi for more money. I don't think there will be a problem. If it weren't for me, and my loyalty to him, he would not have any time off for himself. I am becoming fairly well known in the neighborhood from serving the customers. No bakery has our quality.

Antonio now owns his own horse and wagon and sometimes he even hires someone to help him make his rounds and keep the wagon clean and take care of the horse. When you do come I think he will not stay in the apartment too long. He is looking for an apartment now. There aren't too many in the neighborhood because people keep coming in from Italy. He says he will get a small flat if he has to and then a larger one later on. I promise you, I am not rushing him. It is something he wants to do.

I know that he has plans to buy an apartment building someday. I don't know how he will do it but he is the kind of person who will be able to talk the bank into cooperating, and he is known to be an honorable person. He says he is going to make owning real estate his career. His delivery business is just that, a business. He is good at it only because he is good at business. I think he would succeed at anything and it does not matter to him what he does.

It's not the same for me; I have come to love the bakery business, and I don't want to do anything else. Owning my own bakery has now become my dream and beside you and Ralph, it is the only reason why I work so hard. I want to have a large family too and I want to have a home and take care of everybody.

Stay well and kiss Ralph for me and tell him that I also pray for him every day.

Your husband,

John

4 August 1894

My dearest love, John;

Your last letter sounded so sad. Has something happened? I sense that there is a problem, but I hope I am wrong. Oh, my love, perhaps soon we will be together and no matter how we are forced to live we will fight life's problems together. We are one, you and I. Nothing will ever separate us again. I will not permit it! Our new life in America will be beautiful; we will make it beautiful. We will raise our children and live to see our grandchildren. You'll see, have faith.

No one has made an offer to purchase the house, so I have lowered the price again. Now they will know I am very anxious to sell so if I get an offer it will probably be lower still. Unless it is an attempt to steal the house from us I will accept any offer. It is not worth the time apart any longer to hold out just for money. We will see. I think a tailor from the other side of town may be interested. I think my sewing room and the fitting room are an attraction to him. I have sold everything from the house except our bed and a few utensils, linens, and some clothing for Ralph. He grows so fast that it is hard to keep extra clothing for him. I am not selling any of my sewing equipment on the possibility that the tailor may be interested. It might be an added incentive for him to buy the house although he will have to pay extra for the equipment. The time is getting short, my love, I can feel it.

I am beginning to explain to Ralph that we will be moving and taking a long trip on a big ship very soon. He is getting excited about it. Frankly so am I. It will be a great experience for him and for me too. Every day he asks when we are going on the boat. I have never traveled far from Pietramelara. I have never even been to *Napoli* and that is only about thirty-five miles away. He understands he is going to see his Papa. He asks for you every day. God forbid that I should wish part of my life away, dear John, but I wish the immediate future were over and we were together as a family.

As far as not going to America is concerned, I am sure we did the right thing. The man who bought the farm from us has lost it. The drought was so bad that he could not make the mortgage payments and the bank took it away from him. How sad. But you see, dear John, if we had tried to keep it that might have happened to us. Again, God watches over us.

I hope that you have explained how I feel to Antonio. He must believe I am sincere in wanting him to stay until he is ready to move. I am looking forward to meeting him, and Luigi and his wife Gia. Just think, soon I will be an American and not an Italian even though there was no Italy when I was born. So I will be changing my nationality three times, let's hope it will be the last. Pray for me as I pray for you.

Your loving wife,

Maria

*****

1 October 1894

Dear Maria;

My love to you and Ralph. My heart goes out to you knowing you are living in a house that is practically empty. All your Mama's nice things gone. What will make it worse for you is that there are no nice things in the apartment. You are going to be disappointed, I know it. Antonio and I bought only what we needed, and that's not much. It is true, men live in a house, but a woman makes it a home. You will have a lot of work to do when you come to me.

I am sorry you felt it necessary to lower the price on the house. But I am sure you know what's best. Your father was so proud of it. He died leaving a house and a farm to us and in a few years we lost what it took him a lifetime to build up. It makes me bitter at the government system and its laws. I have lost respect for both of them. We are so helpless.

So many people live here without paying too much attention to the laws that it is almost like living in a separate society. It is also funny. When laws are made everybody nods in agreement and then they go about doing whatever they want, just like in Italy. So many people make up their own rules and no one says anything about the wrong doings if it doesn't affect them. I sympathize with them because I feel the same way. I guess that is the way it is all over the world. But America is not too bad because of the freedom and opportunity we have. But life does not always let you survive if you follow the rules. Sometime you have to do what you have to do.

Well, my love, let me know when you are ready to come, although sometimes, even now, I think I should come back to Italy. It is such a hard choice, but considering everything you have told me about the changes over there, I think America is better.

All my love from your husband,

John

2 November 1894

My dearest love, John;

I waited until now to write as negotiations for the sale of the house were in progress when I received your last letter. So much bickering back and forth. Finally I said, "*Basta*, enough! Take it or leave it!", and that did it. It is sold! The tailor bought it. I had to lower the price again and include all of my sewing equipment to reach an agreement. But it is done. Please don't be upset about the price but I don't think you realize how bad things are here in Italy, especially in small towns like Pietramelara. If I had held out we might not have sold the house and we would be apart longer and I can't live that way anymore.

I have purchased the boat tickets. Ralph and I sail on 25 November from *Napoli* on the SS Alesia and we will arrive in New York on 10 December. At Last! The nightmare is over! You will have to find out how to meet us on Ellis Island, I don't know the procedure, and also check on the ship arrivals in case we are late arriving. I will have Ralph, a small trunk, and a suitcase, and if everything works out, 'it' will not be with me. In case you have forgotten what I look like, I will be wearing the blue hat with the flower that you liked so much. I could not bear to sell it.

After all the expenses were paid I was able to add some more to our surplus so if you look closely you will see that my left breast is a bit larger than my right. And we will be together for Christmas. It will be so wonderful for Ralph to have Christmas with his Papa; he will be so happy. And I will have Christmas with my husband.

Don't write to me anymore, dear John, as I will not be here. I can't wait! Do they arrest people in America for kissing in public?

Your impatient wife,

Maria

Chapter VI

GIOVANNI IN AMERICA 1892

Giovanni was watching the docking procedure from the deck of the ship bringing him to the New World. Fifteen days earlier he had left Naples and, the day before that, his beloved Mariantonia. Odd, as much as it pained him to leave her, he had felt nothing about leaving Italy. Now, on May 24, 1892, he was landing in America and would start a new life for both of them.

There was a great commotion on the pier, shouting back and forth between the deckhands and the men down on the dock. He didn't know that there had been a last minute change and that the ship was docking on the East River side of Manhattan instead of its scheduled Hudson River slip. As the procedure progressed, the rumor spread among the passengers that the ship had landed at the wrong place. The rumor caused a great anxiety among them. Some thought that they had landed in the wrong city, and others even thought that they had landed in the wrong country. It was a while until they were all calmed down.

This was New York City; they were in America. After all, didn't they pass the Statue Of Liberty as the ship entered the harbor? The statue was a gift from the people of France and was erected on what had been called Bedloe's Island and renamed Liberty Island. It stood on a pedestal that was paid for by donations from the school children of America. They sent in their pennies and nickels from all over the country. The statue had only been dedicated in October 1886 and already it had become a symbol of freedom and opportunity to arriving immigrants.

The word was passed among the steerage passengers that after debarkation they would be transferred to the other side of the city, then to Ellis Island for processing. Giovanni hated government interference in his life in Italy and now it seemed as if in America there was no difference. He also resented the fact that it was only the passengers in steerage who were being subjected to this indignity. First and second-class passengers were processed aboard ship and were free to leave immediately afterwards. He could have traveled second class, they had the money, but he had wanted to leave as much money as possible with Mariantonia for her and the baby. He smiled at the thought of where the surplus was kept and laughed because it was the first time he ever remembered being jealous of money.

45

The steerage passengers were assembled on the pier and marched off toward the street. Many were families with children all struggling with their belongings in trunks and suitcases, and some with nothing more than a rolled up blanket tied with rope and slung over their shoulders. Giovanni traveled very light, just a few clothes and toilet articles in one small, black suitcase.

The officials leading the long line of immigrants stopped here and there, and directed them this way and that. Giovanni became more and more agitated. As the group approached the street the attention of the officials was momentarily distracted as they tried to direct the hapless column of strangers to turn left down the street. Giovanni made a spot decision, which was very unlike him. As the line turned left, he turned right instead, and for the first time walked through the streets of America alone. He was free, let them go and process their papers without him.

He found himself on South Street heading north, parallel to the East River. The area was very crowded. The street was busy with horses and wagons going in all directions; there was no order at all. The roadway was lined on the west with warehouses filled with newly arrived cargo. There was a constant commotion. Men were coming and going from the various ship chandlers carrying supplies to the boats docked on the other side. Ships were berthed all along the riverside of the street, some still with sails only, tall masts and yardarms. Their bow spits were overhanging the street almost touching the warehouses on the other side, creating an umbrella effect, almost like an arbor, over the street. The sound of English being spoken all around him was very strange. He had thought he might hear some English on board the ship but the ship was of German registry. So he only heard German among the crew and Italian spoken by the passengers.

There were no sidewalks so he walked in the street, careful not to get knocked down by someone, or worse, a horse and wagon. All the hustle and bustle made him wonder if he had made a mistake in leaving the other passengers. *Maybe I should turn around and go back and catch up with them.*

His indecision and apprehension were interrupted as he heard the familiar, musical sounds of his native tongue. There, on his right, were men working out in the open, in what was the largest fish market he had ever seen. He had stumbled onto the Fulton Fish Market on the East River. The men speaking Italian were working, moving large containers, and dumping fish from one container to another. Others were gutting and cleaning all kinds of fish. There were buckets of clams, mussels, and crabs, and it all smelled like the fish market that it was. Cautiously, he approached the men and began speaking with them.

"Are you just off the boat?" one asked him.

"Yes, I just arrived this morning. Do you know of any farms around here where I could get a job?"

The men all started laughing. "Farms? There are no farms in New York City. How do you feel about gutting fish? You can work here by the day, the boss is always looking for workers and at the end of the day they pay cash. What do you say? Shall I call him over? It may not smell as nice as the open air back home, but at least the fish always look up to you," said one of them with a smile. The others just laughed.

Giovanni jumped at the chance. Before he even realized where he was, he was working in America, in a fish market, as a day laborer. He hated the work but it was a start. The men were friendly enough, maybe too friendly he thought to himself. When the workday was over, as they were standing in line to be paid, another of the laborers approached him.

"So you want to work on a farm? If you want to be a farmer you'll have to go to New Jersey." He pointed west and added, "It's across the other river. Hey, you need a place to stay for the night? I can help you."

The offer made him suspicious. They all seemed too eager to please him and too condescending. He thought of the few American dollars, now hidden in the special money belt that Mariantonia had made for him. He had exchanged his lira for dollars back in Naples. He decided that the prudent thing to do was to collect his day's wages and leave. As he stood in line he thought it was best to get to New Jersey, wherever that was, as quickly as possible. It was seven o'clock in the evening when they stopped working. After getting paid he picked up his suitcase and silently slipped past the group of Italian workers and disappeared west into the city streets.

He still had no idea where he was. He followed the twilight to the west and wound up on the Bowery near Canal Street. Continuing west on Canal he again found himself among people speaking his language. Following the familiar sounds he walked into the heart of the Italian section of New York City and turned right, walking north on Mulberry Street. He bought something to eat from a street vendor and continued up the street. He saw a large, red brick church on the corner of Mulberry and Grand Streets.

It was St. Patrick's Old Cathedral, the first Catholic Cathedral of the city. In the church graveyard is the grave of Pierre Toussaint who would one day be canonized by the Catholic Church. He had been a slave, born in Haiti in 1766 and brought to America by his owner, Jean Jacques Bernards. On her deathbed, Bernard's widow freed him. Afterwards he dedicated the rest of his life to helping the poor and homeless in New York City. Toussaint died in 1853.

It never occurred to Giovanni that all churches in America were not Catholic; he just naturally assumed they were, just like at home. He pushed the door open and entered the vestibule. The interior of the church was dark except for the flickering lights of the votive candles reflecting off the walls. He was tired and sat in the back pew far off to one side. There were a few people in the church and he wanted to be as far away from them as possible.

'*Oh God,*' he prayed, '*I am sorry that I smell of dead fish.*'

He relaxed and sleep overtook him. He didn't hear the sexton locking the doors for the night. They never locked the church doors in Italy. In a few hours he woke up. He had no idea what time it was and was shocked to find that he could not get out. Giovanni thought about his situation and reasoned that they would probably unlock the doors for morning mass.

'*When they open the doors I'll just walk out like I am finishing a visit. Then I'll go to New Jersey somehow and look for farm work.*' He felt more secure now that he had formulated a plan of action. So he curled up on the pew and went back to sleep using his small suitcase as a pillow.

The next morning the entrance bells announcing the start of the five o'clock mass woke him up. On the spur of the moment he decided to remain and attend the mass and offer it up as a prayer of thanksgiving. After the familiar Latin dismissal, "*Ite missa est,*" announced by the celebrant, to which the congregation replied in unison, "*Deo Gratias*", he left the church and walked out into a beautiful, bright, sunny day.

He was worried about the language problem but thought if he just kept saying 'New Jersey' and pointing to the west he could get there eventually. The strategy proved to be successful and by late morning he was on a ferry heading toward Hoboken, N.J. One of the crewmembers on the boat was an Italian immigrant and befriended him. He told Giovanni that he had a cousin who lived in Newark.

"There is a very large Italian neighborhood near the Morris and Essex Railroad Station. I go there to visit my cousin once in a while. It is easy to get to."

"But how am I ever going to find my way? I don't speak any English"

"Don't worry," the man told him, "Here, I'll write it down for you." So the man wrote it down for him in very large letters. He was amazed; he had never seen the letter 'k' before. "The train station is right where we will dock. Show this note to the agent and buy a ticket. Keep looking for the signs that spell N-E-W-A-R-K, the conductor will help you. Then get off the train. When you get off, walk down the steps to the street and turn left. You'll be OK."

He thanked the man profusely, "*Grazie, mille grazie.*" Then with a wave of their hands they exchanged the familiar, "*Ciao,*" and Giovanni went ashore.

With the directions the man had given to him he was able to purchase a railroad ticket. "Look for the sign that spells 'Newark' and then get off." He repeated the directions to himself, over and over. It was a minor miracle that he was successful and he was very proud of himself that he had come so far in two days without knowing any English. Armed with the instructions, he was, by late afternoon, in Newark walking up Broad Street. Just as before he again heard the familiar song of his native tongue. He just followed the sound as though it was a well-marked street map in front of him. Soon he was walking up Eighth Avenue into the heart of Newark's first ward. Dominated by Italian immigrants, it would be where he would live in America for many years.

So fate, chance meetings, fear of the unknown, and hope all conspired to place Giovanni in a neighborhood which would be the setting for his short-lived success, trials and tribulations and ultimate downfall.

He decided to walk the streets and explore his new surroundings. Everyone spoke Italian and he had no trouble nor did he feel he was in a strange place. Idle conversations here and there made him feel even more at home.

'Home, that's a good thought, where am I going to spend the night?' He decided that finding a place to sleep should be his first priority. He stopped his casual wanderings and began to look for signs for a room to rent. *'Thank God the signs are all in Italian.'* Continuing up Eighth Avenue he was crossing High Street trying to find a boarding house. He saw someone attaching a *cercasi uomo* 'man wanted' sign on the shop window of a bakery from which emanated the sweet smell of freshly baked bread. Giovanni approached the man and asked what the job was.

Luigi eyed him up and down and introduced himself as the owner of the bakery. Looking at Giovanni's imposing physique he said, "I need a strong and dependable worker." Luigi was a little apprehensive, looking at Giovanni's almost threatening appearance. Luigi's reluctance melted away immediately as soon as Giovanni smiled. He offered the job to Giovanni on the spot.

"Hard work, long hours, early starts, shoveling coal into the ovens, carrying sacks of flour and sugar and baskets of bread would be required," warned Luigi. The prudent Giovanni thought it best to accept the piece of good fortune and agreed to start the next day. He would look for farm work later on. That evening he ate dinner in a small *trattoria*. It was the first food he had eaten that day. It tasted so good and he ate until he was completely satisfied. It was also the first glass of *vino rosso* he had since leaving Italy.

Employed but still homeless, Giovanni continued along the street in search of a place to sleep. What he found instead was another church named St. Lucy's. It was located on Sheffield Street, between Eighth and Seventh Avenues. This time he deliberately hid and allowed himself to be locked in. Where else, he rationalized, could he find a better and safer place to sleep than in God's house. Besides, it was free. He thought of how far he had come down in the world from the comfortable bedroom he had shared with his wife in their house.

Early the next morning when he walked into the bakery Luigi introduced his assistant to Giovanni.

"I have big orders to fill today. Antonio will tell you what your duties are," said Luigi, and turning to Antonio he instructed, "You take Giovanni under your wing. Go show him where the ovens are."

Luigi's introduction served to let both of them know that in the scheme of things, Antonio would be Giovanni's superior. Neither of them had a problem with that arrangement.

*****

"Come with me," Antonio said, "First let's have some coffee and bread with *marmelatta*. It's homemade by Gia, that's Luigi's wife." They went into the room in the back of the bakery's retail store and ate breakfast.

Antonio was tall with light brown hair, bright blue eyes, and fair skin. He did not look Italian, certainly not in Giovanni's eyes, but he was. Instinctively Giovanni felt that he liked him. As for Antonio, when he first caught sight of the hulking figure in the doorway, he didn't know what to think. But then came that infectious smile and any doubts he had faded away. They started to get acquainted and when they finished eating Antonio led the way out the front door of the bakery store.

Around to the left of the building was an alleyway running alongside the length of the building. It led to a flight of steps then down to a door leading into the basement where the ovens were located. Just inside the door were cans of fresh milk and cream. Luigi had been in earlier and stoked the furnace that had been banked all night. The basement was about forty feet wide and sixty feet long. The ovens and their gaping hearths were along the far wall and took up most of the area. Along the alley wall opposite the ovens were the kneading and cutting tables and proofer, which allowed the formed loaves of bread to rise. Next to the tables were the mixing vats, and then further along the wall to the back wall were piled sacks of flour and sugar.

There were supplies of cocoa, citron, cases of eggs and all kinds of exotic spices stacked everywhere. Even after breakfast the aroma was mouth watering. The furnace stretched deep into the ovens under the stone baking surface. The mouth of the furnace was near the back wall of the basement and to one side there was a coal pile. Antonio pointed to the mouth of the furnace and explained that it was Giovanni's responsibility to keep the fire going.

Antonio turned to Giovanni, "Well, here it is, a little slice of heaven, just for you." He smiled and pointed to the pile of pea coal and a shovel.

"Your job is easy. Take that shovel and make sure the fire never burns out. So start with the shovel now, I have to start baking."

The air was very hot and Giovanni thought that it was actually a little slice of hell just for him. But he thought that it was probably a good place to be on a cold winter's morning.

"I'll show you how to bank the fire tonight." They smiled at one another and Antonio walked around to the hearthside of the oven and began to feed shaped loaves into it. Giovanni took his cue and picked up the shovel. While they worked they could not see each other unless one of them walked to the corner of the oven structure. From time to time Antonio would walk to within sight of Giovanni and tell him to bring up a bag of flour or sugar or whatever else he needed to prepare the bread dough and, later on, cake and pastry batter. It did not take long for them to establish a routine that complimented each other's job.

*****

Giovanni learned very quickly that even in an Italian neighborhood some customs did not survive the immigration process. Most conspicuous by its absence was the two-hour siesta following the large, main, noontime meal. Antonio explained the situation to him. In America, lunch was a short half hour long without any siesta afterward. It was back to work. The main meal was at dinner after the workday was over. That is, except on Sundays or a holiday when there was no work, and the main, leisurely meal was at one o'clock, usually after church was over. He was used to a short lunch during harvest time, but this was May! He wasn't sure he was going to like it, but this was America and he would have to adapt. It wasn't all that bad. At noontime Gia provided lunch for them. Antonio threw a freshly baked roll to Giovanni.

"How about a picnic? At least lunch is free."

They sat down on a pile of flour sacks and the respite also allowed a little time for conversation. For lunch they had a large piece of that special salami called *sopresato* along with some aged, sharp provolone cheese and that exceptional fresh roll, just baked that morning. It was all washed down with homemade wine. Not too much for noontime, just one small glassful which they had to nurse if they wanted to have that one last swallow with the last piece of bread.

"Take a piece of pastry if you want it. In season Gia also brings some fresh fruit. No one eats as well as we do. So, when did you arrive in America?"

"Just two days ago."

"Where are you living?"

"Well, to tell you the truth, I've spent the last two nights sleeping in two different churches. I don't have a place to stay yet."

"Churches! That won't do at all! I live in a boarding house and room with two other men. It's tight but it's cheap. There's a large room down the hall with three men and there is still another cot that's vacant. It'll be four of you but at least you won't get into trouble with the priest. What do you say?"

"That's OK with me, *grazie.*" Giovanni felt flattered that Antonio had taken such an interest in his well-being. They began a budding friendship that was to grow into a special kind of bond. They worked well together even though Giovanni received his work assignments from Antonio. It was a classic case of opposites being attracted to one another. Antonio was the dominant though not domineering personality and Giovanni the quiet, unassuming follower.

In a few days Giovanni's life settled into a routine. He worked six days each week and he ate breakfast and lunch on the job with Antonio. Supper was with Antonio at one of the small, inexpensive restaurants in the neighborhood. On Sundays they explored the city.

Not too far up Seventh Avenue the street ended at a reservoir located between Eighth Avenue and Seventh Avenue. About a half mile farther to the west of the reservoir was the Morris Barge Canal. The area in between was a swampy valley that extended from Eighth Avenue north for about three miles, all the way to Heller Street. There was a stream running through the valley called Branch Brook and it connected several lakes in the swamp.

*****

As Newark's population exploded, the demand for potable water outpaced the meager supply that came from a pond down on Market Street. In 1860 the city purchased the Newark Aqueduct Company and by 1870, in desperation, the city took to using the polluted Passaic River as its water source. Inevitably, by 1875, typhoid plagued the city. In order to satisfy the need for healthy water, the city built a series of reservoirs supplied by deep wells, one of which was built in 1873 on the eastern side of Branch Brook Valley. It was the area commonly referred to as the Quarry and it lay between Eighth and Seventh Avenues adjacent to the Italian neighborhood. But even these measures were insufficient so a very large reservoir system was built in 1892 far out of the city limits, called the Pequannock Reservoir System.

After that the old reservoir in the ward was drained and it became a recreation area for the citizens and was mostly used by Italians in the ward. In the winter, some water continued to accumulate there and when it froze, the reservoir was also used for ice-skating. The city erected a playground around its perimeter for the children. Picnic tables were set up for families and also a building with all the necessary facilities. *Bocce* courts were built for the adult males. At the time, a street was opened up and ran from Norfolk Street, parallel to the valley so that Eighth and Seventh Avenues now became 'T' intersections with the new street. It was called Chattum Street and later on, Clifton Avenue. Clifton Avenue ran all the way north to a stream called Second River, which was the city line between Newark and Belleville.

*****

Antonio and Giovanni spent Sundays at the reservoir area playing *bocce*. Sometimes they would go skinny dipping in the Passaic River and even in the Morris Canal. Then there were walks downtown along the canal and the canal locks to the Farmer's Market between Broad Street and Mulberry Street. On visits to the market Giovanni tried to find work on a farm but was always unsuccessful. As his attraction to baking increased he became less and less disappointed about not finding farm work. It wasn't too long before he stopped looking for farm work altogether. It was now the middle of June and he thought about missing Mariantonia's birthday in July. It made him homesick. He wrote his first letter to Mariantonia and was eagerly waiting for her reply. It arrived in August. She had written to him on her birthday. He was encouraged by Mariantonia's support of his progress so far.

'*So, she is going to call me John, all right, I will call her Maria.*'

He mentioned to Antonio her suggestion that they use English on the job whenever possible. They agreed to help each other this way and had many laughs over their misuse of words and improper pronunciation. However, they got the swear words correct and very quickly. Nevertheless, they agreed that Italian was a much better language to swear in, especially when accompanied by the proper gestures. Antonio didn't like the name John and he continued to call his friend Giovanni, and Antonio remained Antonio. They both liked Maria and so that is what they called her.

As their bond of friendship became stronger, Giovanni became aware that Antonio possessed a superior intellect and had a better education than he had. Antonio thought things through carefully and in great detail. He was a long-range planner. Giovanni came to respect Antonio very much for these qualities and as a result, he tended to follow Antonio's lead. Antonio in turn, assumed the role of the dominant, yet friendly, mentor. It was a perfect match.

It was no surprise to Giovanni when Antonio came up with an idea for them to make some extra money. There was a three-room apartment that was available for rent at 138 Eighth Avenue just a few blocks up from the bakery. He explained that they could put cots in the front room and rent them out to boarders. The rental income would more than pay for the apartment so they could live rent free, and with a kitchen they could cook and eat at home. They would be able to save even more money. Giovanni didn't ask questions, he just agreed to the plan. They rented the flat and moved in on the 1st of October. With money borrowed from Luigi, they purchased some second-hand furniture. They had no trouble finding four boarders.

The friendship between Giovanni and Antonio waxed stronger with each passing day. Their differences complemented each other's personalities. Antonio the thinker and planner was the stronger personality and Giovanni was the trusting follower just as he had been with Maria in Italy. The unspoken arrangements of the friendship fit in well with both personalities and they were content. It was somewhat the same kind of contentment he felt with Maria in their marriage.

They lived this way until the following February when Antonio announced that he was going to start his own business by selling and delivering bread and cakes to stores and restaurants. At first Giovanni was stunned and hurt.

"But I thought we were friends, Antonio," Giovanni said sadly.

"We are and we will always remain friends. Just because I won't work in the bakery anymore doesn't mean our friendship has to change. We're still partners in the apartment, right?"

"Yes, but why do you have to do it at all?" What's wrong with Luigi's bakery? Don't you like working there no more?"

"I like it very much. I've learned a lot from Luigi. It's just that I have to make money for my family. I have two extra mouths to feed than you have. I also want to better myself. I don't want to live in a tenement all my life. Besides, Luigi is going to be my supplier in this venture so I'll still see you at the store and at home. You'll probably even end up with my job and a raise. So, what do you say, are we still friends?"

"Yes we are," Giovanni agreed. He thought, "How could it not be right, he is my best friend."

When Antonio approached Luigi it was with a well thought out plan that included more business for the bakery and a replacement for himself in Giovanni. All Luigi had to do was find another day laborer, an easy task. After explaining the plan in detail to both of them, Luigi and Giovanni were as excited as Antonio, and Luigi agreed to pay Giovanni the same wages he paid to Antonio. It was a good deal for all concerned, everyone came out a winner. It was not that Antonio was manipulative, because he wasn't. It was just that his way of doing business was to leave something on the table for everyone as he improved his lot in life. That was Antonio's way. He thought he had made everybody's situation a little bit better while he took most of the risks. But that would not prove to be completely true for Giovanni.

The added responsibilities that Antonio took on meant that Giovanni was alone a lot more. The loneliness set him to brooding on his need for Maria. He had been so busy trying to make his way and with his long workday, nighttime and sleep came quickly. Now alone, he thought more and more about her absence and his need for her in his bed. While the problem was always on his mind it now became one of need just for a woman, any woman. Fighting the temptation was always aided by his sincere love of Maria and the example of Antonio's fidelity to his Joanna, but it was becoming more and more difficult for him.

Then one night one of the boarders had a little too much to drink and brought a prostitute into the apartment while the three other boarders were asleep in the front room. The boarders were awakened and a fight broke out. Before Giovanni and Antonio were able to resolve the matter the police broke into the flat. Later they agreed that it must have been the gossip that lived next door who sent for them.

But the real tragedy was that Giovanni became acutely aware that the 'ladies' were out there and available for what he found out was a mere pittance. He resisted temptation for a long time but the more he tried to put the idea out of his mind the more insidious and desirable it became.

When he finally succumbed to the temptation for the first time, the feelings of guilt and betrayal of Maria were almost more than he could bear. He resolved that the first time would be the last, but it wasn't. And as the incidents with 'them' became more frequent, it was harder and harder to be discrete about it. Still, he was confident that Antonio would never find out. He never took them to the apartment. He always went to the 'house' down near the Passaic River. But in such a close-knit community nothing was a secret for long, and it wasn't too long before Antonio knew. He never said a word about it to his friend and the subject was never brought up between them. Giovanni soon realized that his thinly veiled secret was out. Out of guilt and embarrassment he stopped attending mass on Sundays.

'Birds of a feather', like all sayings, always contain an element of truth. It was on one of Giovanni's visits to the 'house' that he became acquainted with some of the seedier characters and even criminal elements found in the neighborhood. One day he was approached by a man and asked if he would like to earn some extra money. The man and his friends were loan sharks even though they called themselves businessmen. The term might have been unfamiliar to Giovanni but what they did was not. They reminded him of some of the men he used to see in Italy.

They were looking for someone to make collections. Giovanni's towering appearance made him ideal for the job because he could easily intimidate strangers. They explained that all Giovanni had to do was collect payments from people and turn the payments over. They knew that Giovanni's initial impression would instill a sense of fear in the debtors especially if they did not make payment, just as long as he did not smile.

"What if they don't pay?" Giovanni asked.

"Don't worry. You don't have to do a thing," they assured him, "Just tell us and we will take care of it. Just don't smile, *capisce*?"

The offer was attractive especially since the time required would not interfere with his job at the bakery. He agreed and decided to write to Maria about his additional source of income. Antonio was against the idea from the start. He knew the reputation of the men involved. For the first time Giovanni didn't heed Antonio's advice. After all, he rationalized, he wasn't going to do anything but collect money. He thought that if Antonio could go into business, so could he. Besides, he could quit any time he wanted to. When Maria made a bit of an issue of it in her letters he just ignored her inquiries and continued to make the collections. *'There is no trouble, people pay me on time, so what's all the worry about?'*

*****

In November of 1894, Maria wrote that she had sold the house and was on her way to America. Giovanni received her letter on the 23rd.

"My God," he told Antonio, "She will be here in less than three weeks!"

Antonio reassured him there would be no problem. "Don't worry, my friend, I will be out of the apartment in plenty of time."

"That is out of the question. I insist that you stay with us. You are always trying to make more money for your family. I will not hear of you paying more for rent and taking it away from them. You are my friend and it is my turn to help you. Where would I be now if it weren't for you?" He demanded that Antonio take the front room as they had agreed. He and Maria would sleep in the back bedroom along with little Ralph.

"We will share our meals together. Maria is an excellent cook. She learned from her Mama."

Antonio said no, Giovanni said yes, and for the next few days they each used all the arguments they could to sway the other. Finally, and mostly because Giovanni would not let the matter drop, Antonio agreed, but on a temporary basis only, and for not too long. He did, however, have the discretion to make arrangements to room elsewhere for the first few days following Maria's arrival.

56

Chapter VII

MARIA IN AMERICA 1894

It was unusually warm that day, December 10, 1894 when Maria and Ralph arrived at Ellis Island. Giovanni decided to go into the city early hoping that he might catch sight of them at the pier as they left the ship and before they boarded the ferry for Ellis Island. Because of the mass of people and all of the confusion it did not work out that way. He decided to board the visitor's ferry for the island. He went into the waiting area until Maria and Ralph were processed and released. Three ships arrived that day, one each from Genoa, Naples, and Bremerhaven, and large groups of immigrants were being marshaled like cattle into the processing center. Giovanni resigned himself to a long wait.

Maria, with Ralph and her small suitcase and trunk in tow, became part of the crowd waiting to be called for processing. She was looking for Giovanni but could not spot him in the crowd. Besides, she had to pay attention to the ongoing procedures. She was fearful of missing her number when it was called. When they entered the 'great hall' they were each assigned a number written on a small card that they had to hang around their necks on a string. There was a veritable cacophony of many languages all melding into one unintelligible roar. The two-storied arched ceiling and the walls were covered with white ceramic tile, and with a concrete floor the huge room became a sound box. The roar echoed back and forth and up and down. It was difficult to listen to what was going on.

They were seated on long benches awaiting and dreading the imminent medical examination. She could see officials marking the backs of some of the immigrants with white chalk. *'How degrading, to have someone come up and write on your clothing.'* An old woman sitting next to her recognized the troubled look on her face and, in Italian, clarified things for her.

"My daughter wrote to me about going through Ellis Island and told me about those markings. That man - you see him over there - with the X with the circle around it on his back? He has to take another medical examination. They think there's something wrong with him. And that girl over there," she pointed toward the other side of the room with her crooked finger; the one with the 'C', she may have conjunctivitis. You would do well to avoid being marked by the chalk."

Maria watched the process in horrified bewilderment. An 'X' on that man, a 'C' on that woman and other letters which had no meaning for her. Some were just pushed along without any markings at all.

She had heard many disturbing rumors about the treatment of women who were unaccompanied by husbands or fathers. The authorities were very diligent in this regard not to allow 'those women' into the country. But Maria, with her usual self-confidence, expected no trouble. After all, her husband was outside waiting for her and she had her little son with her. She was not one of 'those', and in her halting English made that very plain whenever the occasion demanded.

Her number was finally called and she went to the indicated booth with Ralph clutching at her dress. There was an official seated in the booth and an interpreter was standing next to him.

"Passport," he snapped and before the interpreter could speak Maria handed the document to him. This was her line of attack on the system. Whenever she understood the official's questions she answered immediately. She stood very tall and proud, yet not arrogant. It worked most of the time and both the official and the interpreter were impressed. The inquisition did not last too long and her demeanor and obvious class did wonders to expedite the process. She and Ralph were shunted off to another area in the 'great hall' waiting their turn with the 'markers of clothes'.

The time was approaching noon and they were given something to eat. It was awful, some bread, a little dried fruit and water. They hardly touched it, preferring to go without. So far Maria was not at all impressed with America. She felt like one of the sheep in a herd back home. The only thing lacking were the dogs and some of the officials came very close to filling that role. She kept straining her neck to locate Giovanni in the crowd, impatient to see his smile, but to no avail.

Eventually her number was called again and she walked over to the medical officer, with Ralph holding onto her for dear life. They were ushered into a small room where the doctors looked at, listened to, and poked various parts of their bodies. She stood stoically through the ordeal. Ralph was constantly looking to her for reassurance. The only problem arose when the doctor tried to examine Ralph for conjunctivitis. He resisted as the doctor tried to roll back his eyelids. Maria, with full authority, said to the doctor in accented English, "No, wait. Me first, then he will not be afraid."

Astonished at her control of the situation, the doctor said, "Of course," and he did as she directed. Ralph, seeing his mother submit to the examination, offered no further resistance when it was his turn.

'*Mama can do anything,*' he thought with admiration. Thankfully there were no chalk marks made on either of them. Soon they were escorted to the next official, with a clean bill of health.

He asked her how much money she had brought with her. There was paranoia among the immigration authorities that many of the immigrants would move directly from Ellis Island onto the welfare rolls. Again, Maria did not wait for the interpreter to speak. She told the official, in English, the amount of her hidden surplus. Taken aback by her immediate reply, the man did not even ask to see the money.

'*Thank God! I won't have to suffer the embarrassment of having to produce the surplus from its hiding place.*'

When at last the long day of examination and waiting was over, she was directed to the staircase leading down to the outer room where the 'sponsors' were waiting.

Admonishing Ralph to hold onto her skirt, they left the 'great hall'. Giovanni had been keeping a keen eye on the stairway coming down from the 'great hall' waiting for them to appear. '*I can't even imagine what little Ralph will look like.*' He recalled Maria's letter telling him about the hat she would be wearing. '*God, did she look gorgeous in that hat,*' he remembered. He could hardly restrain himself from breaking through the barrier and running up the stairs. After hours of waiting he saw them emerge through the stairway door, little Ralph looking lost and frightened, and Maria at his side carrying the small suitcase and dragging the trunk. She did not see Giovanni first; it was he who saw her. '*With that blue hat, just like she told me,*' he thought as he pushed through the crowd toward her. '*God she is beautiful*'

Fifteen days at sea and after the long arduous day she looked as if she had just been on a holiday. The blue hat offset her eyes and its shape complimented her oval face. The dress she wore was blue matching the hat, with big puffed sleeves at the top, then form fitting at the elbow. The bodice was made of white satin trimmed with lace and small blue rosettes. She had labored over it especially for their reunion. Not that Giovanni took much notice. As soon as he saw the hat he was running toward her, but still she had not seen him.

"Maria," he screamed over and over as he pushed his way over to her. "Giovanni, Giovanni," and they were soon in each other's arms and in their ecstasy they momentarily forgot little Ralph who was looking on with wide-eyed astonishment. Tears flooded down their cheeks until their kisses tasted salty. Giovanni was the first to collect himself and he dropped to his knees hugging and kissing Ralph.

Maria was standing next to them wiping away her tears. "It's Papa, Ralph, it's Papa!" They were together again. The long wait was over, almost as if it had never happened.

"Please, Giovanni, let's leave this awful place." Dutifully, he took hold of the trunk. He picked up Ralph and cradled him in his arm. Maria lifted the suitcase, locked her arm around Giovanni's and the family walked out together toward the waiting ferry to take them back to Manhattan. From there it was not too far to the New Jersey ferry slip. They did not even stop for her to see any part of the city. That could come later, some sunny Sunday. For now the only thought was to get home.

When they got off the train in Newark it was nighttime. The temperature was dropping and it was turning cold and windy. They went down the station steps to the street level and started walking up Broad Street. She had no appreciation of her surroundings. She just clung to Giovanni. They had not ceased talking to each other, holding hands as best they could, and kissing, on the ferry, on the train, and now in the street. They gave as much attention to Ralph as they could but it was almost as though he was an intrusion on their reunion.

They retraced the same path that Giovanni had explored when he first came to Newark, two and a half years before. From the railroad station, up Broad Street, left onto Eighth Avenue, and then to the tenement building where Giovanni lived. As they climbed up the stairs the trunk that Giovanni was dragging made a thump, thump, every time it went from one step to the next. Ralph thought that was very comical and he laughed and squealed at every thump.

The door to the apartment opened directly into the kitchen. Giovanni put Ralph down and let go of the trunk. Maria let the suitcase fall from her hand and in the middle of the kitchen they embraced. They did not speak. They just surrendered to the emotion of the moment. It was a long time before either of them heard Ralph.

"Mama, I'm hungry and it's dark in here."

Giovanni lit the gas lamp then lifted Ralph up onto one of the kitchen table chairs. The fire in the coal stove had been banked, and he stoked it adding coal from the scuttle near the stove.

"Soon it will be warm in here, Ralph." He smiled at his son and messed his hair. Maria was watching his every move so she could learn where things were.

"I bought some milk for Ralph." he said, as he walked into the front room. He opened a window and to her amazement, hanging from the window frame, was a metal box taking up the lower half of the window. Giovanni slid the door of the box to one side and pulled out a bottle of milk and some other food. '*A food container, hanging from the window!*' There was no question about it; America was a strange place. But she realized that it was a good place to refrigerate food in the wintertime. She smiled at the ingenuity of it. He showed her where all the utensils were, talking and stopping to kiss her with every movement.

60

The kitchen temperature was becoming warmer. Maria prepared hot oatmeal for Ralph. She and Giovanni just had coffee. Giovanni had ground the beans in a grinder he took down from a shelf. He carefully measured out just the correct amount of the roasted beans and poured them into the top of the grinder. He turned the handle round and round until the grinding sound stopped. He pulled out the drawer and there was the fresh ground coffee they needed. Neither of them had eaten all day but they were not hungry. The stove was heating the entire apartment and it was becoming comfortable.

The unspoken desire for both of them was for Ralph to go to sleep. They didn't have long to wait before he was yawning.

"All right, *mio bambino,* time for bed." Giovanni took him in his arms and into the front room and laid him on Antonio's bed. Maria got him ready for sleep. She looked around the room and her eyes met with Giovanni's. In a low whisper she asked, " Where is Antonio?"

"He will be gone for a few days."

"Well then, let's go into the bedroom and you can see how much surplus I brought to you."

Hand in hand they walked to the back bedroom. He took her in his arms and she felt the warmth of his hands and his body on her. For her it was an ecstasy for which she had waited for two and a half years. She wanted it to last forever and was stunned at how short their lovemaking was. Afterwards, lying on her back in the dark, she could hear his deep breathing; he was sound asleep.

She took in a deep breath and held it as the terrible realization came over her. It may have been two and a half years for her, but it was not two and a half years for him. It was as if a knife pierced her heart. She tried to tell herself that she was mistaken, that it was just the hustle and bustle of their first day together, that they were all exhausted. But try as she might she couldn't bring herself to believe it. The tears rolled silently down the sides of her face.

She hoped that it was not just one woman; that would be too much to bear. She hoped that it was a hundred different women. That way, there was no personal relationship, just an outlet for him. *'Oh God, my first disappointment in America, and it has to be this.'* She rolled over on her side, her back to him, and with tears still rolling down her face she fell into a blessed sleep.

*****

The sound of Giovanni moving about in the kitchen woke her up. It was still dark outside and she could only see the flickering light from the gas lamp in the kitchen as it reflected on the bedroom wall. He was not beside her; he had gotten up without disturbing her.

"Giovanni," she called. She had lapsed back to calling him Giovanni and the name stuck but she remained Maria.

"In here," he replied. She threw the blanket over her shoulders and joined him in the kitchen. *'It was warmer in the bedroom,'* she thought with a slight shiver, *'He must have just stoked the fire.'* He was shaving at the sink.

He turned to face her, "I always get up at four o'clock. I need to be at the bakery by five. I didn't want to wake you but I must leave shortly." He walked over to her and gently kissed her on the cheek.

"Can't I even make something to eat for you before you go?"

"No, that's OK. I always have coffee and yesterday's cakes at the bakery with Antonio. I'll see you at noon. I'll come home instead of eating lunch there. We'll talk more then and tonight we can talk as much as you like because tomorrow is Sunday and we can be together all day."

He continued dressing and she stood there watching him with nothing but the blanket wrapped around her naked body. She yearned for him to pull it off and stay but all she got was a kiss on her forehead instead. He went into the front room, kissed the sleeping Ralph on the cheek, put on his coat and hat, and, kissing her once more on the cheek, he left, closing the door behind him. She stood in the middle of the kitchen as if paralyzed, bewildered, not quite accepting the reality of what had just happened.

'Well,' she thought, *'I have about two weeks before 'it' arrives so I will just have to do something about this situation.'*

She needed to familiarize herself with the apartment and prepare some breakfast for Ralph. No sense in going back to bed. Later she would need to shop for food and that would be her opportunity to explore the neighborhood. She went into the bedroom to dress, and dropping the blanket to the floor, stood motionless before the mirror hanging on the door. She looked at herself for a long time. She knew that she was beautiful and could not understand why he had not taken her for a longer time and for more than once. Then the frightful reason flooded back to her thoughts. With her usual resolve she made up her mind to say nothing.

She would change things back to the way they were in Italy. For the present she needed to get dressed and do what had to be done. She had not taken time to unpack the previous night so she opened the trunk and selected what she would wear that day. Then back to the kitchen. There was still some hot water left in the kettle on the stove so she washed and dressed. She refilled the kettle and placed it back on the stove.

There were some apples in a bowl on the table, and in a cupboard she found the container of oatmeal, a box of raisins, dried figs, coffee beans and, in a brown bag, a half loaf of bread. *'Not very much, but what can you expect in a house without a woman.'* She tiptoed into the front room and quietly opened the box hanging from the window. Again she smiled with amazement at the thing. Inside was a bottle with some milk in it, some butter, a small jar of jelly, and some salami and *prosciutto*. There were no eggs. Well, breakfast would not be a feast but she was determined to make lunch the best she could under the circumstances. *'Tonight I'll make a grand dinner. That should help Giovanni realize what he has been missing.'*

She began to make a mental list of needed items so she could prepare for dinner and for tomorrow's as well. She assumed that here, as in Italy, all the stores would be closed on Sunday. It was a lot to do in one day. She was tempted to wake Ralph in order to get an early start, but decided to let him sleep as long as his little body needed it.

She correctly guessed that the toilet facilities were in the yard at the back of the house, which was why it was called the 'back house'. In the Italian slang of the time it was pronounced 'bacouse' because it was almost impossible for Italians to vocalize the letter 'H'. In fact, it was a joke of the era that the reason so many Italians moved to Brooklyn was because they could not pronounce Manhattan.

She wondered if all the tenants in the building shared the same privy. She hoped there were two, one each for men and women. She moved as quickly as she could while Ralph was still asleep. It was still dark so she fumbled her way down the dimly lit hallway to the back end of the building that led onto a porch. There were stairs to the ground below and also up to the third floor porch. They weren't really stairs in the typical sense. It was more like a ladder, sloped to resemble stair steps. She had to grip both handrails to keep her footing.

To her disappointment she found that there was only one privy. That was acceptable in Italy where it was located behind the house and Papa had planted tall bushes around it and along the path leading up to it. At least there they had some semblance of privacy. But here the comings and goings were out in the open and truly everyone knew everyone else's business.

On her return from the 'bacouse' she was able to get a full look at the rear of the tenement building and the porches off each floor. It was hard to see in the limited daylight but as her eyes adjusted, she was taken aback at how unstable they all looked. All of the porches leaned toward her, giving the appearance of imminent collapse.

She shook her head in disbelief and returned to her flat just in time to hear Ralph calling her name. She had to help him get dressed and then was forced to retrace her steps to the 'bacouse' holding his hands to guide him down the steep steps.

'*Well,*' she thought in despair. '*This is a process that I'll have to organize or I'll spend much of the day going up and down those stairs and in and out of the building. I'll have to work out a schedule.*' Back in the kitchen she prepared breakfast for Ralph and made coffee for herself. With the warm cup nestled in her hand, she began to explore her new living quarters.

She started with the front room. There were two double hung windows overlooking the street. She was amazed that the windows were clean and framed with white, tied-back curtains. Aside from the unmade bed Ralph had slept in, the room was neat and tidy. There was a small dresser with a mirror above it. Next to the mirror was a picture of St. Anthony and to the right of it a small crucifix. She opened the drawers, one by one, and found clean clothing all neatly folded and separated. There was a small rug on the floor. Near one window there was a comfortable rocking chair.

Maria sat down and glanced clockwise around the room, sipping her coffee. The cup felt comfortably warm in her hands. The room was Spartan. There was a calendar and a picture of Pope Leo XIII hanging on one wall. The calendar looked odd to her. At first she could not put her finger on what bothered her. Then it came to her. The first day of the week was Sunday. But that didn't make any sense to her at all. Everyone knew that the first day of the week was Monday. All of Europe did it that way. That was why Saturday and Sunday were called the weekend, then came Monday. It was very confusing.

She resumed her inspection of the room. '*So, this is where Antonio lives.*' She hoped that he was not overly meticulous, the neatness of the room suggested that, but still it had a lived in look about it. For a moment she wondered what he was really like, and for Giovanni's sake, she hoped that she liked him. '*Antonio has done so much for us.*'

Maria didn't like the idea of him living with them, but she realized that the apartment was just as much his as theirs. '*It will work out, I'm sure. After all, the arrangement is only temporary.*'

She walked into the kitchen and talked with Ralph to reassure him about his new home. Now that he would not have a back yard to play in she felt sorry for him. '*Well, that is another sacrifice to contend with as the price for coming to America.*'

"Where's Papa?" he asked with a somewhat lost look in his eyes.

"He's working today," and she quickly added, "But it's not like before. Papa will be home for lunch and dinner, and tomorrow we will be together all day. We will go to church together and have a big Sunday dinner, just the three of us."

That seemed to satisfy him. She gave him some more hot oatmeal and a little bread with some jelly on it and he continued with his breakfast. She left him and walked into the bedroom. When she saw the unmade bed she sighed over her reaction to Giovanni's lovemaking.

Beside the bed the only other piece of furniture was a dresser. It did not even have a mirror over it. She opened the drawers and saw Giovanni's clothes all in a jumble. Everything pushed aside and on top of everything. No order at all. But that was like him. She remembered that even in Italy she always had to pick up after him and keep his clothes straight.

The room did not have a window; neither did the kitchen. She wasn't going to like that. It meant leaving the bedroom door open all the time. But what would they do at night when Antonio was in the front room? There was a door between his room and the kitchen and she hoped that he would have the discretion to close it.

She didn't want to think about that just now so she continued to study the bedroom instead. There wasn't even a rug on the floor. She would have to make that a priority. She was very disappointed but thought that she could make the room much more inviting with very little effort.

Ralph called to her that he was finished with breakfast. She took out the lettered blocks and brought them into the kitchen and placed them on the table.

"Here, play with Papa's blocks for a while and then we are going out to see the stores."

Maria took a quick inventory of the kitchen. It was becoming lighter. She extinguished the gas lamp and then continued with her exploration. There was not much. The men evidently had bought only what they needed. There was no warmth, not even a picture on the walls, only in the front room. She would have to leave it as is for the time being. Even the dishes were a collection of odds and ends. Nothing matched; it was all purely functional. That would have to suffice for a while, a very short while.

She put more coal on the fire and banked it. There was only a little more coal left in the scuttle and she wondered where the main supply was kept, something else to ask Giovanni at lunchtime.

Maria went back to the bedroom and she got Ralph's coat and hers. Picking up a small purse she realized that Giovanni had not left her with any money. She unpinned the small handkerchief from inside her brassiere and took out some of the American money she had exchanged for her lira in Naples. She had no idea how much cash to take out. She guessed at what she thought would be needed and put it into her purse. The balance went back to its hiding place. She closed the door behind them and she and Ralph descended the back stairs for the third time that morning. Another stop out back and then out the front door this time.

*****

She stood on the front steps of the building and looked around in order to familiarize herself with the immediate neighborhood. She really couldn't get lost. The address was burned into her memory from all the letters she had written to Giovanni. She was in an Italian-speaking neighborhood so there was nothing to fear, not that it was in her nature to fear anything. Besides, she possessed a working knowledge of English.

She remembered from the previous night that to her right Eighth Avenue sloped gently down hill east towards Broad Street. Looking directly across the street she saw the end of Factory Street. It was only one block long between Eighth and Seventh Avenues.

She was surprised to see that all the buildings were constructed of wood! Wood was very expensive in Italy; there were no forests to speak of. Construction there was of brick usually faced off with stucco, and of course, if one had the money, there were marble and tiles. Wood was a luxury in Italy. But here, in what she deemed was a poor neighborhood, wood was everywhere. She thought that was astonishing.

Maria was satisfied that she would have no trouble finding the building again. She took Ralph by the hand and they started off. They crossed the street and she turned around to get a better look at the tenement where they lived. There were three stories. She remembered from her trips 'out back', that there were four apartments on her floor, two on either side of the hallway, and four on the first floor, and probably the same on the third floor. That meant twelve families lived in the building not counting boarders if there were any. The potential problems with the 'bacouse' took on an even more ominous logistical problem. She thought it odd that she did not run into anyone in the building. *'Oh well, there will be time to meet the neighbors later. Just now I have to go food shopping.'*

Crossing the street again they walked down Eighth Avenue toward Broad Street. They crossed Sheffield Street, then Boyden Street. The next street was Summer Avenue that ended at Eighth. That's where she found Luigi's bakery, on the same side of the street where she was walking. She looked through the shop windows to see if she could see Giovanni but he was not there. He was probably down in the basement at the ovens. There was no one in the store except a middle-aged woman whom she guessed must be Luigi's wife, Gia.

The store had a glass entry door recessed in the middle of the building. There were show windows extending out from either side of the doorway. On the windows, in a graceful arch, was the name Luigi's in large italics

66

and under his name was simply 'BAKERY'. In each of the show windows there were tiers of glass shelves lined with all kinds of cakes and pastries on white doilies.

Looking through the window she could make out a wooden counter at the back of the store and behind it wooden shelves. The shelves were piled high with all shapes of bread and rolls. To the left and right there were glass showcases containing more cakes, various kinds of pastries and piles of cookies on doily-lined trays. The aroma made her mouth water. She was tempted to go in and introduce herself but thought better of the idea. She would let the introductions be made by Giovanni.

Continuing with her exploration, they walked past High Street and then John Street on her right then on to Broad Street where they had turned the night before. She turned to the left on Broad Street, past Clay Street and then left again and walked up Seventh Avenue. On her right she passed Webster Street, then High Street and Summer Avenue, both of which went through to Eighth. Then came Stone and Wood Streets. Just a little past Wood, on the left was Sheffield Street, where for the first time, she saw St. Lucy's Church.

The church was in the middle of the block on the west side. She decided to make a visit of thanksgiving. As she approached the building she became disappointed by its plainness. It was a rectangular, wooden building with a small bell tower at the northeast corner. *'Hardly a campanile,'* she mused. Inside there was no marble, no artwork or stained glass windows. Later she found out that St. Lucy's had only been erected in 1892. But even in small Pietramelara, the three churches were of brick covered over with stucco and decorated in and out with marble and tiles. Artwork and statuary were everywhere. But of course, Pietramelara's churches were centuries old, not like St. Lucy's.

The church was empty. She smiled, recalling that Giovanni slept here the first night he arrived in Newark. She did not have much time so she just lit a votive candle, said a short prayer, and they were out on the street again. She turned left back to Seventh Avenue and headed up toward the reservoir and the picnic area where Giovanni and Antonio played *bocce.* She decided not to walk that far, so she turned left onto Factory Street and found herself back on Eighth across from her tenement. They had walked a counterclockwise circle around the heart of Newark's first ward.

'That was very interesting, but now I better get some shopping done before lunch.'

The sidewalks were beginning to fill with people. There were peddlers in the streets, some with pushcarts and some with horse and wagon. Other housewives were beginning to go about their daily chores and the neighborhood was coming alive, bustling with activity. Peddlers interrupted her walk, trying to sell their wares. She politely shook her head 'no' and continued on her way. Ralph was holding her hand for dear life.

In front of her was a man looking up and shouting. She looked up and saw a basket with money in it being lowered by a rope. *"Scusa, per favore,"* he said, as he stepped around Maria. He took the money and in its place put a head of lettuce, some tomatoes, and a cucumber.

Maria was awestruck. *'What kind of place is this?'* She pulled Ralph's hand and started walking down the street once more. Just a few doors from her house she found a fruit store. She went in and introduced herself to the proprietor. He gave her a warm welcome to America and his shop.

He wore a dark brown, bulky woolen sweater. A full white apron hung down from his neck that tied around his waist. He had a gray felt hat on his head and he wore woolen gloves with the fingertips cut off.

They talked as she made her selections and he told her the price of the items she chose. It was a quick course in economics for her. She knew the rate of exchange between the lira and the dollar and her quick mind was able to grasp the value of things. Of course, the man knew Giovanni and Antonio and spoke highly of them. He gave an apple to Ralph.

Maria told the proprietor that she was *La Scrittore* and would be available to write for clients. She also informed him that she was fluent in many dialects. He promised to spread the word around to his customers.

Maria watched him closely as he wrote down the prices of her purchases using a brown paper bag as a pad. When he finished adding the list he put the pencil to rest behind his ear as he smiled at her. He put the items in the bag and she gave him what she thought was the proper amount. She was off a little bit in her calculations but said nothing; she would add it up herself later at home. The bag served not only for carrying her purchases but it was also her receipt. She had to get used to the dollar and cent system. *'Giovanni is right; it is confusing.'* In Italy there was only the lira; there were no parts.

Farther down the street she found a grocer. She did the same thing, purchasing what she needed for the noon meal. Again she introduced herself to the owner. He was dressed almost identically as the *fruittivendolo.* He promised to tell everyone that she was *La Scrittore.*

'Well, not bad. I did my shopping and got in some free advertising too.'

The lack of refrigeration in the late nineteenth century necessitated frequent food shopping. Most Italians were raised on fresh fruit and vegetables. Indeed, their diet bordered on that of a vegetarian. It was not unusual for housewives to food shop twice a day in order to prepare the noontime meal and dinner with fresh food. And of course, there were the ever-present street peddlers with their carts and wagons.

In Newark most of the fresh produce was supplied by outlying farms past the town of Bloomfield especially those in west and north central New Jersey.

*****

Much of the produce was delivered to the Central Farmer's Market via the Morris Canal. As the canal approached Newark it ran parallel to the western edge of a swampy area through which flowed the Branch Brook. There were a series of locks along the waterway as the canal descended to sea level. The last set of locks in Newark was located on Warren Street just before the huge market. The market itself was located between Broad and Mulberry Streets. The canal went right through and under the market-place.

The original canal was constructed from 1825 to 1831 and a few years later an extension to Jersey City was put into service. The initial construction brought canal boats from Phillipsburg on the Delaware River to Newark. The western entrance to the canal was about twenty miles south of the famous Delaware Water Gap. Contrary to popular belief the river was not named after the Delaware Indian Tribe. It was actually the other way around. The river was named after Lord de la Warr, the governor of the Jamestown colony in Virginia. The name Delaware came to be applied to almost all of the Lenape people who lived along the river. The Delaware River also came to be the political boundary separating New Jersey from Pennsylvania.

Originally the canal was used to ship high grade New Jersey iron ore west to the anthracite iron furnaces in Pennsylvania's Lehigh Valley. It was also used to ship coal east to the Newark and New York City markets. In its heyday, the canal contributed a great deal to the economic and industrial growth of Newark.

In the 1870's the canal's use as a water highway was mostly taken over by the railroads and barge activity waned. Nevertheless, the canal continued in use for many years bringing farm products to the Newark Farmer's Market. Wholesalers then delivered the food by horse and wagon to the retail stores in the surrounding area. Enterprising peddlers would also purchase the produce and sell it retail, street-by-street and door-by-door in the ward and surrounding areas.

*****

When Maria returned home she started up the stairs. Then remembering the 'bacouse' problem she took Ralph 'out back' first. *'This is going to be a problem. I just know it!'*

On her way back up the stairs she met the neighbor who occupied the apartment adjacent to hers. She introduced herself and they chatted a bit. The woman seemed likable enough but Maria got the impression that it would not be necessary to repeat anything she told this woman to any of the other neighbors. This one, she was sure, would take care of that. Maria assumed that it was probably she whom Giovanni suspected as the one who had sent for the police that night of the trouble.

If Maria wanted to maintain any semblance of privacy, she decided that she was going to have to be careful of what she said inside her apartment and how loudly she said it. In her mind she imagined the layout of the apartments and concluded that her bedroom shared a common wall with this neighbor's bedroom and that the windows of the neighbor's large room were off the porch and faced the yard and the privy. *'Well, whenever we make a trip out back this one would certainly know it.'* Maria felt a pang of nostalgia for Italy. She wondered what the other tenants were like and resolved to be aloof yet friendly.

While her neighbor was chatting away, she had a good look around the hallway. The walls had wainscoting about three feet high and topped with a chair rail. It was painted to simulate mahogany. Above the rail the plastered walls were painted white and the ceilings were covered with sheet metal that was embossed with a design of squares. Her apartment was similarly decorated and she assumed that the flats were all alike. The hardwood floors were coated with floor oil. It was very simple and clean.

At the ends of the hallways there were windows on the street side except for the first floor where the front door was located. On the backyard side of the hallways, there were glass paned doors opening onto the porches. That was good. It provided all of the light that was needed during the day. For nighttime needs there were gas lamps at the foot and head of each staircase. She wondered who turned them on and off and who paid for the gas. She would find out later when Giovanni came home. There were a lot of questions that she needed to ask him.

Chapter VIII

TOGETHER IN NEWARK 1894

After she returned to the apartment she set the kitchen table and prepared lunch while Ralph played in the front room. She had purchased
some polenta so there would be something hot along with the vegetables
and fruit. She cut some tomatoes into wedges and made a tomato salad
with onions, a few cloves of garlic, olive oil, wine vinegar and sprinkled
with oregano. She put the salami and *prosciutto* on a plate and put the loaf
of bread off to one corner of the stove to warm it. There was no cheese so
she made a mental note to buy a large wedge of provolone and also some
Romano cheese to grate over pasta. She made sure the ever-present kettle
was filled with water and in its place on the stove for Giovanni to wash.
She wondered if he would bring any cake or pastries home with him. Finally, with the table set, and a moment to herself, she sat down and cried.

None of the plates matched and what was there was inferior. It made
her think of all Mama's good dishes and matching platters, all gone. She
wished she had made an attempt to ship them to America but knew that
would have been impractical. Even if she had tried, she knew from watching the way luggage and trunks were tossed around on the ship and docks
that everything would have arrived in pieces anyway. Of course, it was
not really the dishes that were making her upset.

She began wondering if they really did make a big mistake in coming
to America after all. This dingy, wooden neighborhood could not begin to
compare with the colorful stucco and tiled homes on *Via San Giovanni*
where Papa's house was. And, oh God, the church, what a disappointment
that was! Such thoughts were to plague her for many, many years.

Ralph, pulling on her dress and complaining that he was hungry,
snapped her back to reality. He was getting bored with his blocks and she
added to her mental list to get an additional toy for him to occupy his time.
Without a back yard she realized that he was going to be more demanding
of her time.

"In just a little while Papa will be home and we will eat. Just be patient."

No sooner had she said the words than she heard his footsteps in the
hall. When the footsteps stopped she was able to hear him talking with the

neighbor next door. They must have met on the stairs, or more likely she was waiting for him. She never should have mentioned that Giovanni was coming home for lunch. Maria was appalled that she could hear every word of their conversation. *'Well, goodbye to privacy, we might as well be living in a glass house.'* But she did have some recourse, so she wiped her eyes with her apron as she walked to the door and opened it.

"Giovanni, we are waiting for you. Lunch is getting cold."

She glared at the woman who was called 'The Tongue' by the neighborhood gossips. Maria wanted to let her know that the interruption was not welcome. Perhaps the mild scold to Giovanni would prevent her from lurking about in the future, but Maria doubted it.

Giovanni walked over to Maria and kissed her and they moved, with his arm around her waist, into the kitchen. He was carrying a bag and he took out the contents and put them on the table. A small bottle of red wine, freshly baked bread, a cake, and some cookies for Ralph. He reached for them and that earned him a light crack on his hand. "After lunch, not now." He pouted but it did not sway Maria's firmness. She threw her arms around Giovanni's neck and kissed him again, more than a hello kiss and this time he responded in kind. *'Good,'* she thought, *'We are making progress.'*

He walked over to the sink. There was a rubber stopper on the end of a chain that, in turn, was attached to the faucet so it would not get lost. He inserted the stopper into the drain and poured some hot water from the kettle into the sink. He began washing his hands and asked what she had done all morning. As she prepared the polenta she gave him a run down of her shopping spree, *la spesa*. He congratulated her for finding her way around so easily. He also spoke well of the grocer and the vegetable man, and, yes, that was Gia, Luigi's wife, behind the counter in the bakery store.

They ate. She talked and he listened. She had a litany of questions ready for him. His answers were in his usual abbreviated manner.

"Where can I go to get meat and chicken?" she asked.

"There is a very good sausage store on High Street near Eighth," he explained. "It is the first place where Antonio began to sell bread whole-sale. Also, if you walk up Seventh, one block past Sheffield Street, there is a fresh poultry store on Cutler Street."

"Where is the post office? I need to know that if I am going to be *La Scrittore*, like I've been telling people."

He wasn't sure he liked the idea but he let it pass. He directed his attention to Ralph and was surprised at how well he talked.

"You really have done a good job in taking care of him by yourself." Taking her hand in his he smiled at her. "I am also grateful to you for making sure he knows who his Papa is."

She squeezed his hand and smiled back at him. It was nice to see his face light up again. But enough of that, she still had many questions to ask him before he left.

"What about the gas lamps in the hall? Who lights them every night?"

"One of the families on the first floor, in the back, act as superintendents for the building. They get money off their rent for keeping the halls clean and the lamps lit at night."

She thought, *'Even more eyes!'* then said, "When will I meet Antonio?"

"Monday after work, so you will have to prepare dinner for the four of us."

"Maybe we'll meet him at mass tomorrow. What time does it begin?"

"There are five masses on Sunday and they start at eight o'clock and then every hour till twelve."

"Well, that's very convenient. Let's try for the eight, and then we won't have to fast so long. We should be back by nine and we can have a light breakfast."

"Oh, I meant to tell you earlier. I gotta do my extra job in the morning, so you'll have to go to mass alone with Ralph. But don't worry. We'll spend the afternoon together in the picnic grove near the reservoir. They got swings and see-saws there so I'm sure Ralph will enjoy it." He got up from the table and kissed her on the forehead. "I gotta get back to the bakery now. We'll talk at dinner tonight."

"You didn't leave me any money this morning before you left for work, so I had to use some of our surplus."

"That's OK. I have savings in the bank on the corner of Seventh and Garside, next to the post office. You take what you need, and the rest we will put in the bank on Monday."

"What about coal for the stove?"

"Oh yeah, I forgot to tell you. We have a small coal bin in the basement. It's for our use only, so it's caged and locked." He pointed and said, "The key is on a nail over there near the door. Make sure you lock it every time you go down there. If it isn't kept locked some of the neighbors will just help themselves and that stuff's very expensive."

He picked up the scuttle, took the key from the nail, and walked out the door. He returned shortly with a new supply of coal. He washed once more, kissed Ralph, and then held her close. *"Stanotte*, tonight," he whispered in her ear and left for work.

After clearing the table, she and Ralph went out again to do some more shopping, but not before the usual detour to the backyard. She had planned to roast a chicken for dinner so first they went to find Cutler Street. The poultry store was filled with cages of live chickens. The cackling was deafening. The store was crowded with women all getting ready for the weekend meals.

By the time it was her turn, she had already picked out the bird she wanted and pointed it out to the store clerk. He opened the cage door and grabbed the cackling chicken and brought it out to the back of the store. There he wrung its neck with his bare hands, slit its throat, and let it hang over a long sink on a hook by its legs to bleed. Then he put it into a tub of hot water. That helped to make the job of plucking most of the feathers a little easier. She would have to finish the job at home. He wrapped the bird in some paper, put it in a bag, and handed it to her. The whole process took fifteen minutes.

Thank God it didn't take longer, the stench was awful and she could see Ralph was not looking very well. She wondered what it must be like on a hot summer's day with flies and all. She shook her head from side to side. She didn't even want to think about that. She was going to tell the proprietor that she was *La Scrittore,* but thought better of it. It would have to wait for another time when he was not so busy and might be standing outside on the sidewalk. Just now she had to get Ralph and herself out into the fresh air.

'*What a place!*' In Italy killing a chicken was done outdoors, in the open air. But in here! Even she was beginning to feel a little queasy. She was becoming more and more disillusioned with America. With all the land she wondered why everything was so crowded in one place. Of course she did not quite appreciate the fact that she was a farm girl in a big city and would have to adapt.

Then it was back to the grocers, the butcher, and finally, the sausage store. Tonight she would make the tomato gravy for tomorrow's pasta. And there was plenty of wine left. She passed a hardware store and realized that she had not seen a roasting pan in the cupboard so she went in and bought one. At each store she introduced herself. All of the proprietors knew Antonio and most of them knew Giovanni. She made sure that they all knew of her availability to write letters

Home again, via the 'bacouse', she and Ralph climbed the stairs exhausted. She put him in bed for a nap. After cleaning the chicken she prepared it with a beaten egg and sausage stuffing and put it in the oven for slow roasting. She went into the front room and sat down to rest in Antonio's rocking chair. She began to take stock of her situation.

There was the problem with Giovanni. What to do? She detested confrontation. She thought it best not to approach him with her suspicions but rather to make a life for themselves that would be attractive to him. Then, of his own accord he would stop any liaisons. She was not quite able to put her finger on it, but she felt that somehow there was a fundamental change in his character. Being the pragmatist that she was, she tried to

74

view the situation objectively. Perhaps it was she that had changed but she thought not. Perhaps she had dreamed for too much; that was possible. She would have to work on that too.

Next she thought about Newark. She was very disappointed by where they were living. She was used to much better and she knew the adjustment would prove difficult for her. But if they worked together the situation might just be temporary. Maria had never believed that the streets in America were paved with gold but she expected it to be better than it was.

Then there was the problem of Antonio. She had not even met him but she knew that the present living arrangements could not last too long. But what about their financial position? Could they do it without Antonio sharing the expenses? Besides, they should not ask him to pay half when in reality he should only pay one fourth.

Too many unanswered questions. Although things were not what she would have liked, they were not intolerable. She did not want to make snap decisions. She thought it better to wait until she had a more detailed understanding of the situation. But she was sure that at some time, somewhere, they would buy a house of their own. Whether Giovanni remained a baker or tried farming again would remain to be seen. That would be his decision.

Then there was her apprehension regarding that Sunday job. That would have to be a priority discussion. She did not like it. It had a dishonest ring to it. It just did not seem right to her. Also, she had to get him back to attending church so they could go to mass as a family. She had her work cut out for her but she decided to tread softly and slowly while she worked out the solutions. She knew she could not push Giovanni too far. She would have to lead and motivate him.

Summing it all up in her mind she concluded that the streets in America were definitely not paved with gold; what the streets were paved with was what the horses left.

*****

When Giovanni came home dinner was ready and they sat down at the table. Conversation was light and on a level that included Ralph as much as possible. After dinner she cleared the table and began to prepare the gravy for tomorrow's dinner. It was a time-honored recipe, passed on through the family, which Mama had taught her. It was also a time consuming process. She tied an apron around her waist, let out a deep sigh, and started.

Peeled plum tomatoes were strained through a colander into a large saucepan. Salt and ground black pepper seeds were added. Fresh basil and parsley were added in season but in the winter she used dried leaves.

She put the pan on the hot part of the stove to bring the tomatoes to a boil and then moved it slightly to the side so that it would simmer. In the meantime Maria prepared the meat in a large bowl. Freshly ground beef, pork, and veal, crumbled bread, salt, black pepper, parsley, minced garlic, and an egg were mixed by hand. Then the *polpette* (meatballs) were formed but she kept a handful of the mixture aside to use later. In a large cast iron frying pan she sautéed some fresh garlic and onions in olive oil along with a generous quantity of parsley.

When the garlic and onions were browned she removed them from the frying pan and fried the *polpette* and *salsicce* (sausage) in the hot oil. When the meat was not quite cooked through but well browned, she put it into a dish for later. Then she took the meat she had set aside and put it into the hot oil and mashed it with a fork so that it crumbled into very small pieces. To the hot oil and crumbled meat she added tomato paste and water and stirred it into a smooth mixture making sure to scrape the side of the frying pan because that was where the flavor was. When the thick mixture was smooth and brought to a boil she added it to the sauce-pan and stirred it into the simmering tomatoes. She added a little more water into the frying pan to assure that the entire flavor was added to the saucepan.

Then the cooked meat was added to the gravy and it was allowed to simmer for hours. The last spices that she added were oregano and a little anise seed. The gravy was stirred often to prevent it from catching on the bottom of the saucepan. When the gravy was finished cooking, the pan was covered and moved over to a cooler part of the stovetop and allowed to stand overnight. It always tasted better the next day. However, in the summertime the gravy was prepared in the morning.

This process was repeated three times each week as they always had pasta on Tuesday, Thursday, and Sunday. While she was cooking, the apartment was filled with a mouth-watering aroma. So was the entire building for that matter since all the housewives were doing the same thing, each with their own special recipe.

The biggest problem she had was preventing Giovanni from stealing meatballs and dipping bread into the pot. '*My God,*' she thought, as she stood guard with a wooden spoon in her hand as a weapon, '*If I don't stand over the pot there won't be anything left for tomorrow.*'

*****

Giovanni spent the evening getting to know his son. By the time she finished in the kitchen it was bedtime for Ralph. When he was asleep they sat at the kitchen table and talked. It was almost as if they were getting reacquainted. She was vivacious and he was subdued. At least that much had not changed. And he still had that disarming smile that she loved so much. But she could not help noticing that he had difficulty maintaining direct eye contact with her. *'All right, what has happened has happened.'* She hated it but understood. She was determined to make it as easy for him as she could and herself as desirable as possible, not only for their bedroom, but also as a housewife and mother.

The longer they talked the closer they became. It was like old times as they conversed hand in hand across the table. He had not eaten so well in years and the wine gave him a heady feeling. Once again he was with his beloved Maria Antonia. It was a new start. In his heart he decided to break clean from the 'house' by the river.

'Never again,' he vowed to himself.

"What do you think of the woman living next door to us? I have the feeling that she's the building gossip."

"You are very observant, Maria. I think she is the one who sent for the police that night of the trouble. I'm sure of it. So is Antonio. The woman just has a wagging tongue. There is no malice in it." She was not so sure of that. She thought that it would be better not to become too familiar with that one.

He sensed her disappointment with where they lived and told her that he agreed but it was the best they could do for the present. All they needed was time. Then she mentioned Antonio.

"Giovanni, how will this work out, our living with Antonio I mean? He will be in our family but not part of it. This apartment precludes any real privacy that should only be within a family."

"I agree that something will have to be done. I think we can make it on our own. I have decided to ask Luigi for more money. I am important to his business now and he needs me more than ever. Luigi might even need a second laborer. There is too much work for just the three of us. Besides, Luigi is enjoying his time off. Also, I have my Sunday job and I'm saving all of that money." Secretly he knew that they could save even more if he stopped going to the 'house'.

"Antonio will only stay for a little while. I think he's already making plans to move out soon. He's done so much for me. I just can't ask him to leave now." She did not like the situation but promised not to make an issue of it for the time being.

It was getting late and she decided to put off any discussion about the Sunday job. Not only was there something about it that she feared, but it also prevented him from going to church with her. Surprisingly, since she was usually the aggressor, he got up and turned off the gas lamp, took her by the hand and gently pulled her toward the bedroom. In silence he undressed her and they got into bed as though they were still in Italy. For a long time afterward they clung to each other and whispered their feelings until sleep overtook them both.

*****

Ralph woke them up early in the morning. He wanted to go 'out back.' Giovanni told Maria about the chamber pot under the bed. '*Good, it is too early and too cold to go outside.*' Giovanni got up and stoked the fire. When he returned to bed Ralph was next to Maria so he got back into bed with the boy between them. They talked until daylight.

They established a routine for washing and dressing. She would get washed first, then begin preparing breakfast while the 'men' washed and dressed. But today was Sunday so there would be no breakfast until after church. '*How can Antonio fit into this family routine?*'

There was still plenty of time for them to leave for the eight o'clock mass. Giovanni went off to his Sunday job saying he would return at noon. Maria decided that they should dress in their very best in order to make a good first impression among the parishioners. She brushed out Ralph's little suit and dressed him. For herself she picked out the blue dress that she wore for Giovanni.

The windows in the front room were covered with frost. As she dressed she could hear Ralph scratching his letters on the frosty windows with his fingernails. They put on heavy winter coats to keep warm. Thankfully Maria had made woolen scarves and gloves for the family.

Maria had planned a large Sunday dinner for one o'clock. After dinner she wanted the family to take a long, late afternoon walk, perhaps up to the reservoir. As they went out the front door, she could feel it was going to snow. The clouds were low and dark and the air was heavy and damp. It was cold, and there was no wind. It was very still. Ralph was laughing over seeing his hot breath condense into a white fog as he huffed and puffed. They crossed the street and walked toward Sheffield Street to St. Lucy's.

Once inside the church, the flickering candles and gas lamps gave her a better view of its interior. Wooden pews lined both sides of the main aisle. That was a departure from her old parish church, *San Nicola in Annunziata*, which had no pews. Almost everywhere in Italy everyone stood for the entire mass and they kneeled on the cold, marble floor. Inside St. Lucy's there were a few statues. St. Mary to the left of the altar and St. Joseph to the right. A large crucifix hung above the altar. On a step near the pulpit there was a statue that Maria assumed was of St. Lucy.

Maria recalled from her classes in church history that St. Lucy was martyred in Sicily about 304 A.D. during the persecution of Emperor Diocletian. She is the patron saint of those afflicted with diseases of the eyes.

The church was crowded. Maria looked around but she did not see any of the few people she had met the previous day. She even looked to see if she could recognize Antonio from Giovanni's description, not sure she would even know him if she bumped into him. She saw no one that she recognized. After mass she and Ralph walked directly home.

Giovanni was not there. She and Ralph had a simple late breakfast. She didn't want to spoil their appetites for Sunday dinner. After breakfast she put him in Antonio's room with his train and wooden blocks. Once he was quiet and playing she went into the kitchen and started to prepare for dinner.

Maria moved the pot of gravy over to a warmer spot on the stove and also put a large pot of slightly salted water on the hottest place. She made a small *antipasto* from the salami and *prosciutto* that was left over along with small wedges of provolone. Maria had purchased some red peppers and roasted them in the oven and now she prepared them with olive oil, garlic, and salt and served in a separate dish. She sprinkled the peppers with some oregano and added parsley as a garnish.

Giovanni returned at noon as he had promised and promptly at one o'clock they sat down at the table and started to eat dinner. With slices of Luigi's fresh Italian bread and some wine to wash it down, they enjoyed a quiet time together as a family eating *il primo piatto,* the first course of antipasto and peppers.

The pot of water had come to a boil and as they finished the *antipasto* she got up and tossed handfuls of pasta into the water. She stirred the pot with a long handled wooden spoon until the water came back to a boil in order to keep the strands of spaghetti from sticking to each other. Every once in a while she would stir again. Occasionally she dipped a fork into the boiling water and lifted one strand from the pot and pinched it to determine if they were cooked. *Al dente* was the preferred way. When the test told her it was time, she lifted the pot off the stove and poured the entire contents into a waiting colander in the sink to drain, then back into the pot to be mixed with a little gravy to prevent the pasta from sticking.

The spaghetti all went into a large serving platter. A few spoonfuls of gravy spread evenly over the top and *il secondo piatto* was ready. She placed the platter in the middle of the table on top of an overturned soup dish. It was easier to serve the spaghetti from an elevated platter. Giovanni and Ralph watched in approving and impatient silence. Toes were tapping and stomachs grumbling.

Maria placed a stack of three dishes in front of Giovanni and he served out the spaghetti in each, first for Ralph, then Maria and lastly, for himself.

They each sprinkled some grated Romano cheese on the steaming pasta, then a little crushed, hot, red pepper, and a final ladle of gravy were spread over the top. With fork and spoon in hand they mixed the pasta in their dishes. The aroma was as magic. After the spaghetti she served *il terzo piatto* of meat balls and sausage on a platter together with a large bowl of fresh, green salad, mixed with olive oil and red wine vinegar and sliced *pomodori*. A basket of Luigi's fresh bread complimented the meal.

Set next to Giovanni there was a bottle of red wine from which he poured a glass for Maria and himself. For Ralph there was a glass of water into which he put a few drops of wine. The water turned pink and the boy enjoyed drinking 'wine' with Mama and Papa. The entire dinner was a family ritual; there was no deviation.

After dinner and once the table had been cleared, they bundled up for outdoors and went walking up toward the reservoir. When they returned she planned to serve coffee and the cake that Giovanni had brought home. It was cold and the wind had picked up from that morning. They walked up Eighth Avenue, turned right onto Factory Street, and then left up Seventh Avenue.

They crossed Clifton Avenue and walked around the reservoir. Maria was impressed by the height of the circular brownstone exterior wall. Ralph was running ahead and climbing onto the picnic benches. The children's swings had been taken down for the winter, but the seesaws were still there. Because of the weather, no one was playing *bocce* on the several courts. Maria was further impressed by the entire recreational facility that the city had provided. Because it was so cold no one else was there and they had the area to themselves.

They walked for just a little while longer and then it started to snow. The flakes were fine at first, like powdered sugar, and then slowly they became much larger. Ralph was in a state of joyous wonder. Looking up and holding his mouth open he caught as many flakes as he could on his tongue. The ground was cold so that none of the snow melted. Almost as if by magic the landscape was quickly covered with a white blanket.

"*Fa bella,*" she said, "How beautiful and clean the snow turns everything." As much as Ralph was enjoying eating the snowflakes they thought it better to return home, so they coaxed him into agreement with a promise of hot cocoa and cookies.

So passed her second day in America and the third night was as good as the second. She drifted to sleep thinking that finally, tomorrow, for dinner, she would meet the great Antonio.

Chapter IX

ANTONIO 1894

Antonio had been born on June 6, 1858 in the small town of San Sossio Baronia, located about sixty miles west of *Napoli*. It is in the province of Avellino, in the region of Campania, in what is present day Italy. Like Maria and Giovanni he was actually born in the Kingdom Of The Two Sicilies. He was twelve years old when Italy was unified under the monarchy of King Vittorio Emmanuele II. When he immigrated to the United States, arriving in New York on May 2, 1892, aboard the SS Britannia via Naples, he was almost thirty-four years old. Fairly well educated, and with a great deal of self confidence, he possessed that pioneer spirit that moved people to the New World from all over Europe in the great migration around the turn of the nineteenth century.

He was tall and fair, with bright blue eyes. Not many people would take him for Italian, and if they did, most would assume that he came from up north, perhaps as far north as Piemonte near the French and Swiss borders. His education and social stature also laid claim to a northern background. He was soft spoken and unassuming but manifested a quiet inner strength. He walked with the poise of an aristocrat and he had a charisma that exuded self-confidence that was completely without arrogance. He was always well dressed, bordering on the *grandee*, yet never ostentatious. There was no question about it. Antonio had class.

In contrast to his demeanor, Antonio had come from a hard working peasant family. His personal struggle had been not just for survival but also to lift himself from his parent's lowly status in life. And so he worked as an apprentice baker. He thought that with a trade he could go anywhere. But that did not satisfy his desire for mental growth. He continued his education on a self-learning program and his social contacts were with the local intelligentsia. Even so, he was not satisfied with what life had to offer in the small parochial town of San Sossio Baronia and so he decided to go to America.

Leaving Italy was not an easy decision for him and his wife, Joanna. They did not have the wherewithal to bring a family of five to America and then hope that he would be able to support all of them while he found a position. Once the decision was made for the family to leave Italy, it was planned that Antonio would go first and send for his family when he became established. They were among the tens of thousands who opted for this strategy. So he went alone, leaving behind his wife, with their son, Francesco, and two daughters, Emanuella and Theresa. They would live with Joanna's father and mother. It would be difficult starting over again in a strange land, but he had the advantage of entering the United States with a trade.

Antonio had a cousin, Francesco, his son's namesake. It was he who sponsored Antonio's immigration into the United States. Francesco had come to America three years earlier, in 1889.

*****

In 1889, Ellis Island was not the reception center for newly arrived immigrants coming into New York City. Francesco was processed through Castle Clinton located on a small island in the Hudson River just off the western shore of the island of Manhattan. The islands were connected via a 300-foot causeway. Castle Clinton was built on a former fortress that had been constructed just prior to the War Of 1812 with England and it was part of the fortification system protecting New York Harbor. From 1844 to 1855 it was known as Castle Gardens and was used as a concert hall with a promenade atop its eight-foot-thick sandstone walls.

During this period the water between the island and Manhattan was displaced by a landfill that created Battery Park. From 1855 to 1890 Castle Clinton was an immigrant-processing depot where many immigrants entered the United States. However, the increasing immigration necessitated much larger facilities and in 1892 Ellis Island was opened to the incoming masses.

*****

Francesco, five years older than Antonio, had settled in Newark, New Jersey and worked there as a skilled foundry worker. There were some small foundries in the 'down neck' section of Newark along the Passaic River and he had no difficulty finding work in one of them.

Francesco met Antonio at Ellis Island and took him to Newark. It had been decided that Antonio was going to live with Francesco and his family temporarily until he became settled. Francesco was very loyal to the extended family even to the extent of obtaining a position for Antonio in a local bakery shop on Eighth Avenue. A friend of Francesco's named Luigi owned it. Luigi would prove to be Antonio's mentor.

Luigi and Gia lived in an apartment above their bakery. The baking ovens and equipment were in the basement of the building. He did the baking alone and she worked in the retail shop above. They were among the first Italians who had arrived in Newark in 1852. That was even before Castle Clinton was the point of entry. Their arrival was actually administered by the State of New York and amounted to little more than signing into the country. Now in their early fifties they had resigned themselves to having no children.

Luigi's business had grown due to the excellent bread, cakes, and pastries that he baked. The business had become too much work for just him and Gia. Therefore, finding Antonio was a gift from heaven for Luigi. Thankfully, because of Antonio's apprenticeship in Italy, it took only a few weeks before he was able to adapt to the operation and become a valuable assistant. In that short time he became the son they never had.

Francesco and his family were living in very cramped quarters and Antonio's addition to the family only served to make matters more uncomfortable. After only one week of working at Luigi's, Antonio decided that he must move out on his own very quickly. He dreaded telling his cousin that he found another place to live. He was afraid Francesco would be insulted and take his plan to move as a refusal of his hospitality. Antonio did not want to seem ungrateful. However, Francesco was happy for Antonio because the change coincided with one he was about to make himself. He had been looking to advance himself for some time and just after Antonio arrived Francesco had received an offer from a company in Youngstown, Ohio. It was from a large steel mill with much better opportunities than those in a small foundry in Newark.

Francesco spoke English very well and was literate in both languages. There were a lot of non-English speaking Italians working as laborers at the Ohio Steel Company, and along with his trade knowledge he thought he might obtain the kind of position he wanted. He wrote to the mill applying for a foreman's position and they accepted. He had just the qualifications they were looking for, someone who was knowledgeable in the steel industry and who was bilingual and could supervise the Italian workforce.

Antonio was relieved by the news in spite of the fact that his reunion with his cousin was cut so short. After less than two weeks in Newark, Antonio was employed, left his cousin's apartment, and moved into a boarding house where he shared a room with two other men. It was far from ideal, but it was a good start. Within a month Francesco and his family left for Ohio. It was a sad parting so soon after being reunited but they promised to keep in touch with each other.

Shortly after Antonio started working for Luigi, Giovanni was hired. The two employees took to each other immediately and formed a close friendship. The mutual attraction between the two could not seem more improbable. They were complete opposites, not just in personality but physically as well. Giovanni, while not sloppy, was not much concerned with his appearance. Antonio, to the contrary, was a meticulous dresser. Even on the job he was well groomed, always with a clean apron tied around his waist. He wore a clean, white baker's cap that even the demanding Luigi did not do. They just did not go together, these two, but they became the closest of friends in a very short time.

It was at Antonio's suggestion that they became partners in an apartment. Their lifestyle improved slightly and Antonio felt that they would become something in the community. Therefore, it was a great disappointment to him when, after the incident with the boarder at the apartment, Giovanni became involved with the prostitutes in the 'house' down by the river. Far from being naïve or prudish, Antonio thought that Giovanni was inviting trouble. It was a difficult situation for Antonio. While his marriage to Joanna was not what could be called a love match, nevertheless he missed her and decided to remain faithful to her.

He did not flaunt this morality because deep inside he was sometimes envious of Giovanni's indulgences. But he held out. He never mentioned his concerns to Giovanni. The subject was never broached between them. Being judgmental of others was not Antonio's way.

However, when Giovanni became involved with the seedier elements of their society and the loan sharks of the neighborhood, Antonio thought that this impinged on any future plans they might have together as business partners. Therefore he felt he now had a justification to talk with him about it. Antonio spoke to Giovanni without trying to force his views on him. He told Giovanni that he did not want to be associated with those kinds of men, even indirectly, and implored Giovanni to reconsider and break off his connection with 'them'. This also meant, by inference his visits to the 'house' down by the river.

Giovanni was adamant about retaining his new part-time 'job' and Antonio, disliking confrontation, let the matter drop. He still liked Giovanni and they remained very close friends, but he no longer included Giovanni in any of his future business plans.

Antonio corresponded frequently with Joanna and was now even receiving some notes from his oldest daughter, Emanuella. Joanna was beginning to sense that their daughter was not happy about leaving Italy for America. She wrote to Antonio about this potential problem so he began to enclose separate letters only for Emanuella. He was trying to play the role of father and advisor from thousands of miles away. He was certain that when the time came he would be able to convince her that her future lay in America with the family, not in Italy. Like most immigrants he overestimated his ability and underestimated the problems and the long absence was taking its toll on the family.

He was also shocked when he came to the realization that the streets in America were not paved with gold. All America offered was opportunity but no help. He had to make his own way in a culture that was not only foreign but also sometimes inhospitable to him. But that was true for all nationalities that had immigrated. That was the reason he concluded, for the development of close-knit, ethnic neighborhoods in the evolving American cultural landscape. Their xenophobic fears forced them to huddle together in common neighborhoods such as Newark's first ward was for Italians.

Antonio's mind was always planning for the future and open to recognizing opportunities. One day, while making a purchase in a sausage shop, he noticed that the store did not sell bread.

"How can anyone eat sausage without fresh Italian bread?" Antonio asked the owner. "Why don't you sell bread?"

"I'm not a baker," was the reply.

That was the opening Antonio needed. He convinced the proprietor to offer bread in his store and buy the bread from him wholesale. He would become the middleman as long as he could convince Luigi to cooperate and be his supplier. When Luigi gave his blessings Antonio embarked on his new career. Before long he was selling to other small storeowners, then restaurants, and finally to non-Italian stores in the surrounding neighborhoods. After all, everybody liked Italian bread, but the non-Italians did not want to venture into 'that' section of Newark.

'If they don't want to come here, I'll go to them,' Antonio thought to himself, and that is what he did.

The venture expanded rapidly. At first he had to make deliveries on foot using a pushcart, but before long he was able to rent a horse and wagon on a *per diem* basis. After a while he was in a position to purchase a horse and wagon of his own, which he kept garaged in a barn down on Clay Street, not too far away from his tenement.

Antonio was just getting his business venture off the ground when Giovanni told him that Maria was on her way to America. The timing was not good for Antonio. He was not ready to send for his own family or even to move, but he told Giovanni he would move anyway. This precipitated a small argument between the friends, and reluctantly, Antonio agreed to stay for just a little while. After all, Giovanni was giving him only three weeks notice of Maria's arrival, and he did own half the apartment. But he insisted that he would arrange to live elsewhere for a few days after she arrived. She was expected on a Friday, he would be gone until Monday evening.

Antonio wrote to his cousin in Youngstown and informed him of his plans and asked his advice. By this time Francesco had been in Ohio for over two years and was doing well. He was very successful at being the liaison between the mill management and the Italians. Not only was he able to protect management's interests, he was also able to help his fellow countrymen become established. He had even rented a large house that he converted into a rooming house. Francesco and his wife and their two daughters occupied the first floor and he had seven boarders living on the second and third floors.

He replied to Antonio's letter encouraging him in his business venture. Later when Antonio wrote that Giovanni's wife was coming to America, Francesco likewise supported his idea to rent a place on his own and he also suggested that he try to buy a house as soon as possible, maybe a rooming house or even an apartment house.

"Real estate is the key to success in America," Francesco advised. Antonio decided that he would look for an apartment as soon as possible. Purchasing was just out of the question for the present and he would be unable to run a rooming house on his own; maybe later when Joanna was with him.

Antonio saw Giovanni at the bakery the day after Maria and Ralph arrived. "Congratulations, my friend, on your good fortune. I'm sure I will never see you again now that you will be spending all of your time with Maria."

He hoped that Giovanni would understand this comment was veiled advice that he should stop his visits to the 'house'. He also hoped that the fear of Maria finding out through the gossip network in the neighborhood would be an added incentive for him to straighten himself out. Once the visits to the 'house' stopped, Antonio felt his friend would sever his association with the loan sharks. Their reputation started out bad but was now getting worse and he was very concerned for Giovanni's welfare. When their downfall came Antonio did not want to see his friend go down with them.

It was a touchy situation. He could say only just so much to his friend. Giovanni was an adult and, while passive, could still tell people to mind their own business. He knew from conversations with Giovanni that Maria had written to him expressing her disapproval of his 'Sunday' job. Perhaps, as she became more familiar with the personalities of the ward, Maria would be able to convince Giovanni of the immorality of it, not to mention the risks.

On the Monday evening after the arrival of Giovanni's family, at the end of a long and tiring day, Antonio headed back to his flat. He was looking forward to finally meeting the beautiful Maria. He almost walked right into the flat but at the last moment caught himself. He thought it would be prudent to knock on the door first. It was ludicrous really, standing in the hall, knocking on the door for permission to enter his own apartment.

Chapter X

GIUSTINA 1895

Maria was preparing dinner and wondering who would be the first to come home, Giovanni or Antonio. She wanted it to be Giovanni. She felt it would be a little awkward to manage self-introductions. Ralph was playing in Antonio's room and she suddenly thought it would be better for the boy not to be in there. She moved him into the back bedroom just as she heard footsteps in the hall. She did not recognize them as Giovanni's.

"It's him," she gasped, as she quickly brushed back her hair with her hands and smoothed out her apron. Then, taking a deep breath, she stood erect in front of the stove facing the door. She wanted to make a good first impression. She was surprised to hear a knock on the door.

"Who on earth can that be at this hour? It can't possibly be Antonio knocking on his own door," she muttered half aloud. She walked to the door and opened it. She pressed the palm of her hand to her cheek and breathed out a soft, "Oh!" when she saw his tall, lean, body framed in the doorway.

She recognized immediately that it was Antonio. He fit exactly the picture she had formed of him from Giovanni's descriptions. In a fraction of a second she took in all of him. Standing there with his shoulders back and his head held high he almost had a military bearing. But he was not massive like Giovanni. His brown hair was wavy and well groomed. His work clothes were neat and clean even after a full day's work. In spite of his soldier-like appearance he gave the impression of being a soft, gentle man. His skin was very fair yet had a soft, tanned glow to it. But above all it was his piercing blue eyes that were his most disarming feature.

"Maria," he said in a very pleasing, euphonic tone, "It's me, Antonio." She instinctively held out both arms to him and they embraced each other, and in the doorway, they kissed each other on one cheek and then the other.

"My goodness, don't you have your key?" Maria wanted to set the parameters immediately that he was not to feel intrusive in his own home. He lived here and moreover he owned half of whatever was in the apartment. She had made up her mind that he was to know that while he lived there, he was not to feel as though he was a boarder. Besides, she had taken an instant liking to him and hoped that he felt the same way about her.

Dinner was almost ready and she motioned him to the kettle on the stove so he could wash. She continued preparing dinner while she watched him at the sink. There was some idle talk and then he went into the front room. She was relieved of her previous anxiety when he closed the door. No need to worry about that.

She refilled the kettle so that Giovanni would have hot water when he came home. In a few minutes Antonio returned to the kitchen in a change of clothing. She was pleased that he was not coming to the table in his work clothes. It would lend a little elegance to the meal. *'There was no question about it. Antonio had class.'* Giovanni always washed and sat down in his work clothes. She recalled how in Italy, they always had dinner in the dining room after Papa bathed and changed his clothes.

Maria had put on a better dress than normal for the occasion. Several months before she sold the house she made as much clothing as she could afford. She knew that she might not have access to a sewing machine for a while and also thought that dress material would be more costly in America. For this first dinner with Antonio, she wanted to look a little more special, and chose a purple dress with a detachable yolk. She decided to wear the yolk for their first meeting. She didn't want to seem too intimate by not wearing it, and besides it was a bit cold, and it covered her neck and kept her warm. The dress was detailed with a darker purple and a black ribbon was tied around her waist, the ends of which touched the floor. The fabric of the dress was pleated around the back and trailed just slightly behind her. It was one of her favorite dresses and she wore it proudly.

Maria made a mental note that she had better be fairly well dressed for dinner while Antonio lived with them. She smiled as she thought that maybe some of the class would rub off on Giovanni, but she doubted it. Still, while they were not well off with a formal dinning room, they could at least have a pleasant time at the table rather than just take care of the need to eat. They both sat down to wait for Giovanni and they became acquainted with each other. Conversation came easily between them and each listened attentively when the other spoke.

When Giovanni arrived, true to form, he washed and sat down in his work clothes and they had dinner. Table talk was very interesting and stimulating but mostly between Maria and Antonio. Giovanni was his retractable self, contributing very little. At times, the three of them would direct conversation to Ralph who seemed very pleased that they were paying some attention to him. The boy appeared to be very comfortable with the situation.

After dinner they enjoyed coffee and some fresh pastries that Giovanni had brought home. When the conversation turned between Antonio and

Giovanni, Maria could not help but look back and forth between them. Slowly, almost unconsciously, she began to make comparisons. That was not the proper thing to do, and with an almost guilty feeling, she shook her head from side to side to drive the thoughts out of her mind. As they continued with their men talk she began to clear the table and tidy up the kitchen. In a little while Antonio excused himself, put on his coat, and went out with a pleasant, *"Buona notte."* She wondered where he was going and again dismissed the thought. It was none of her business.

*****

Ralph was four years old on January 6th and the four of them had a pleasant birthday party for him. Giovanni baked a special cake for the occasion and Maria bought a toy for him. She dressed him up and the four of them had a grand time. She was grateful that Antonio had bought a small toy for him and took the time to take part in the family event.

Everything was going along quite nicely between the four of them. In the middle of January 1895 she woke up one morning and realized that 'it' had not arrived on schedule. She was surprised. Only a few weeks with Giovanni and the first sign of pregnancy already presented itself. She didn't want that now, the timing was wrong. It was going to severely complicate matters. Remembering her mother's advice when she became pregnant with Ralph she decided to say nothing until the following month. Giovanni did not even notice that she was always available.

Since coming to America, she had become the initiator of their sex life and he just participated whenever she made the overtures. She often felt unfulfilled afterwards. She was not comfortable with that aspect of their lives, it was not like it had been back in Italy. She attributed it to the possibility that, when they were in bed, Antonio was in the front room or if he was out he could walk into the kitchen at any minute and they would hear him. Then there was Ralph sleeping on a cot in the corner of the bedroom. But that was no problem because he slept the deep, undisturbed sleep of the young. This particular concern was resolved when Antonio offered to have Ralph's cot moved into the front room.

"I really don't mind," Antonio offered. "After all, my room is the largest room in the flat."

The boy thought it was a great idea because he could look out the windows.

"Thank you, Antonio. I am grateful for your concern." Maria was slightly embarrassed by Antonio's sensitivity. She readily agreed thinking that the new arrangement would be one less hindrance to their lovemaking, but it made no difference. The change did not seem to faze Giovanni one way or another. She didn't want to think about why he was not coming to her.

After the February miss Maria told her husband that she was pregnant and would probably have the baby in late September. He was both elated and apprehensive. This turn of events would certainly require a reappraisal of their living arrangements. They decided to wait a little while longer before telling Antonio. They were sure his reaction would be to move out immediately and they wanted to afford him as much time as possible to relocate.

Giovanni was concerned about their finances and Maria about the loss of the companionship that she and Antonio had developed. They related to each other intellectually, something that was absent in her marriage. When she thought about it, she realized that in Italy she had not noticed this lack between Giovanni and herself. But then everything was rosy. In retrospect she was coming to the conclusion that she should have married a best friend and companion. If love followed, so much the better. Even if it did not, she would be living with a best friend and intellectual equal.

She started to brood about this void in her marriage and was coming to realize that she had married for love alone. Now it was somehow not quite enough. The bloom was slowly coming off the rose, but it was not a flash of insight that brought her to that conclusion. The growing feeling was insidious and it took a long time for her to be aware of what it was. She still loved her husband. But the terrible gnawing paradox in her mind was created by her admiration for Antonio and his personality that contrasted with Giovanni's lack of companionship.

*****

Most of Maria's time was occupied with household chores and with Ralph. Also, word of mouth was spreading throughout the neighborhood about her ability to write and it was paying off. She was gaining a reputation as *La Scrittore* and was developing a nice, steady clientele. She kept her patrons at arms length, on a strict business level. She did not want to become personally involved with any of them. It was a 'for fee' service that she provided and she expected payment on the spot, no credit. She remained aloof yet dependable and cordial, always calling her clients by their surname, giving them a sense of dignity in spite of the fact that they were non-literate. One of the qualities of her character was this trait of sensitivity toward others.

Maria often took Ralph to the picnic grove around the reservoir to play, as did most of the other mothers in the neighborhood. It was during one of these visits that she met Giustina who also brought her children to the grove. One day they happened to sit on the same bench and they became

90

acquainted while they watched the children play on the swings and see saws.

"I'm from Pietramelara, do you know it?"

"I think so, isn't it over in Caserta, near *Napoli?*"

"Yes it is and where are you from?"

"We are from Calabritto in Avellino. My husband works in the construction business. Those are my two boys over there playing with your son. What does your husband do?"

"He works in a bakery. He works for Luigi, down on Eighth Avenue."

"Oh yes, I know the store. We buy our bread there."

They spoke for quite a while, trading personal information and about their children. They met this way several times and it wasn't long before they were inviting each other back to their respective homes for coffee in the late afternoon. The relationship developed very quickly into a close bond and each found comfort in her newly found confidant. Very quickly Maria and Giustina became inseparable. They confided to each other their joys, fears, disappointments, and the intimate details of their marriages. They became as sisters

It was Giustina who suggested that Maria could lie about Ralph's birth date and that she could enroll him in school that fall.

"Do you think I can get away with that?"

"I think so, he looks as though he is five and he certainly seems smart enough."

Maria's tutoring had seen to that, and he was also becoming bilingual very quickly. She was pleased with how rapidly the child adapted to change. She decided to try it, and in July Ralph was registered in the Seventh Avenue School for that September. She had no trouble, they didn't even ask for a birth certificate, something that was not available anyway.

The school was on the corner of Seventh Avenue and Factory Street, only two blocks away. It was very convenient. *'That will be a big help.'* The baby was due about the time school opened and she would be relieved of some of the pressures of taking care of both Ralph and the infant.

*****

Maria always wrote letters for her clients at the kitchen table. When she was finished she collected her fee, which included postage. Once a week she purchased the stamps she needed and mailed the letters from the post office next to the bank on the corner of Seventh Avenue and Garside Street. It was very convenient, only a few minutes walk from her home. Everyone in the post office knew her and she never failed to use the opportunity to tell even more people about her services. After some small talk she would go next door to the Bank & Trust Company to make a deposit of her fees, Giovanni's Sunday job income, and whatever was left over from his bakery salary. Their savings were increasing, slowly but surely.

*****

An Italian immigrant named Salvatore had founded the bank. He had arrived in Newark in 1885. He started out like most everyone else who had come to America, poor and with high expectations. He began selling steamship tickets and making travel plans for a growing clientele. He was the first travel agent in the ward. Eventually he established a bank because most clients left money with him for safekeeping. He also arranged to have funds transferred to Italy for families back in the 'old country'. There were always rows of steamer trunks lined up outside his bank, and they had to be navigated around in order to go inside. Maria often found herself saying one last goodbye to a neighbor or client while she was doing her banking. The bank had also become a meeting place for the neighborhood.

*****

Antonio frequently corresponded with his family in Italy and his cousin Francesco in Youngstown, Ohio. After dinner he would sit at the kitchen table and write to them. Sometimes, if the three of them were there, they would talk and have a late espresso after Ralph had been put to bed. As Maria's pregnancy progressed she was finding that, more often than not, she and Antonio would be alone in the kitchen. Giovanni was growing more indifferent to her and often was not at home. She and Antonio began spending more and more evenings together. He sympathized with her obvious loneliness but could say nothing about the situation. He wondered if she knew where Giovanni was going when he was out at night. But it was none of his business and the subject was never discussed between them.

Antonio looked forward to the little time they spent together. It filled a need for him to be able to communicate with someone on his level. Often, as a favor, Maria would post his letters for him on her weekly visits to the post office and pick up any replies he received. She did not correspond with any of her relatives in Italy. They had never been that close. It was through Antonio's correspondence with his wife and her own letter writing for clients that she was kept up to date with affairs in Italy. Over time these late night talks became very important to both of them.

*****

One night when Maria was alone and sitting in the front room thinking things through there was a knock at the door. She walked into the kitchen and over to the door. Before she opened it she asked, "Who is it?"

A strange voice from the hallway inquired, "Signora, I am looking for *La Scrittore*, is that you?"

As she opened the door she said, "Yes, I am."

A very young man was standing in the doorway. She guessed that he was about eighteen, no more. He wore very shabby clothes and his heavy jacket was in need of mending. He was holding a cap in his hands that he was wringing back and forth. He had a long, rectangular face with partially sunken eyes. He was pale and seemed almost undernourished. He looked so humble standing there twisting his cap. His shoulders were slightly stooped. He was obviously very embarrassed. Her immediate thought was, '*Oh, the poor boy.*'

"How can I help you?" Maria asked.

"Signora, I want to write a letter to my mother, will you do it for me?"

"But of course. Please come in and sit down," and she pointed to one of the kitchen chairs. She always tried to make her clients as comfortable as possible. She knew that they always felt ill at ease having to admit that they were not literate. But of course that was never mentioned; they both knew why *La Scrittore* was needed to write a letter for them.

He sat down and as she walked over to the cupboard to get her stationery, pen, and a bottle of ink she asked, "Where are you from?"

"I'm from a small fishing village in Calabria. My grandparents and my mother live there. My father died about two years ago. He was a fisherman and worked on the boats. There was a storm and the boat never returned to port; they were all lost."

"Oh, I'm so sorry for you and your Mama. So why did you come to America?"

"We are very poor and my mother did not want me to work on the boats like Papa so I came here because all there is in my home town is the boats. I wanted to make enough money to send for my mother but now I want to send her a letter and tell her no."

"How old are you?"

"I am sixteen, Signora. I need your help. I never went to school and I don't even speak good Italian. He reached into his jacket pocket and took out a small coin and put it on the table.

"This is all I have, Signora, is it enough?"

Maria looked at the small coin. It wasn't even enough to pay for the postage let alone for her supplies and her services. She hesitated a bit. She did not want the word to get out that she was a soft touch. She was tempted to tell him that it wasn't enough but she could not bring herself to say it.

When she first became *La Scrittore*, Maria had vowed to herself that she would never become emotionally involved with any of her clients. She never asked questions nor made suggestions. She wrote what was asked of her, no more, no less. But this boy, this child, she wanted to reach out and hold him tightly to comfort him. It took all her strength to restrain herself.

"Of course it's enough. Don't worry, I'll write the letter for you."

She put a sheet of paper on the table in front of her and uncorked the bottle of ink. Then she laid a pen point wiper on the table and dipped the pen into the ink, tapping the side of the bottle to clear the pen point from any excess ink.

"Now, what do you want to say? Just talk like your Mama was sitting here and you were talking directly to her. I'll slow you down if you start to talk too fast." She poised the pen and he started to speak, to unburden himself was more like it.

18 August 1895

Cara Mama;

I hope that you are well and *nonno* and *nonna* too. I am well. *La Scrittore,* here in Newark, is writing this letter for me.

Mama, things are not working the way we want. I could not get a good job for a long time. Because I don't speak any English and even my Italian is not good people don't want to hire me. I don't even do good arithmetic. The best job I could get was sweeping the streets after the horses. It didn't even pay enough for me to live on so I did odd jobs around the neighborhood. America is supposed to be a Christian country but the people don't act like it. There is so much hatred toward different people from Europe, especially the Irish and Italians.

Mama, three days ago I got another job in the Farmers Market. I unload all the food and stuff from the barges in the canal. Now I eat much better because I just take what I want, mostly fruit and vegetables. There is a broken window on the side of one of the buildings so at night I go back and climb through the window and sleep somewhere in the market.

Mama, I love you and I don't tell all of this to you to make you upset. I am living this way because I don't have to spend any money at all. I am saving everything. When I get enough I am coming back home. I will work the boats just like Papa. It is a much better life for someone like me and I will be happier. Because things are so bad here I think it is God telling me that He wants me to go back home, so that is what I have decided to do.

So Mama, don't come to America; you won't like it either. I will come home as soon as I can.

I love you, Mama

Giacomo

Maria made no comment about the letter. It was his private business and to speak about it would be an intrusion into his private life. She assured him that she would post the letter soon and that his Mama would probably get it in about three or four weeks. Again she wanted to mother him but she resisted.

'*Let his Mama take care of that when he gets home.*'

When Maria got into bed that night she could not shake the memory of the boy from her mind. He was so young and he believed that God was shaping his life. Witnessing such profound faith had a very deep effect on her.

As she was falling asleep she recalled the story about the visionary, St. Theresa of Avila. Once, in a vision of Jesus, she complained to Him that life was so hard on His people.

He said, "That is the way I am with my friends."

Theresa quickly retorted, "Well then, it isn't any wonder that you have so few."

Maria always thought that it was very impertinent of St. Theresa to talk that way, but now she realized that the saints have such a relationship with God that they can speak their minds as among friends. She fell asleep with tears in her eyes.

Chapter 11

AUGUSTA 1895

By her fifth month, Giovanni began to come home later and later for dinner. Sometimes he would not show up at all. Often, if he did come home, he went out after dinner only to come back very late after she was asleep. He rarely touched her. He just got into bed and fell asleep. By the sixth month, sex between them stopped altogether and conversation between them turned from lukewarm to indifferent. She told herself that it was her bulging belly or perhaps he thought he would harm the baby. But she knew she was grasping at straws for an explanation to excuse his behavior. Bewilderment and disappointment slowly turned to bitterness as she was forced to accept the fact that he was turning elsewhere.

*****

Her work as *La Scrittore* and the neighborhood gossip mill had made her aware of the seedier side of the community. She knew about the 'house' down near the river. And although no one ever told her that Giovanni was going there, it was not hard for her to figure out where he was when he was not at home.

All of her dreams and plans were being destroyed. She had tried her best to repair the damage that their long separation had caused. Although she never confronted him, she hoped that she and family life would have been enough of an attraction for him to see that everything he wanted was right there in front of him the whole time.

It was not her way to rant and rave about his treatment of her. She abhorred confrontations. She began to harbor feelings of inadequacy. Was she still attractive? Was she a good cook? Did she look after him enough? She ran the gamut of emotions from disappointment to anger, and finally self-pity. In desperation she confided all of her feelings to Giustina, and her dear friend confirmed her worst suspicions. For a long time Giustina had wanted to tell Maria about it but she could never bring herself to inflict such hurt on her dear friend. And yet, now that Maria had brought up the subject it still grieved her to tell Maria what Giovanni did with his free time.

"Oh, Giustina, I am in such a quandary. I feel as though it is my fault, but I don't know what I am doing wrong."

"Maria, believe me, it is not you. I have watched you and you are all that a man could want. It is a mystery. But, as hard as it is for you to accept the rejection, that is not the only problem. He is getting in deeper with those *animali* he works for on Sundays. They are bad people. I don't know what you can do about that situation either. I tell this to you not to add to your burdens but to warn you of a potential problem."

"Yes, I know. I've tried to reason with him but I can do nothing. Oh, Giustina, I am beginning to fear for Ralph and myself and now I will have a new child to fear for. Please pray for me. I think only God can help me now."

*****

When they told Antonio of her pregnancy he informed them that he was looking at an apartment that would become available soon. It was at number 4 Garside Street just a few blocks away. He told them he was going to move on June 1st, long before the baby was due.

Maria reckoned that their total income was more than adequate so they would have no trouble without Antonio's contribution. It just meant that they would save less.

Although she liked the additional security afforded by saving the extra income from Giovanni's Sunday job, she was still determined that the job would have to go. She knew he was not giving her everything. She thought that he most likely withheld whatever he needed for his extramarital sex. She said nothing about it to him as they both played the game.

Maria made up her mind that after the baby was born he would have to give up working for 'them.' She would demand it no matter what the consequences. She knew what his wages were from the bakery. That would be enough money for the four of them. Once the newborn baby was in her arms and he had to explain to her why he needed extra expense money he might reconsider what his behavior was doing to the family.

She wasn't sure that this strategy would work either. She thought constantly about the deteriorating family situation. She realized the possibility that she probably had already lost her husband and that she might have to settle into a life of living with him but without him. She wondered if she should try once more to save her marriage; or if it was even possible. Maria's rock through all of this anguish was the friendship of Giustina and the companionship of Antonio.

On June 1st Antonio rented the other apartment and moved out. However, he visited Maria and Giovanni very often. She made sure to invite him for dinner as often as she dared. She thought that this tactic would also be a way of keeping Giovanni at home. It worked sometimes but not always. When it did not she and Antonio had dinner alone with Ralph and continued with their long talks and late coffee afterwards.

*****

The baby was born sooner than expected on the first of September 1895. Maria was preparing dinner when she felt the pain of the first contraction. She called to Ralph to run and get Giustina and tell her that the time had come. Giustina arrived with the midwife and they made preparations for the birthing. Giustina sent Ralph to the bakery to tell his father.

'At least he should come home from work this evening!'

When Ralph returned he was sent to Giustina's house to stay there for the night. Giustina and the midwife were in the bedroom with Maria when Giovanni came home. He went in to Maria and then sat at the kitchen table and waited. They all waited as the contractions became more and more frequent. Maria maintained her stoic self throughout the birthing.

Finally, Giovanni heard the midwife call out to him, "It's a girl."

He went into Maria as Giustina and the midwife worked over the baby on the other side of the bedroom where they had set up a small table for that purpose.

It did not occur to Maria or Giovanni why they were huddling over the baby, and why they did not show the baby to them, and why they didn't hear any cries from their newborn daughter. Then Maria heard the midwife reciting the ritual prayers of baptism, "Augusta, I baptize thee *In Nomine Patris, et Filii, et Spiritus Sanctus.*" She knew then that something was wrong.

"Why are you baptizing my baby!" she screamed. Tears flooded her eyes until she couldn't see anyone in the room. There was no reply and she screamed it again. Giovanni let go of her hand and rushed over to the table where the midwife was standing over the baby. Giustina walked over to the bed.

"Maria," she whispered. "The baby has died. It was a girl and she just stopped breathing. There was nothing we could do. We baptized her with the name of Augusta, just as you had planned to do."

Maria was inconsolable and she became incoherent. She was muttering, half in Italian, half in English. Giovanni had to restrain her from trying to get up and go to the baby. Giustina and Giovanni ministered to Maria while the midwife silently did what she had to do. Giustina and Giovanni remained with Maria until, exhausted, she cried herself to sleep.

Giustina left Maria's side just long enough to go home and make arrangements with one of her neighbors to care for her family and Ralph. Then she returned to Maria to take care of her. Giovanni did what he could but the time for his being able to communicate with his wife had long since passed. He did not know what to do or say. He remained in the kitchen and Giustina sat on a chair in the bedroom next to the bedridden Maria. The midwife carried little Augusta's body into the front room and laid her on the sofa and covered her lifeless body with a sheet. She left saying she would notify Michele, the undertaker, and Father Conrad, the pastor of St. Lucy's.

Giustina was still with her friend when they heard the knock on the door. They looked at each other and Maria began to cry. They both knew who it was. Giovanni opened the door for Michele.

"*Buona sera*, Giovanni." They embraced as Michele offered his condolences.

"*Buona sera,* Michele." He pointed to the bedroom, "Maria is in there."

He walked into the bedroom and bent down and kissed Maria on the cheek. "*Buona sera, mia cara Signora.* How are you feeling?"

"Oh, Michele, I never thought I would ever see you under these circumstances, that's for sure. I'm as fine as anyone can be."

"Well, don't you worry, I will take care of everything. I will bring baby Augusta back tomorrow morning before everyone starts coming by. I'll also make arrangements with Signor Torino to have her photograph taken, just for you, *cara mia.*" It would be the only remembrance she'd ever have of her baby.

Tears welled up in her eyes again. "Thank you Michele, you are very kind. Everyone could use a friend like you in an hour of need."

He walked into the front room and gently picked up Augusta's body and left. Later that evening Father Conrad came by to offer his sympathy. He spent some time with Maria in prayer and counseling.

"I will make the arrangements for the funeral mass and burial with Michele. It will have to be on Saturday, we cannot do it on Sunday. But you must promise not to come, it will be too much for you, and you must think of your son. You must take care of yourself; God will take care of Augusta. Do you promise me?" She nodded a reluctant yes. When he left, Giustina went in to Maria.

It was Thursday and Giustina stayed for the night, sleeping as she could, sitting upright in the chair alongside the bed. Giovanni slept on the sofa in the front room. The next morning Giustina urged Giovanni to go to work.

"Go, Giovanni, go; there is nothing you can do here. I'll stay with Maria until you return." Acquiescing, he kissed Maria on the cheek and left for work.

About mid morning Michele returned as he had said he would. He placed Augusta in the front room, in her beautifully satin lined coffin, on a small bier. Alongside he placed a bunch of flowers, and on a small table, a bowl with some money in it. With kind tenderness, he said aloud, "Here you are, *bella*." It was a custom to help the family with funeral expenses. He also left a registry book and he was the first to sign it.

By mid afternoon neighborhood women began to stop by to pay their respects and to sign the book and leave small amounts of money in the bowl. Some brought food for the family. The bereaved were not allowed to cook. The women went in to the bedroom to see Maria. Giustina refused to allow her to get up. Giovanni buried himself in his work. Shortly after he arrived at the bakery, Antonio stopped by to pick up his day's supply of bread and pastries.

"Good morning, Giovanni. I'm surprised to see you here today. I thought you would be cooing over the baby."

"Antonio, the baby is dead. It was a girl and we named her Augusta, after my grandfather, but now she is gone." Tears started to form in Giovanni's eyes, but he quickly shook them away.

"Oh, Giovanni, I am so sorry. How is Maria taking it?"

"She is very bad. She was screaming and crying. She was saying things, I don't know what. I didn't know what to do for her."

"Who is with her now? Are you sure you should be working?"

"Her friend, Giustina, is with her and she promised to spend the day. She insisted I go to work today. I think maybe I'm no good at home right now, but I'll go home early."

"How can you say that, Giovanni? You're the baby's father. Maria needs you by her side, no?" Antonio's voice was sympathetic, but a quick flash of anger came over him. "No," he thought, "Even though Maria's my friend, it's really none of my business what goes on between the two of them."

"But I'm no good with words, Antonio. Giustina knows the right things to say. I think I just make Maria more upset. That's why I came to work today; I'll see her later. Giustina will be there."

"Well, I'll stop by too, as soon as I finish today's deliveries. Again, I'm really sorry dear friend. You two will recover, just give it some time."

*****

By late afternoon dozens of people came by to pay their respects but the only face Maria wanted to see, no, needed to see, was that of Antonio. Always good to his word, as soon as his workday was over, he rushed to her bedside. He arrived at the apartment about four o'clock.

"Go home, Giustina. You must be exhausted. I'll stay with Maria until Giovanni gets home."

Needing the respite, she agreed. She kissed the still dazed Maria on the cheek. "I'll come back tomorrow after the funeral and I'll stay all day. On Sunday Giovanni will take care of you." She nodded to Antonio, said "*Ciao,*" and left.

Antonio sat in the chair next to the bed holding Maria's hands in his. He said all the things that should have been said by a loving and caring husband. He consoled her and he cried with her, and hand in hand they talked. Mostly they tried to make sense of it all. Their firm religious beliefs accepted God's will but their emotions rebelled against it.

The two of them often talked about religion and philosophy so the subject was not new between them. The longer they spoke the closer they drew to one another. Each realized that what they were feeling went beyond friendship and companionship. Their mutual awareness of the situation was frightening.

They loosened their hands and just stared into each other's eyes. He sat there quietly for a long time knowing that his feelings were unacceptable yet too frightened to talk about them. To talk about them would make the situation dangerous even though it was now too late to stop how he felt. Maria was becoming frightened and was also afraid to speak. Their eyes told each other that the emotion was mutual. They sat there, physically separated but emotionally as close as a man and a woman could be.

The moment was interrupted as they heard Giovanni entering the kitchen. He came into the bedroom and Antonio was relieved to have not only the excuse to leave, but also the strength to get up and do so. He told Giovanni that Giustina had gone home and would keep Ralph overnight and return with him tomorrow. Giovanni thanked him. Antonio turned and smiled at Maria who managed a weak smile with tears in her eyes.

"*Arrivederci*, dear friends. I will pray for both of you." He walked through the kitchen and out the door.

Giovanni prepared something for her to eat and wanted to bring it in to her. She refused saying she wanted to get up and go in to see Augusta. He protested but she would not listen. He helped her into the front room, half carrying her. For a while they stood silently by their Augusta and cried.

"Come, Maria, you must eat something," and he coaxed her into the kitchen and helped her into a chair. She ate very little and they talked very little. They sat quietly and stared into space. She began to feel nauseous. She realized that she had pushed herself too soon and needed to get back to bed. He picked her up and carried her back to bed. He tried to make her as comfortable as possible.

She watched him as he fussed over her and the blankets. She felt numb. She had been with him since before Mama and Papa died and now she felt nothing for him. She never felt so guilty in all her life though she knew she shouldn't. She had done nothing wrong. She had invited nothing. Just a few weeks ago she was plotting a course to save her marriage and now she did not care. She blamed it on post pregnancy emotions and the tragedy of Augusta's death.

She also resolved to do nothing about Antonio. That would have to die as quickly as it had come alive, just like the baby. She fell asleep promising herself never to think of Antonio in that way again. Still, she hoped that she would see him again very soon.

Chapter XII

MARIA AND ANTONIO 1895

Giustina returned the next morning about six o'clock. She decided not to bring Ralph with her. He was doing well at her house playing with her children. After Giovanni left for work she and Maria discussed the matter and both agreed that Ralph should stay at her house for a few more days.

It was necessary to have the burial that day because tomorrow was Sunday. Giustina prevailed on her friend to remain at home.

"Maria, you cannot endanger yourself. Let Giovanni go alone. He can do what must be done, and as for Augusta, well don't worry about her, she is already a saint."

Giovanni returned early to get ready for the mass. Maria still wanted to go with him but they prevented her from doing anything that would be so physically and mentally stressful.

"You can go to the cemetery when you feel up to it," they told her.

Giovanni had purchased a family plot through Michele in Holy Sepulcher, the Diocesan cemetery over on Central Avenue. In a little while Michele came and the coffin was sealed and he took Augusta away to St. Lucy's. Maria had never felt such pain, not even when Mama and Papa had died. She was part of them but Augusta was part of her, and that is how she felt. Part of her was gone. Giovanni left and Giustina remained to help her friend.

Giustina busied herself with the household chores while keeping a running conversation with Maria. She went from the kitchen then in to change the bed linen and back to the kitchen to put the laundry in the sink to soak. She helped Maria wash and change. When the apartment was cleaned and in order she sat down next to Maria and they talked.

Their friendship had grown to the point that they were each able to sense the mood of the other. Giustina could read in Maria's face that something else was bothering her besides Augusta's death. Not wanting to dwell on the death of the baby, she turned to happier thoughts of what they would do during the next few weeks.

"School will be starting soon. That means that Ralph and my two boys will be away for most of the day. We can share taking them to school. We can pack a lunch for them so they won't have to come home at noontime. Maybe we could alternate days or weeks. *Va bene,* OK?"

"That will be fine, Giustina."

"Then, while they are in school, you and I can shop together; maybe go to the reservoir on our own. We can spend the day together just having a little fun. How does that sound to you?"

"That would be nice, Giustina." She looked at her friend and tried to smile. "We will have good times together, I know."

Tears started to well up in Maria's eyes again. '*Will they ever stop?*'

Giustina went over to her and sat on the bed so that she could hold her friend, rocking her gently back and forth. "Oh, come here. Rest your head on me. I am always here for you. I know things look desolate now. Just let your feelings out, *bella*." She held her friend silently as tears fell from her eyes also. When Maria calmed down she let go of her and just held her hand.

"Thanks Giustina, I don't think I would have made it without you."

"What about Giovanni? How is he taking it all?"

Maria wiped her eyes with her fingers. "To be honest, I'm not really sure. He doesn't talk about it too much. I'm certain he is devastated about the baby. Beyond that I don't know what's going to happen to us. What I do know is that I am going to try to convince him to give up working for those bad people. Then I'll see if I am able to rebuild some sort of life between us." Giustina encouraged her. She was frightened about what could happen to Maria if Giovanni wasn't careful.

As Maria spoke about her plans she could not help but think of what life might have been with Antonio. Again pangs of guilt consumed her. She shook her head from side to side to drive the thought out of her mind. She was tempted to tell Giustina what was troubling her but felt it would only serve to keep the feeling alive and she wanted to kill it. Besides, why burden her friend with the knowledge?

Maria felt ashamed of her thoughts about Antonio, even to herself. She felt as though life were playing a dirty trick on her in the midst of her tragedy. Maybe Antonio would come to his senses and be able to stop it before it even got started. She hoped so. She tried to tell herself that it was all one-sided, that he did not have the same feelings, but she knew she was trying to delude herself. She promised herself she would never say anything. She did not need this additional problem in her life.

'*Oh Giovanni, please come back to me and make me come back to you.*'

When Giovanni returned from the cemetery, Giustina left for home. As she was leaving she said she would ask Father Conrad to bring Holy Communion to her after mass the next day. He was fluent in Italian and could comfort her in her bereavement. Giovanni walked over and sat on the corner of the bed feeling very ill at ease; he didn't know how to handle the situation.

Mostly he felt guilty because he thought his sins had brought this awful tragedy on the family. He felt her eyes on him as he walked in and out of the bedroom. He made small talk and Maria remained almost silent. Her eyes followed him as he moved in and out of her sight. All she could think of was that she needed the Giovanni of old and he was not there for her. It was Antonio who softened the blows that fate had lashed out at her.

'*Why, why? Why Antonio and not Giovanni, why turned around one way when it should be the other?*'

Giustina had prepared dinner for them before she had left and Giovanni was heating it and setting the table. Again he asked if she wanted to eat in bed. She said no, she wanted to get up. He helped her to the table and they ate in almost complete silence. What little communication there was between them concerned Ralph and the arrangement she had made with Giustina for his care. He thought it was a good idea. After another excruciating silence Maria brought up the subject of his second job.

"Giovanni, please, I think it's time to give up your Sunday job. We don't need the money and I don't like what it is doing to our family."

"No, it's good money and the work is easy. The money I make saves for our future."

"But what about the reputation of the men you associate with, especially that Rocco? Your alignment with them will only lead to trouble. Those are bad people and are not to be trusted. Their only god is money and power. But you, Giovanni, you are different from them, you are better than they are."

"No, they are not so bad. They are real nice to me and they pay me really well for what I do. I'm not going to give it up just yet. I can handle them, no problem. We need the extra money."

They went back and forth over each other's arguments. It went on and on, the first real argument between them, but the problem remained. She thought it best to end the discussion. At least the subject had been laid out in the open. There was no sense in repeating herself. Playing the part of a nag would serve no purpose. She decided to wait a while and talk about it again if some opportunity presented itself.

*****

After a few weeks she was almost back to her energetic self. School had started and for the first week Giustina brought her boys and Ralph to school each morning and picked them up in the afternoon. The following week Maria took on the chore. She didn't have any trouble. Maria and Giustina spent the days together except for the time they needed to spend at home attending to household responsibilities. In the evening, Maria had to allow time for her letter writing; she did not want to lose her following.

From time to time Antonio would stop by. Each of them looked forward to the little time they spent together. Often she invited him for dinner.

"Why should you eat out when you can enjoy a good home-cooked meal?" she told him. It did not take too much urging for Antonio to agree. She was a fantastic cook and besides he wanted to see her. She always told Giovanni when Antonio was coming to dinner. Sometimes he was there and sometimes not.

They were putting themselves into temptation's way. The visits became more and more frequent and lasted longer. Maria was fearful that the relationship was becoming dangerous and that she should stop inviting him over, but her almost complete estrangement from Giovanni made her yearn for Antonio's company all the more.

Slowly her body began to look and feel normal again and she waited for Giovanni to approach her, but he did not. When she tried to initiate intimacy between them he often rebuffed her claiming he was exhausted from work and needed to get up early. But his tiredness did not prevent him from going out at night. At times he did not even come home for dinner.

When she questioned him, his explanation was, as usual, the extra job. He also claimed that he needed some recreational time with his male friends. It was a feeble explanation.

She thought to herself, '*What about recreational time with our family? What about time with me? What about just being home? He can't even look me in the eye! Oh, Giovanni, don't you realize that I know you are lying to me?*'

It was so evident that he preferred what he was getting from the 'house' rather than from her that she stopped trying. She was not going to beg for what was rightfully hers. The feeling of rejection was hard to bear. She stood naked in front of the mirror and took a good look at herself. She knew she had a beautiful body and that her two pregnancies did not affect her appearance. She could not understand why he was not attracted to her body if not to her.

During one of Antonio's visits Maria asked him outright if he knew about the type of people Giovanni was working for on Sundays.

"Oh, Maria, I have known for a very long time. I know it is none of my business, so I've tried to stay out of it. I did warn him at the outset, but he was adamant."

"I'm worried, Antonio. Those are not good people to be associated with. I fear for him and I also fear for myself."

"I agree. The biggest problem of all is that he does not see what he is getting himself into. He does not understand the dangers and he is so easily influenced by others. You know how he is. Rocco, the leader, is the biggest problem. He seems nice on the outside, but you'd do best to avoid him. He is very dangerous and not to be trusted. He will turn on you in a minute no matter who you are."

"I've already talked to Giovanni about it but he is certain that there is no real danger."

She was wary of saying too much even to Antonio but she needed to be relieved of her concerns. Telling Antonio somehow helped to get it out of her system. She hadn't told Antonio about any of her marital troubles before but now it seemed easy to talk about it.

"Things are not going too well right now between us. I feel very alone in this marriage. Sometimes I feel about ready to give up trying to mend the rift between us. Other times I feel I'm just being silly and I try to make a go of it."

He urged her to continue to try to get Giovanni to break off with Rocco. She promised that she would. He offered his sympathy, kissed her on the cheek and left. No mention was made of the 'house'.

Winter was approaching and there was still no sign from Giovanni of any desire for her. She kept telling herself that it was okay, that she could adapt. But then Antonio would show up for a visit and they talked and after he left she felt both aroused and guilty.

*****

On one very rainy day in early December Antonio came to visit her in the early afternoon. They exchanged greetings and stood silently facing each other there in the kitchen. Their eye contact was almost hypnotic. Nothing was said for a long time nor did either of them move. Their emotions rose to fever pitch.

He knew he had fallen in love with Maria. He didn't care anymore. She was beautiful, she was intelligent, and he wanted her. Moreover, she was there. He moved toward her. Her name danced in his head and played with his heart.

'How could I have been so blind? How could have I waited so long?'

She became frightened. She knew she couldn't stop what was happening. She didn't want to stop it yet in her mind she was screaming, no! Then, as if awaking from a deep dream, Maria slowly shook her head and in a whisper, almost a moan, she said, "No, Antonio, no."

"Maria," he whispered over and over in reply, as he slowly stepped closer to her. That was all, only her name.

Again she moaned, "No, Antonio, please no." There was complete silence as they stood staring at each other, struggling with the moment. She could feel his blue eyes piercing her very soul. He wrapped his arms around her waist and gently drew her close, all the while staring at her. He touched her hair and ran his fingers down her neck and shoulder. Tears began to fall down her cheeks as she lifted her hands to his face, caressing his cheeks, all the while staring deeply into his eyes.

He pulled her closer and his embrace took her breath away as she sobbed and moaned simultaneously. He kissed her hard on the mouth. It was pure ecstasy for her and she reciprocated as his hands found her breasts and squeezed gently. There was no turning back now and he pulled her into the bedroom and undressed her. She stood motionless as he undid each button until all of her clothes slipped to the floor. He took a step backward to drink in the vision of her naked body in front of him. He was awestruck by her beauty. It was Maria who had to break his trance. She moved slowly to the bed and got under the covers. He undressed and followed her. Soon they were holding each other, kissing and professing their mutual love.

For a long time afterwards they lay silent and motionless, clinging to each other. When they finally spoke it was to tell each other that what they had done was wrong. They shared their guilt feelings along with the knowledge that neither had ever felt this way before. Maria once thought her love for Giovanni was complete, but even now she knew that this was something different, stronger, more intense. She might have loved Giovanni but this was an entirely new experience for her, a peaceful bliss she had never known before.

The rainstorm intensified and there were bolts of lightning just like a summer storm. The claps of thunder made her cling to him all the more. Once more they made love but this time nothing was said afterwards. He got up and she followed. Quietly, even pensively, they dressed. He held her once more, kissing her full on the mouth and left without saying a word.

She cried as she heard his footsteps fade down the hall. She ran to the front room, looked out the window and saw him dash through the rain across and up the street.

'Oh my God, what have I done!' She resolved that it would never happen again but even as she did so she knew that it would.

Thankfully Giovanni did not come home until long after dinner and by that time she and Ralph were both asleep. At least she did not have to face him the way he had faced her after so many of his infidelities.

The liaisons between Maria and Antonio went on through the holidays. She surrendered to the reality that she was desperately in love with Antonio and he with her. She decided to confide what had happened to Giustina. She chose the time and place very carefully. She wanted to make sure that her friend's reaction wouldn't be noticed by anyone. So she waited until after the holidays when they were at the reservoir one Saturday in January while the children were playing in the snow.

"Giustina, I have a confession to make to you."

"What's the matter? I've thought for some time that something was wrong. You know you can tell me anything."

It was so difficult for her to say, even to Giustina. She had to fight back the tears. She squeezed her eyes shut and took in a deep breath.

"I'm having an affair with Antonio."

Giustina was stunned. Of all the things that could have been bothering her friend, this was the one thing she never suspected.

"Maria, how on earth did you ever let such a thing happen?"

She could no longer hold the tears back. She began to sob uncontrollably. She opened her eyes and looked directly at Giustina.

"I really don't know myself. One minute I'm in Italy with a new baby who has doting grandparents, a loving husband, and the next I'm living in a shack with a husband who hardly speaks to me, let alone touches me. Antonio was there for me. I needed him. I fell in love with him and he fell in love with me. I tell you I don't know how it happened, it just did."

"Maria, dear. You have to end this now. Disaster will strike your house if you do not."

Even as she said it Giustina realized that her friend would not, could not listen. While she did not condone her friend's affair, neither was she judgmental. She had a happy married life and could imagine what a trauma it would be to lose it. She did not say it but she felt that most of the fault lay with Giovanni.

'*Damn him!*' But she kept that comment to herself; she did not want to proffer any excuse for Maria to rationalize what she was doing.

"Whatever you do, Maria. You must be very careful about this. You can't be too discrete. This is such a small neighborhood and you know how much people love to gossip."

"I will, I promise you. You are such a dear friend. Thank you for being so understanding."

Maria wondered what would happen to her if Giovanni ever found out. Giustina was saddened by her friend's predicament and hoped that the affair would wane as time passed.

Maria and Antonio were unaware that his visits and the sound of their lovemaking did not go unnoticed by the wagging tongue that lived next door. Through the year the affair became known in the neighborhood but no one ever mentioned it to Giovanni or Maria or Antonio. The three of them did not suspect that they were the topics of hushed gossip. That is, until just before Christmas of 1896.

Chapter XIII

ROCCO 1896

On the first Saturday of December in 1896, after work, Giovanni met with Rocco in his restaurant. He walked into the dimly lit café located on the ground floor of a tenement building and looked for his boss. There were a few scattered tables here and there surrounded by small, bare, wire-back chairs. The decorations may have been sparse, but the clientele always made the café colorful and the food was excellent. There were a few patrons having dinner and some of Rocco's underlings were seated at the bar sipping wine. Giovanni acknowledged them with the respect that their individual position in the association demanded. He found Rocco seated alone at his customary table in the far corner, with his back against the wall. Even in his own establishment he had to protect himself.

Giovanni sat down across from Rocco and ordered a glass of wine from the waiter. After the required pleasantries were exchanged, Rocco complained, "There are too many people not paying on time. We gotta do something about these deadbeats, *capisce?*"

"Well Rocco, I tell you as soon as it happens. I can't do any more than that."

"Sure you can, Giovanni. You can twist a few arms, you know, threaten them a little. Rough them up even, if you have to; scare the hell out of them. I want them to know who's boss around here."

Giovanni's mind flashed back to past conversations he had with Antonio and Maria. "No, Rocco, I won't do that. That's not my way. I collect money for you and that's all. I don't want no part of nothing violent."

"Maybe you don't understand me, Giovanni. You ain't got a choice here. I want my money, and you're going to get it for me one way or the other, *capisce?*"

Their conversation grew louder and louder. Soon they were drawing the attention of Rocco's men seated at the bar. Giovanni finally realized the predicament he was in and thought this was his chance to end it. Maria and even Antonio wanted him to get out.

"Look, Rocco, this was not in our agreement. I won't do nothing violent and if that means that I have to stop working for you then I quit. I won't hurt nobody. I never did anything wrong and I'm not going to start now, especially just for money. Keep your job!"

"No one quits on me! You will do as I say," Rocco shouted, as he pounded his fist on the table.

"No I won't," snapped Giovanni. He was on his feet now. "I am an honorable man, and I don't want your money anymore."

Rocco turned red with embarrassment that quickly gave way to rage. How could anyone disrespect him this way? He jumped up from his chair. How could anyone have the temerity to talk to him in that tone of voice? His associates were listening intently, appalled by the scene. The patrons in the café stopped eating and turned to stare at them.

"Honorable?" Rocco shouted with mock laughter, "How honorable is it down by the river, huh? How honorable is it when you go down to the 'house' by the river and your wife and her boyfriend are in your bed while you work!" Rocco saw the look of shock on Giovanni's face.

"Ah, don't pretend to me that you don't know about your wife whoring around with your friend Antonio!"

Giovanni's reaction was automatic and the punch knocked Rocco down, and before he hit the floor blood was gushing from a broken nose and split lip and some of his teeth were on the floor.

The customers were horrified. Rocco's men were stunned into immobility. How could Giovanni have dared to show disrespect for 'a man of honor' such as Rocco? How could anyone dare to strike a man in Rocco's position?

"You'll pay for this!" Rocco yelled to Giovanni as he stormed out of the restaurant's entrance doors. "You hear me, you're gonna pay bad, Giovanni!"

Rocco's accusation made Giovanni fume, even though he refused to believe it. At the same time he had the normal male reaction to such an accusation. His anger grew to the boiling point the closer he got to home. He was in full rage when he got there. He stormed up the stairs, two at a time, and barged into the kitchen. Ralph was playing in the front room and Maria was cooking at the stove. He slammed the door behind him and she whirled around at the sound. As soon as she saw his face she knew that he had found her out.

"Is it true?" he yelled.

"Shhh, the neighbors will hear!"

"The hell with the neighbors! Is it true about you and Antonio?"

She had feared and expected that at some time he would find out. Deep down she knew it would be just a matter of time. Still, now that it had happened, she was surprised. She knew that there was no denying the truth. Not able to look him in the face, she lowered her head and whispered, "Yes, it's true."

His hand stung across her face. She expected it and tried to prepare herself, but it still came as a shock. The force of the blow knocked her across the room and against the far wall. She slid down the wall, landed on the floor, and braced herself as he started towards her. She was trembling looking up at his towering figure. Suddenly he stopped and slumped onto one of the chairs, putting his elbows on the table. He laid his head on top of his hands and began to cry with big, heaving sobs, not only for what she had done to him but also for what he had done to her. Maria sat on the floor, leaning against the wall, not daring to move. She watched him as the sobs became deeper and deeper.

"What have I done?" he kept repeating over and over. She began to cry too.

When he stopped she said, "What have we done?" It was more of a statement of how far they had fallen from their love back in Italy rather than a question. Neither of them moved for a while nor were they aware that Ralph was standing by the doorway to the front room watching the entire spectacle.

"I'm hungry, Mama," he said, with a worried look on his face. They both came back to their senses and she broke the silence.

"Let me feed the boy and we'll talk about this later."

She finished cooking. The boy ate alone. Neither of them ate anything. They just sat at the table while Ralph ate. After she cleared the table she put Ralph to bed a bit earlier than usual.

She came back to the kitchen. Giovanni was seated at the table with his back to the door. She sat down across from him, facing the door, her hands folded on the table. For a long time neither of them spoke. It was he who spoke first, in a lowered, almost beaten down voice.

"My wife and my best friend, I don't believe it."

"I am so sorry, Giovanni. I never meant for it to happen. I am just so sorry. You were gone so often. I was lonely and Antonio befriended me. We never meant for any of this to happen."

She was careful not to mention any of his extramarital affairs; neither did she try to blame him. He knew what he had done; she knew what she had done. She thought that it would serve no purpose to deflect all the blame onto him. Nothing would be gained by hurling recriminations at one another. Her attempts at explaining what happened were interspersed with heartfelt apologies and pleas for understanding and forgiveness. What could he say, who had the greater fault?

He looked at her straight in the eye. "You know about the 'house' on the river, don't you?" She nodded yes. "Well, I have been there; you are not alone in your guilt."

She was quick to add that his infidelity was not the reason for her actions. Tears rolled from her eyes.

"I have fallen in love with Antonio. I am sorry that I can't control my feelings. But I should have been able to control my actions. That's where my guilt is."

"And what about me? Don't you have no love for me no more?"

"Oh, Giovanni, you must know that what we had has been over for both of us for a long time."

"No, not for me," he protested.

"Oh, Giovanni, be honest with yourself, listen to what you are saying. I have not been what you wanted since I arrived in America, maybe even before."

He had no reply nor did he attempt one. They just sat there, starring into space.

Suddenly, Antonio burst into the room without even knocking. She was stunned into rigidity. Giovanni whirled around, "What are you doing here?" He rose menacingly from the table, "Did you come to gloat over me?"

Maria jumped to her feet. "Wait," she screamed. "Please, Giovanni, sit down." She turned to Antonio and looked directly into his eyes so that he would get the message that it was dangerous for him to be there.

"Antonio, please leave immediately." She hoped that he would get her full meaning, that he would read the warning in her eyes. Staying could only add fire to the situation and it might turn ugly. So that there was no doubt in her pleading she added, "He knows about us, I told him everything. Please, for my sake, leave now."

"I beg your forgiveness, both of you but that is not why I am here." He turned to Giovanni. "Please don't blame Maria. This is all my fault."

"Antonio, that's not fair. We are all to blame, each one," she interrupted. "None of us has the right to hold the others accountable. We are all guilty. We have all wronged the other. Now please go!" Giovanni stood up. He was incredulous, unable to speak either to his unfaithful wife or to his deceitful friend.

"All right, I'll leave. But first I must tell you why I came! Giovanni, you are in grave danger."

"What are you talking about?" Maria demanded.

"Please, Maria, let me finish. Giovanni punched Rocco at the restaurant and hurt him badly. He did it in front of Rocco's men and even worse, in front of his customers."

She whirled around to face Giovanni. "You idiot," she yelled at him, almost involuntarily.

Antonio interrupted. "Please, Maria, I don't think he fully realizes the consequences. Giovanni, listen to me! By now the entire neighborhood must know what happened. Rocco feels disgraced, that his honor has been damaged. He cannot let the incident pass if he is to maintain the respect of his men and his control over them. He needs to have them fear him, and the people too. Giovanni, don't you understand? They are going to kill you. Do you understand what I am saying? Rocco is going to kill you!"

Maria gasped; she fully understood the danger of the situation. Giovanni, on the other hand, just yelled, "Let him come. I can take care of myself."

"No, Giovanni, you still don't understand. Rocco isn't going to kill you. He will have someone else do it, but everyone will know that the order came from him. In that way he will save face, and in their perverted way his honor will be restored. People will fear him even more. You won't even know who is coming after you."

When it finally sank in, Giovanni slumped onto the chair, utterly defeated, temporarily forgetting Maria's infidelity. He realized that he was a doomed man.

She wrung her hands and half moaned, "Oh God, what are we going to do?"

Antonio said, "There is only one way open. Giovanni must leave Newark immediately or he will be killed. Make no mistake about it, it will happen, but I have come up with a plan that I'm sure will work." At this point Maria and Giovanni were willing to listen to anything. They both looked at Antonio in anticipation of a miracle. In a hushed voice, Antonio explained the plan that had started to form in his mind as soon as he heard the bad news.

"Right now, tonight, before dawn, Giovanni must leave this house. You have to get out of Rocco's reach immediately. We will wait until the tongue next door goes to sleep. Tomorrow is Sunday and I doubt very much that even Rocco would do anything on a Sunday." He continued, sarcastically, "After all, he and his men go to church with their families on Sunday." They had no religion, these men, but they needed to maintain an image of respectability and benevolence in the community.

Antonio continued to outline his plan. "Now listen closely. I will hide you in my wagon down at the barn. No one will suspect that I would help you now. You will have to stay there all day and tomorrow night too. Maria, pack as much clothing as possible for him, and enough food and water to last until Monday morning. You will not be missed until you don't show up for work on Monday morning and by then Luigi will have already heard the bad news."

"I will tell Luigi that you have fled back to Italy and that you are on a boat or hiding in New York. I don't know where. Luigi will then advertise for another laborer and promote one of his help to take your place. That will lend credence to the story. Luigi can be trusted. I'll make my usual rounds by myself with you hiding in the wagon all the time, right under their noses. I will tell my man to go help Luigi in the bakery so we

114

will be alone in the wagon. I have many customers downtown and I can take you to the railroad station unnoticed. There you can board a train for Philadelphia and then on to Youngstown, Ohio. I will write a letter to my cousin Francesco explaining the situation and beg him for his help. Francesco can be trusted; don't worry about that. I will ask Francesco to help you get a job in the steel mill."

"I know Francesco will cooperate because he has no use for those criminals, he is an upright and honorable man. He calls them *animali*. I won't tell him anything about Maria and me. It would serve no purpose. Once I hear from Francesco that you are settled, Maria and I will make plans for her to join you, wherever you are."

"Luigi, Maria and I will support the rumor that you've gone back to Italy. Maria, you will openly make plans to join him there. You must sell all of your furniture. In fact, I will buy it from you. Then you must purchase a ticket for Naples at the travel agent's office in the bank, and withdraw all your money asking for lira not dollars. That will become common knowledge very fast and strengthen the story. Then I will accompany you and Ralph to New York and put you on a train to Philadelphia. Giovanni will meet you there and bring you to Youngstown."

Antonio explained further that all the arrangements could be made through Francesco. Most people who knew Antonio knew that he kept in touch with Francesco. They could stay in touch with each other through Francesco once it was determined that Rocco believed the story. Antonio was sure that he would because forcing Giovanni back to Italy was almost as good as killing him. In fact it was probably better because there would be no unsolved murder to contend with. Publicly, Rocco would have restored his sense of honor. For all intents and purposes Giovanni would have been disgraced as far as Newark was concerned and it would count as a lesson to anyone who tried to cross Rocco in the future.

Maria was dumbfounded by the plan. She also recognized the genius of it, but that was Antonio, quick and thorough. Except for falling in love with her, he was always the master of any situation and at least three or four jumps ahead of everyone. With the exception of a few minor details to be worked out, they all agreed that the plan was their best option.

Giovanni, now concerned for his life and his family's welfare, forgot their mutual infidelity and he acquiesced. There was no time to lose. He began to pack as Maria put in a bag enough food to last all the next day while he was hiding. Quietly now, so as not to awaken the gossip next door, they made the final preparations. Antonio was helping her and as she packed the food, their eyes met. The look between them asked for forgiveness from each other, declared their undying love, and said goodbye, at one and the same time.

When Giovanni was ready to leave, she handed him all the money she had on her. It was not enough so Antonio handed him more. Tears were rolling down her cheeks.

"Oh, Giovanni, I am so sorry," she said and she pushed both of them out the door.

Chapter XIV

YOUNGSTOWN & JOSEPHINE 1896

14 December 1896

Ciao Francesco;

The man delivering this letter to you is my very close and dear friend, Giovanni. You will recall that I mentioned him to you in my letters. He is the one I went into partnership with in the apartment and also we have worked together for many years in your friend Luigi's bakery. I am sending him to you and I ask a very great favor. Through no fault of his own he has gotten into trouble with Rocco. You remember Rocco and the kind of person he is. As a result it is very dangerous for Giovanni to remain in Newark.

He has a wife and son here. His wife's good friend and I are going to spread the story that he has returned to Italy in the hope that Rocco will stop trying to find him. I ask that you take him in for a little while. Either help him to locate somewhere or better still, get a job for him in the steel mill, if you can. If there is any expense let me know and I will send the money to you.

Once he is settled, his wife will leave Newark and pretend to join him in Italy but instead she will go to be with him, wherever that may be. Dear *cugino*, I know that this is a great imposition I put on you, especially involving people you don't even know, but I implore you, do this favor for me. You know that if the situation were reversed there is nothing I wouldn't do for you. These are my very dear friends and I am indebted to him.

It is important that he have no direct contact with his wife because the mail goes through the neighborhood post office near the bank. Any letters to her from him should be put in an envelope and then that envelope addressed to me as having come from you. I will see that she gets it. Likewise, any letters from her to her husband will be given to me and I will mail them to you to give to him. I am sorry for this subterfuge but it is necessary; believe me. People in the post office are used to mail going back and forth between you and me so I don't think anyone will suspect anything unusual.

I hope that you and your family are well. I miss seeing you; you helped me so much in the past. My bakery delivery business is progressing very well. I plan to send for my family in about a year. In a few years I think I will be able to buy an apartment building of my own.

Stay well, my dear cousin,

Antonio

*****

18 December 1896

Ciao cugino Antonio;

Your package has arrived and everything has been explained to me. I have arranged all matters, and the additional packages can be sent to me at any time. Just write to me and advise when they will be shipped. Ship them to general delivery at the railroad station in Philadelphia and I will arrange to have them picked up there.

I am very happy to hear that your business is doing so well. I am overjoyed that you are sending for your family. Soon you will be a family man again. Remember, Antonio, nothing can replace the family. Too bad that it has taken so long. How glad you will be to see your son Francesco, my namesake. I was always grateful that you named him after me. How old is he now? He must be about eight or nine, and little Theresa must be five or six. Emanuella must be getting to be quite a lady. Francesco should be able to help you on the wagon on Saturdays and during the summer.

I am doing well here. I have been going to night school and my English is becoming very good. I am also working with a speech specialist and slowly my accent is disappearing. I have been promoted twice since I got the job. I am now an assistant shift manager. I don't work in the mill any longer. I don't know which I like better, being in the mill or paper work. But, in addition to my own advancement, I also have the opportunity to help our fellow countrymen. So many of them are taken advantage of and I stop it where I can. We are hiring more men now and I am able to hire some directly, which, for your information, I just did recently.

I am renting a very large house and taking in boarders. We live on the first floor and they all live on the second and third floors. But I am in the process of buying a one family house and that leaves the boarding house available for some energetic person to rent and run. I think I have found the right person who just recently came to Youngstown so I might be moving soon.

Stay well and kiss Joanna and the children for me when they arrive from Italy.

Cugino, Francesco

*****

13 January 1897

Maria;

We are back to writing letters again. Antonio's cousin has been like an angel from heaven to me. We must not write to each other directly. That is why this letter is in the envelope with Francesco's letter to Antonio. When you reply to me give the letter to Antonio and let him mail it to me with one of his letters to Francesco. I am so sorry that my behavior to you and with Rocco has caused this great trouble for us. Tell Antonio that I am grateful for what he has done to help me out but I don't want to have anything to do with him ever again. What has happened has happened, between us and between you and me. That can't be changed.

When I got here Francesco took me in immediately. He loves Antonio very much and would do anything for him. Francesco has a very good job at the steel mill and he rents a very large house here. They use the first floor for themselves and rent out the second and third floors to boarders. I have my very own small room on the third floor. Francesco got a job for me at the steel mill. I am doing common laborer's work. Just now I am shoveling coke into the furnaces. The work is very hard and very hot and very dirty. I hate it more than I did the fish market when I first came to America. But it will have to do and I am very grateful to Francesco for the opportunity. We are becoming friends.

I have very good news. He bought a one family house and will be moving his family soon. He says he can arrange to have the lease on this house turned over to me and we can run the boarding house. I remember the problems Antonio and I had taking in boarders in Newark. But now I have a little more experience and the house is very large so we would not be in too much contact with them. I would need rent money to give to the man who owns the house plus a security deposit and to pay Francesco for the furniture that the boarders use. You will have to buy furniture for us when you get here. We have enough money in the bank so we can do it. I said yes to the offer and everything is ready.

It will be hard work for you but we do not have to provide any meals, only keep the bedding and the rooms clean. So Maria, make the arrangements to come here as soon as possible and let me know when. Take the earliest train to Philadelphia on a Saturday and I will meet you at the train station. Francesco will arrange for me to have the Saturday off from work. Then we must take the next train back to Youngstown. I will have to be at work on Monday morning. I am sorry but there was no time to consult with you on all of this. It was necessary to say yes immediately or lose the opportunity, so I have already committed us to the deal.

Giovanni

*****

23 January 1897

Ciao cugino Francesco;

I hope that you and the family are well. How can I thank you for all that you have done for my friends? Your help is beyond my expectations. It is a relief for me to know that they will soon be together and established. His wife, Maria, has let me read the letter she received from him. We are taking care of everything here in Newark

So far it seems that Rocco has accepted the story of the return to Italy so I am sure that there will be no trouble from him. Enclosed is a letter from Maria to Giovanni. Please give it to him. I am sure that she will handle the travel plans expertly. She is a very competent woman and knows how to take care of herself.

Stay well, dear cousin. I pray for you and your family. I am sorry we do not live closer together. Some day we will meet again, I am sure of it.

With all love and respect,

Antonio

*****

23 January 1897

Dear Giovanni;

How hard life is. We have certainly had our share of trouble and most of it is our own doing. Yet somehow God always sends someone to help us. Especially he sent Antonio even though we betrayed you. I am sure God is angry with both of us for that. Forgive me Giovanni, and Antonio too. He is grief stricken over what has happened and so am I. So we are in trouble again and God sends Francesco. Again you surprise me in making the arrangements for the boarding house with him. You did the correct thing. Do not worry about the extra work; I can handle it.

I will leave a week from this Saturday on the earliest train from New York. Antonio thinks it is better to go to New York and then to Philadelphia rather than leave from Newark. He is afraid we might be seen. Also, his hired hand will take us to the railroad station in Newark and he will see us get on the train to New York so if he is ever asked that is what he will say. The ship I bought tickets for does not sail for a few weeks later. We just told people I am going to stay in New York until then.

That allows Antonio time to cancel the tickets and get a refund. We should arrive in Philadelphia at noon. When you meet us you will have to make arrangements to transport two trunks and two suitcases to the Youngstown train.

I closed our bank account and took most of the money in lira as we planned. I gave the lira to Antonio and he gave me dollars for it. He will exchange the money again in New York after I leave. Also, Antonio gave me the money for the furniture. He tried to be overly generous but I refused. What I accepted was fair. You had better open an account at the bank there; I don't want to have the cash in the house. Then I can make a deposit on Monday after we deduct what we owe the landlord and Francesco.

Don't bother to register Ralph in school. I think I made a mistake in starting him so early anyway. We will register him in the fall in the first grade.

Giovanni, don't be angry, but I confided what we are doing to Giustina. I trust her, it is like telling myself; it will go no farther, she won't even tell her husband. She is my friend; I had to do it. Also, it will be to our benefit to have her report anything to us that we need to know. I know we can depend on Antonio but she will hear things that only women talk about among themselves. I will see you on Saturday, February 3rd.

Ralph misses you very much and it will be good for him to have a father once more. I worry about him, being moved around so much, but this time we will stay settled in Youngstown.

Maria

6 February 1897

Dearest love, Antonio;

I miss you so much. I should not be writing things like this to you any longer but I cannot help it. Being with you all night the night before I left was pure ecstasy for me. Now that last time will be our last time. I will probably never see you again and that is pure agony for me. Please don't acknowledge any of your feelings for me in any of your letters. If you want to write to me make it a 'newsy' letter because I will show it to Giovanni. However, I think you should write to him directly. That way he can give the letter to me to read. If any response is required he can do it. If it is necessary for me to communicate with you privately I will have to resort to writing to Giustina and pretend that I am writing just to her. I do not want to put this additional burden on her, so let us use this method for dire emergencies only.

Yes, dear Antonio, I confided everything to her. Don't be angry, there is no worry, and she can be our mutual friend for exchanging information about each other but only if it is necessary. But, dearest Antonio, I think we should not use her to exchange letters regarding our mutual feelings. We must let them lie still and not make matters worse by writing to each other about things that will never be. But, my love, rest assured that the love I feel for you I took with me and it will remain with me forever. Now that's the end of it, I will say no more and I beg of you to respect my wishes and promise you will say no more.

I am telling Giovanni that this letter to you is just to thank you for what you have done so that we can establish a life here. He may not believe me but he is not pressing me to read it. He did meet me in Philadelphia as planned and we made it to Youngstown in one piece. Your cousin Francesco has been a Godsend, literally. By the time you get this letter he and his family will have moved and we will be running the boarding house he had. Youngstown is a very large city and newer than Newark. The only problem with where we live, on Waverly Avenue, is that the street parallels the railroad and sometimes the noise from the trains can be annoying. However, I am getting used to it already. The work of caring for the rooms of seven boarders is a little difficult but I will soon have it down to a manageable system.

When you see Giustina tell her that I will write to her and enclose the letter with the next one that Francesco sends to you. Giovanni is slowly getting over what happened so that maybe there will be some kind of life for us together. I don't know, but I hope so. It is so odd to live with a man who gives the appearance of being in complete control but in reality is not, he just follows along with whatever comes his way.

Thank God that hard work always solved things for him, and he is working very hard at the steel mill, of all places. I know that his soul aches for the bakery, but for now, that is impossible.

Antonio, this one last time,

All my love forever;

Maria

*****

3 March 1897

Dearest Antonio;

Even though I said I would not, I am writing to you through Francesco and Giustina because I have some startling news. I am pregnant, I am sure of it. The problem is that I have not been with Giovanni since three months before Augusta died. He is avoiding me and there is nothing I can do about it. There wasn't enough time to mend that rift between us. I have no option open now except to tell him. Soon he will be able to notice my condition and it is better if I tell him before he realizes it for himself.

When I tell him there will be no choice but to acknowledge you as the father. I was shocked when 'it' did not come on schedule. I think the baby will be born in late September. I waited until I missed the second time just to be sure. There is no doubt about it and no sense in putting off telling him. I am writing this to you now and tonight I will tell him. God help us, I don't know what his reaction will be. I was hoping to start a new life here but now this will make the situation even worse than it was.

He has been very quiet since we moved here, even for his personality. I think he is brooding over what happened, all of it, not only you and me. I think he is having a very difficult time putting everything behind him and I know that he hates working in a steel mill. I will not write to you again for a very long time. Please don't write to me! It would serve no purpose and I don't want to put Francesco in any kind of embarrassing position. He still does not know about us and I want it to remain that way.

After I tell Giovanni he might write to you, I don't know, but I doubt it. When you see Giustina please tell her what happened, just now I don't have the courage to write to her. My God, what a tangled and complicated web we have created for ourselves! It is true; there is retribution in this life, not from God, but from our very selves.

If you ever do get the opportunity to write to Giovanni again let us know if the trouble with Rocco is completely forgotten. Sometimes I fear he is only pretending to accept the story of our flight to Italy. As if we don't have enough things to worry about, we still have that sword of Damocles hanging over our heads.

Be happy, my love, no matter what happens. Again, my love, please don't write to me.

Always,

Maria

*****

12 March 1897

Maria;

My God, will it never end? I saw Antonio today and he told me of your condition. How foolish you were. I never pointed my finger at you, that is not for me to do, but my God, Maria, couldn't you see the danger in front of you? It is so unlike you not to consider possibilities. You must have been blind.

Have you told Giovanni? If you did, what was his reaction? This kind of thing can provoke a man to violence, even a non-violent man like him. Everyone has a limit. I pray that he didn't do anything stupid. Be careful, Maria, I told you to be careful once before but you did not listen to me. Listen now!

And now you are in trouble and I am not in a position to help you, my dearest friend. All I can do is pray for you, which I do every day. Write to me as soon as you can. I don't think you should write to Antonio any-more. Don't include any letters to him in your letters to me. Why take the chance? I will tell him whatever you want him to know. So far you have not asked me to keep anything from him so we share whatever you write. Please don't make us keep secrets between us.

I miss our times together, you and me, and I wonder if we will ever get to see each other again. Maybe someday I will be able to make a vacation trip out to see you. I know that you will never be able to come here again. I am sure that Rocco has accepted the story and is content with thinking he won over Giovanni. But that would change in an instant if he ever found out the truth.

Stay well, dear friend, and may God help and bless you.

Giustina

15 March 1897

Antonio;

Maria has told me she is pregnant with your child. The news was so devastating to me that I could not even get angry. I am a defeated man. I have no wife and I have no friend. I feel alone and abandoned in a strange country. I have seriously thought of taking Ralph and going back to Italy leaving Maria to her own fate. I see no future for me with her. It is only the distance between us that prevents me from doing you harm. You were my best and only friend. But as I write this letter, I try to find the truthful answer to what has happened. I see where I have been part of the evil that has come down on my house. I was addicted to the 'house' on the river. I cannot explain it but it had a hold on me that I could not shake. Even after Maria arrived in America I could not keep away. I tried but I guess I am weak. That is not an excuse but it's what happened, *mea culpa, mea culpa, mea maxima culpa*. But you! You are more to blame than even Maria or myself. You were my friend and I would have trusted you with my life. But none of us has clean hands.

I hit Maria again when she told me. It was the wrong thing to do. She was frightened and defenseless and I took advantage. I am sorry for that and I blame you for that too. What to do, I don't know. For now I will do nothing. Maybe time will help heal all our wounds, but I will never forgive you. You are no longer my friend and I never want to hear from you again. But, you helped me when I came to America and you helped me in my trouble with Rocco. Now we are even, quits, *finito*.

I don't want Francesco to find out about any of this. He is an honorable man and well respected in the mill and in the community. I will do nothing to bring dishonor to him. He loves you and I don't want to hurt him with the truth. As far as the world is concerned the baby will be mine. But don't write to me anymore, and you can explain that to Francesco any way you want. I work like a dog in dirt here instead of a clean bakery surrounded by the aroma of baking bread. That is my punishment, my penance. I hope that yours is equally as bad.

Giovanni

10 June 1897

Dear friend, Giustina;

I hope that you and all of your family are well. I miss you very much. I have not made any friends out here. I am very busy keeping the house clean for all the boarders. I feel so sorry for them, all alone, trying to earn enough to survive. All of them are single men who, for the most part, left Italy to escape the conscription into the army. They cannot speak English and they rely on Giovanni and me to help them. Of course, Francesco is next to God in their eyes. I write letters for them, most are non-literate. I also try to teach them English, but they are young and have no incentive. Can you believe it; they are trying to save enough money to buy a bride in Italy. There are agents out here who make such arrangements, just like in Newark.

I have delayed writing, waiting for things to quiet down a little. The night I told Giovanni about the baby he became incensed and hit me again. In my guilt I thought he had a right to do it. He wanted to punish me for doing exactly what he did at the 'house'. While I don't excuse myself, he is guiltier than I. I was, and still am, in love with Antonio, something that would never have happened if he had been home where he belonged. He did what he did out of lust. What a weak argument for me to use to justify what I did. God help us!

He wrote to Antonio and severed their relationship. That saddens me the most, I think. Well, it is done and cannot be undone. What I did was wrong. I did not heed your advice, although, if you can believe it, I did try.

I don't know what will happen here. He goes to work and comes home for dinner. He never goes out. We hardly ever speak to each other. What time he has after dinner he spends with Ralph. They have a very special kind of relationship. When they are together I am excluded, almost an outsider. But I have Ralph during the day. It will be difficult to send him off to school in the fall. But I will need the time because that is when the baby is due. I am in dread of Giovanni's reaction when he sees the baby. I hope that it will be a girl so that there will be no sibling competition between the children. I also know that he is still at a loss over Augusta and so am I. Oh, Giustina, pray for me, I feel so alone in the world.

Maria

14 September 1897

Dearest friend, Giustina;

The baby came early on the 6th. It is a girl. I have named her Josephine Augusta. She is a beautiful baby with very light brown hair that I am sure will darken in time. She has Antonio's coloring but my brown eyes. She is a good baby, nurses well, and is no trouble at all. Thank God Ralph has accepted her without any difficulty. He goes to school now and the first thing he does when he comes home is go look for her. He is fascinated to watch her breast-feed. The procedure must be a revelation to him and I think it is healthy for him to watch so he knows what things are for. Giovanni has not said much but he does go in and looks at her from time to time, but he will not pick her up. I think that will change as she develops a personality. I was afraid he would take Ralph away from me and go back to Italy, but I don't feel he thinks about that now, if he ever did.

Francesco was able to get a better job for him at the mill. Not much better, but at least he isn't shoveling coke any more. He works in the maintenance department. It is still a dirty job but better and he earns a little more money. He never goes out with the men. I tried to get him to go play *bocce*, but he won't. He stays home all the time. I think maybe he doesn't trust me anymore. He still has not come near me and it is now over a year since we were together. Whenever my body gets back to normal I am going to do my best to change that. Now, for the children's sake I will do whatever is necessary to protect the family.

Word of my writing letters for the boarders has gotten around and I am *La Scrittore* once again and I have a clientele that is larger than the one I had in Newark. I save all of the money. I bank all of the rent money too. I hope that one day there will be enough for Giovanni to open a bakery somewhere. I don't care where; it's a big country. I am also making lunches for the boarders to take to work and I make a little money there and I save that too. I also make sure they eat properly. I am going to make as much money as I can and save it for Giovanni. My only salvation in this life will be for him to be happy in his work again. If he is, maybe some of his happiness will spill over into our marriage.

How wonderful it would be if you could come to see me. I would come to see you in a minute if it weren't for Rocco. I have not heard from Antonio and I don't want to. Please tell him about Josephine and that I will dedicate my life to providing for her.

Maria

15 December 1897

Dear friend, Maria;

Buon'Natale to you and to your family. Congratulations on Josephine. I was pleased to hear that Ralph had no trouble accepting her. I was so afraid that he might have heard the gossip here in Newark. But even if he did I don't think he is old enough to understand. I am happy to report that the whole affair over Rocco is forgotten. It is yesterday's news. No one has mentioned the incident for months. They have moved on to more current dirt and there is plenty of that.

I see Antonio on the street from time to time, and sometimes at Luigi's. He was elated about Josephine and wanted to write to you but I talked him out of it. I told him I would tell you how he felt about the baby. He said nothing else but I can see he is having a very difficult time getting over you. However, he looks very well. You know him, always dressed like he was going to a banquet.

I see Gia often. She asks if I hear from you. I lie and say once in a while. She sends her regards. I don't see Luigi too much; he is mostly down at the ovens so I only see him if he happens to be in the store. Antonio still buys his bread from him and has built up quite a business making deliveries especially to restaurants downtown. He has someone working for him full time now. I think he is getting rich, but you can't tell, he always looked rich even when he was poor.

The rumor is that we will be getting a new pastor after the first of the year. We don't know whom, but we think it will be an Italian. The German is a good priest, but just because he speaks Italian doesn't make him think like one. Still, you should have seen the San Gerardo Feast in October. It was the best we ever had.

I am laying the groundwork to come to see you by telling people that I have relatives on Long Island that I want to see. I don't know yet how I will explain it to my husband, but I will think of something.

Stay well, dear friend, and kiss Josephine for me.

Giustina

Chapter XV

A NEW BEGINNING 1898

The Christmas holiday was over and January 1st rang in the new year of 1898. Neither Maria nor Giovanni could believe how quickly the time had passed since coming to Youngstown. Ralph was doing well at school, not a top scholar but still he was doing well and he was no trouble. Josephine, now over four months old, was beginning to become a joy to watch as her personality developed. Her presence in the house seemed to have a soothing effect on Giovanni. Maria was thankful that he did not resent that she was Antonio's child. She hoped against hope that he would come to look on her as God's gift to replace Augusta. It was a great deal to ask, but she prayed that Giovanni would.

Christmas had been pleasant enough. She did not expect it but Giovanni surprised her with a present. He gave her a woolen scarf and a matching muff. She had knitted a beautiful sweater for him. He was really making an effort to renew their relationship and she was cooperating at every turn, grasping at every opportunity to please him without appearing to be condescending. As good a cook as she had been she had become better still and he had never eaten so well. He began to look forward to their family meals that she served with elegance and ritual.

Because of his job in the maintenance department of the mill, he came home dirty and smelling of oil and grease. The first thing he did now was to bathe and she always had hot water ready for him. Also he took to dressing up a little for dinner. This change in his behavior pleased her very much. She wondered if he was doing it in an attempt to upstage Antonio or because he had to dress in clean clothes anyway. She hated herself for making the comparison and it was a constant struggle for her to keep such thoughts out of her mind. They developed a routine of dressing for dinner and she also felt it was a good example to Ralph.

Maria made the house as comfortable and pleasant as possible. She made no close friends and spent all her waking hours being a housewife and mother. She wrote letters very often, some in the afternoon but mostly in the early evening for the workingmen and also for her boarders. She had gained such a reputation that the boarders stopped calling her Signora and even when they addressed her in person, they always called her *La*

Scrittore. When she wrote at night, Giovanni spent his time with Ralph and Josephine.

He had actually come to the point that he would pick her up. In her prayers she thanked God that Josephine was a happy baby, rarely crying, and sleeping the night through very soon after she was born. Maria saw a daily improvement in her relationship with Giovanni but she was still waiting for him to come to her at night.

They slept in the same room but in separate, single beds. Sometimes she lay awake for hours waiting for him to come to her but he did not. In her resolve to make it happen, she determined not to be the aggressor because she feared it would push him farther away. She would wait; his pride had to heal, she understood that. In the meantime she made herself as desirable and as attractive as possible. She made sure that he was in bed before she undressed. She knew that he was watching. Again she thanked God that she had the kind of body that quickly returned to its former beauty after each birth. It would happen, she was sure. It was only a matter of time.

*****

Giovanni's dream was to get out of the mill. He desperately wanted to go back to baking. He kept a constant eye open for a job as a baker. He had no luck in that pursuit. He did get a few offers but they were only as a laborer at the ovens and the pay was less than that from the mill. They were starting to come to the conclusion that the only way for him to get work as a baker was to open his own shop. They decided not to spend any of the boarders' rent nor her income from letter writing. Even the little extra she earned making lunches for the men was saved. They lived on his mill income. It was a tribute to her competency that they were able to do it. He was not going to leave the mill unless the pay was at least the same.

They celebrated Ralph's seventh birthday in January. Giovanni outdid himself baking bread and rolls and a superb birthday cake. The cake decoration was a work of art. They invited Francesco and his family for dinner and the party. Ralph had the time of his life being the center of attention. Francesco was greatly impressed with Giovanni's baking skills. He assumed that Maria had done the baking and was surprised when he was informed that it was Giovanni. He knew that Giovanni and Antonio were bakers by trade but he did not know how good they were until the party. He knew that Luigi was a master at the trade and he was amazed that he was able to teach Giovanni so well in so short a time. Luigi never accepted less than perfection in his shop. Francesco was aware that Giovanni, although grateful for his job at the mill, was not happy there. Now he knew why. At the mill the man was out of his element. Having

130

made a vow to help all of his countrymen whenever possible he made a mental note to see if he could do something more to help him.

*****

They lived quietly and uneventfully on Waverly Avenue in Youngstown, Ohio. They lived in a section of the city that was originally a separate village called Briar Hill. It was incorporated into Youngstown in 1889, but the people still referred to themselves as living in Briar Hill. The house was more than adequate. The neighborhood had at one time been upper middle class but then the railroad built a spur along one side of the street and the houses were sold off one by one and converted into rooming houses.

*****

20 May 1898

Ciao cugino Francesco;

I hope that you and your family are well. Things are going very well for me in Newark. My business has grown beyond my expectations. I have moved to a larger apartment on Boyden Street. I am writing because I know that you will be pleased to hear that I have written to Joanna telling her to come to America. I have not yet received a reply but I am sure she is making travel arrangements. I expect a letter shortly.

We are having trouble with Emanuella. She still doesn't want to come to America. I don't know what to do about it. If I force her to come we might have a problem child on our hands. I want so much to see her, my first-born.

Joanna's mother and father say they will take care of her as if she were their own child. I believe they will. I am beginning to think it would be better to let her stay in Italy but I am trying very hard to persuade her to come and so is Joanna. Perhaps when she is older she can judge for herself if she wants to stay here or return. She is ten now and in a couple of years she could visit Italy. We will wait and see what happens.

Stay well, dear cousin. I pray for you and your family. Some day we will meet again, I am sure of it.

With all love and respect,

Antonio

Maria knew from her mother's example how to make a bright, inviting home. The atmosphere in the house became more and more inviting as she put her talents to work. Here she at least had something with which to work. Large rooms with plenty of windows and the furniture they bought from Francesco was all they needed. The house had been electrified and wonder of wonders there was a toilet in the basement that was connected to a sewer line in the street. No more trips to the 'bacouse' on cold or rainy nights. Giovanni began to settle in and slowly he became increasingly attentive to Maria.

One night, in the middle of June, she awoke to feel him getting into bed with her. '*At last,*' she thought. She let him take the lead and cooperated fully. They made love in silence. Afterwards he made no attempt to go back to his bed nor did they speak with each other. He fell asleep in her arms. She could not help herself, but she thought that it was not the same as with Antonio. Would she never rid herself of the past? She squeezed her eyes shut and drove the thought out of her head. She quietly cried herself to sleep realizing that she should be grateful and content with what she had. The next day, she purchased a double bed. From then on they began functioning as a family unit and times were beginning to look good.

On Sundays the family would have a large family dinner at one o'clock, after church. She thanked God that Giovanni had started attending mass once more. If the weather was pleasant they spent the latter part of the day walking through the city. Giovanni even started to push the baby carriage with Ralph holding on. Maria purchased a sewing machine and began making all of their clothing and they looked elegant, far beyond their means.

'*My God,*' she thought, '*He's beginning to strut a little when he pushes the carriage.*'

They walked with her arm locked in his. She smiled as she watched his transformation from a hurt and defeated man to a proud husband and father. He had completely accepted Josephine. Antonio was never mentioned. Thoughts of him still came to her very often and try as she might she could not avoid them completely. So she just accepted them as part of her life, a part that was long ago and far away. She neither avoided the memories nor surrendered to them. It became a comfortable state of mind for her.

The passionate love she had once had for Giovanni never returned but she found herself married to a gentle and caring man. Many women who were madly in love with their husbands did not have that. Love may be more exciting at times, but she thought that contentment was more secure and much more comfortable. She decided she had been lucky and vowed never to do anything to destroy her life again. Although he had expressed

132

his love for her when he was writing to her in Italy, Giovanni never again said he loved her. She knew that was gone from his life too.

On rainy Sundays they spent their time at home with the children. Often Giovanni would bake something special for dinner and they would have a grand time. He became so content that on these occasions he would often fall asleep in a chair. Josephine would go in for her nap and Ralph would play with his toys.

It was a quiet time for Maria, but also a dangerous time. She would reflect on her life, thinking about Mama and Papa and how it was before they died. Back then America was a place far away and held no attraction for her. Her simple ambition was to grow old with Giovanni and live in peaceful contentment in Papa's house with the farm as their subsistence.

No matter how she tried or what she reflected on, thoughts of Antonio would somehow manage to creep into her meditations. When her thoughts about Antonio turned to sex she usually made a great effort to push them from her mind, but once in a while she let them linger and indulged herself in fantasy. Afterward she had deep feelings of guilt and was irritable the rest of the day. Giovanni simply wrote it off to woman's ways. She also knew what she was like at these times and she thanked God it did not happen often. She remembered the old, Italian saying, *L'amore fa passare il tempo; Il tempo fa passare l'amore* - Love makes time pass; Time makes love pass. She would wait.

*****

15 July 1898

Dear Maria;

I have not heard from you since last September. I hope you have not forgotten your old friend. Please write soon and tell me all that has happened.

Antonio's family has just arrived from Italy. They are very nice and his son seems to be a fine young boy and the daughters are beautiful. Antonio is very proud. Yes, the oldest child finally relented and came with them. I don't understand her reluctance but that's the way it is. They are living on Boyden Street now. He got a much larger flat there.

But, my dear friend, I must tell you that the gossip concerning you and Antonio has reached Joanna's ears. It didn't take long. I have only met her a few times, mostly at mass. While she seems very nice I get the impression that she has a volatile personality. My guess is that there is trouble in Antonio's house over the whole affair. I hope that I am wrong, but I don't think so. When I see them together at church I just sense a lack of warmth between them. We should pray for both of them.

Newark is growing so fast. You would hardly recognize it. Our neighborhood is very crowded now. There are new tenements going up all over.

The archdiocese of Newark has decided to build a cathedral. It will be located on Sixth Avenue between Clifton Avenue and Ridge Street directly across from the new high school. It will be huge, almost taking up the whole block up to Park Avenue. It is called Sacred Heart Cathedral. They are bringing stonecutters over from Italy. No one here can do the job. All the altars will be carved in Italy and shipped over here. I don't know where the money is coming from. It will be a beautiful building and I am sure it will add to Newark. But we will still be in St. Lucy's parish.

That's about all that is new here. Write soon.

Giustina

*****

Time passed quickly for Maria and Giovanni as they settled into a routine of enjoying family life in Youngstown. Josephine had turned one year old in September of 1898 and Ralph became eight in January of 1899. Maria and Giustina continued to correspond using Antonio and Francesco as intermediaries. Neither of them wrote about Antonio and Maria was grateful that as much as she still loved him she had become able to cope with the situation. Her life was far from perfect but it was also a far cry from that dreadful night when Giovanni was forced to leave Newark.

*****

10 July 1899

Dear Maria;

We are all well here and hope that you and your family are well also. This is just a short note to update you on the cathedral.

In June we had the ceremony for laying the cornerstone. Some of the walls are up and I can't believe how big it will be. There will be two very high *campanili* just like the ones in *Milano*. The newspapers said there were over fifty thousand people here for the ceremony and I believe it. The archbishop was here and many bishops from all over the country, all in their purple vestments. Even two of the cardinals came. It was magnificent. I never saw so many priests and nuns in my life. It was a

134

spectacular day. You would have enjoyed it. I thought you might be interested so I am enclosing a picture and the article from the Newark Evening News.

Stay well and let me know if Giovanni ever writes to Antonio.

Giustina

*****

One of their boarders was a young man named Luca. He had been living in Youngstown for five years and had worked at the mill all that time. He was an Italian Jew. His ancestors had emigrated from Spain to Rome centuries ago during the anti-Semitic persecution that had started in 1492 during the reign of King Ferdinand and Queen Isabella. In Rome, they lived in the ghetto. The Jews were not allowed to own land outside the ghetto and as a result many became merchants and bankers. Some of them became wealthy but that was not so for Luca's family. They were poor day laborers.

With no prospects on the horizon Luca had immigrated to America, the land of opportunity, and had settled in Youngstown. He became a boarder in Francesco's house and worked in the mill. Francesco used to write letters for him and read the replies to him. When Giovanni took over the house from Francesco, Maria became acquainted with Luca. Although he was uneducated and non-literate he had a driving ambition to do in America what he could not do in Italy. Luca wanted to own land and he found a way to do it.

One rainy Sunday he asked Maria if she would write a letter for him to a friend. They sat at the kitchen table while Giovanni and the children played in the parlor. Luca dictated and Maria wrote.

17 November 1899

Mia cara Marta;

I am well and I hope that you are the same. Since I last wrote to you I have completed the necessary time to live in America in order to file a Declaration of Intent to become an American Citizen. That means I became eligible to apply for free land in the western part of this country. There is a law here that provides the land. This I have done and I have been approved to receive 500 acres to raise cattle. If I remain on the land for five years it will be mine.

Marta, I know that we were both very young when I came to America but through the past five years we have held onto our friendship. Since, in

135

your last letter to me, you told me that you have not married, I now want to ask you if you will marry me. We had a lot of fun growing up together and we are very compatible. In fact, I know that we are the best of friends. I would like to spend my life with you. If you feel the same then I ask you to come to America and together we will build a life here.

I have saved as much money as I could over the last five years and I can afford to send for you. That will not leave very much money left over and our life will not be easy. But we will have something that we could never have in Rome. We will be landowners. It will be virgin land and we will have to build from nothing but I believe we can do it. While there is some hatred for us here in America, it is nowhere near as much as in Europe. This is a free country and here we can become anything we want and live wherever we want.

I will need to know from you very quickly because I must leave for the west as soon as I can. If you say yes then I will send money to you and you can make arrangements to come to New York. I will meet you there and together we can go directly to our land.

Marta, as hard as it will be, it is a golden opportunity for me and if you say yes, it will be so for you too. You know that you have nothing in Rome and the land will be our security here. I will always respect you and I am confident that our friendship can grow into a love that will bind us forever.

Your loving friend,

Luca

*****

Maria was greatly impressed by Luca's ambition and determination. After he went up to his room Maria became intrigued with his plan. She didn't know what law he was talking about but if it were true maybe Giovanni could make an application for some farmland and they could be farmers again, just like in Italy. She was willing to do anything, endure any hardship to get things back the way they were in Pietramelara.

'If we can get back to farming maybe it will erase what I did with Antonio and make things right again.'

The next day, while Ralph was in school, she took Josephine in the baby carriage and visited the library to research this law that Luca had spoken of. That is how she became familiar with the Homestead Laws that originated in 1862. As she understood it, they too could make application for free land out west.

But it was a short-lived dream because when she spoke to Giovanni about it, he was not interested. He said he did not want to give up trying to get a job in a bakery. He had lost all interest in farming. She was disappointed and while she was brooding over his refusal to consider farming again the most unexpected thing happened.

Just after Thanksgiving the job offer as a baker came from the most improbable source. It came from Francesco. After Thanksgiving they invited him and his family for a Sunday dinner. Again Giovanni outdid himself with baking. After dinner, with Josephine in bed for a nap, and the older children playing in the parlor, the adults sat at the table and enjoyed a leisurely espresso.

Francesco told them of an acquaintance who was the owner of a very large restaurant in the center of the city. Maria and Giovanni had heard of it but they had never been there. It was far too expensive for them. They reserved their few nights out for the local *trattoria*. Francesco explained that the restaurant's pastry chef was going to leave his job for a much better one in Philadelphia and a replacement was needed. So he told his friend that he knew of an excellent baker and asked if he would be interested in meeting Giovanni. The restaurateur had said yes. Giovanni was completely surprised, in fact speechless. It was Maria who asked how much the job paid.

"I really don't know," replied Francesco. "But first he wants to meet Giovanni and sample his skills. I know it is a good job. They only serve lunch and dinner, so the hours are acceptable. The job is for six days a week, the restaurant is closed on Mondays, so it would require working weekends. That's the downside."

Maria thought that they would have to give up their Sunday ritual, but they could make up for it by having their special family time on Mondays instead. That is, except during school time.

"If you are interested I could set up an appointment for you," Francesco gently offered.

Both Maria and Giovanni were in a slight daze, thinking what the opportunity could mean for their future.

"If things don't work out or if you decide not to accept the offer if one is made, there will be no hard feelings between us. You are not obligated to me in any way. And there is no rush. My friend and his pastry chef are good friends themselves and the chef is leaving on very good terms. He promised he would not leave until his replacement was found and he worked with him for a week or so."

"Think about it and let me know during the week," said Francesco. Then he and his family left early in the evening so that Giovanni and Maria, with their heads spinning, could talk over the proposal.

As she busied herself cleaning up the kitchen, Giovanni remained seated at the dining room table, thinking of the opportunity. He would shout out a question to her only when she was in the kitchen and she had to walk back to the dining room to answer quietly. While he mulled over her reply she went back to the kitchen only to have another question yelled at her. She returned again. After a few trips back and forth she recognized an opportunity to test his reaction if she became the aggressor again. She walked back to the dining room one last time and told him if he did not leave her alone she would never get the dishes done. And she still had to get Josephine and Ralph bathed and put to bed.

"Why not wait until we go to bed and we can discuss the matter properly." She paused deliberately and then added, "Afterwards."

In a moment Giovanni jumped up off the chair telling the children that it was time for bed. She thought, 'It worked.' Now she would be a lover to him once more.

They talked long into the night. It was still Giovanni's dream to own a bakery. That was why they were saving and sacrificing. They weren't close to having the necessary funds although their savings increased with each passing week. But at the present rate it would take a few years before they were able to equip a bakery and still have enough to carry them until they became established. To buy an existing bakery would require even more resources since its value would be so much higher. However, an interim job as a baker for someone else would put him back in the trade, with all the contacts, and get him out of the hated mill. At last, for the first time in years, there was a second 'afterwards' before they fell asleep.

By Wednesday they had decided that he should try for the job if the pay was as good as, or hopefully better, than his earnings at the mill. Francesco set up a meeting for Giovanni on that Sunday morning at the restaurant. The departing pastry chef interviewed him in great detail. The chef was not Italian and the interview was both difficult and comical. Evidently he was very friendly with his employer and they decided between them that Giovanni would have to pass his scrutiny before he even talked with the boss.

The pastry chef decided that on the next Sunday Giovanni should come in for the day to work at the restaurant and he would see what Giovanni could do. The job would pay more than he was getting at the mill. The hours were very attractive. He would start early in the morning and bake the day's requirements. He did not have to remain there for the dinner crowd. He could finish up late in the afternoon. He left with high hopes and a feeling of accomplishment.

Chapter XVI

FRIENDS AGAIN 1900

1 January 1900

Dearest friend, Giustina;

Buon'Natale and a happy New Year for 1900. I pray that you and your family are well and happy. We are doing very well here and the wall between Giovanni and me has completely fallen down. We are a family again. Josephine was two in September and this month Ralph will be nine. They are a lot of work but I love them, they bring untold joy to my life. I am sure you get as much pleasure from your children. Isn't it wonderful?

I have some good news. Giovanni went for an interview last month for a pastry chef job in a large restaurant in downtown Youngstown. Francesco set it up for him. They liked what he did and they offered him the job. It pays even more than the steel mill and the hours are better. It was funny; the night before he went to see them we both scrubbed his hands and fingernails. I was afraid we were going to scrub his skin off, we laughed. We just couldn't get them clean. All that grease! Anyway that did not prove to be an obstacle and they offered the job to him.

He has already started and the pastry chef who was leaving worked with him for a week. He learned how to bake some French bread and pastries too. The owner likes the Italian bread and pastries that Giovanni showed him and he has added them to the menu. It is great to have him come home smelling of bread and cake instead of dirt and grease.

We are so happy. Antonio's cousin has been very good to us. I often wanted to write to Antonio and thank him but I think it is better if I don't resume any contact with him just now. I hope he and his family are well. If you do see him tell him that Josephine is a beautiful girl and she has his coloring but my eyes.

Stay well, dear friend,

Maria

15 January 1900

Dearest friend, Maria;

How wonderful to hear from you. I never did get an opportunity to come to see you last year but maybe this year. I am so happy to hear that everything is working out well for you and Giovanni. How is the new job? Well! Pastry chef at a famous restaurant, aren't we coming up in the world! Maybe it will be his career. Being in business for one's self is not easy; all those worries. This way he only has to think about his job and I am sure he thinks he is in heaven. Good luck to both of you.

Our new pastor, Fr. Joseph, has the church very well organized and the people love him. We have a lot of societies functioning very well. He is wonderful with the children. The only thing is that he is a little bit of a dictator. It has to be his way and he does not leave himself open for ideas from other people. However, he is a good man and he is doing a lot for the parish and the best part is that he is from Italy so he understands us all very well.

I saw Luigi the other day and he does not look well to me. He says that middle age is creeping up on him and he is just tired. Do you believe it, he is sixty years old. I should talk; the years are creeping up on me too.

I saw Antonio at church last Sunday. He looks as handsome as ever. I could not speak with him too long as his family was with him. Joanna does not like me because I am your friend. I did get a few words with him when she walked away. He was sincerely moved to hear of your comments about Josephine. I think it pains him that he has never seen her. He wanted to write to you many times but thought better of it and I said that he did the right thing in not writing.

Stay well, dear friend. Let's hope that someday we will meet again. I have many friends here in Newark but none of them mean as much to me as you do. It hurts that we are separated.

Giustina

*****

Maria had just finished reading Giustina's letter when her boarder, Luca, burst into the kitchen. Maria saw the letter he was clutching in his hand.

"It's from Marta, I know it. Please read it to me! Hurry!"

She took it from his hand and ripped the envelope open, she was as excited as he was to learn what his Marta said.

"It is from Marta, it's dated two weeks ago."

140

2 January 1900

Mio caro Luca;

You have no idea how happy your letter has made me. I know that you always considered me as your best friend and you were also mine. What you never knew was that I always loved you, even when we were children, but you never said anything. It hurt so much when you left for America. I thought I would never see you again. And now your letter has taken all the hurt away. I too want to spend the rest of my life with you.

You don't have to send any money to me. I have saved all that I could through the years. I will be able to pay for my ticket. I already have my passport because I was going to come to America, too, when I could. You are right, there is nothing here for people like us.

I have already purchased my ship ticket on the SS Italia and I will arrive in New York on February 18th. You can meet me at Ellis Island and we can go directly to our land.

How wonderful our life will be.

I love you Luca,

Marta

*****

Maria threw her arms around Luca. Tears of joy were running down her cheeks. As they embraced she could not help but think that this was the first time she ever showed her emotions to any of her clients over their letters.

"Oh Luca, I'm so happy for you"

Through tears in his eyes he clasped Maria's hands and started kissing them. *"Grazie, La Scrittore, Grazie, grazie, mille grazie."*

He left and she could hear him running up the stairs to his room, two at a time. She thought how wonderful it was that best friends were going to marry. It made her think of Antonio and she violently shook here head from side to side to drive out the thought.

21 March 1900

Dear friend Maria;

   I have some startling news. Rocco is dead! They murdered him right in front of his restaurant, on the sidewalk, in broad daylight. Can you believe it! The police don't know who did it but the rumors are pointing to certain people, especially the ones who have taken over the loansharking business. They are now running gambling games and we hear that they own the 'house' down by the river, too. They are animals and we should pray thanks to God that Giovanni has nothing to do with them anymore. Anyway, Rocco is gone and I don't think they care two cents that Giovanni gave him what he deserved. So it looks as though your fears are as dead as Rocco. Besides, everybody forgot about the incident a long time ago.

   You would be surprised at how the neighborhood has grown. Italians are coming over in droves. I don't know where they are going to put them all. They are beginning to cross over Bloomfield Avenue toward the Forest Hill section and also on the other side of the Morris Canal into Belleville in the Silver Lake section. Newark is becoming very crowded and downtown has more new stores and buildings than you can imagine.

   I met Antonio on the street the other day and we were able to talk a little longer than the last time we met. His bread delivery business has really grown. He has two wagons now. He no longer owns the horses; he says it is better to hire them. He says someday he won't even use horses so better get rid of them now. He says someday he will be using trucks. But that's Antonio, always thinking about the future. I told him that I had written to you and passed on his best to you and Josephine. He says he misses his friendship with Giovanni and hopes someday to reestablish it. I told him I hoped so too. It was odd the attraction between those two opposites.

   His Joanna is pregnant and is due in August. Well, that's all the exciting news I have about Newark for you.

                        Stay well, you and yours,

                        Giustina

142

2 June 1900

Dear friend Giustina;

I apologize for not writing sooner. One would think that with all the letters I write for others I could squeeze one in for you. It was certainly a welcome shock to hear about Rocco; God forgive me for saying it. I told Giovanni but he made no comment one way or the other. I think that part of his life has long since left his memory. Now that you have told us about Rocco, I think he feels like that is what could have happened to him and he just wants to put all of those people out of his mind. He is becoming very conservative in his thinking. You should see him when we go walking with the children. He literally struts down the street. I think he is becoming a bit pompous, too. I don't like that in him and I try to point out to him that he gives the impression that he has a very high regard for himself. I will have to work on that new aspect of his personality.

His new job is working out very well. He loves his work and the customers love his cakes and pastries. He is gaining a bit of a reputation and I think that is what is going to his head. His boss praises him no end and has given him a raise already. Giovanni is even thinking of getting rid of the boarders. He says they are too much work for me and that he would like the house for us alone. I keep asking him what we would do with such a large house? Sometimes he can't think past his nose. I will have to work on that too. The boarders are not that much work, and besides, I want the extra money to save for our future. He still talks about his own shop.

There is one downside to this job, however. It's his boss' son. I have met him and he is not a very pleasant person and the daughter-in-law is even worse. He works in the restaurant as the headwaiter and he is always flaunting his position. His father keeps him in check but if he ever gets control of the business he will ruin what his father has worked so hard to build. Giovanni has already had one run-in with him, but the father thinks the world of Giovanni, as do the other chefs, especially the head chef. Oh well, I guess nothing is ever perfect.

I am so happy for Antonio. Maybe some day I can get Giovanni to write to him. By the way, I still think we should communicate through Francesco, at least for a little while longer.

Maria

20 July 1900

Dear Friend Giustina;

Well, I'm pregnant again. I expect the baby to come next year in March. It is very welcome news. In those early years, after I had Ralph, Giovanni and I were separated because he came to America first. Then after I came over our second baby died. Then I had Josephine by Antonio and it took a long time to reconcile with Giovanni. Now we are having a new baby and it will be ours and it will strengthen our bond. I pray that everything goes well. Pray for me, dear friend.

Stay well, you and your family,

Maria

*****

1 September 1900

Dear friend Maria;

I saw Antonio this morning and I am rushing to write to you. He said he was going to write a letter to Giovanni and was just trying to get up enough courage to do it. It is obvious that Giovanni's hatred and anger towards him is very painful. I think he has gotten to the point that he cannot remain quiet about it any longer. Even though they will probably never meet again I don't think he will ever be at peace until somehow he rights the wrong or at least makes an attempt. I am writing so that maybe you could pave the way. I know that you want them to reconcile and so do I.

I was very happy to hear that you are expecting. I think it is good for your marriage even though Giovanni has come to accept Josephine as his own. But that is not quite the same.

Stay well dear friend and take extra care of yourself and let me know if Antonio writes to Giovanni.

Giustina

144

20 September 1900

Dear Giovanni;

Please, dear old friend, do not destroy this letter in your anger, please read it. I must first tell you of my deep and sincere sorrow and regret for what I have done to you. I very humbly beg your forgiveness. I went to mass yesterday and I prayed. How can the rest of my life be content when this great evil exists between my friend Giovanni and me? I tell you the truth, dear friend, God spoke to me in the heart. I must crawl to you on my hands and knees and tell you how I feel. I only wish I could do it in person but since I cannot I must write to you.

Through this letter I put myself back into friendship with God and beg you to let me do the same with you. If you feel that in your heart you can forgive me then please write to me.

One more thing, dear friend, what happened between Maria and me was because I truly fell in love with her. Nothing was done out of lust or a desire to do you dishonor. I still love her very much, and I hope that you do also. There is nothing wrong in that. It was only that I did something about it when I did not have the right. Please try to understand. While we cannot help what we feel we can still choose to do what is right and honorable. I did not choose correctly or wisely. My shame is hard to bear and the loss of your friendship worse still.

I pray God you will write to me,

Antonio

*****

15 October 1900

Dearest friend Giustina;

Well, we are going to move. Giovanni is doing so well that we can afford to save without having to take in boarders. I tried to talk him out of it but he was adamant. Last month, one of the very rich customers of the restaurant asked if Giovanni could bake for a special dinner he was having at his home. Giovanni really outdid himself and the man was so grateful that he gave him a big tip. He also praised Giovanni so much that he got another raise plus he is going to receive part of the headwaiter's tips, only a very small part, two percent. That is what the old pastry chef got. The son is enraged, but the father insists. He is trying to teach his son that good employees must be taken care of but I don't think the son gets it. Some day he will be in trouble, I know it, and I can't stand his wife.

Anyway, Giovanni found a smaller one-family house for rent at 1240 Meade Street but it is still larger than the space we kept for ourselves in the rooming house. We should be in by November 1st, so make a note of the new address. I think you could write to me directly now, just put the letters in the post office on Broad Street, don't use the one near the bank, for safety's sake. However, I will still write to you through Francesco for now.

Josephine was three years old last month. She is getting to be quite a lady. She is becoming fussy about her clothes. Ralph is the opposite, all boy. I have to make him change and put on old clothes when he comes home from school or he would ruin everything.

Did Joanna have her baby? I'm sure she must have by now. How wonderful for Antonio. I haven't broached the subject about Giovanni writing to him. I am sure he has forgiven Antonio by now. That is not the problem. He considers Josephine to be his now and I think that by keeping clear of all contact with Antonio he feels more secure about her. I think that is like sticking your head in the sand but I am not going to try to do anything about it now. Some day she will have to be told. It would be terrible if she found out from someone other than me. I will wait.

Perhaps the right moment will come for me to say something about Giovanni writing to Antonio, then again perhaps not. How sad. It is the one last thing I would like to rectify. Then, I think we will all be free from the past.

Stay well, dear friend,

Maria

*****

27 December 1900

Antonio;

I was very surprised to get your letter. I have thought about it for a long time. And I decided I should write to you. It is very difficult for me to tell you what my emotions were when I read it. I am mixed up about you. The last time I saw you the only thing that held back my anger was the matter with Rocco. You helped me with that grave problem and now that it is gone I only remember how I felt about you.

The truth is I still cannot believe that you took my Maria and even worse that she consented. But I have had time to think and I realize that I am to blame too. If I truly want to be fair then I must admit that the three of us are equally at fault. We each have our excuses. No sense in listing them now. What has happened has happened and cannot be undone.

Forgiveness comes very hard for me. I want to forget about the whole affair. My mind tells me to forgive but my heart resists. But I also need forgiveness from Maria. I know that she has given it to me and now I must follow her example and do the same for you. I went to mass on Christmas and I think God spoke to me in my heart also. So I have decided to do it. You ask for my forgiveness and I give it. Now I can call you friend once more.

We will probably never see each other again and that is sad. I am thinking of moving even farther west, maybe Chicago. Now it is my turn to thank you for all you have done for me. Without your cousin Francesco I am sure I would be dead. If not, my marriage would be gone and my dear son Ralph would have suffered. Now I live and have a family and a good job.

Your new found friend,

Giovanni

*****

29 December 1900

Dear friend Maria;

I hope that your family is as well as mine. We had a very nice Thanksgiving and Christmas and I hope you had the same in your new house. I am mailing this letter directly to you there. Just to be sure I did not put a return address on the envelope, but I really don't think we have a problem.

The animals are too busy fighting among themselves as to who the headman will be, *il capo*, they call him. He now runs Rocco's restaurant and he will be in charge. I don't know if they paid for Rocco's business or just took it over. They make their own laws, those *animali*. Besides, who would they pay? Rocco didn't have a wife or any children.

Joanna did have her baby in August. It was a girl and they named her Grace. She was baptized in September. Antonio invited me but I didn't go. I told him it would only upset his wife. He understood. I still think that there is trouble between them over the past. He sends his 'warm personal feelings' to you.

Luigi is not very well. He still goes to work but he relies more and more on the help. Gia tries to manage the best she can. She has to watch the employees every minute. She said it is not the same as when Antonio and Giovanni worked for them. But at least the quality of the baking has not suffered. While Luigi does not do much work he does make sure that everything is still baked his way. It is too bad that we had to deceive him. He is disappointed that Giovanni never sent a letter to him from Italy. Only Antonio and I know where you are. The rest of the neighborhood thinks you are in Italy, that is, if they think about it at all.

They are making rapid progress on the new Sacred Heart Cathedral. And Maria, the city is draining the swamp behind the old reservoir and they are building a huge park. They are going to leave the lakes. The park will extend from Eighth Avenue all the way north into the Forest Hill section. The plans have been printed in the newspapers and I am enclosing the article from the Newark Evening News. They have named it Branch Brook Park. Newark is growing very fast. You wouldn't recognize downtown. There are new department stores, but I still like Hahne's the best. And now we have electric street lights although most areas still have gas lamps. It is beautiful at night. I miss the time we went shopping downtown together and the lunches we had.

Francesco must be a very straightforward man. For him to give you all the help he has given speaks very well of him. Still, I think he will be very glad that he does not have to forward my letters to you any longer. Maybe someday you will not have to write to me through him. I am going to try my very best to come and see you for a short visit this year.

By the way, Antonio has moved to a much larger apartment over on Wood Street very close to Seventh Avenue.

Your very best friend,

Giustina

Chapter XVII

MICHAEL 1901

6 February 1901

Dear friend Giustina;

Well, here I am waiting for the baby to be born. I can hardly wait for the event. I know that Giovanni will be so happy to have another child between us.

It is a shame that good news is often accompanied by some bad news. Giovanni's boss died suddenly last week. It was an unexpected shock. He wasn't sick at all. It was a heart attack. His son has taken over management of the restaurant although the mother owns it.

I see only trouble ahead. The son is very arrogant and has an undeservedly high opinion of himself and his business abilities. He is not well liked by any of the employees. On top of that his wife is a spendthrift. Thank God we have sacrificed and saved as much as we could over the years. If Giovanni must leave his job, or worse get fired, we will have enough resources to survive on until he can find something new. We are already watching for any openings in his trade anywhere, even if he has to start a new bakery from scratch. He is thinking maybe Chicago would be a good place for us to go. I dread having to make another move but it may be our only recourse. We'll see.

Well, dear friend, we hope that things will remain as they are, at least until after the baby comes, but it will be stressful. Please pray for us.

Stay well, you and your family,

Maria

5 April 1901

Dearest friend Giustina;

Good news, I had a baby boy on March 29th. He is healthy and I am also well. I have named him Michael after my father. Giovanni is elated. If I told you he was getting pompous before, you should see him now. He has developed an ego that is almost obnoxious. He is always bragging about his job and now, with Michael, there is no holding him back. I don't like this side of his personality. I am surprised that I never saw it before. I think that his soft-spokeness and gentleness were a cover up for his insecurity. Now that things are well and we have money in the bank and no debt he no longer feels insecure. I keep telling him that he is no better than other people, just more fortunate, but it doesn't seem to sink in. And now he talks too much. That is another change in him. He was always so quiet. Maybe I am misreading the signs but it is almost as if a hidden personality is emerging.

With Michael arriving on schedule, the timing is good. School will be over in three months and Ralph will be home all day and the baby will be a little more manageable. I will need that with three children. Josephine is three and a half years old now and has taken to her new brother and tries to imitate me and be a mother to him. Ralph was ten in January and is too caught up in boy's games to be too concerned about Michael.

I suppose you know by now that Antonio has written to Giovanni. He showed the letter to me and he decided to respond. It took all my strength not to cry in front of him as I read it. I know it was difficult for him to write back. He really agonized over it for three months. I was afraid to say too much.

I didn't want him to think I was trying to influence him one way or the other. I was afraid he might misinterpret my motives and change his mind. I said very little and only when he asked me. But I think he did the right thing by writing back to Antonio. He did not show me his reply to Antonio but from his actions I am sure they are friends again as much as can be. I am happy that this last wound has been healed.

If you see Antonio, and you have an opportunity to ask him about it, I would like your comments on his reaction.

Stay well my dear and loyal friend,

Maria

9 July 1901

Dearest friend Maria;

How happy I am for you with your new son Michael. I am also happy that Josephine has accepted him so well. Sometimes that can be a problem with the youngest ones.

When Antonio gave me your last letter we were able to talk a little. He was so relieved when he got Giovanni's letter. I did not read the letter but evidently they are friends again. How wonderful. Now we can all put the affair behind us and with Rocco dead maybe someday we will see each other again. He said he was going to write to Giovanni again soon.

I told Antonio about your new Michael and how Josephine was acting like a little mother. He was very attentive and kept asking about her. I didn't have too much to tell him but it is obvious that he has very strong feelings about her. You know, dear friend, some day you will have to tell her who her father is. It will be better for all involved to have it come from you rather than for her to hear it through gossip. Even though you live in Ohio you can never be sure that the distance will keep the truth from her. Sorry to bring it up but you should think about it.

Stay well, dear friend, and have a wonderful birthday.

Giustina

*****

20 July 1901

Dearest Giustina;

I hope that you and yours are well. Little Michael is growing daily and Josephine plays mother to him all the time. Whenever he cries she always comes to call me to feed him. She just sits and watches me nurse him. The process fascinates her.

Thank you for your birthday wishes. Thirty-six years old, can you believe it? It is true, life is so short, and we have our ups and downs.

Things with Giovanni's job are getting very bad. The son is not doing well. He downgraded the quality of the menu but kept the prices the same. He has even cut the quality and variety of the cakes and pastries that Giovanni has built a reputation on. He saves the leftover baked goods and serves them the next day, something his father would never do. He always gave the leftovers to the employees to take home. Giovanni is furious and says that some of the old time regular customers have stopped patronizing the restaurant. The son is just bleeding the business and I'll bet his wife spends more than they make. I feel sorry for the mother. It is obvious that it will only be a matter of time before they are in trouble.

Giovanni is now looking very hard for a new position or possibly a location to start his own bakery. He talks a lot about moving to Chicago. We will see what we will see.

Well, dear friend, until next time stay well,

Maria

*****

6 September 1901

Dear friend Giovanni;

Congratulazione e saluti from Newark. I saw Giustina last week and she told me about your new son, Michael. She also told me about your troubles with your new boss. I am sorry to hear about it but it allows me to approach you about something.

Dear friend, I am sorry to have to tell you that our mutual friend and benefactor, Luigi, is very ill. He can hardly spend time at the bakery. Gia takes care of the store and I help out in the ovens as much as I can. Between the three of us we can just about keep things going, even with two other employees, but they don't work the way you and I did. I have my own business to take care of and I buy everything from Luigi. I have tried to talk him into selling out, but out of pride he refuses to do so. But he really has no choice.

Giovanni, I know that if you offered to buy the bakery he would sell it to you. I know that this suggestion will come as a shock to you, but if you agree I know we can work out the details. First, Luigi owns the building. You could rent from him and he and Gia could continue to live upstairs. Second, you would solve your personal problems concerning your job. Third, I would still have a good supplier. You see everyone would benefit. I don't know how much longer Luigi has to live and even he knows the end is not too long off. If you buy the business and rent the store he will be able to die knowing that we will take care of Gia. They have no one. They always looked on us as their sons. We owe it to him for the help he has given us in the past.

152

Think about it dear friend but don't delay. I am afraid that there is not too much time. Also, rest assured that if you do decide to come back to Newark our friendship will never be violated again.

Your dear friend,

Antonio

*****

20 September 1901

Dear Giustina;

Have you spoken with Antonio recently? He wrote to Giovanni and wants him to buy Luigi's bakery. I was shocked. I am so sorry to hear about Luigi's condition but for him to suggest that we return to Newark! I cannot believe it! At first I thought Giovanni would be angry but he had the letter in his pocket for three days before he showed it to me. He must have been thinking about it all that time. I am upset that he didn't share his thoughts with me and I understand why. He wants to do it but he is afraid to have me be near Antonio again. I finally had to bring the subject up because he was avoiding it.

I told him I would never do anything like that again. I promised and I begged him to do whatever he wants to do. After a few days he made the decision to return to Newark. We were very honest with each other, almost brutally so. I told him I still had strong feelings for Antonio but that they were under control. I promised no Antonio and I made him promise no 'house' and no bad associations. We start again clean or no Newark. We made a new pact together almost like getting remarried. He is going to write to Antonio and tell him to make the deal.

Giustina, one more time I need your help. After the deal is made please tell everyone that we are returning from Italy. I don't want to take any chances of putting Francesco in a bad position. Also it would put you and Antonio in a bad light if we tell people about Ohio. If the deal is made I will write to Antonio and tell him what we must do so as never to bring trouble and dishonor to our families and friends again.

Stay well dear friend,

Maria

2 October 1901

Dear Antonio;

    You can imagine how I felt when I got your letter. I am sorry about Luigi. We have talked over all of the reasons to accept or reject your idea. Believe me, dear friend, your offer is the answer to all of my business troubles out here. As for any other matter I say that is all behind us and Maria is confident that she can control the situation. She was very blunt about her feelings for you but she assures me that she makes the choice never to act again. Well, dear friend, you have told me the same thing. That being said it all boils down to you and Maria. Now it is your turn to choose. You must make the decision. Maria says yes and if you say yes then I say yes. So, you make the deal or not. I leave it to you. No hard feelings one way or the other. If you do make the deal I can come at a moments notice. I owe nothing to my employer. Besides, I don't think he will be in business much longer anyway. If we do this, Maria insists that you tell everyone that we are coming back from Italy. That way we cannot hurt Francesco and her friend Giustina.

    Don't do anything about Luigi's employees. It may be that they do not work well because Luigi has not been there to supervise them. I will see when I get there. Let me know what you have decided.

Your grateful friend,

Giovanni

Chapter XVIII

THE RETURN 1901

As soon as Antonio received Giovanni's letter he went to see Gia and explained his idea to her. "What do you think, Gia? Do you think Luigi will accept it? We all know that he is sick and that the bakery is his life. But I am also afraid that he might think we are all giving up on him."

Gia looked at him as an angel from heaven. "Oh, Antonio, listen to me. Luigi and I have talked about his bad health for some time now. We both know that his time has almost come. He is very worried about who will take care of me, but he is also in deep depression because he knows that the bakery will have to be sold off. He worked so hard most of his life to build it up and the thought of having it sold is weighing him down."

"We always regretted not having any children. I am so sorry I could not give a son to Luigi. That's why we were so happy when you and Giovanni were working for us. We both felt that we had two sons in the business. Luigi told me once that it was too bad that you two did not want to buy the bakery when his time came. Don't you understand, Antonio? Luigi will be elated and relieved at the idea. It will make him happy for what little time he has left and I can be happy with him. I am so grateful to you and Giovanni for giving us happiness during this last time. Now, how fast can Giovanni get back to Newark?"

They went upstairs and she repeated to Luigi what Antonio had told her. Tears fell from his eyes as he embraced Antonio. "I have prayed for this, you have no idea. When can Giovanni come?"

"Soon, Luigi, very soon." So the deal was struck then and there. It was agreed that Giovanni would buy the business and equipment and rent the store. They would continue to live upstairs and Gia would work in the store. Everyone came away with something. That was Antonio's way.

Antonio sent a letter to Giovanni the same day he met with Luigi, telling him to come as soon as he could. If he came immediately then Luigi and Gia would have to be told about Ohio to explain his arrival so soon after the deal was made. Antonio knew that they could be trusted and was sure Giovanni would agree.

Once more Giovanni and Maria made plans to separate temporarily. They planned for him to go on while she stayed and sold off all of their furniture and packed what they wanted to take. He apologized for putting all the moving responsibility on her shoulders but she told him it was the better thing to do.

"After all," she said, laughing at him, "I am the only one with enough experience to do the job. You go and close the deal with Luigi while there is still time. How much notice will you give for leaving your job."

"None," he blurted out. "I have no obligation to that greedy son. If it was the father it would be different but I owe nothing to his son," he said contemptuously.

She agreed about him having no obligation but she was uneasy about the tone of his voice. It had the ring of revenge in it and that was a bit worrisome to her. But she let it pass because they had other more pressing matters to attend to regarding their own family and the move. He told her that if he was going to make the change at all he was going to leave for Newark the next day.

"Why delay it? There's no reason," he told her.

He was chomping at the bit. With all things considered she agreed. They sent a telegram to Antonio telling him when Giovanni was leaving but they did not know exactly what time he would arrive.

Sometimes his decisiveness really surprised her. His personality had definitely changed. No more the follower yet not quite the leader. Maria considered this midway transition in his personality to be dangerous. She feared he could become overconfident and make rash decisions. She conspired with herself to be more observant and even manipulative if need be to prevent any foolishness. However, in this particular case she also felt impatient to get started. She gave him all the support she could muster and told him how proud of him she was. They spent the evening packing what he would need to take with him.

That night, for the third time in their marriage he took her twice and she felt confident that their marriage was now on solid ground once more. They had a common goal to work toward. She fell asleep thinking she could control any situation that might arise with Antonio.

The next day, before he left for the train station, they had time to rehearse the stories they would tell people in Newark. They decided to say that Giovanni had fled Newark and returned to Italy because of Rocco's threats. She joined him there but they remained only a short time and then returned to America and settled in Ohio. They sought out Francesco and he had helped them get started there. Josephine was born in Ohio, a few weeks after they arrived. In Youngstown they became close friends with Francesco and his family. After that, they would be able to conform their story to the truth. Michael was born in Ohio. Maria kept in touch with Giustina and that was how they found out that Rocco was dead. By then Giovanni and Antonio had reconciled, albeit through the mail. When Antonio wrote about Luigi's illness they made an offer to purchase the bakery and he accepted. Antonio brokered the deal. Giovanni came back first and Maria followed as soon as she was able. That seemed to cover all of the bases and at the same time protect everyone who had participated in the subterfuge. They were sure the story would not raise any eyebrows in the old neighborhood.

Then there was the problem of Josephine's paternity. They felt they could explain the situation to Ralph; he was old enough to understand. But Josephine was another matter. They felt that at her age she would be too innocent to grasp the complexity of the situation. So they decided to tell Ralph first about Josephine for fear he would find out anyway when they returned to Newark. Maria wanted to tell him, but no, Giovanni said he would do it. They argued about it but in the end she prevailed. She insisted that she would be telling Ralph something about herself rather than have it appear that Giovanni was telling him a disparaging story about his mother.

"If he reacts badly, let it be towards me, not you," she reasoned. She did not want to do anything to harm the relationship between father and son. "I'll tell him before we join you. If it seems the right time I will tell Josephine also."

Maria promised to explain to Francesco why they were moving and apologize for Giovanni not saying goodbye. She would also tell Giovanni's employer that he had quit and was out of town.

By noon, a very happy Giovanni boarded the train to Philadelphia, gloating over what would happen when the great pastry chef didn't show up for work. It gave him a sense of power to retaliate for the ill treatment he had received recently. He had never experienced being able to get even before and he liked it.

'*Let them eat leftover cake!*' This was a new Giovanni who, for better or worse, would assert himself.

*****

When Antonio told Joanna that Giovanni and Maria were returning to Newark to buy Luigi's bakery her reaction was extreme to say the least. She accused her husband of having engineered the whole plan as a subterfuge to get Maria back to Newark. She felt even more convinced of this when he also told her that he was arranging for Giovanni to lease an apartment just a stone's throw away from where they lived. In fact, it was so close that Joanna could see the building from her front window. The severity of the arguments between Joanna and Antonio had affected the family. The older children knew of their father's infidelity and now 'that woman' was coming back.

Tension in the household increased to the point that Emanuella demanded that she be allowed to return to Italy. She had never wanted to come to America in the first place and was the least able to adjust to her new surroundings. She refused to learn English and was doing poorly in school. She was sinking into depression and losing weight. Neither Antonio nor Joanna could remedy the situation. She demanded that they let her go. Reluctantly they agreed. As Joanna saw it, Antonio was entirely to blame for the problem with Emanuella.

So, as Maria was preparing to come back to Newark, Emanuella was returning to Italy. The atmosphere in Antonio's house was barely tolerable. He would not leave his children and it was impossible for Joanna to leave either. Where could she go?

*****

There had not been enough time to alert Antonio to the exact time Giovanni was to arrive in Newark. So, unannounced, he went directly to Antonio's house on Wood Street. Giovanni was amazed at how the city had grown since he had fled to Youngstown that frightful night five years ago. He walked up Market Street from the Pennsylvania Station. The station was down near McCarter Avenue and on the mainline Pennsy system that routed trains through Philadelphia. When he got to Broad Street he was impressed by the city's progress.

'*Mama mia.*' he observed, '*Electric lights and trolley cars!*' Rather than try to find out which trolley to take he decided to walk to Antonio's house.

He turned up Broad Street and soon passed the Delaware, Lackawanna, and Western Railroad Station near Orange Street. Until recently it was called the Morris and Essex Railroad. Now it was popularly referred to as the DL&W. It was the station connecting Newark and Hoboken with the ferries that crossed the Hudson River to New York City.

As he walked under the trestle of the DL&W, he continued up Broad to Eighth Avenue, the same route he had taken that day long ago when he had first arrived in Newark. He laughed to himself as he remembered looking for that city with the funny letter "K" in its name.

'*Well,*' he thought, '*This part of the city hasn't changed much. A few more houses and stores, but it's still the same old neighborhood.*'

*****

It was late evening when Giovanni knocked on the door. Antonio opened it. They stood facing each other with Giovanni's massive frame filling the doorway. There was a moment of hesitation. Antonio was a bit

158

apprehensive of what might happen, but then Giovanni flashed his famous smile and he knew they were brothers again. They embraced in the doorway before Antonio invited him in to meet Joanna. The introduction was awkward.

As soon as Antonio had received the telegram he had told his wife that Giovanni was coming back to Newark that very day. Although she did have a little time to prepare herself, she did not handle the situation well. Her coldness was evident and embarrassing to Antonio. Giovanni felt embarrassed too. However, with no place to go he stayed the night.

Very early the next morning the two friends went to see Gia and Luigi. It was a tearful reunion. Luigi rebuked Giovanni mildly for keeping his whereabouts a secret for the past few years. But that was quickly put aside; such was their relationship. Giovanni left it to Luigi and Antonio to take care of the necessary legal papers. He did not have the patience for such matters. All he wanted to do was to get to work. He excused himself saying he was going down to the ovens that very minute.

"Wait," said Gia, "I'll go with you and tell the men that you are the new owner. Then I'll open the store."

Within a few minutes Giovanni was once more at work down at the ovens. But now he worked for himself. He had made it, what he had wanted ever since he came to America!

'Who said the streets in America are not paved with gold!'

After work Antonio took him to a vacant apartment at 114 Seventh Avenue. Antonio thought the space would be more than adequate for Giovanni's family. It was just around the corner from St. Lucy's Church and very near Wood Street where he and Joanna lived. Vacant was the right word. The previous tenant had stolen all of the furniture and had run off without paying a cent to the landlord. Antonio was friendly with the owner of the building and introduced Giovanni to him with a fine recommendation.

The building was three stories high and it contained six apartments, two on each floor. Each flat occupied the full length of the building from the street side to the rear and a common wall separated them. This one was on the second floor with two large, double hung windows in the parlor room overlooking the street. Across the street and down a little, Seventh Avenue intersected with Wood Street. That was where Antonio lived with his family. His apartment was also on the second floor.

The flat consisted of a parlor, dining room, kitchen, and three bedrooms. The floor plan was referred to as a railroad flat because the rooms were all in a line off a long interior hallway. The apartment was not as spacious or as private as the house in Youngstown but it was much better than the one they used to live in over on Eighth Avenue years ago. Gio-

159

vanni thought it was more than adequate for the family so he leased it then and there.

The building had been electrified and there was a large, coal burning cooking stove in the kitchen. The city had just run a sewer line down Seventh Avenue and all of the houses were connected to it. However, there was no toilet facility in the apartment. That was located in the basement, there for the use of all the tenants. Not the ideal, but better than a 'bacouse'.

*****

Giovanni felt very uncomfortable because of Joanna's cold reception. He decided that he did not want to return to Antonio's apartment that night. He told a protesting Antonio that he would spend the night alone in his new, unfurnished apartment. Giovanni spent his first night back in Newark sleeping on the floor using his suitcase as a pillow, just like he did when he first came to America. The next day he mailed a letter to Maria and told her to come whenever she was ready.

He was now a shop owner, a merchant. There was no doubt about it; the 'Rocco affair' was old and forgotten news even with those who had worked for Rocco. No one mentioned it and a lot of the new residents in the ward did not even know about the incident. There was a new 'il capo'. He owned Rocco's restaurant and ran 'things' in the neighborhood and even beyond. No one cared what had happened five years earlier.

Giovanni worked very hard, putting in long hours at the bakery, while he waited for Maria and the family to arrive. Things down at the ovens were not the way Luigi had taught Giovanni and Antonio. Giovanni soon set that straight, not so much as a result of his managerial abilities, but because he had Luigi's example to follow. He just did what he had been taught. It was not necessary for him to replace the two employees; they quickly fell into step.

Gia continued to work in the store as an employee so that was one problem he did not have to worry about. Occasionally Luigi made an appearance and gave his nodding approval, but for the most part he remained upstairs, looking out the window onto Eighth Avenue watching the people parade.

Within two weeks the bakery was functioning properly and his largest customer was Antonio. He had two wagons now and purchased large quantities of bread, cakes, and pastries. Giovanni spent what little spare time he had doing his best to ready the apartment for his family. There was a furniture store on Broad Street and the proprietor promised to deliver whatever Maria chose on the same day she ordered it. It would be hectic

160

for a few days after she arrived but they had done it before and they could do it again.

Maria expected to register Ralph and Josephine in school when she arrived. The school was called the Seventh Avenue School. It was only one block away from the apartment. One block past the school was the new Branch Brook Park. St. Lucy's was also very close, just around the corner. It would all be very convenient.

Giustina, elated that her dearest friend was coming back, offered to care for the children while Maria did what needed to be done to establish a home. Giovanni, Giustina, and Antonio waited for them to arrive.

*****

Maria decided to tell Ralph about Josephine before they left the house in Youngstown. She tried to prepare herself for the ordeal, rehearsing just how she would tell him and trying to anticipate answers to the questions she knew he would ask. She wasn't even sure Ralph knew about sexual relations although she suspected he had some idea of where babies came from, especially after she had carried Michael for nine months. She did not know if Giovanni had ever broached the subject with Ralph.

'*How stupid of me not to have asked Giovanni.*'

"Ralph, come sit next to me for a moment. You know we are going back to Newark very soon. I want to ask you what you remember about the people and places there. I know it was a very long time ago for you, and you were very young back then. What can you tell me about our time there?"

"Well Mama, I remember going to school. The teacher was very nice and we used to play catch out in the back."

"What about my friend Giustina, do you remember her?"

"She used to take us to school sometimes. She had two boys I used to play with after school, up near the reservoir."

"That's right, honey. Now what about the house we lived in?"

"It was cold, and there wasn't much room in it."

"Do you remember the 'out back' where I would take you every day?"

"No, but I do remember looking out the window."

"Yes, the window in the front room. Do you remember anything else about the front room?"

"No."

She tried to elicit as many memories from him as possible hoping he would mention Antonio. After she exhausted this tactic she asked him directly if he remembered Antonio.

"What about Antonio, the man you used to share the front room with before he moved away? He used to play with you when Papa wasn't home. Do you remember him at all?"

"No, Mama, I don't remember him."

She didn't know if she quite believed him, they had spent so much time together. She wondered if he was avoiding admitting to the memory because he knew something or perhaps he just buried the memory in his subconscious, a sort of denial tactic.

She paused. "Well, I have something very important to tell you about him." She took a deep breath. "Antonio is Josephine's father."

He looked at her directly in the eyes for a moment. She wasn't prepared for what he said next.

"But Mama, then who is her mother?"

She was stunned at his unexpected question. Recovering her composure she maintained direct eye contact with him and in a hushed voice she said, "I am."

She watched him intently, looking for the slightest reaction, but his face remained expressionless. Then he turned his face away from her and he sat there staring into space.

"Oh." That was all he said. Then he said that he was tired and wanted to go to bed.

She wanted to reach out to him and hold him close but he was gone. It was one of those rare times when she did not know what to do. She had hoped he would have cried so she could have taken him in her arms, something that would have brought some physical contact between them, but nothing. She decided, or more correctly it was decided for her, to say nothing more. She was convinced that he did not know or suspect the truth before she told him. Telling him was the hardest thing Maria ever had to do, even harder than having to tell Giovanni.

'Will it never end?' She felt that the punishment did not fit the crime; it was excessive. She did not sleep that night. Time, she hoped, would heal the wound for everybody.

Her explanation to Josephine was equally without response. Maria did not press the issue with her because she was not sure if the child understood. But at least she planted the seed and she hoped it would one day grow in Josephine's mind to full knowledge of who her father was. At least Josephine was somewhat aware of the truth if the matter ever came up when they got back to Newark.

*****

Once again Maria sold off all of their furniture. It would mark the third time she had done it in the last seven years. She packed all of their

162

clothing and took the train to Newark via Philadelphia. The season had changed and it was late fall. The train ride through the autumn colored fields and woods had a calming effect on her. Gazing out the window of the train she reflected on all that had happened to her since her marriage and her arrival in America. Four children born, one by the man she fell in love with, three by her husband, and one dead. She felt guilty for what she had done to Giovanni, especially in light of Ralph's reaction.

'It would have been better if I had never met Antonio.'

When she got back to Newark she was going to live in close proximity to Antonio again, almost across the street. She knew that every day she would have to fight the battle to stay away from him while the deep feelings of love still persisted inside of her.

'It would have been better if I had never left Italy.' But by that logic it would have been better if she had never met Giovanni; better to have never been born.

'But that's stupid, unrealistic, schoolgirl thinking,' she told herself. She knew that it was useless to think about what could have been. Yesterday was yesterday and could not be changed. The reality was that she was on a train, heading for Newark. She vowed that from then on she would determine her own tomorrows and not surrender to what an insensitive fate might toss her way.

Michael's cries of hunger snapped her back to the present. She began to nurse him with Josephine staring intently as usual. Ralph had been very quiet since she had told him about Josephine. She could not get a reaction from him. Thank God there did not seem to be any change in his attitude toward his sister. She would have to take special care of the problem once they were settled.

Giovanni met them at Penn Station. Antonio had lent him one of his wagons and also a driver. It was rather amusing having a driver come get them with a wagon painted on both sides with Antonio's name but filled with Giovanni's bread and cakes. The children thought it was great fun to be able to ride in a horse drawn wagon. Giovanni looked so proud seated up front, taking care of his family, and Maria was pleased.

Within an hour they were unloading the trunks and carrying them up the one flight of stairs to the flat. It would become Maria's home for the next nine years. Had she had the slightest inkling of what would happen in those nine years she would have turned around, right then and there, and gone straight back to Ohio, or better still, to Italy.

Chapter XIX

RELAPSE 1902

Maria decided to lie about Josephine's age and enroll her in school as soon as she returned to Newark. She had only turned four the previous month. She had lied about Ralph's age before and thought it was a mistake but with Josephine she felt more secure. The child was very advanced for her age and she looked like she was five so they got away with it. It was such a common practice that in first grade there were more four-year-old than five-year-old children. Josephine also had the advantage, as did Ralph, of being bilingual. They both seemed to adapt to their new environment quickly and there did not appear to be any problem with their classmates regarding Antonio. This was a good sign because it meant that the subject was not discussed in the homes. Michael was too young to even be aware of the change in his surroundings. With the older children in school, Maria set to work establishing a home for the third time since she arrived in America.

The reunion with Giustina was as long-lost sisters finding each other again. Her help was immeasurable. They resumed their relationship and spent as much time together as family responsibilities allowed. Maria had not seen Antonio since her return about a month ago. He was conspicuous by his absence. She went out of her way to avoid seeing him. She knew why he was staying away but she also knew that it was just a postponement of the inevitable meeting. Even if they both worked at not meeting each other it would only be a matter of time before they did. The neighborhood was too small and their houses were too close to avoid it.

'*Where will it be?*' she wondered. As it turned out it was in the park.

On Saturdays Ralph worked with his father at the bakery. Maria, like all the housewives in the ward, spent the morning shopping for supper and Sunday's dinner. Often, with Michael in the carriage and Josephine playing mother by helping to push it, they had just enough time to visit the park. She relaxed sitting on a park bench with the carriage close by while Josephine played with the other children. Maria enjoyed the open space and the trees. On clear days the blue sky reminded her of Pietramelara and the farm and she indulged herself in the nostalgia of days gone by.

One Saturday she looked up and there he was, standing tall, a short distance up the path, watching Josephine play. Antonio said nothing. He just

164

looked at Maria. He sat down beside her, but not too close. Their gaze lasted only for a moment. It was Maria who broke the silence with a smile and a warm greeting.

"Hello, Antonio, how are you?" She thought how good it was to see him.

"I am well, thank you. You look as beautiful as ever. Are you settled into the apartment yet?"

"Yes, it is a very nice apartment, thank you for finding it for us. And thank you for the peace between you and Giovanni and the arrangement with Luigi,"

"No, it is I who thank you for going along with it. I was afraid that you would oppose the purchase of the bakery. Now we are all taken care of and our friend Luigi is grateful that we have provided for Gia. Is that Josephine playing over there?"

Maria looked into those blue eyes and simply nodded, "Yes, it is."

He thought to himself, '*How beautiful she is, just like her mother.*' But he said nothing more as he thought also of his new daughter, Grace, at home. The conflict of his thoughts hurt him very much. Maria watched him as his eyes followed Josephine running and jumping.

"I know that you come to the park from time to time. I was watching for an opportunity to see Josephine. I needed to see her, and you."

"I understand that, Antonio, but you must never do it like this again. If we ever meet again it must be in full view, on the street, or at church, even some social event, never this way. No matter how innocent it is it would be misunderstood by anyone watching. I don't want to leave my family, myself, and even you open to any more gossip. We have caused enough trouble for our families and I never want to let that happen again. It must not happen again. Do you understand what I am saying?"

"Yes, I do understand. But I must see Josephine, even occasionally. Please don't shut me out of her life. At least let me have that much." He paused, "Does she know?"

"Yes, I've told her, although I am sure she does not understand completely. In time Antonio, in time, but Ralph knows."

He nodded in understanding. "Will you call her over so I can get a better look at her and hear her voice?"

"No, now is not the time and certainly not the place. We will meet on the street soon, I am sure, and you can talk with her then."

There was no need for them to say what they both still felt toward each other, their eyes said all that was necessary. As much as he wanted to be in her company he agreed that it would not be prudent to remain with her any longer. He stood up, not taking his eyes off her, tipped his hat, bowed slightly, and in a hushed voice said, "*Arrivederci,*" to which she replied, "*Ciao.*" He turned and walked up the path.

It hurt deep inside her seeing him leave that way. It upset her very much. It was difficult to hold back the tears. But no, never again would she surrender to her emotions. It's over! She promised herself she would not add to the damage she had already caused. She put all the blame on herself, not admitting even to herself, that she too had been a victim.

*****

Their lives settled into a family oriented routine and everyone became busy preparing for the holidays, first Thanksgiving, then Christmas. Maria and Giovanni had invited Luigi and Gia for Thanksgiving Day dinner. Antonio and Joanna had them over for Christmas dinner. They were all thankful that they had shared the holidays with them because Luigi died shortly after New Year's Day of 1902. The whole neighborhood came to pay their respects to Gia, but it was Antonio and Giovanni who took care of her, just as they had promised.

The bakery was now on a solid footing. Giovanni introduced to his customers some of the French bread and pastries that he had learned how to make in Youngstown. His reputation was gaining more and more momentum. 'Giovanni's Bakery' was the place to go for the best breads, cakes, and pastries. The accolades only served to inflate his ego all the more; he was bursting with self-admiration. Antonio was more than satisfied because his customers responded with even more business. The two friends were becoming prosperous.

After Luigi's death it seemed logical for Giovanni to purchase the Eighth Avenue property from Gia. She took back a mortgage and the monthly payments were more than enough to take care of her needs. She continued to work in the store and in return Giovanni allowed her to live rent-free in the apartment above the bakery. Antonio was in complete accord with the arrangements and Gia became as a member of both families. So the debt of gratitude to Luigi was paid.

*****

Maria remained concerned about Ralph. He still did not evidence any reaction regarding Josephine's paternity and he had said nothing about seeing Antonio. Would he recognize him if they met? What would he say if he did? Sometimes Maria and Josephine would run into Antonio on the street or at the store but she never pointed out to her that he was her father. That would have to come later, but at least the child was somewhat prepared if some child should tell her. Children can be so cruel without even realizing it. Maria was sure that Ralph must have seen Antonio at the store on Saturdays. But if he did he never mentioned it.

For a while life was good in Newark. They were in a large city and as they were assimilated into the American culture, they still retained the flavor of their heritage within the neighborhood's Italian culture. They all felt that they had the best of both worlds.

*****

The area of Newark where they lived had originally been part of the Eighth ward but later on it was designated as the first ward on the tax maps. That is how it was referred to in ordinary conversation. They called it the first ward but most often people just called it 'the ward'. Irish immigrants originally settled in the neighborhood but slowly they had moved out as the Italians moved in. By 1900 the ward was almost one hundred percent Italian. It was also called Little Italy and was famous for its many fine restaurants and food stores. It was where you went to buy fine imported cheeses and olive oil. The bakeries were renowned for their excellence. It was a lively, closely knit, ethnic hub. The ward grew as more relatives and friends immigrated. Many came from just a few towns in Italy, mostly from the region of Campania. That was why the ward was influenced so much by the Neapolitan culture. For the most part everyone was a relative or if not, a *pisano*. The term properly means 'one from the town of Pisa' but in the vernacular of the time it came to mean people who came from the same town or region in Italy.

*****

The downside of the ward's social structure was that it was the base of the mob in New Jersey. Centuries before in Italy, some men had secretly banded together to protect themselves and their families from an oppressive government. They called themselves *La Societa' della Mano Nero*, The Black Hand Society. Over time, because they were responsible to no one but themselves, their lofty idealism gave way to criminal behavior and they became the oppressors. Immigration did not change their ways and in America they developed into a subculture that attracted the criminal element within the Italian society. The organization possessed its own hierarchy.

The members of the mob were of like personalities. Hating honest work they preferred to beat the legal system by living outside of it. They had their own rules and organization. Their meetings became the support group for a mutual admiration society. The young toughs of the neighborhood showed extreme deference to the adults associated with the mob. For them it was important to cultivate and have connections. The more connections one had the more powerful one became. In fact, that is how

167

people outside the inner circle called the mobsters. It was said of them that they were 'connected'.

Favors were traded, IOUs were closely watched and counted and held in reserve for a time of need. The system held a perverted attraction among some men. They had an ability to organize and work, making a living by not working. Well-dressed dandies, they strutted about the ward like nobility surveying their domain. They thrived on their own self-anointed importance. They jealously guarded their position within the chain of command. Those on the 'way up' coveted higher status. No position was ever secure. Ambition and greed made everyone vulnerable. The 'connected ones' constantly looked over their shoulders and sat down with their backs to the wall.

Loansharking, gambling, and prostitution became their sources of income. Having a mistress was a sign of manliness and pride. They treasured their perverted sense of honor above all else. These 'connected' men had to develop a dual personality. In order to justify their lifestyle they became ardent family men. They treated their wives with great respect, at least publicly. They loved and protected their children, especially the girls. For appearance's sake most even went to mass on Sunday, priding themselves over the amount of financial support they rendered to the church and always with the most public display possible.

The overwhelming majority of people in the ward avoided the mob. However, it was a very attractive way of life for a very small minority. Their misdeeds became common knowledge and they caused difficulty all out of proportion to their numbers. However, to those few, the lifestyle was their addiction.

*****

Unfortunately, Giovanni was one of those to whom the 'connected' way of life held an addictive attraction. His previous loose association with Rocco made it easy for him to slide back into his old ways and he soon became addicted once again. Except it was different for him this time. He was a merchant now and he did not need the money. He was attracted by the camaraderie and the power. It made him feel important and he relished the admiration bestowed upon him by the toughs. It inflated his ego and in his mind added to his identity over and above that of being a successful merchant. The bakery gave him respect but no power. The most tragic thing about it was that he did not have to do it; he wanted to do it. The way he saw it, reestablishing contact with the mob made him a man of honor. It wasn't long before Maria found out. She tried to talk him out of going back down that road.

168

"Giovanni, I am hearing rumors that you are hanging out at Rocco's old restaurant again. What are you doing over there?"

"I'm just catching up with some old friends of mine. That's all. We go way back."

"I know all about the 'old friends' that you are spending time with and the kind of people they are. Giovanni, we made promises to each other before we left Ohio, remember?"

"Yes, yes," he said with a wave of his hand trying to dismiss her protests. "I remember, but it's different this time. I'm not the same lowlife groveling around for a few dollars. I don't need their money. This time they respect me."

"How can you be so blind? They respect you now and they'll kill you later, in the wink of an eye, if it suits them. The first time they don't want you they will get rid of you. Giovanni, come to your senses."

"Look, Maria, I'm not going to argue with you no more about it. This is my house and I do as I please. You're not going to tell me what to do and who to see and that's final."

She was shocked at the 'my house' comment. Where was his sense of sharing? Now that he was financially successful was she to be denied her role in working toward a common goal? She was incredulous at how little time had elapsed after returning to Newark before he slipped back to his old ways. He was completely oblivious to the change in himself and his reversion to the behavior that drove her away from him and into Antonio's arms in the first place. The way Giovanni saw it was that he was successful, a good father, and a respectful husband. She only saw the danger of being thrust once more into the role of the spurned wife. She was afraid he might succumb to his previous addiction for the 'house' by the river.

She did the best she could to avert the inevitable but the inevitable did happen, only this time it was worse. Now he had the money to indulge himself on a grander scale. The 'house' was for dirty lowlifes, not for well-connected and established men like him. He would carry on with his liaisons elsewhere. He came to her less and less and finally he stopped altogether. The rejection confirmed her suspicions that he was turning somewhere else; back to the way things had been when she first arrived in America. She was devastated, hardly able to comprehend what happened to the marriage that she had tried so hard to restore. As time wore on she gave up and no longer tried to maintain any intimate relationship with him. Instead she immersed herself completely in her relationship with her children.

She thought back to her early school days and the Sister who had helped her learn English as she waited for Giovanni to call her to America. She resolved that the education of her children would be the most important project in her life. Unusual for the time, and because she was educated herself, she began helping her children with their schoolwork, especially with their language capabilities. It was amazing that as she did so, her strong Italian accent became less pronounced and it became a pleasure to hear her speak English with only a slight continental flavor. It added to her poise, self-confidence, and above all her aura of class.

The result was that she and the children became fluently bilingual. Homework and conversations at mealtimes were always spoken bilingually, questions in one language, answers in the other. This playful and intellectually challenging banter brought Maria and her children closer. Even Michael seemed to relish the game.

Because of Giovanni's constant absence from these family pastimes he was, by default, slowly becoming estranged from the family except for Ralph. Ralph worked every Saturday with his father at the store and a special closeness grew between them. On Saturdays it was Maria, Josephine and Michael who were together. On Sundays, the entire family gathered for dinner after mass. She was determined that with or without her husband this was one tradition she would continue. On most Sundays Giovanni was home because he had nowhere else to go. However, he no longer attended mass even though most of his friends did. She resented that the children did not have him as a role model in this regard. Ironically she found herself right back in the same place she had been when Augusta died, eight years before.

For Antonio matters were not much better. Joanna never forgave him for being the father of Josephine. Outwardly they maintained an appearance of parents living within a family. Privately, love waned between them. In time all intimacy ceased in their marriage too. Antonio did as Maria did. He buried himself in his business and with his children's interests. He lived with his wife but without her. Joanna too centered her attention on her children.

There was an undeclared truce in both families. But however serene the situation seemed to be, it was an explosion waiting to happen. As it turned out, the San Gerardo Feast, in October of 1902, became the fuse that, once lit, set off the explosion with all its dire consequences.

Chapter XX

LA FESTA 1902

As with all church affairs nothing ever happened without that core group of the congregation who volunteered to be the driving force behind the event. Both Maria and Antonio were part of that group, so that as preparations for the San Gerardo Feast Day began, it was inevitable that they would come in contact. Committee meetings were held in the church basement. Other volunteers were present so they felt they were safe and a certain, special, and different relationship began to form between them. They looked forward to the weekly business and planning meetings and as the date of the event neared the committees met more and more frequently. Working together at the church seemed to satisfy their need to socialize outside the family.

As far as their sexual desires were concerned, they suppressed them and that only added to their stress. They each told themselves that they could do it. They did not realize that their humanity worked against such a platonic relationship and made the situation a constant and heavy cross to bear. They braved it out.

After the meetings they took to stopping at a coffee house for a *caffe-latte* and a piece of pastry. They would pick a small table in a quiet corner not because they did not want to be seen but because they wanted no inter-ruptions or distractions of this little time they had together. They spoke of literature, music, philosophy, and religion. They never mentioned their feelings for one another. They knew, and their eye contact confirmed, what they would not say or do.

The relationship remained platonic, almost spiritual, and it was in this manner that they were also able to cope with their familial problems at home. They even made plans to go down to the Court House together to file their Declaration of Intention papers to become citizens. For Maria these meetings were almost a complete fulfillment of her desire to be with him, but not quite. For him the ache of his empty arms was a constant battle.

The feast that year was a grand affair. It lasted for three days, from the opening ceremonies on Friday night through to the closing prayers on Sun-day night. The usual food carts and booths were everywhere, packed together lining the curbs on both sides of the streets. Seventh and Eighth

Avenues, from High Street up to Clifton Avenue across from the park were blocked off from traffic, as was Sheffield Street where the church was located. St. Lucy's was the epicenter of the activities. A bandstand was built in the middle of Sheffield Street opposite the church steps where the dignitaries sat and the band played. There were bright, colored, oil lights hanging across Sheffield Street. The entire lengths of Seventh Avenue and Eighth Avenue had electric lights strung across the streets from house to house. At night, looking down the length of the streets, the white, green, and red bulbs added to the spectacle and increased the air of festivity.

The smell of food cooking was mouth-watering. Frying sausages and peppers, the aroma of tomato gravy with meatballs and *bracciole*, the mussels in marinara sauce, steamed clams, all melded into an aroma that was unique. Everywhere there were candy stands intermixed with pastry booths selling *zepelle*, *sfogliatelle*, *pasta-croce*, and coffee stands selling *espresso* and *caffelatte*. And the wine, oh how it flowed, like water from the tap. The entire neighborhood turned out for *La Festa*, as it was referred to in the vernacular. The streets were so crowded that it was almost impossible to cross from one side to the other. People came from miles away, not only just to witness the spectacle, but also to be a part of it.

In the evenings there was a processional march starting at the bandstand in front of the church. Out in front there was the band followed by the dignitaries of the ward. The altar boys dressed in white surplices and carrying staffs topped with candles followed them. Immediately behind them another boy carried the main staff topped with a gold crucifix. The pastor, Father Joseph, fully vested with an alb, stole, chasuble, and biretta, was close behind. Then came the statue of San Gerardo, the patron saint of Caposele in the province of Avellino, the same province that Antonio had come from.

*****

Although Pope Pius X did not canonize Gerardo until 1904, the people had regarded him as a saint before then. He was the son of a tailor who died when the boy was 12, leaving the family in poverty. Gerardo tried to join the Capucians, but his health prevented it and instead he was accepted by the Redemptorists as a lay brother. When falsely accused by a pregnant woman of being the father of her child, he retreated to silence; she later recanted and cleared him, and thus began his association as patron of all aspects of pregnancy. He was regarded as a wonder worker and was reputed to be able to bi-locate and read consciences. He died in 1755 of tuberculosis. He was 30 years old and was immediately venerated as the patron saint of Caposele. The Italian immigrants brought the tradition of

172

devotion to him when they arrived in America. His feast day was especially celebrated in the first ward of Newark.

*****

The statue was on a platform carried on the shoulders of some of the men of the parish. It was considered a high honor to be selected as a bearer. The men were dressed in their Sunday best and the expressions on their faces were of humility and piety, as befitting the occasion.

The procession started each night at the steps of St. Lucy's Church. They marched a half block north and turned right down Seventh Avenue to High Street. Along the way the procession stopped temporarily at makeshift shrines so the devout could give an offering to the church and say prayers and make petitions. Women threw rose petals to the statue and gave offerings of gold and jewelry, and men draped dollar bills all over it. Hundreds of people walked, often in bare feet, behind the statue carrying lit candles as an act of penance. As the procession passed the booths all commercial activity ceased and everyone lining the streets blessed themselves with the sign of the cross and also genuflected as the statue passed in front of them.

Each parade made a clockwise circle around the core of Little Italy in the ward. The procession turned right at High Street over to Eighth Avenue and turned right again and processed up Eighth Avenue to Clifton Avenue, across from Branch Brook Park. Turning right again they marched north along Clifton Avenue and passed Aqueduct Alley and Drift Street to Seventh Avenue then right down Seventh Avenue to Sheffield Street, ending where it started at the steps of St. Lucy's. Then, gathered around the bandstand, the closing ceremonies and prayers were led by Father Joseph. Everyone who was able attended the festivities.

For the feast, Giovanni had constructed a food stand and set it up outside his bakery on Eighth Avenue. He sold his famous Italian and French pastries. He and his men were busy from early morning until late at night working at the stand. He also supplied bread and rolls to other food stands so they had to shuttle back and forth between the bakery and the stands in order to keep everyone supplied.

Maria had arranged for a baby sitter for Michael so that she could attend to her duties as a volunteer. Ralph was busy helping his father, and Josephine, now five years old, sat in a chair next to Giovanni's stand, entranced by the wonder of it all. Joanna was also attending the feast and had her baby Grace with her. Her daughter, Theresa, and son, Frank, were old enough to be on their own.

Antonio was with Maria attending to all the details for which they were responsible, along with the other volunteers. It was a joyous time espe-

173

cially since everything was going so smoothly. It was also exhausting work and by the final procession on Sunday night, they were both tired and exhilarated.

Their adrenaline was flowing from the excitement. They were at the back of the parade of people as it wended its way back up Eighth Avenue toward the park for the last time. As the procession turned onto Clifton Avenue, Antonio took Maria by the hand and led her across the street through the entrance to the park. He was walking so fast that most of the time he was pulling her along. They walked down around the reservoir to the lake, then to the boathouse. She did not protest. Her emotions, like his, were at fever pitch. The park was deserted and dark but for the light from the full moon. He took her around to the back of the boathouse where the picnic tables were. Without speaking a word they embraced in passionate kissing, lost in the bliss of being together again.

"Oh, Antonio," she moaned as she felt his hands on her body.

He began to undress her. She stood motionless neither helping him nor hindering him from what he was doing. In a minute she was standing in front of him, completely naked. He looked at her, standing there bathed in the bright moonlight. She was like an apparition of Venus. He did nothing for a very long time. He stood in front of her just staring. She did not move, letting him drink in the beauty of her body knowing that it pleased him so much. She was intoxicated with the moment. They made love, there in the park, in the moonlight, on one of the picnic tables.

Afterward they lay silent in a tight embrace. It was Maria who broke the spell as she got up and began to dress.

"Come, Antonio, we must get back before the feast is over."

He said nothing, and following her lead, he dressed. He took her hand as they left the boathouse and headed for the street in silence. As they approached the exit from the park she let go of his hand and they walked down toward the church.

They had been gone from the procession for less than an hour but no one had noticed. They got to the church just as the closing prayers were being recited. They separated and mingled with the other working volunteers to complete their assignments. They did not see each other again that night.

When her work was finished Maria walked over to the bakery expecting to see Giovanni at his stand, but it was closed up. She went home still feeling the ecstasy of the night. She looked in on the children. The three of them were sound asleep. She went into her bedroom; Giovanni was not there. He did not come home that night. She was too exhilarated and exhausted to think about it and felt too guilty to wonder where he was. She could not sleep so she went into the front room and sat in the dark by the window looking at the windows of Antonio's house.

174

Antonio had returned home to find the same situation. Everyone was asleep. He went into the parlor and sat down and looked out the window toward Maria's apartment. He was too excited and troubled to go to bed. He sat for a long time thinking of Maria and wondered where she was and what she was doing. It was one of those very rare occasions when he didn't know what to do. He was in an untenable position. All he could think of was that he must not do anything that would bring further hurt to his children. He could not and would not. Running through the gambit of possible solutions he even thought of what his cousin Francesco would think if he did anything to disrupt the family. What about the teachings of the church? Marriage was forever, for better or for worse.

Across the street his beloved Maria was going through the same agonizing thoughts. It was remarkable how much alike they were. Maybe opposites do attract but for them it was their similarities that were the attraction. Their lovemaking was the expression of a pure love for one another. To disrupt their families would be an act of self-indulgence that neither of them could justify. So who should suffer, the innocent children or themselves? Who was to blame for what they felt for each other? In the end, independently, sitting alone in the dark, they decided that they had to accept their lot in life and protect the children.

Each stared across the street at the other's darkened windows. She finally fell asleep sitting upright in the chair. Antonio fell asleep in the chair where he was sitting thinking that Francesco was right, *alla famiglia*. There was no replacing the family.

Chapter XXI

OGDEN STREET 1903

The entire neighborhood was busy preparing for the holidays but all too soon Thanksgiving, Christmas and the New Year of 1903 were come and gone. Since the San Gerardo Feast in October, Maria and Antonio were not together again nor did they try to meet. Their mutual feelings of guilt precluded any attempt at another tryst. The night of *La Festa* had been a spontaneous intimacy brought on by the excitement of the moment. The fact that they were unobserved was a minor miracle. She vowed to herself that it must not happen again under any circumstances. They only saw each other during casual meetings on the street or during church activities.

Ralph had turned twelve in January and Josephine was now a precocious six. Little Michael was going to be two very soon. Her maturing family kept Maria occupied with household responsibilities. In the evenings she was kept fairly busy as *La Scrittore* for her growing clientele. Although she sometimes wrote letters during the day, for the most part it was after dinner. Usually men came to the apartment alone to have her write to their wives in Italy but increasingly married couples came together in order to stay in touch with their friends and relatives. Often they would bring letters they received and she read to them aloud. It was not as easy as reading letters back home in Pietramelara because in the ward there were the dialects of people from all over Italy.

When the Roman Empire had ceased to exist so did the political infrastructure on the Italian peninsula. Small city-states were formed. Travel was difficult and dangerous. Communication between towns was seriously impeded. These problems had a great impact on language. Over time Latin ceased to be the mother tongue and was replaced by many dialects. The immigrants brought their dialects with them to the ward.

Consequently, the correspondences Maria was reading for her clients were often written in dialects that were very different from hers and also from classical Italian. She was forced to translate from one dialect into her own or into classical Italian and then back again. It was always an intellectual challenge and she relished the mental gymnastics. Sometimes she wrote replies immediately; other times her clients would return to have her write their reply letters and then she had to do the translating again.

176

Although Maria adhered to her policy of not becoming friendly with her clients, she enjoyed the work very much and took a personal interest in their letters and replies. It kept her informed of current affairs in the old country. Certainly it helped pass the time when she was alone. On occasion someone from Pietramelara or nearby towns would need her services and she was able to read about some things and some people she knew of first hand. Often the memories plunged her into a deep, melancholy mood. She would think of her hometown and her childhood on the farm; time with Mama, and Papa's strong arms lifting her into the air, the sweet smell of the farm and the bright, clear days and the crisp, starry nights. She indulged herself in nostalgia. She recalled memories of those heady days when she first met Giovanni and the ecstasy of her first years with him, Ralph's birth, painful memories of Papa's death, then Mama's, and all that had happened to her since then. It was her whole life flashing before her eyes. It gave her pleasure and pain. She would try to drive the thoughts away. Often Maria fell asleep weeping; dreaming of what life could have been if she had met Antonio first.

During the day she often thought of Antonio, wondering where he was and what he was doing and thinking. She missed their conversations while slowly sipping a cup of espresso, sometimes with a little anisette or lemon peel and an occasional pastry. She had no one with whom she could converse on the level that she could with Antonio. She laughed to herself remembering how they used to banter back and forth in four languages, English, classical Italian, and the two different dialects with which they were each raised. They used to tease one another by refusing to translate some of the more difficult idioms, forcing the other to make wild guesses. It was a lot of fun.

But now she no longer was able to indulge in this playful repartee. At times she felt as if she were locked up in prison with no way out and no visitors. Her strong friendship with Giustina helped but their conversation was, for the most part, women's talk, interspersed with the local current gossip. They went food shopping together and often went downtown for an afternoon when the children were in school and she could get a sitter for Michael. These visits came nowhere near to satisfying her intellectual needs.

Financially, things were going well at the bakery. Giovanni was generous with her, almost to a fault. She knew that this was his way of salving his guilt. In a way she almost felt sorry for him; he was missing so much. Maria knew that he was addicted to whatever kind of sex he was getting from his lady friends. Surprisingly she no longer cared about it. Her only fear was that he might get into trouble with his 'connected' friends and that would be a reflection on her and the children. For herself she was able to enjoy some of the better things in life.

Over time she stopped sewing and bought clothing for herself and the children during shopping trips downtown. On occasion she purchased something to brighten up the apartment but she didn't spend everything Giovanni gave to her. She began to build a little nest egg for her own security and the children's. She even stopped depositing her earnings as *La Scrittore* in the bakery account and kept the cash. She told no one, not even Giustina. Giovanni was too caught up in his dual life to even notice. In spite of guilt feelings about doing it she thought it was the prudent thing to do. As the nest egg grew she thought it better not to have the cash in the house so she opened a savings account at a bank downtown in her name only.

Maria's life was slowly passing by. She was far from happy but she was content and felt secure. She took delight in the children, played games with them, and helped them with their schoolwork. The bilingual games they played helped her as much as it did them. Ralph was still quiet toward her and did not join in the conversations as much as Josephine did. Even little Michael delighted in the games with his limited vocabulary. They laughed at him when he would get the languages mixed up and call things by incorrect names but he joined in and had no trouble laughing at himself. He was such a joy to be with and everyone loved Michael.

Maria was concerned over the problem of Ralph not having fully adjusted to Josephine's paternity. Her heart ached because of what she had done to him and she felt helpless in overcoming this emptiness in their relationship. She was frustrated but realized that she would have to adjust to living with Ralph while not living with him just as she was forced to do with Giovanni. She was thankful that at least he and his father were close and Ralph did like to work in the bakery. But then again she had reservations about that. She didn't know if Giovanni's friends frequented the store; she did not want 'them' to have an influence on her son.

But she didn't have to worry about that. Ralph took in what he saw and was strong enough, like his mother, to reject what he did not like. What he did not like were his father's friends. He also did not like his mother's past relationship with Antonio and especially he did not like Antonio. As far as Josephine was concerned, he loved her dearly and imputed no blame to her. And like everyone else, he loved and enjoyed Michael, that happy child who lit up the room for everyone. On balance, Maria was grateful for the peacefulness in her home and did all she could to keep the happy sibling relationships in her family.

She saw Antonio from time to time but never by prearrangement. Passing each other on the street was unavoidable. Although she had once told him that he was not to avail himself of the opportunity, she purposely went to the park on some Saturdays with Josephine and Michael hoping he would be there. Sometimes he would come by and they would chat briefly. Her paranoia about being seen with him slowly faded. Antonio took great pleasure in watching Josephine play. It was obvious that he loved this child that he and Maria had between them. These meetings were very infrequent and lasted for only a short time.

Sometimes too, while she was in the bakery to pick up some bread or cake, Antonio would be there. They were cordial but formal toward each other because Gia was always present. Whenever such chance meeting occurred, Giovanni was always down at the ovens, supervising and baking. Gia would always have a warm embrace for them and the three would exchange pleasantries for a few minutes. Then either Maria or Antonio would leave while the other lingered on a while to talk with Gia.

On one such chance meeting, in the early afternoon, of a beautiful early June day, Antonio invited Maria for a cup of coffee. Gia exclaimed how wonderful it was that they were all such close friends and how proud Luigi would have been. Maria was boxed in and without a ready excuse she was forced to accept.

Antonio held the door open for her and they both nodded, *"Ciao,"* to Gia as they left.

They strolled down the street toward a café. Maria refused to let him take her arm. She was upset with him, and he knew it. She was convinced that all the eyes of the neighborhood were watching them. Of course no one gave them a tumble. Still she felt very self-conscious. She was angry because he had taken unfair advantage of her in front of Gia. She decided that when they got to the coffee house she would tell him exactly how she felt. They walked in silence and entered the café. Maria went directly to a table in the middle of the floor. She did not want him to select one that was secluded. He recognized the rebuff. Nevertheless he held the chair for her as she sat down. He did not do anything to show his disappointment.

Before Maria had a chance to berate him he cut her off by engaging in general conversation. He spoke in a loud enough voice that could be overheard by the few patrons at nearby tables. He asked questions to which simple propriety required a response. Again he put her in a situation whereby she could not do anything except respond to him. He was finessing her and she knew it. She couldn't help smiling at his tactic. She knew him so well.

Her agitation slowly diminished. She became more relaxed as she began to enjoy his company. Eventually their voices dropped to just above a whisper. The other customers did not even know they were there. Besides, he and Maria were speaking in English and the others used Italian.

Her initial desire to criticize him for his rouse gave way to expressing her fear that it was dangerous for them to be seen together.

"Antonio, people will see what they want to see. Don't you understand that?"

He made no reply. He just shrugged his shoulders. They continued with their conversation. The afternoon was slipping by. A man at a nearby table stood up and announced to his companion that it was three o'clock. Maria jumped up from her chair and exclaimed, "My God, I need to be home when Ralph and Josephine return from school. *Ciao*, Antonio." She was out the door before he even had a chance to say goodbye.

Maria was able to make it home in time, dismissing the baby sitter and apologizing for being late. She was hardly settled in when Josephine came home and told her that Ralph went to the store to help Papa. She gave Josephine and Michael something to eat and began preparing supper. Sometimes, but not often, Ralph and Giovanni might come home together for dinner and they would have a family meal. But most often Giovanni came home late and ate alone as she sat and played with the children. Then he would go out to be with whomever. He would return after she was asleep only to wake up early to leave for the ovens. In spite of the way he treated her she always awoke to make coffee for him while he washed and dressed. On a few occasions when they had a family supper, he would not go out afterwards. Instead he played with the children. By the time she bathed Michael and readied him for bed there was little time left for them to speak with each other and when there was time the conversation invariably revolved around the mundane affairs of running a household.

This night it was different. Giovanni retired early and she sat down in a chair in the parlor. She gazed out the window over to Wood Street and could see the lights on in Antonio's apartment. Her mind was drawn back to the pleasant afternoon they had spent together. She had no regrets, no sense of guilt for having spent time with him. She wondered what he was doing. She fantasized that he was at his window looking over at hers.

Months had passed before they met again, and it happened in the same way. This time it was not by accident. Antonio waited purposely until he saw her go into the bakery. He entered and again, in the presence of Gia, he invited Maria for a *caffelatte*. This time she was delighted to see him and eagerly accepted his invitation. They left Gia and talked excitedly as they walked to the coffee shop. This time she didn't give a thought to who might be watching.

She allowed him to pick out a secluded table where they stayed for a couple of hours. The hot coffee felt good in the crisp, cool weather of late autumn. They were completely oblivious of their surroundings, only aware of each other. Even during the lulls of conversation their eyes spoke to each other. She realized that their conduct meant a complete and mutual surrender. They no longer cared what the insensitive world thought. He

180

wanted to be with her and she wanted to be with him. They did not know where or when it would happen but were sure it would. She was dizzy with excitement. They made no plans that day. She would leave it up to him. He told her that he would contact her soon and she understood his meaning. But for now she had to leave to be home for the children.

*****

Antonio rented a small, furnished room up on Ogden Street near Fourth Avenue. It was in the German section of Newark near enough for Maria to walk yet far enough away from the ward and the stores where she shopped. The chances of their meeting anyone they knew on the street would be remote. He did not like using a fictitious name with the landlady and wondered what Maria's reaction would be when he told her what he had done.

The next time they went for *caffelatte* he told her about the room. He looked at her intently trying to read her face. He was so afraid that she would become insulted or angry but she just listened without any indication of how she felt. He gave her directions to the rooming house and pressed the keys into her hand, one for the front door and one for the room. She never turned her eyes from his as she accepted the keys and put them in her purse.

His relief was so obvious that she felt compelled to say, "Oh, Antonio, don't you know how much I love you? Did you think I was going to be angry because I know that you love me as much? Aside from our children we both have nothing outside of ourselves. I don't even think God will be angry with us."

He reached for her hand again and held it as she spoke. He gently squeezed it in acknowledgement of her acceptance. She withdrew her hand from his as a signal to him that they were not to show any kind of affection in public.

'*Well,*' he thought, '*The rules have been established.*'

Her response relieved any anxiety he had. Neither of them felt any guilt. As far as they were concerned, their deep and sincere love for each other justified their actions. As they left the café Antonio whispered a time and day to her. She discretely nodded assent without speaking. They had just arranged their first rendezvous.

Chapter XXII

THE COLLECTOR 1903

The secret life between Antonio and Maria had started. The deceptions of maintaining a seemingly casual relationship in public did not bother them. They were together and that was all that mattered. Any guilt they might have had was buried deep in their subconscious minds. Their rationalization was that their loveless marriages were traps from which they needed to escape occasionally.

They met often, but with no fixed schedule. Plans to meet were made whenever they saw each other in the neighborhood. A short, whispered time and date was all that was needed. The intrigue added to the excitement of the romance and the spontaneity of it all made them even more attracted to each other. Antonio still tended to his family and his business. Maria had her family to care for. They put their children first and did not neglect their responsibilities. But when it came to their respective spouses, they did only what was demanded of them and that was very little.

They had little difficulty arranging meetings when school was in session. During the summer break it was more difficult but they managed. Antonio, of course, could make his own time. Maria used her trips downtown for shopping as an excuse to be away from home. To help maintain the façade, Maria occasionally went downtown with Giustina. On such occasions she also stopped in to make a deposit at the downtown bank. Giustina never commented on Maria's stops at the bank. She put two and two together and guessed that Maria was building a savings of her own. She knew nothing of the secret trysts between Maria and Antonio.

The furnished room was on the first floor in the rear, of a three-story house located on a quiet street. Most of the people in the neighborhood were of German descent. Italians never had the need to venture into that part of the city. It was no small feat that Antonio was able to rent the room from the German landlady in the first place but he paid cash for a month in advance. That quelled any dislike she had of having an Italian in the house. Besides, he seemed to be clean enough for her standards.

Maria would walk down Seventh Avenue to Broad Street. Then, instead of taking the trolley downtown, she crossed Broad and wended her way through the side streets to Ogden Street and then up toward Fourth Avenue. Rarely did she pass anyone on the streets and never anyone that she recognized. Usually she arrived first and let herself into the room. It was sparsely furnished but contained all that they needed. She was tempted to add to the furnishings and decorate it a little. Fresh flowers crossed her mind but she thought better of it. She knew what the room was for. It was definitely not a home.

Antonio would arrive a few minutes later and they were together for two, maybe three hours. Sometimes they spent their precious hours together only in conversation but not often. Their love for each other usually erupted into passionate lovemaking as soon as they were together. Conversation was for afterwards.

They made it a point to read the same books while they were apart and discussed them in their private time together. They spoke very little of her family except for his questions regarding Josephine. His separation from his daughter weighed heavily on his mind. Whenever he asked about Josephine Maria kept the mundane matters from him and told him only of the pleasant things. As well as she knew him she did not fully understand the ache he felt because he could not be with the child they had together.

Sometimes when they met on the street they would go to a quiet café and have a *caffelatte*. These infrequent meetings started out only between themselves but soon it was arranged to have others join in so that an eclectic, intellectual, social group formed. Consequently the neighborhood saw them together in the company of others. Therefore, they were able to increase the number of times that they could be in each other's company.

They enjoyed the company of their peers and the rapport satisfied the social needs that could not be fulfilled by their spouses. During this time, along with some of their friends, they finally completed the naturalization process and they became American citizens early in 1904.

Giovanni could not have cared less with whom his wife associated. In fact he was actually grateful to see her find friends who were on her own intellectual level. It relieved him of another marital chore that he was not capable of fulfilling anyway. He suspected that Maria might be seeing Antonio again. Most men of 'honor' would have been furious if their wives were unfaithful. Giovanni did not think about it often, but deep down he knew that it was he who first broke the promises they made back in Ohio. He deluded himself into feeling that if he ignored his suspicions there would be no mutual accountability. And his suspicions of his wife's infidelity made it easier for him to do whatever he pleased. He knew he did not have any justification for his behavior. He thought that as long as she was discrete, there would not be any problem.

*****

183

Giovanni's accent was still heavy and he made no attempt to correct it. Even though he was making rudimentary gains in reading some English, it was only what he needed to run the bakery. He couldn't see any reason to apply himself. His intellectual growth stagnated.

Joanna constantly rebuked Antonio for his past behavior and this harshness left little room for any companionship between them. She neither forgot his past indiscretions nor made any attempt to repair her damaged marriage. It seemed to Antonio that she enjoyed her role as martyr.

In addition to her anger, Joanna unconsciously used her husband's affair as a rationalization for not sleeping with him. After her daughter Grace was born Joanna's sexual desires had diminished and then finally subsided altogether. Even though she was physically capable of bearing more children, Grace would be her last child. Antonio of course had no need to make any demands of her anymore. He was completely satisfied with his relationship with Maria, sporadic as it was. He was in love with her and that was that.

The four of them settled into double lives that time mellowed into a tolerable routine.

On some Saturdays Maria continued to take Josephine and Michael for a walk in the park when Ralph was working with Giovanni at the store. Whenever it was possible she would tell Antonio in advance so he could come by to see the children. He tried to develop a friendly relationship with Josephine and played park games with her. So Josephine came to know him fairly well but not for whom he was. Maria could never find the right moment to point to Antonio and say 'Antonio is your father,' but she wondered if Josephine was beginning to suspect that he was. These park visits were rare and lasted no more than a half hour or so. It was incredible that they went unnoticed.

Giovanni found complete satisfaction socializing with his 'connected' friends. He preferred spending time in Rocco's old restaurant to sitting in his claustrophobic flat. Talking with members of the mob, paying honor to each other, breaking the law with gambling, loan sharking and the rest was like a meeting of the mutual admiration society.

He was not high up in the hierarchy of the organization but he was not on the bottom rung of the ladder either. Though he had to show respect and deference to his superiors, he in turn received like behavior from his inferiors. He was in his element. It gave him a sense of identity, which, for some reason, he did not feel he had even as the owner of a successful business and the head of a family. He relished his role in the organization and he became more pompous than ever, especially as the bakery thrived.

He had little difficulty satisfying his sexual needs. He used an apartment on the second floor above the restaurant that had been set aside for

184

that purpose. These *animali* traded women back and forth among themselves, like chattel. Now he only went down to the 'house' by the river on rare occasions.

*****

It was a cold day in December when Gia passed away. She wasn't sick at all; it was a sudden heart attack. In her will she forgave the mortgage debt that Giovanni owed to her. She left a like amount to Antonio and then split the remainder of her estate between the two of them. It was her way of saying thank you to the 'sons' she felt belonged to her and Luigi. After she was buried Maria suggested to Giovanni that they move into the apartment over the bakery and give up the one on Seventh Avenue.

"Why should we pay rent when we own a building with an empty apartment?" It was more of a statement than a question. Giovanni would not hear of it.

"I don't want to live in the same building where I have my business. It just isn't right for a man in my position. I'll probably rent the apartment but for the time being, I won't do anything."

That wasn't his real reason. It wasn't long before he began using the apartment for meetings with his friends. They played poker for amusement and also for business. He started a game for the organization. After deducting his allotted share, he turned over the balance to the organization. He also used the apartment for a floating crap game under the same terms. The set up made him more important to the organization and he moved up a rung on the ladder and this pleased him more than his share of the bets.

Now he stopped visiting the 'house' down by the river altogether and instead used his apartment for assignations with his lady friends, and there were many of them. It was far more convenient and less expensive. In time Maria found out why he did not want to move the family into the apartment over the bakery.

The members of the mob were well known for their exploits, both real and fancied. How they loved to have the stories of their deeds recounted with increasing embellishments in each retelling. It filled the cups of their egos to the rim, flowing over.

Giovanni's behavior after Gia died became the final straw. Maria no longer cared what he did or with whom. She stopped cooking for him every night. If he came home she would prepare something for him but she no longer planned on it. She gave up on the idea of moving the family to Eighth Avenue and never mentioned it again. She no longer wanted to live with him and she made her feelings very obvious. He just shrugged it off and did as he pleased.

She told herself, '*As long as he continues giving money to me, let him waste what is left as he pleases.*' More often than not, Giovanni spent the night at the apartment over the bakery and Maria continued to live in the rented flat on Seventh Avenue.

She had her children and she had Antonio. He had his children and he had Maria. They felt like parents to Josephine and shared that relationship as much as possible. Ralph was another matter. He hated Antonio and continued to remain distant from his mother. The meetings on Ogden Street remained a secret from everyone. This was due not only to their discretion, but also to the fact that they both had spouses who did not care.

*****

One afternoon while Maria was preparing supper there was a knock on the door and Maria asked, "Who is it?"

A woman's voice replied from the hallway, "I want to see *La Scrittore.*"

Maria opened the door and said, "I am *La Scrittore.* Come in. Please sit down," and she pointed to a chair, "What can I do for you?"

"*Signora*, please, I would like you to write a letter for me to my father in Italy. Will you do it?"

"Of course." Maria opened a drawer in the china cabinet and took out her pen and a bottle of ink, some writing paper, an envelope, and a pen wiper. She sat opposite the woman at the kitchen table. Maria wondered why she had never seen the woman before. She guessed that the woman was about twenty-five years old. She wore a thin gold band wedding ring. She was modestly dressed in old but well cared for clothes. She was very plain looking. She was fingering her wedding ring and acted extremely nervous, her eyes shifting from side to side.

"Something has happened and I need to write to Papa. Can I trust you? It is very private."

"*Signora*, if you ask around the neighborhood you will find that I never talk about my client's private affairs. In fact, no one will ever know that you have even been here unless you say something. So just go ahead and say what you want as if you were writing the letter yourself."

"*Grazie, signora*, I am so frightened. I am not from this neighborhood. I live over on Cabinet Street near St. Joseph's Church. I walked all the way over here so that no one would recognize me. I heard about you from someone I know."

"Well, don't worry about me. Just try to calm down and we will begin when you are ready." Maria's tone seemed to have a soothing effect and within a few minutes the woman nodded and she began to speak.

186

"My father doesn't know how to read or write so we will have to mail the letter to my aunt and she will give it to him."

20 March 1904

Dear Papa;

I am in trouble and I want to come home. I don't have enough money for the steamship and I am asking you to send it to me. I have been living alone now for about three months. I know that you didn't want me to marry Stefano. I should have listened to you. But I thought if we came to America he would change and we could live here without any fear. He promised he would not gamble anymore and get in trouble like he did in *Napoli*. We both got jobs here and I thought we could save and have a family.

I didn't know that right after we got here he started to gamble again. I thought he was putting our money in the bank but he was gambling it all and even money that we did not have. I didn't find out until one day a man came to our apartment and wanted to see Stefano. He wasn't home so the man told me that he came to collect money that Stefano owned some men in another neighborhood not far from here. He said to tell Stefano to get the money or there would be a lot of trouble.

The man scared me. He was a big man, almost a giant and he was very mean to me. He said he would be back and that we should have the money ready. I told Stefano what happened and he admitted to me that all our money was gone and that he owed so much more and that he didn't know where we were going to get it. Oh, Papa, all my hard work and now I have nothing. We had a big fight and I told him that I was going to leave him and go back to Italy.

The next night the man came back and when Stefano told him that we did not have the money the man hit Stefano and beat him right in front of me. He said that Stefano had to have the money in one week or he wouldn't need any money no more. Papa, I was so scared. I yelled at Stefano again. He slammed the door and went out. Papa, that was almost four months ago and I haven't heard from him since. I don't know if he is dead or just ran away. Papa, I want to come home.

The little money I earn is just enough to keep me alive. I'm living with a neighbor. She is helping me. I need money to come home. Please forgive me for not listening to you and Mama.

Regina

As the woman was dictating Maria was becoming frightened. She suspected that the incident had to be related to the mob in the ward. The man that the woman was describing could be Giovanni but she doubted it. Giovanni was not violent and wouldn't frighten a woman like that. But there was another man that everyone in the ward knew was a 'collector'. He was a terrible and violent man. She was sure his name was Mario. Then the realization hit her.

'*Oh God, Mario works for Giovanni!*'

Maria struggled to control her breathing. It was difficult for her to keep her composure. Her hand was shaking as she continued to write. Regina was sobbing and wiping her eyes with a handkerchief that was knotted to hold her few precious coins to pay *La Scrittore*.

When the letter was finished they both stood up. Contrary to her professional code, this one time, Maria embraced her client in a gesture of sympathy. Actually Maria also needed some support at that moment.

"*Grazie, signora,*" whispered Regina, unknotting the damp handkerchief. She handed the coins to Maria.

"*Grazie,* Regina *e buona fortuna.*"

After Regina left Maria's mind began racing. She walked over to the table and placed both hands on it for support. Her knees felt week. She looked around at all she had shared with Giovanni. She could not help thinking about the small, sparsely furnished room on Ogden Street that she shared with Antonio. She hated herself for making the comparison. She shook her head violently to shake the thoughts from her mind.

She was overwhelmed by fear and emotion. It was impossible for her to delude herself. There was only one conclusion. It became crystal clear to her that Giovanni had ordered Mario to give a beating to Stefano.

'*Oh Giovanni, you have become an animale just like them!*'

CHAPTER XXIII

TERROR 1904

Maria decided for the first time she would violate a confidence and tell Antonio what happened. The next time they were together at Ogden Street, Maria told him about the letter.

"Maria, you are right, they control all of the gambling and loan shark business in all of Newark. That woman's husband must have been indebted to them. And Maria, you are right about Mario too. He works for Giovanni; everyone knows it. Giovanni doesn't make collections anymore but he is the one who is responsible. He has a couple of thugs who work for him and that Mario is the worst. It must have been him, he is the only one who fits the description."

"What should I do?"

"Maria, be practical. There is nothing you can do. Giovanni won't change now. He doesn't even live with you anymore. Maria, forget it. It doesn't concern you so don't get involved. Let's hope that the woman's father sends her the money and that you will never see her again. You can't do anything."

"All right, I'll forget the whole thing."

"Maria, I must tell you that sometimes I think I am just as bad as they are. Here I still buy my supplies from Giovanni knowing that he is in with those crooks. I do it for the same reason that all of his customers do. He bakes the best bread and cakes in Newark. I feel guilty sometimes."

"You must not feel that way. I take money from him and I don't feel guilty. I just feel that it comes from the bakery and not from his other life."

*****

In July 1904 'it' did not arrive on schedule. From the very first time when she was twelve 'it' never failed to arrive on time except when she became pregnant. This time she did not have to wait for the second month to be sure. She knew immediately what the problem was. It happened, or more correctly did not happen, on the Friday before the Fourth of July celebrations.

She felt as though her whole world was crashing down around her. She could not even begin to speculate what would happen. She had not been with Giovanni for over a year, going on two. This time she was deathly afraid of his reaction. He would not care, she was sure of that, but his pompous vanity and the pride he had of his standing with his comrades could turn him into a raging animal. Horrible thoughts filled her mind. Would she have to flee from the city to only God knew where? What about the children? She felt completely out of control, as if she were sinking into a bottomless pit. The only thing that sustained her was that she knew Antonio loved her and that he would somehow save her. He always did.

She and Antonio had not made any advance plans to meet. They trusted to a chance meeting in order to set a time to rendezvous. Antonio was very busy because of the holiday and she did not run into him until late the following week at the bakery. She only had time to whisper a time and date to which he discretely nodded yes.

Maria was late by almost three weeks and she would be almost five weeks into her pregnancy before she could tell Antonio. The waiting was almost unbearable.

It was raining when Maria set out to meet Antonio. She allowed herself more time than she needed for the walk. Holding an umbrella she walked as quickly as she could and hoped that he would be in the room when she arrived. She got there early and this time Antonio was unusually late. She sat in a chair to wait for him. Time seemed to have stopped and she sat there in the dim light, looking out the window, staring out into space, through the rain. She realized that her life was now in a shambles. Everything would become public knowledge. She told herself that there were no excuses for her actions. She truly loved Antonio but their present relationship was self-indulgence, pure and simple, and it had now brought her to the brink of disaster. She was afraid of what Giovanni would do to her when he learned of her pregnancy. As she sat watching the rain falling outside the window, her mind ran the gambit between guilt and justification. Then she heard Antonio's footsteps in the hall.

He entered the room and instead of the usual warm greeting he was anticipating he saw her sitting in the chair staring out the window. At first she did not move. Then she slowly turned her head toward him. Their eyes met from across the room and he sensed that there was a serious problem. He shut the door behind him and stood still for a moment then he took a step closer to her.

"What? What's wrong?" It was all he could bring himself to ask.

There was a short hesitation as her eyes began to fill with tears. "Antonio," she whispered, "I'm pregnant."

He was stunned into silence but managed to walk over to the window. Without uttering a word he sat on the edge of the bed opposite her.

"I'm sure of it, there is no doubt."

They sat across from each other for a long time looking into each other's eyes. All he could see on her face was total despair and hopelessness. He rose and knelt on the floor in front of her and put his arms around her waist. She did not respond. She just sat there with her hands folded on her lap. His embrace was not enough. His arms did not console her and she began to sob uncontrollably.

As she started to feel some self-control return, she pulled away from his arms. Sniffling and wiping tears from her eyes with the palms of her hands she looked toward the floor as she said, "Maybe I should try to get an abortion. I understand I can go ……"

"No!" He cut her off in mid-sentence. His voice became louder. His response was automatic. "I will not hear any more about that, it's murder." His objection was partly founded on his religious convictions but also his fears for her safety. "You could be seriously harmed or even killed in the process. Most women either hemorrhage to death or suffer physical scars, not to mention the emotional trauma. The answer is no!" It was almost an order rather than an answer. Because her beliefs and fears were the same as his, she let the suggestion drop. She was beside herself.

"Oh, the children. The shame! How can we continue to live in the neighborhood? Your wife and Giovanni! Joanna at least has been faithful to her marriage vows even though Giovanni has not. And look at us - look at what we have become! Meeting here like this, in secret, in this… this place." She looked around the room. She could feel her emotions rising again.

"I hate this room. It's not a home. No matter what others have done to us, the fault is ours. We can blame no one but ourselves." Antonio just looked at her. She was still shivering from fright.

"Shh, shh, Maria." He lowered his voice as he held her tightly trying to help her regain her composure. She put her arms around him and buried her face in his shoulder. Her sobs were intermingled with deep, gasping breaths in her attempt to calm herself. He said nothing and began to analyze their predicament, searching for any possible solution. Even in the most dire straits Antonio always managed to analyze and think clearly. It didn't take him long to come to the conclusion that there really was no solution. Not this time. All they could do was choose a course of action that would cause the least amount of additional damage.

Slowly a glimmer of an idea formed in his mind, not a solution, but a course of action. He pushed himself away from her and looked up into her eyes.

"I think maybe I have an idea of what will happen. It is certainly not going to solve the problem but we might still be able to work things out between the four of us. But the first thing you must do is to forget who is to blame. Now is not the time to do that, and besides, we're going to get enough of that from Giovanni and Joanna, not to mention the finger pointing from the neighborhood."

Maria sniffled once more looking down at him, her large, brown eyes bloodshot from crying. He let go of her and stood up. He sat down again on the bed, opposite her. He began to talk in a soft consoling voice and she listened intently, hoping for a miracle.

"You and Giovanni are almost completely separated now. He spends so much of his time in the flat above the bakery. My guess is that once he is told he will make the separation complete and final and go live there permanently. Maria, he will move out on you, a complete break! I am sure of it. He probably wants out of your marriage anyway. This will be his excuse. If that's what happens, then you must continue to live in your apartment with the children."

"Maria, you are going to need some financial help."

"No," she yelled at him. "I am not going to be a kept woman!"

"Maria, be practical. Listen to what you are saying. I have never offered money to you before. But now things are different. The new baby will be mine as well as yours. We must share the responsibility. And besides, Josephine is mine and I have a responsibility to her too. The money is for the children, not for you! I am sure Giovanni will provide for Ralph and maybe Josephine since he regards her as his own."

She tried to interrupt him with objections. But she knew they had no substance and so she just listened.

"As far as Joanna is concerned the situation can be no worse than it is at present. She is living with a husband for whom she has no love. Her children are her life. She no longer cares what I do or with whom. Believe me, I know. She never misses an opportunity to tell me so."

"I don't know if Giovanni will continue to sell to me. There are other bakers who would jump at the chance to be my supplier. But I don't think he will do that. He would lose the largest customer he has and he needs the income to live the way he does."

He thought to himself, *'That is what they did, those connected ones. Business was business.'* Antonio was pretty sure that even Giovanni would think that one through.

"Oh, Antonio, the scandal that will break out into the open. I can just picture the gossips drooling over the whole mess."

"Well, that cannot be avoided. There is nothing we can do. We will just have to suffer through it."

192

"What about Giovanni when I tell him? He will be furious with me. He has hit me twice before and I am afraid he will do it again. He is so physically powerful. Suppose this time he can't control himself?"

"This time you will not be alone. This time I will be with you, we will tell him together. Then I'll go and tell Joanna. What happens after that, well, that is out of our hands. All we can do is hope and pray for God's forgiveness."

There was nothing else to say and they both stared out the window into the rainy day. The rain stopped and it seemed to be nature's way of telling them that it was time to leave and do what they had to do. They had to go and pay the piper.

*****

"You bitch," Giovanni hissed, "How could you disrespect me this way?" His hands were locked into fists and his arms were shaking by his side. He looked at Antonio.

"I should have expected this much from you. I should never have trusted you again after the last time. It was a set-up, wasn't it? All this talk about getting me back here to help me buy the bakery. All you wanted was her! You bastard, you even used Luigi. The only reason I don't kill you is because you make money for me. You're lucky Antonio, you and your whore."

He turned and faced Maria. "As far as you are concerned I don't care what happens to you no more. You can beg on the streets for all I care or stand on the corner like the *putana* you are. Maybe you can make a living that way. You won't get a penny from me. I'll pay for the children, that is my way, but for you, nothing. Rocco was right. You are a whore!"

That very night Giovanni moved out completely and went to live on Eighth Avenue above the bakery. They never discussed the given fact that the children would be left with Maria.

Antonio went home and told Joanna. She cursed them both. She told Antonio to get out or get his own bed. She said that she didn't care what he did. She ranted and raved for hours. The saddest part of all was that the children were home and they heard the airing of the entire sordid mess. Antonio struggled to tune out Joanna's litany of his transgressions. He realized that he had lost his children regardless of where he lived.

*****

Finances between Giovanni and Maria were not discussed. Every week he sent money to Maria through Ralph. Ralph continued to work in the bakery after school and on Saturdays. Giovanni also gave his son a generous allowance for his work. Business between Giovanni and Antonio remained the same. Early each morning Antonio sent one of his hired hands to the bakery to pick up the daily order and pay for the previous day's supplies. The arrangement had not been discussed. Antonio just thought it was the better way to handle it. He never set foot in Giovanni's store again. Giovanni and Maria never met or communicated afterwards. The matter might have been settled between the four, but for the neighborhood it was just getting started.

*****

How quickly the news traveled! It didn't take long before the scandal reached Giustina. Sadly, she had to hear it on the street. Maria had been too afraid to face her friend and tell her. As soon as Giustina heard about it she became furious and stormed into Maria's apartment.

"Maria, what on earth have you done? Are you crazy?" She pointed to the window, "Do you know what is going on down there because of you? The whole neighborhood is talking about it."

"Giustina, I love him. Giovanni has left me for good and I know my name will be dragged through the mud. The worst part is what my children will go through."

"You're damned right that's worse. What the hell were you thinking? Didn't I warn you about this years ago? My God, Maria, you're right back where you started after Augusta died. Didn't you learn anything? How long has this been going on?"

"About a year and a half."

"How? How did you manage it? Where did you meet?" Maria merely waved her hand in response. She couldn't tell even Giustina about Ogden Street.

Realizing she wasn't going to get an answer to that question, she said, "Well I suppose you're lucky you've gotten away with it for as long as you have." She looked at her friend. Maria was crying.

"Oh Maria, come here. I'm sorry." Giustina reached out and hugged her. "I'm just desperately worried about you, that's all. You're like a sister to me, and that means that sometimes you get treated like one. It'll be all right. You are not going to avoid the scandal, that's already started, but I will always be your friend. You are going to need me now more than ever."

"I'm so relieved, Giustina. I was praying that you would stand by me. I have been so worried about the children's welfare and Antonio's reputation, and on top of that, I was worried that you would hate me and that I would have nobody left in this world, even though I deserve as much."

194

"Well, Maria, you can't get rid of me that easily. I'll be here for you. I hate what you have done to yourself and your family but I don't hate you. Now why don't you make some coffee for us and we'll sit down and you can tell me all that happened, all right?"

*****

Maria became the scarlet woman. *Putana*, they called her, whore, and worse, but never to her face. They called Josephine that *putana's* bastard. Joanna's children joined in with the name-calling. Josephine became an easy substitute target for their hatred of Maria and their bitterness toward their father. Outside the family, little blame was imputed to Antonio because he was a man. In fact, in some circles he was admired. It was all Maria's fault!

Giovanni now had full freedom to associate with his friends without worrying about Maria's nagging, not that he had paid much attention to her objections anyway. He also completely indulged himself in his sexual desires. He invited whomever he wished to his apartment and made no attempt to conceal it.

Antonio visited with Maria almost every day but only while Ralph and Josephine were at school. There was no intimacy during these visits. They reassured each other that everything was all right. Maria told him that she was coping with the situation and that he was not to worry. He wanted to be as much of a support figure for her during the pregnancy as he could. But this mutual consolation lasted only during the visits. They could not alter the reality of the situation.

Ralph despised Antonio. He developed a love/hate relationship toward his mother. However, that did not change his relationship with either Josephine or Michael. Maria was grateful for that. She agonized over her family's condition as she waited for the pregnancy to end. Unlike most mothers-to-be this was not a happy time for her.

Giustina's friendship was like a rock that Maria could cling to for safety. She was an endless source of strength to Maria. Even though Antonio still loved Maria he cursed himself for what he had done.

The months dragged on until that fateful day of April 21st in 1905, when the twins were born.

Chapter XXIV

TWINS 1905

Maria had gained more weight during this pregnancy than in any of her previous ones. She attributed it to being a little older. After all, she would turn forty in July. Because she was also carrying very high she believed that the baby would be a boy. It appeared that she was going to carry to full term. Giustina concurred with this diagnosis. Even the midwife who was to attend the birthing agreed. The baby was expected in early April. When the expected date passed each succeeding day was spent in imminent expectation. It was more of a relief than a surprise when the contractions started on the 21st. She was preparing breakfast for the children when she felt the first twinge of pain.

After her first contraction she sent Ralph to fetch Giustina. On her way to Maria's, Giustina alerted the midwife and they arrived together. Giustina got Ralph and Josephine ready for school and sent Michael to a neighbor to be cared for. Maria went into hard labor about eight o'clock, just after the children left.

Through experience they all knew what to do. Maria groaned with every push. The birthing was proceeding very well. The midwife was confident that it was going to be an easy birth. She and Giustina stood ready as the baby's head appeared and then very quickly the body.

"Maria, it's a boy!" screamed Giustina with delight. The midwife cut the cord and Giustina carried the new born over to the side table.

"Oh, my God! There's another one," yelled the midwife. "Come on, Maria, push some more. That's it. Good. Push. Good. It's a boy too!"

They were dumbfounded. There had not been the slightest suspicion that it would be a multiple birth. The twins were born a little after ten in the morning. There had been no complications. The boys appeared healthy and Maria was doing surprisingly well.

When the children returned from school about four o'clock, Maria was too tired to speak with them so Giustina told them about their twin brothers. Ralph looked at them but showed no reaction. Michael hardly knew what was going on, but Josephine was ecstatic. Giustina wanted the three of them to go home with her, but Ralph insisted on going to the bakery to work with his father. He said he would stay there that night and go directly to school in the morning. The midwife agreed to remain through the night to care for Maria and the twins.

"Maria, don't you worry about anything. I'll make arrangements for someone to take care of Michael. I'll come back in the morning once I get Josephine off to school with my boys. When I return we can send the midwife home."

"Oh thank you so much, my dear friend."

"Maria, the boys are beautiful. They have clear skin without a blemish. Their coloring is very fair, just like Antonio's. They are so alike I can't tell them apart! I tied a piece of cloth around the ankle of the one that was born first. It was the most amazing thing I ever saw. You get some rest. We will take care of everything."

"*Ciao*," they said to each other as Giustina left.

*****

Antonio was unaware that Maria had gone into labor and he had gone off to work as usual. There was no way to get a message to him. He knew that Maria was past the full term date and he had been stopping in to see her each afternoon for the past week as early as business permitted. When he arrived, Giustina and the children were already gone.

The midwife met him at the door and told him of the twins. He rushed into the bedroom to see Maria. She was in a deep sleep brought on by utter exhaustion. He didn't want to wake her so he turned and walked over to the boys who were also asleep. He stood over the makeshift cribs and gazed down at them. He stared at them for a long time. He was shocked almost beyond comprehension. It was over. He couldn't believe that there were two. He left the midwife to continue her work and walked into the front room. He collapsed into the chair near the window overlooking the street. He looked across Seventh Avenue and could see his apartment building.

'*Oh my God!*' he exclaimed half aloud, '*What a mess I've made of all our lives.*' He had a wife who hated him, children who probably despised him, and the reputation of both his family and Maria's lay in tatters. His children still paid him the respect due to a father but beyond that he did not know what they felt. '*How will they treat me now?*' he wondered.

His old friend, Giovanni, hated the ground he walked on. Even Giustina had lost most of the respect and admiration she once had for him. And Maria, asleep in the bedroom with their twin sons not yet a day old, what was going on in her mind? Did she wish she had never met him? Maria would be completely alienated by the neighborhood now. Feelings of despair and isolation crept over him. He felt hopeless and at a loss to cope with the mess he had created. What to do? Fear of tomorrow started to bury his remorse for today. He was boxed into a corner. There was no way out.

Thank God that Maria was asleep and could not see him in this state. He knew he could not keep his feeling of desperation from her. She would be able to read it in his eyes. He didn't want to frighten her any further. He hoped she would sleep through the night so that he could get his wits together.

He wondered how far the news had traveled. Ralph would have told Giovanni as soon as he got to the bakery. Did Joanna know? Probably. News of this sort traveled like wildfire in the ward. When he did not get home by dinnertime Joanna would guess where he was. He was sure of it. For a moment he wondered where he would sleep that night. What of his children, Frank and Theresa, did they know? His daughter Grace was not yet five and would not understand, and thankfully Emmanuella was back in Italy, but he knew that Joanna would waste no time writing to her. He would have to face all of them; there was no escaping that. And the bitter confrontation with Joanna that was yet to come, what he wouldn't give to be able to avoid that!

'*Maybe an attempted abortion would have been the better course,*' he thought to himself. But he knew deep inside he could never have brought himself to be a party to that. It would have been murder, pure and simple, and as it turned out a double murder at that. Besides, Maria was alive and well and that was all that mattered.

'*Oh God, Your punishment for our sins is swift and sure. But why must the innocent suffer along with the guilty?*'

He was so deep inside his thoughts that he didn't hear the midwife enter the parlor.

"Antonio, Antonio," she said softly, "Maria is awake and she is asking for you."

It was an effort for him to get up from the chair. Suddenly he felt very old. He wanted to see his beloved Maria but at the same time he had to force himself to walk to the bedroom and face her. He did not want to look into her eyes. She would expect him to produce one of his miraculous solutions and this time he had none.

The midwife discretely remained behind in the parlor as Antonio went into the bedroom. He walked over to Maria and took her hand as he sat on the bed, as close to her as he dared. It hurt her to see tears fall from his beautiful blue eyes. They said nothing to each other for a long time and then she broke the silence and whispered to him.

"Well, my love, we really did it this time."

"Maria." he confessed, "This time I have no plan. For the first time I don't know what to do,"

"Neither do I Antonio, neither do I."

198

One of the boys began to cry and the midwife came back into the bedroom. It was a signal that Antonio should leave. He bent over and kissed Maria on the cheek.

"Let me go home and face that situation and I will come back as soon as possible. I'll try to return later tonight if I can, if not, then I'll try for tomorrow. But tomorrow is Saturday and I will be very busy and may not be able to come to you. So I may not be able to see you until Sunday." He left, but this time there was no cheerful, *ciao*.

He walked out of the building and crossed the street to go home to face his family. Twilight had given way to darkness. He stopped at the corner and looked up at the lighted window that was his parlor. How was he going to face his wife?

Self-recriminations began to blacken his thoughts. He had never seen himself as a selfish person before. Now he thought that is exactly what he had become. There had been choices, nothing was ever forced on him, yet he had chosen Maria. It struck him then that what Giovanni had done to Maria and his marriage he had done to Joanna and his marriage. He was no better a man than Giovanni! It was too late now; the damage had been done and could not be reversed. Yesterday was yesterday. He hated today and he dreaded what tomorrow would bring.

He had to go home - there was no escaping that. It was where his children lived, where his wife lived, and where he lived. He saw his life as ended but in no way would he try to avoid his responsibilities. He had to care for his family and somehow take care of Maria and the children that they had between them. He shrugged his shoulders and with a sigh of resignation, stepped off the curb into the street and headed for home. Each step was an agonizing choice between going home and running away. But running was impossible. For now he could only go home and face reality.

'Now,' he thought, '*Now I know how Jesus felt when he carried His cross to Golgotha.*'

Chapter XXV

THE DECISION 1905

Antonio walked down the hall to the door of his apartment. He squeezed his eyes shut, threw his shoulders back, took a deep breath, and went in. Joanna was sitting at the kitchen table. As soon as he shut the door behind him she jumped up and started screaming at him.

"So you finally decided to come home! I'm surprised that you even remember were you live! Why didn't you stay in your other house with your *putana* bitch? What did she do, throw you out? Twin bastards you gave her this time, huh? Are you going to give her triplets next time? How could you do this to me and the children?"

The children were huddled together in the parlor listening to every word. Little Grace was cowering behind her brother for protection. Theresa was horrified. Francesco was angry and bitter. But the emotions of her children were not enough to stop Joanna. In her wrath, she didn't think of how her behavior was affecting them.

"It's bad enough when I came here I found out that you had a whore that you gave a bastard baby to. But you couldn't leave her alone, could you? No, not you! When you brought her back from Ohio you had to give her two more bastards!"

Her words were so vicious that Antonio could hardly believe what he was hearing.

"Where do you go with her? Do you have another house someplace where you sleep with your *putana*? Maybe you do it in the hallways at night or maybe even in the 'bacouse' where you both belong!"

He hoped that she would stop screaming out of pure exhaustion. But she was relentless. All she could think of was that she was trapped in a scandalous marriage to a man who had another woman and, oh God, another family!

Antonio remained stoic. He didn't think he had a right to say anything. His silence only served to fuel her hostility. She continued ranting and raving and cursing Maria. As an automatic self-defense mechanism Antonio began to shut out her screeching voice as though he were not there.

Suddenly he found himself comparing his wife to Maria. He had never done that before. How terrible of him to do so now, but he could not help judge this peasant woman to whom he was married against Maria with her superior intellect. Maria whom he loved and Joanna whom he tolerated. Maria with whom he indulged himself and this wife he wished he did not have. He began to feel sorry for himself. He had never experienced self-pity before but then he had never been so out of control of his life either.

He began to resent his lot in life and the emotions he had for Maria, emotions he never sought and was unable to repress. It was a nightmare and he couldn't wake up. Life was playing a dirty trick on him and he felt that he didn't deserve it. Regardless of what he had done this was too much, he couldn't bear it.

'No,' he thought, '*I am not going to take all the blame on myself. I was born into this time and place and among these people. I did not seek to hurt anyone; I am entitled to some happiness and contentment too.*'

Joanna was still screaming at him. She started to pound on his chest with her fists and that brought him back to reality. He grabbed both of her hands to stop her. Her eyes were livid with anger, like the eyes of a wild animal. She was hysterical.

"So, what are you going to do now? You take one bastard and she takes the other, that *putana*; that whore? Why not," she yelled, "You're sharing everything else with her, why not the bastards too?"

Joanna had gone mad with anger. Her behavior stiffened his back and gave him resolve. He was going to do what he wanted, salvage something for himself. His reaction was automatic, and unpremeditated.

He shook her hands back and forth and shouted back at her, "Yes! Yes! That is exactly what I am going to do. I am going to bring one of them here to live with us and I am going to raise him as my son!"

That shut her up and she stood in front of him, her mouth wide open in disbelief of what she had just heard him say. She became speechless staring at him as though he were from a different world. They stood glaring at each other.

In a subdued voice, she hissed at him, "You wouldn't dare! You haven't got the guts to do something like that! You would not dare!"

He hissed back at her, "Oh yes I have and I will do it tomorrow!"

After he had thrown back at her what she had thrown at him, he let go of her hands and stomped out of the kitchen where they had been fighting. He went into the parlor where the children had been huddled together, listening to every word of the bitter argument. He hardly saw them run out past him into the kitchen.

He couldn't believe what he had just said. Take one of the twins away from Maria! Take a newborn from its mother! Bring one of their sons into his house where his wife and family lived! He sat on the sofa folding his hands between his knees slowly rocking back and forth. The entire family was stunned by the horror of it all. The silence in the apartment was deafening.

He heard Joanna moving about in the kitchen. He assumed she was making something to eat for the children. He wasn't hungry and couldn't eat anyway.

He did not move, he just sat there as the thoughts of having one of the twins as his own started to grow in his mind. The more he thought about it the more attractive the idea became. If he could no longer be with Maria then he could at least have one of their sons. How could he do it, how could he not do it? He began to sell the idea to himself, considering the pros and cons. And that is exactly what he decided to do, this changed Antonio, this man who, in a few hours, became obsessed with a desire to have a son from Maria.

He searched his mind for reasons to justify such an act. Maria, in her circumstances, could not handle the twins by herself, plus care for Ralph, Josephine, and Michael too. She would be alone without a husband. Ralph was almost old enough to care for himself. He would not be too much of a problem. But how could she care for the others without any help? My God, Michael was not yet of school age! Antonio began to sell himself on a plan that, as he saw it, made practical sense.

But would it be possible? If he took one of the twins who would care for it? Joanna would never cooperate. He could hire a wet nurse to care for the child. His business was such that he could afford to be home early every day and during the day the children would be at school at least until late June.

The children! What would their reaction be to the horrible mess? He realized that what he was contemplating would alienate them for good. He could not blame them for that.

Then he thought that maybe, if over time he remained with the family and never went out or ever saw Maria again he might be able to salvage some kind of relationship with them. He would have to work extremely hard at being a thoughtful and loving father. He would have to give up Maria and she him. There was no doubt about that. All the children would have to come first but he and Maria had already agreed on that. He could never make it up to Joanna, but at least, if he ended the affair, and stayed home whenever he was not working, he might be able to placate her to some extent. His plan was sketchy. The details would have to be worked out as time went by. For the present he saw it as the only solution for Maria and a last chance to have something of her for himself. But could he convince Maria?

He slept very little that night on the sofa and habit got him up at four o'clock. He washed, changed his clothes, and then left for work. Usually Joanna was up making coffee and a small breakfast for him but not today.

He left without eating anything. She did not get out of bed until after she heard him leave. By the time he arrived at the stables his hired hands had already hitched up the horses to the two wagons and were getting ready to leave to pick up the day's order from Giovanni. He gave money to one of the drivers for payment of yesterday's order. He did not know if they knew what had happened the previous day. They said nothing but the usual greetings. He also did not know if Giovanni would have anything ready for them. He might refuse to sell to him any longer and just send them back empty-handed. It was a chance he was forced to take and he sent them off.

However, as he had suspected, the wagons came back loaded with the day's deliveries and the drivers started their rounds. It was business as usual. Money was money.

It was Antonio's practice to alternate days riding on each wagon. As his driver unloaded the day's order he would chat with his customers and over the course of two days he was able to visit with all of them. The customers paid for the deliveries on the spot and at the end of the day he would take the receipts from his drivers and make a bank deposit. On Saturdays he had the added chore of settling with the stable owner and paying his help and doing his bookkeeping. Sometimes he would make sales calls to prospective customers so he did not ride the wagons.

This Saturday was no different except that he performed his duties by rote, not thinking of what he was doing. His mind was focused on how he was going to persuade Maria to let him have one of the twins. As soon as his work was finished he headed for Maria's house. On the way he went over his arguments one by one. He analyzed each objection she could possibly make in order to have a reply ready.

'*How does one ask a mother to give up one of her children?*'

But therein lay the strength of his argument. They were his children too. He had as much right to them as she did. If there had been only one, the situation would have demanded that the child remain with the mother. There was no question about that. But there were two. Since he had the same rights as she did it would be reasonable for them to each have one. It was an incredible argument. Was he deluding himself into thinking that it was justifiable?

He and Maria had shared so much together and now it appeared that their relationship would be ended forever. He convinced himself that it was right that they should share this last common part of their love. Besides, they lived close by. They could each somehow manage to see the other twin and he especially wanted to see Josephine. That was another argument; she would have two of their children, he would only have one. They could work it out; they would have to.

In a flash of hope he decided not to give up the room on Ogden Street. How could he think of such a thing at this time? But the idea invaded his mind of its own accord; he did not seek it out. He had always been able to talk to Maria about his most private thoughts. He could explain, maybe not immediately, but sometime in the future, that they could use the room to visit from time to time and see the children together. God! What was he thinking? Did he want to see the children together or did he want Maria? He vacillated between the two desires. In the end he decided to keep the room and say nothing to Maria about it. If he could broach the subject someday he would, if not then he could always give the room up and she would never know. He decided that he would wait and see what happened.

*****

By now he assumed that the entire neighborhood knew about the twins and they would be watching, some in shock, some in disappointment, some salivating over the new scandal. He would have to tough it out and do what he thought he had to do. As he approached Maria's building he felt the eyes of the entire ward on the back of his head even though he saw no one. He knew they were hiding behind curtains, watching his every move.

'Maybe I'm becoming overly suspicious.'

He walked up the stairs and let himself in. The midwife was still there and it occurred to him that she had not been paid for her services. He took care of that matter and gave her something extra. She told him that she needed to leave and that Giustina had promised to return soon. He thanked her and told her it was all right for her to go, he would stay until Giustina arrived.

As she was starting to leave he asked, "Signora, do you know of a wet-nurse who might be available for hire?"

"Yes, as a matter of fact, I do. She is a fine woman. Unfortunately she just lost a child at birth. I'm sure she would consider the job."

"That would be a tremendous help. I would appreciate it if you can arrange a meeting for me as soon as possible."

"Fine," she said. "I'll see what I can do for you and let you know."

"Grazie, ciao," he said as she left. He closed the door behind her and then went into the bedroom to see Maria. She looked so pale and drawn, almost lifeless, lying there in bed. He smiled to her as he walked over to look at the twins. They were asleep. He returned to Maria and sat on the edge of the bed and took her hand. He could not help himself and slowly bent over her and very gently kissed her on the mouth. With their lips still touching she whispered, "Oh Antonio, what a mess."

"I know, I know," is all he could manage to say. He sat up still holding her hand. They began to talk just as they always did, openly and without reservation, each respecting the other's words.

"Have you given any thought to naming the boys?"

204

"Not much," he said, "But I would like one of them to be named Antonio, the one born first, if that's agreeable with you,"

She nodded in assent. "I'll name the other one Pasquale, I always liked that name." She tried to speak further but her lips only formed the words, nothing was audible, it was just too emotional for her.

He let go of her hand and gently placed his fingers over her lips and whispered to her, "Shhh Maria. Don't say anything yet. Please let me speak and say what is on my mind and what is in my heart."

She nodded yes. She couldn't say anything anyway. She looked deep into his eyes as he started to unburden himself.

"Maria, we are in an untenable situation. I don't know what will happen to us. I only know that I love you and always will and I believe that you feel the same for me. So what can we do? Should you and I run away and leave our children? I say no to that and I cannot even begin to conceive that you could ever have such a thought. That is not an option, it's not for you and it's not for me. What then? We must stay and face our responsibilities. Should I leave Joanna and move in here with you? If I do then you lose Ralph and Josephine and possibly Michael and I lose Francesco and Theresa and Grace. I don't even want to think about Emmanuella in Italy. No, that is not a solution either. The only thing I can think of is for you to stay here in this apartment and for me to stay in mine. We will have to be strong in spite of what people will say and think. Will our friends abandon us? I think they will even if they don't want to. It will be forced on them by the society in which we live, a society that we cannot leave. There is no other way."

She tried to speak but he would not let her. "Listen, my love. I have wracked my brain. There is no other way. My livelihood is here. I can't start over somewhere else. What would you have us do, try to take all of our children and run? Impossible! It is also impossible for you to manage your household as it is. Ralph and Josephine are in school so that helps, yes, but they will be home for the summer in less than two months. Even now you will have Michael and the twins to care for. It cannot be done."

"Then there are the finances to think about. I am sure Giovanni will support Ralph and Michael and possibly Josephine; he said he would. He will not support the twins and for sure he will not support you. But remember, dear Maria, as though you could possibly forget, Josephine and the twins are mine as well as yours. We have equal rights, you and I. Therefore, I have the right as well as the duty to take care of them. This I will do and even you cannot stop that. This leaves no one to care for you. I know, I know, you are able to take care of yourself, maybe later but not now. So on this I will tolerate no dissent, even from you. I will support Josephine, the twins and you."

The look of horror on her face said it all. "No! No! No protests on this matter," he continued. "The matter is closed. As far as you and I are concerned I leave that to the fate that only the future will reveal. See my love, your silence only tells me that even you have no valid argument against all that I have just said to you. What I have just outlined has been forced on us by the circumstances. There is no other way! It is the only solution for us, the only way to care for the children."

She lay there speechless and horrified. She was now going to be a kept woman! Antonio had feared that would be her immediate reaction, this proud, independent woman he so loved. He hoped that she would understand that he was offering to help her financially after their relationship had ended, not during it. There was a difference and he was sure that it would cross her mind.

She was searching for words of protest but at every thought she could only see that any other way would be an added hardship for the children. She had caused enough of that already. She could take care of herself. She was still *La Scrittore* and she did have a little savings that no one knew about, but that wouldn't last very long. She knew she could not support herself and five children on those resources. She was an experienced seamstress, she could get a job in the garment industry, but then who would take care of the children and right now she needed to be at home to nurse the twins until they could be weaned. And Michael would not start school until September. *'Oh God, what a horrible mess!'*

All of these thoughts raced through her mind as she sought to protest against what Antonio was saying. She felt as if the very walls of the room were closing in on her. She needed a valid argument against him but she could not think of anything. Antonio knew her well enough to read the expression on her face. He knew she was thinking it through just as he had. He waited until she had silently exhausted every alternative in her mind. She could see no alternatives. Her silence was surrender, although not agreement. Neither of them had to say it; they knew. The matter was settled in their eye contact. It was done.

'Now,' he thought, *'Now is the time to tell her that I want baby Antonio.'*

"Maria," he whispered, again taking her hands in his, "There is one more thing." He looked deeply into her eyes and a horrible sense of foreboding overcame her. She was filled with fear. She readied herself for what she was sure would be the final break between them.

She thought, *'He doesn't want me anymore!'* What else could it possibly be? She had thought of everything else. She had covered every contingency, she was sure. Nothing else needed to be discussed. She waited. She knew that something dreadful was about to happen.

206

"I hope that you and I can still share what we have had even though that does not seem likely, at least not for the foreseeable future. For now and maybe forever we cannot have each other as we have had. I know the thought is as painful for you as it is for me. We both know that out of everything we have between us, the one most important thing is our equal share in each other. We always treated each other as equals."

"But, my love, think for a minute. If something from what we have had together cannot be salvaged then I go home to a wife who hates me and to children whose love and respect for me is probably gone. You do not have Giovanni anymore and have not had him for many years even though I know you tried your best to make amends to him. He wanted something else in life, not you. So, in that respect you don't lose anything. You have Ralph and Michael as something from him and you have Josephine and the twins as something from us. Listen to what my heart is now saying to you, my dear love, my dear Maria. You will be left with something but I walk away with nothing and I walk to nothing. Do you understand what it is that I am saying to you?"

She began to grasp the magnitude of what he was saying. But there was nothing that she could do about it. Through all of their present trials she had been thinking only of the children and their love together. Fleetingly she thought of herself, but now, for the first time, she realized that she had not thought of Antonio apart from herself. Regardless of what they had together he was still an individual person and, like everyone else, to some extent, traveled through life alone. She thought, '*That is why we all need something, someone, while we are here.*'

"Oh Antonio, now you will be alone and I can do nothing."

He looked at her intently and squeezed her hands and whispered, "Yes there is Maria. You can do something for me that will make my loneliness bearable."

"What is it? Just tell me, my love, you know I will do anything for you."

He hated himself for having lured her into the trap. He always regretted not having Josephine as his own. It was an ache he felt every day. He didn't want to feel that way about little Antonio too.

In an almost inaudible voice he pleaded, "Maria, give Antonio to me. I want to take him home for my own. I want a son we had together."

Chapter XXVI

SEPARATION 1905

Did she hear correctly? Was this all a bad dream? What was he asking? Give up her child! She had already given up one to death but in that there had been no choice. God does what God does. She had never understood that but had come to accept it. But this was different. He was asking her to voluntarily give up one of her sons whom she had carried inside her for nine months and for whom she had suffered the pains of birth. How could Antonio think such a thing, let alone actually ask it? That was thoughtlessness and Antonio was not thoughtless. But then she was not thoughtless either.

Maria began to consider what he had said and slowly she came to understand why he had asked such a thing. It was true; Antonio would walk away with nothing. For the first time she felt pity for him, this tower of strength that she always leaned on for support. Now he was pleading, no, begging, for something that only she could give.

The thought of deliberately giving up a son was almost unbearable. He deserved to have something. Could she bring herself to help him in this way? Was her love for him stronger than her love for her child? It was also his child. She had to consider that. Her mind raced through all the objections and arguments. She found it too much to contemplate. She shook her head violently from side to side trying to drive away the mental pain. She began to sob uncontrollably, deep sobs, her chest heaving, and a choking feeling in her throat. She could say nothing. He felt remorse for the pain he had just inflicted on her. He was tempted to change his mind.

'No, not this time, I need to think of myself. Maria will have to realize that it is only fair to share the twins.'

The birth pain had been hers; he could do nothing about that. But that was over and now life had to go on. He wanted something from it all so he kept his silence as he watched her struggle through the anguish of having to make a choice and come to understand that what he was asking was just and fair.

Finally her face seemed to relax a little and she looked directly into his eyes. He was still sitting on the bed holding her hands.

"Oh Antonio! How can I say yes to such a request? How can I say no? The truth is that I cannot say either. You know what you are asking.

208

You know that what you ask is a knife piercing my heart. I know that you know. You have thought it through before you asked me, that is your way. I know you love me, dear Antonio. Never forget that, I know you love me. So my love, I do a terrible thing to you. I cannot keep Antonio from you and I cannot give him to you. It's not out of weakness that I don't choose and it's because I can't choose that I do a terrible thing to you. Forgive me, Antonio. You make the decision and I will abide by it."

It was the one reply that he had not anticipated. She was not sharing the choice. She was placing it all on him. As he reflected on her reply he understood. There was nothing else she could have said. In a way she was sharing her pain with him and his with her. They would both have to suffer from the decision he made.

It took a few moments before he replied and when he did he spoke slowly and deliberately. Still holding her hand he whispered, "Then I want him." He stood up and said, "I will make the arrangements as soon as I can."

She said nothing as her sobbing stopped. It was over, it was done and she thought, '*Oh God, help us all.*'

Giustina entered the apartment and walked into the bedroom. She had heard nothing of their conversation. She saw her friend lying in the bed and Antonio standing beside her. Antonio turned around and faced her. The look of disappointment on her face said it all to him. '*So Giustina will be the first friend I lose.*'

"Giustina, Maria has something to talk with you about. I have to leave now. There are arrangements I need to make. *Ciao.*" He walked through the kitchen, down the stairs, and out into the street.

*****

He went directly to the midwife's house. She answered the door and let him in. "Yes," she said in reply to Antonio's question, "I have contacted the woman and she has agreed to be hired as a wet-nurse. She will be at Maria's apartment whenever you want her to start."

"Well, actually she's to go to Maria's for a few weeks. Then I am bringing one of the babies to my house to live with me. After that she is to come to my house to feed him. I don't know the exact date. Do you think that will be a problem for her?"

She was not prepared for what Antonio had just told her. She had seen and experienced many things in her profession but even she had to admit to herself that this was a new one.

"Well," she said carefully, "I don't think it will be a problem as long as she will not have any difficulties with your wife." She said it with a trace of sarcasm in her voice but Antonio let it pass. He needed her help. He assured her that there would be no problems; he would take care of it.

"Will she also be willing to take care of the baby during the day?

"I think so, she has no other children, and I am sure she and her husband could use the money."

"That's fine and we will have to work something out for the night feedings. I'll let her know when the baby has been moved. In the meantime ask her to go to Maria's. Also, there is another matter I want you to do for me. We have named the baby that I am taking Antonio. Please make an official record of his birth and record me as the father and Maria as the mother and I want a copy of the birth certificate so make out two."

Again she was shocked and told herself that nothing in the world would ever shock her again. He paid her for her additional services and left for home. It was late and he realized that he hadn't eaten in twenty-four hours and he was hungry.

His apartment was dark. No one was in the kitchen or the parlor. The family was asleep. He poured a glass of wine for himself, cut a large wedge of cheese and then a thick slice of bread. He went back into the parlor, sat in the chair by the window, and began to eat. He shook his head at the irony of eating Giovanni's bread. The sadness of it all drove him to tears. He felt he could sink no lower; his self-esteem was gone. He had lost everything. But at least he would have Antonio. It would take a few weeks to be sure the baby could be moved safely, but he was sure that by the middle of May, little Antonio would be with him. When he finished eating he got up from the chair and washed. He lay down on the sofa and mercifully fell into a deep sleep from complete exhaustion.

He awoke at the sound of Joanna getting the children ready for church. He had forgotten all about mass. He didn't want to go and he was sure she did not want him to go either. Instead he decided to see Maria for just a little while. He wanted to return home before mass was over. He thought it might be an opportunity to spend some time with the children and help them understand what he was doing, that is, if he could.

Antonio took his time washing and shaving to give Joanna the opportunity to leave without him. She didn't even bother to ask him if he was going to church. As soon as Joanna and the children had left, without even stopping for breakfast, he went to see Maria. She was already awake and dressed and was sitting in bed, propped up by two large pillows. Ralph had taken Josephine and Michael to church and she was alone with the twins. He told her that he would not stay too long. "I wanted to see you and the boys, even for a little while."

He told her about the wet nurse. "She will be over some time this morning and you can work out a schedule with her. I will take Antonio when it is safe to do so."

Maria said nothing. He knew how much she was still hurting about giving up one of her sons and he felt heartbroken about it. Again he thought of changing his mind but he reasoned that it was the best arrangement for them. They would all have to adjust to it. He looked at the twins, and he asked which one was Antonio. Maria got up from the bed and with his help she shuffled over to the makeshift crib that held both babies. She leaned over one of them.

"This one," and she pointed to the one on the left. "I've dressed them in different clothes to tell them apart. They are unbelievably alike. As I told you, I've named the other boy Pasquale.

He felt a momentary twinge of guilt at the thought of separating them but he dismissed the thought as quickly as it had come. She said that she wanted to go into the kitchen so he put his arm around her waist to help her. Then he put his other arm around her and they embraced in a warm, gentle, loving kiss. They sat down at the table and talked a bit.

"Antonio, there is one thing I want done before you take Antonio. I want the twins to be baptized together. I want to ask Giustina and her husband if they will be godparents. Is that all right with you?"

"Of course, I would be proud to have them do that. Have you asked them yet?"

"No, not yet. I wanted to ask you first. Antonio, I think Giustina is angry with you, but I am sure it will pass; just give it time."

"I will, I would never do anything to break up your friendship with her and you can tell her that I would be most pleased it they will be godparents to our sons. There are no other people that I would want."

"Good, I am happy that you agree. We will not have a celebration, we will just let them take the babies to the church and return them home. After that, if everything goes well, you can take Antonio."

She burst into tears and he picked her up off the chair and held her close for a long while until she stopped crying. Then he let go of her and turned away, opened the door, and left for home. He left her standing in the middle of the kitchen. She felt her knees beginning to give way and she had to reach for the table for support. She started to cry again, uncontrollably.

'It's done,' she thought, *'It's over between us. No hope for any kind of relationship any more.'*

Again, as she shuffled back into the bedroom and got into bed, she thought of the children and how they would suffer. She sat upright against the pillows and looked over at the twins. It was then that the idea first entered her mind.

She mumbled half aloud, *'It's time to move out of the neighborhood. It's time to move on with my life, what's left of it. It's not going to defeat me, I will survive somehow; I will not be vanquished.'* She resolved to move her family as soon as possible.

*****

Antonio returned home just before Joanna and the children did. He was sitting in the parlor when they came in. Joanna went directly to the kitchen to prepare a light breakfast. They had fasted for communion and they were hungry. While they ate she began to prepare Sunday dinner. When they were finished with breakfast Francesco and Theresa went into their bedrooms without speaking to Antonio but little Grace came to him and sat on his lap. He feared that the problem with the older two might be beyond repair. He called to them and they obediently came into the parlor and stood before him. In the best manner he could muster he explained that they were going to have a new baby in the family.

"I know it will be difficult for you but I am asking you to try to accept him as your brother and make the situation as easy as possible. I know there might be some problems with the other children in school. Believe me, I am very, very sorry about that but if you just ignore them they will stop after a while. Will you do this for me?"

They nodded yes. But he knew that it was only an obedient acceptance of what Papa asked. When he was finished speaking to them they left the room and went back to their bedrooms. Joanna said nothing although she was able to hear every word that was spoken. When dinner was ready she called to them to come to the table.

It was the usual large Sunday dinner and what little conversation there was between Antonio and the children was strained. Joanna did not speak at all. When dinner was over she put a large bowl of fresh fruit and another filled with walnuts and almonds on the table. Normally there would be lively talk as they shared desert but today there was only quiet.

Finally, Frank summoned the courage to ask when their new brother was coming to live with them. "Probably in a few weeks," was all that Antonio could reply. Joanna shot a quick look at her husband.

Taking strength from Frank's courage, Theresa spoke for the first time. "What's his name?" Antonio looked at his daughter as the almost inaudible words came trembling from her mouth.

It hit him then what a blunder he made in naming the baby after himself. But he answered quietly, "Antonio. His name is Antonio."

Frank got up and left the table before Antonio could finish his sentence. He wanted to say that his first son was named in honor of cousin Francesco. He heard the door close as Frank left the apartment. Joanna glared at her husband in disbelief. He hadn't thought about the reaction that his first-born would have because he had named Maria's son after

212

himself. He realized that it was a thoughtless and insensitive thing for him to have done.

'Well, it was a stupid thing to do but it can't be undone. We will all have to make the best of it. I'm not going to change my mind! Antonio is mine and I want him for myself.'

*****

Maria roamed through the apartment as if in a stupor. The wet nurse came over just after Antonio left. The two of them nursed the twins. The boys were asleep by the time Ralph, Josephine, and Michael returned from church. She gave them some breakfast and began to prepare Sunday dinner. Ralph said he wasn't hungry and was going to his father's house and he left. He did not ask permission he just said he was going. Maria could do nothing about it. She was still feeling weak and it was an effort to work in the kitchen. But Josephine, acting the mother, helped. During dinner Maria told Josephine and Michael that one of their new brothers was going to live with Antonio.

"He's my father too, isn't he?"

"Yes he is."

Josephine didn't say anything more and four-year-old Michael, of course, couldn't even follow the conversation.

The wet nurse had left after the first feeding and she returned as Maria was cleaning up in the kitchen and gave her some help. They nursed the twins while Michael and Josephine were playing in the parlor. Maria lay down on the bed for a nap and cried herself to sleep. Ralph did not return home that night.

On Monday Josephine dressed herself and helped Michael to dress. She also fed herself and Michael. Maria got up and walked into the kitchen and marveled at how Josephine assumed some of her duties. For the first time Josephine walked to school alone. Her children were growing up and suddenly Maria felt old. Somehow she got through the day. The coming and going of the wet nurse helped to break up the monotony.

Antonio came to see her in the late afternoon. He told her what had happened at his house. She told him that Josephine had said, "He's my father too, isn't he?"

"Well," Maria said, "Now she knows."

"I'm sorry, but at the same time I am happy that she knows. I have come to love her very much. Promise me that you will not shut her out of my life."

"Yes, I promise, and you must do the same for me with little Antonio. I also want him and Pasquale to have a brother relationship. I don't know how we will do it but we must do it."

"Is he strong, our Antonio?"

"Yes, he is very healthy and strong, they both are. He nurses very well and cries very little. He is a happy and contented baby."

"If it is agreeable with you, let's call him Tony."

"That will be fine. I really don't like nicknames but Tony has a nice ring to it."

"If he is able, let's plan to move him right after the baptism. Have you talked about it with Giustina?"

"No, not yet, but I expect she will be coming over sometime today, I'll ask her then."

"Then, I'll leave now and see you sometime tomorrow." He kissed her on the mouth. In her heart she believed that it was a good-bye kiss. Then he was gone. Giustina arrived later and reluctantly agreed to be godmother to the twins. She said she was sure her husband would agree also.

"It will give the wagging tongues something else to cackle about, but don't you worry, you mean so much more to me than anyone else. When do you want to do it?"

"In about two or three weeks. I don't want a party or anything. Just the baptism, that's all."

"All right, I will make the arrangements with Father Joseph."

*****

Two weeks later, after the twelve o'clock mass, Giustina and her husband brought the twins to St. Lucy's and they were baptized. They brought them home immediately afterwards. The wet nurse was there and she took care of the boys. Maria insisted that they stay for some coffee and pastries. They ate in almost complete silence and left as soon as they could. Later that evening Antonio stopped by and she told him that the baptismal rite had been performed. They agreed that after work the next day Antonio would come and take Tony home with him.

She was sorry that she hadn't arranged the baptism sooner. She had become attached to the boy in just the little time she had with him. She deliberately made sure that she nursed him all the time while the nurse fed Pasquale. It was a stupid thing to do but she could not help herself knowing that soon he would be gone.

'Well. It will be all over tomorrow.'

After school the next day Josephine began playing mother and helped around the house. Maria was preparing Tony to be moved. She had bathed him and dressed him to go outside. She wrapped him in a blanket and waited. Antonio arrived on time. She had the baby ready and was holding him in her arms when he entered the apartment. She handed the baby to him. He gently kissed her on the cheek and started for the door.

They did not speak art all. She followed him as he left and she watched him from the open doorway as he started down the hall and then down the stairs.

When he was out of sight she rushed into the parlor and watched through the window as Antonio walked across the street. When he disappeared around the corner her knees gave way and she slumped into the chair. She began to sob, her chest heaving at each gasp of breath. She did not remember how long she was sitting there; everything was a blur. She came to her senses when she heard Josephine's voice.

"Mama, Pasquale is crying, I think he's hungry."

"Bring him to me, sweetheart."

Josephine did as she was told and handed Pasquale to her mother. When he was cradled in her arms she took out her breast, and there, sitting by the window, looking across at Antonio's window, and with Josephine watching in absolute wonderment, she began to nurse Pasquale. As she continued with the feeding her entire life seemed to pass through her mind.

'*Oh, Giovanni,*' she moaned, '*How you failed me!*' She looked down at the contented Pasquale. '*Well,*' she thought, '*This will be my life from now on, only my children.*'

*****

In a few more weeks her body returned to normal and she was able to tend to her family on her own. School closed for the summer and although Ralph was living with her, he spent his days working with his father. Josephine was an enormous help to Maria, especially watching over Michael.

For the first time since the twins were born, Maria ventured outside. Although she was a marked woman as far as the neighborhood was concerned, no one said anything to her. She pushed Pasquale in the carriage and did her usual shopping. When time permitted, she took the children to the park but always in the middle of the workday. She didn't want to run into Antonio. She didn't think she was ready to handle that emotional situation. But that meant she would not have the opportunity to see Tony. The paradox tore her apart.

A few months after the twins were born she expected that 'it' would arrive and when nothing happened for the next few months afterward she realized that she was going through menopause. She sailed right through the change without any complications.

'*So, now on top of everything else, I am also getting old. Soon no one will want me.*'

She half laughed and said out loud, "Well, 'it', you came early and you are leaving early and that's that. At least I can't get into trouble anymore."

*****

The children enjoyed the summer and the trips to the park filled their need to run wild in children's games. She was pleased to see that there were no enmities between her children and their playmates. Children forget quickly. The adults also tired of the scandal as a topic of daily conversation and went on to more current gossip. However, she was ignored in the neighborhood and only tolerated by the shopkeepers. She felt as though she were being shunned by society. At church, the congregation looked at her as if she had no right to be there.

In the fall, when the children were back in school, she would have more time and she planned to look for another place to live then. Michael would also start school and she would only have Pasquale to take care of for most of the day. Josephine was looking forward to the responsibility of bringing Michael to school, home for lunch, back to school and then home again when school let out for the day. Maria was always there for them whenever they were home. Ralph would be a freshman at Newark High School. He would go directly to the store after school and work there and on Saturdays as well. Giovanni properly compensated his son as if he were any other employee.

By September, Maria was able to spend most of her free time with Giustina and looking for a new place to live. Her letter writing had fallen off sharply. Some of her clients remained loyal but not very many. She thought that in a new neighborhood this work would pick up once more. Besides, she was going to need more room. She planned to start a seamstress business as soon as she moved and she would need a fitting room. She wanted to be free from the financial help she was getting from both Antonio and Giovanni.

Maria never saw Giovanni again after the twins were born but he did send money home with Ralph every week as he promised. Ralph also brought home some of the staples that she needed; bread, flour, eggs, sugar, along with some cake and pastries too. Antonio sent some money in an envelope each week by Giustina who did not want to be a messenger of this sort and only agreed to do it because she thought it was a good way to keep Maria and Antonio apart.

Maria was surprised by how well she was able to get along with this financial support. She felt a sense of guilt because she was even able to add a few more dollars each week to the little nest egg she had been accumulating in the bank downtown. It would help when she found another apartment. She dreamed of a new beginning, to be able to hold her head high once more. There were times when she still wished for the simpler life in Italy with Giovanni or wondered what life would have been like if

216

she had met Antonio first and married him. But these were fleeting thoughts now. All of that was over and she was optimistic about building a new life on what she had left over from the old one.

Her plans did not work out as quickly as she would have liked. The rest of 1905 slipped by and then also 1906 and still she lived on Seventh Avenue.

From time to time she did run into Antonio on the street. He implored her to bring the children to the park and promised that he would bring Tony. On rare occasions she agreed. She did not want to see him that way but she felt obligated to let him see Josephine and Pasquale and the truth was that she wanted to see Tony. It was a wonder that she never ran into Giovanni. She guessed that he was doing his best to avoid her and the truth was that she was doing the same.

Her life went on uneventfully until, that is, that day in November of 1907, when Giovanni was murdered.

Chapter XXVII

MARIO 1907

Rocco had been the head of the mob in the ward for many years by the time Giovanni started to work for him on a part-time basis, even before Maria immigrated to America. The altercation with Rocco had forced Giovanni and his family to flee from Newark. Rocco felt vindicated for having forced them out of Newark to, as he believed, Italy. His honor was restored and he continued to head the organization unrestrained for the next five years. Rocco had never married and his closest relative was his widowed sister who also lived in the ward. She had an only child, Mario, who worked for his uncle in the mob.

Mario was a huge man, standing almost six and a half feet tall and weighing about 250 pounds. Physically he was very powerful. He was completely uneducated and unfortunately had a limited degree of intelligence to help him offset his lack of education. However, he could follow orders and Rocco kept him on the payroll. Rocco paid him whatever he needed for himself and something extra for his mother. Consequently he was paid far more than his worth which led him to believe he was very important in the scheme of things. Mario was very loyal to his uncle.

During the time Giovanni acted as a collection agent for Rocco, there were times when some of the debtors could not or would not make timely payments. As instructed, Giovanni informed Rocco that he had not collected the payment. Whenever that happened, Rocco sent Mario out to see those who had defaulted on their loans. Mario usually resorted to physical assault even before he asked for payment. After Mario got through with them, they paid immediately and if they could not, they raised the money somehow or fled out of town. Mario was the ultimate enforcer for Rocco in the loansharking operation.

Whenever Mario was not making collections he just hung around the restaurant. People would greet him, but not because of what he was but because of his uncle's stature. He misconstrued this attention as being an act of respect. Nothing could be farther from the truth. In fact, Rocco himself referred to his nephew as 'the dummy' but always privately, never to his face. Whenever Mario's enforcement tactics were needed, Rocco would yell to him, "Mario, *vieni qui*! Come here!"

At that command Mario knew that he was going to get an assignment from his uncle and he would strut toward Rocco with his head held high, leaving the others, who had no assignment, at the bar or at a table. Such instances inflated Mario's sense of pride and he mistakenly thought that he was high on the list of those who worked for the mob. Over time he began to look on himself as Rocco's heir apparent. What a fool he was not to recognize his true status and that he was no more than a lackey for his uncle, looked upon with contempt by the members of the mob.

When Rocco was murdered by rivals within the organization Mario could not believe that he was passed over as head of the mob. By now they had become organized enough so that individuals were given titles to mark their ranking. Having never been given a title, he should have known where he stood. Still he was shocked when he was not made the new *capo* to replace his uncle.

Shock turned to bitter disappointment, then to anger, and finally to a plan of attack. He thought that he would be able to organize some of the mob and execute a coup and take over the organization. He confided his plans to his mother who had the good sense and influence to explain the circumstances to her son. She was able, with much cajoling, to talk him out of any overt action. But he never accepted the rebuff and his anger smoldered and festered inside him. He did not know who it was that murdered his uncle but he guessed it was the new *capo* or one of his henchmen. He promised himself that if he ever found out who it was he would avenge his uncle's death, which had cast him into the role of a nothing.

*****

Giovanni had all the intentions of building a new life for his family when they returned to Newark. After all, now he was a businessman. He had attained the dream that had started soon after he went to work for Luigi. Their apartment on Seventh Avenue was more than adequate and he had his Maria back. Ralph and Michael were his and he had come to look upon Josephine in the same way. His friendship with Antonio, while never the same as before, was nonetheless, more than just a business relationship. It was obvious that Luigi's successful business would continue on, not for any innovations on Giovanni's part, but because he followed to the letter what Luigi had taught him. Consequently he attained a certain status in the neighborhood and it served to further inflate his ego that had first begun to show itself after his success in Youngstown.

Some old friends from his Rocco days began to stop by to purchase bread or pastries and they would talk about the 'good old days'. Giovanni started to patronize the restaurant again and he found himself enjoying the male companionship in which he had once delighted. They were very cordial to him. Giovanni knew that Maria would not accept him going back with 'them' and he kept them at arms length for as long as he could, or more accurately, for as long as he wanted. But little by little he began to go back to his old ways but this time even more so.

He started to make investments with them especially to fund the 'bank' for crap games from which he was given his cut. The casualness of it progressed more and more and before he realized what was happening he became an outright member of the organization. He became 'connected'.

The underlings began to show deference to him and that only served to further feed his ego. He loved this show of respect. As ironical as it was, he in turn, liked showing respect to those who were higher up in the hierarchy than he was. It was a camaraderie that he reveled in, their mutual admiration society.

He argued with Maria about it and he so much as told her to mind her own business; that he would do as he pleased. After that it was no great leap for him when he began to indulge himself once again at the 'house' down by the river.

After Gia passed away and Giovanni refused to move his family to the apartment above the bakery, his marriage became as nothing to him. When the twins were born he moved out on Maria and went to live in the apartment on Eighth Avenue.

Next to his business and sexual indulgences, he spent all of his time with the mob. Now that he had some financial resources he was also able to fund some of the loansharking. While he never made loans directly he was nevertheless considered as part of the bank, and he took his small cut from the exorbitant interest they charged. Because of his prior experience as a collector for Rocco, Giovanni was given the responsibility of making collections and therefore became Mario's direct boss. The step from a passive bill collector to the boss of the enforcer was a logical advancement for him. When he became Mario's superior, some of Mario's resentment of the higher ups was focused on Giovanni.

There was nothing Mario could do about his lot so he just did as he was told and continued to brood over his position and how he had been cheated out of his legacy. Now and again he could not contain himself and he would vent his rage by making his feelings known to the lowest ranking members of the mob.

"You know, if I was running things guys like us would be getting a bigger cut," or, "How come we don't get invited to the big dinners? I would treat all the guys the same just like my uncle did," or, "My uncle really knew how to run things."

There was always some complaining among the lowest caste, 'soldiers' they were called. The higher ups just ignored such grumbling. They looked on Mario as a malcontent and didn't pay any attention to the 'dummy'. That treatment only made Mario angrier. Still, he was tolerated as long as he did not express his feelings in the wrong places and continued to rake in the payments from the deadbeats.

One time Mario talked about his poor treatment in the wrong place and in front of the wrong people. *Il capo* feared that if Mario's bad behavior continued, it might cause a problem. It was decided that he must be told to keep his mouth shut once and for all. Since Mario worked directly under Giovanni it fell to him to tell Mario to keep quiet or else. Giovanni said that he would take care of the matter.

Giovanni set up a private meeting with Mario. As soon as they met Giovanni began to berate him mercilessly. He started right out by yelling at him, calling him a dummy and a loudmouth.

"Mario, you are a jackass, you know that? Why do you keep talking about your uncle? He's dead. What's wrong with you? You stupid or what? And another thing, don't talk no more about your place in the organization. You're lucky you're still here at all. Let me tell you something. The only reason you're here is because you take care of the deadbeats real good. Now I'm only telling you once. You do as you're told and keep your big fat mouth shut, *capisce*? You know how I took care of your uncle? Yeah, well make sure the same thing don't happen to you!"

Of course Giovanni was referring to how he punched Rocco in the nose and broke his teeth so many years ago but Mario completely mistook the comment. What a colossal error it was for Giovanni to be so vague. In Mario's mind, not only did Giovanni seem to be a threat to his own life but also Mario now thought that Giovanni had identified himself as Rocco's killer. On both scores Mario was mistaken. But that didn't matter, it was the way he saw it. Now Mario was sure he had found out who had killed his uncle.

Mario thought, '*That dirty bastard, he came back from Italy and killed my uncle.*' He even convinced himself that Giovanni pretended to go back to Italy when all the time he was hiding out in Newark. With Rocco out of the way Giovanni could come out of hiding. Mario realized that there were a lot of gaps in his theory. '*So what,*' he thought, '*He killed my uncle. He told me he did it!*'

Mario promised Giovanni that he wouldn't talk about Rocco anymore. But, from that moment on he resolved to avenge his uncle's murder. He decided to kill Giovanni and at the same time remove what he perceived to be a threat to himself. Mario was just stupid enough to do it.

After their meeting, Mario started stalking Giovanni. Mario was regularly on the street making collections so it was easy to take time to be sure he knew what Giovanni's movements were, day and night. Soon he knew Giovanni's pattern of behavior. In the daytime he was always at the bakery and at night he was either at the restaurant or in his apartment. He was separated from his wife and lived alone. On the nights when there wasn't a meeting or a card game at his apartment, Giovanni usually had a woman with him and that meant that his son was not there. A rudimentary plan took shape in Mario's mind, and crude as it was, when he was ready he acted.

It was cold and raining very hard the first Wednesday night in November when Mario knew Giovanni had one of his lady friends in the apartment. He was willing to kill them both if he had to. After all she was only a *putana*, and a street whore at that. He waited in a doorway across the street from the bakery. His eyes were on the window of the apartment above. He shivered in the cold; his coat collar turned up around his neck and his hands, one clutching a pistol, in his pockets. He was waiting for the woman to leave or the light to go out which would mean that they were both sleeping. He waited a long time, his patience buoyed only by the hatred in his heart and his determination for revenge. It was past one o'clock in the morning.

Mario thought, '*Maybe they just left the gas light on.*' He decided not to wait any longer and just as he started to cross the street he saw the woman leave through the front door. He jumped back to his vantage point and waited to see what she was going to do. She opened an umbrella and walked away from him down Eighth Avenue toward Broad Street and the river.

'*Lucky for you,*' he thought. When she was out of sight he crossed the street and was ready to force his way into the building. But it was not necessary. She had left the front door unlocked. He walked in and quietly closed the door and locked it. He stepped stealthily up the stairs, two at a time, and tiptoed toward the door, ready to barge in shooting. The door was slightly ajar, another piece of good luck for Mario. He could see the flickering light from a gas lamp inside. As he reached the door, he could hear Giovanni snoring loudly.

'*Ha,*' he said to himself, '*The bastard's sleeping, he must have had a good time. Well, it's your last.*' He was familiar with the apartment. He had been there several times before. He entered and found a towel in the kitchen. He drew his pistol and wrapped the towel around it. He tiptoed into the bedroom.

He stood still for a moment looking across the room at Giovanni's naked body sprawled on the bed. Mario walked closer until he could almost touch him. For a moment he was tempted to rouse him. He wanted Giovanni to know why he was going to die and who was going to kill him. But even asleep, Giovanni looked menacing so Mario decided not to wake him. He just pointed the gun at Giovanni's temple, almost touching him with it, and squeezed the trigger.

222

Giovanni's head jerked up and he opened his eyes and gasped. Just for a second Mario thought that he hadn't done the job properly. He was just about to squeeze the trigger again when Giovanni's body sagged and he stopped moving. He had died instantly. The bullet never exited his head and there wasn't even any blood on the pillow. Mario had been so obsessed with killing Giovanni that he hadn't given a thought to what he would do afterwards. Now that it was done, he began to panic. In his agitated state of mind, he did things that no reasonable man would think he could get away with. It was his stupidity that drove him to act without thinking.

Mario picked up Giovanni's shoes and dropped them on his body. Then threw his clothes on top of the shoes and rolled the whole lot into a blanket. He tossed the load over his shoulder. He walked through the kitchen, extinguished the gas lamp, and carried the load down the stairs and out the back door of the bakery. Then he walked down the alleyway and peered out into the street, looking up and down Eighth Avenue. It was still raining very hard and the street was dark and deserted. He boldly walked down Eighth Avenue, crossed Broad Street, and continued down to the river all the while carrying what looked like a rolled up rug draped over his shoulder. It was only by luck that he was not spotted by anyone.

When he reached the river he walked out onto one of the piers extending from the bulkhead. When he got to the end he dumped Giovanni's naked body into the water. He wrapped the clothes and shoes in the blanket and took them home. There, over a period of days, he burned everything.

The body was found in a cove on Sandy Hook almost a year later. It was unidentifiable.

*****

The next morning was Thursday and Giovanni's employees began their work at five o'clock as always. While it was unusual for Giovanni not to be there when they started, it was not a complete surprise to them. It had happened before. They stoked the ovens and took the formed loaves from the proofer. They had already started baking when one of them went upstairs and knocked on the door to rouse Giovanni. The door was unlocked so he went inside calling out Giovanni's name. When there was no response he walked through the apartment. In the bedroom he saw the empty, unmade bed and assumed that Giovanni had gone off somewhere. He didn't have time to look for his boss. He returned to the ovens and the men continued with their work.

Right on schedule, Antonio's wagons pulled up and the drivers loaded the day's order. One of the workmen accepted payment for the previous order and put the money in a drawer in the back of the store. Then they stocked the shelves in the store with the day's baked goods. By now it was time to open the store and still there was no sign of Giovanni. One of them stayed in the store to serve the retail trade while the others started to prepare for the next day and bank the fire.

Ralph was sixteen now and was attending Barringer High School up on Ridge Street across from the uncompleted cathedral. The school was originally called Newark High School when it was built in 1899 but just recently it had been renamed in honor of one of the city's educators. Ralph usually went directly to the store after school, walking over Clifton Avenue and then down Eighth.

Ten year-old Josephine attended Seventh Avenue School. She was in the fifth grade. Six-year old Michael went to the same school. She always waited for him and took him home to Mama and Pasquale.

Today was no different. Ralph took over in the store so the staff could finish up at the ovens and get ready for Friday. Ralph had never worked the store alone before; his father always came up from the basement to check that he was doing OK. He was confident he could do the job without any supervision. When the day was finished he locked up the store and before he headed home, he went up to his father's apartment. Seeing nothing amiss save for the unmade bed, he locked the door and went home to his mother. He took the cash left by Antonio's driver and the day's receipts home with him and put them in the back of one of his dresser draws. He had the good business sense to leave a little cash at the bakery for the next day. He said nothing to his mother about his father's absence. They had never discussed Giovanni after he moved out.

On Friday there was still no Giovanni and the same routine was repeated. On Saturday Ralph went to the store early in the morning. This time, at the end of the day, he locked up everything for the weekend. Again he took the receipts home with him and put them with the other money in his dresser drawer. Again he said nothing to his mother. On Monday the employees realized that no one had been in the building since they closed up on Saturday. Since Giovanni didn't have anyone to account to, his disappearance had not been noticed by anyone except the hired help. When Ralph came in from school they told him. Giovanni had been missing for five days! That had never happened before. When Ralph went home he told his mother that no one had seen his father since last Wednesday. He told Maria about all the money he had hidden in his dresser. She was incredulous and became frightened. Maria saw no sense in berating the boy for not having told her sooner; it would serve no purpose.

"Ralph, stay here and watch the children. I'm going out to see what I can find out. I won't be long. Just be sure to stay home and don't let any of the children out. Please, just do as I say."

She walked as quickly as she could, almost running, to the stables where Antonio rented the horses down on Clay Street. She was hoping against hope that he would still be there. She met him on the street as he was leaving the stables to go home. He was startled to see her and he became apprehensive as he realized that it was not just a chance meeting.

"Antonio, have you seen Giovanni?"

"No. Frankly I've been avoiding him as much as possible. Why, what's wrong?"

Maria told him what Ralph had told her. "It's just not like him to disappear like that for five days let alone not tell the help or even Ralph."

The look on Antonio's face frightened Maria even more.

He said, "Go home and take care of the children. Don't let them out. I'll see what I can do to find him. I'll come by later and tell you what I find out."

She did as he suggested. Antonio went directly to the bakery and tried all the doors. They were all locked. No one answered his knocking or calling out. He knew where one of the workers lived so he went to the man's house.

"It's true," the man told Antonio. "We haven't seen or heard from him since we closed up on Wednesday. We didn't even get paid on Saturday."

"OK, I'll take care of that. You continue working as usual and I'll try to find Giovanni. If I can't find him I will come to the bakery tomorrow when my wagons arrive. I'll pay you then."

The first place that occurred to Antonio to look was the 'house' by the river. He thought that there was a slight chance that Giovanni was there or at least had been. He knew where the house was, everyone did. Reluctantly he knocked on the door hoping that no one would see him. He did not want to go in and when a woman opened the door he just stood there and asked to speak to the person in charge. The last thing he wanted was for people to think that he frequented the place. The woman said that she owned the house. He told her that he was a friend of Giovanni and asked if he had been there.

"If you're such a friend how come you don't know where he is?" She wasn't about to say anything to strangers about any of her guests. She had to protect their privacy after all.

"It's just that he has been missing for a few days and I was wondering if maybe you've seen him recently."

She certainly did not want to get mixed up in any missing person problem so she told him the truth, more for her own protection than to help Antonio.

"I haven't seen him for months. You know he has two places, one for his wife, and one for his women. He doesn't need my services anymore."

Antonio didn't know if he should believe her or not. But then again, it didn't make any sense for Giovanni to stay here for five days.

It occurred to Antonio that only a few people were aware of Giovanni's absence, the men at the bakery, Ralph, Maria, and himself. He thought of his own employees. To whom did they make payment?

Antonio almost ran to the house of one of them. He told his employee that Giovanni had not been at the store for the past few days and wanted to know to whom he had made payment. The wagon driver said he gave the cash to one of the bakers. Rushing back to the baker's house again, Antonio questioned him about the money. Thinking that Antonio was accusing him of stealing, he said, "I gave it all to Ralph, every day, all of it. Go ask him yourself if you don't believe me."

"I'm sorry, I didn't mean anything by that, I'm just trying to find Giovanni. I'll come to the store with your wages tomorrow. In the meantime, if Giovanni shows up, please tell him to contact his wife." That was when Antonio began to fear for the worst. Repeating his instructions for the men to continue working as usual at the ovens and the store, he left and went to see Maria.

She had a sense of foreboding as soon as she let him in. She could see the worry on his face. By now the children had eaten supper and were in the parlor. Ralph was studying and the others were playing. Maria and Antonio sat at the kitchen table and in a hushed voice he explained what he had done and that he could not find Giovanni anywhere or anyone who had seen him in the past few days. He said that he didn't want to go to the restaurant and make inquiries so there was a remote possibility that he was there. If not, maybe the people at the restaurant might know where he is but he doubted that very much.

"Maria, no one has seen him since last Wednesday, no one. I have looked all over." He emphasized his explanation in such a way to be sure she understood that he had also checked at the 'house' down by the river.

"What do you make of it?"

"I don't know except to tell you that I don't think his absence is voluntary. After all, his business is unsupervised; supplies and materials must be ordered. Almost a week's deposits have not been made and the help have not been paid. By the way, you will have to pay them tomorrow, I promised. Better still, give the money to me and I will do it the first thing in the morning to keep them from becoming more upset. Maria, I have to tell you that I fear for the worst. Those animals he associates with; who knows what they might do if sufficiently provoked?

"Should we call the police?"

"No, I don't think so, not yet. Maria, I think you must be prepared for the fact that he has been killed. If that is so then it would be best to say nothing. No on else will say anything, they will be too frightened. We should wait it out and see what happens."

She let out a deep breath. "I knew that something would happen to him some day. I warned him, but he wouldn't listen. I felt it would all come to a bad end that time I wrote the letter for that young girl, remember? Her husband got beat up and we wondered if it was Giovanni or that other hoodlum, Mario."

Maria marveled at her reaction. She was calm, no emotion at all. She felt nothing. "Oh Antonio, what's wrong with me? I feel nothing for Giovanni. I'm sorry if he is dead, but aside from that I feel nothing."

"Listen Maria, you should not feel guilty about this. He left your life long ago."

"What do you think I should do now?"

Antonio's mind was already racing, thinking of a plan of action. He started talking even as the plan took shape in his mind.

"Listen, I'll go to the bakery tomorrow morning and explain to the men that Giovanni is missing. You send the children off to school and then see if you can get Giustina to care for Pasquale, or better still, get a sitter if you can. You are going to need one for a long time if Giovanni doesn't show up. Then come to the store as soon as possible and be prepared to work there for the day. I'll also explain to my men that Giovanni is missing and that I'll be spending some time at the bakery to help you out. When I leave here, I'll go home and tell Joanna. Be assured, by tomorrow night the entire ward will know that he is missing and the rumors will begin to fly."

"If the police ever get involved then let it be a report from someone else, not from you. If they don't get involved by a week from now, only then go to them and report Giovanni missing. Just tell the truth - that you and he are separated and you were not sure if he went away for a few days."

"I will make arrangements to supervise the bakery for part of the day and you will have to make arrangements with the sitter so that you can spend as much time at the store as possible. I will order the needed supplies and Ralph can relieve you as soon as school is out. If Giovanni does not show up in a few more days, and I don't think he will, then we can make further, more permanent arrangements. There is really nothing else we can do but wait and see what happens. Maria, these are dangerous men, let's not provoke them. If they are responsible for Giovanni's death, assuming that he is dead, then let's wait before we make any permanent decisions."

Maria relied on him and she listened carefully as he spoke. He always came up with a well-thought-out course of action whenever a crisis developed, and he did it with lightening speed. It was Antonio's way. She knew in her heart that Giovanni must be dead.

Maria said, "All right, let's do as you suggest, but now I think that you should leave and not come back here again. I will see you at the store tomorrow."

He agreed and left. After he was gone, Maria called to Ralph and asked him to sit at the kitchen table. Josephine followed him but Maria asked her to go back to the parlor and keep Michael and Pasquale occupied.

"Ralph," she began, "I must be honest with you. Your father is missing and we cannot find him. No one has seen him since Wednesday. I am frightened for him and I am doing all I can to find him. If I can't find him soon I am going to go to the police and report him missing."

Ralph just stared at her. He was becoming frightened and she could see it in his eyes. For the first time in a long time she reached out to him and he came into her arms. *'Oh my God,'* she thought as she held him tightly, *'It has been so long since he needed me and now he is mine again.'* Her eyes filled at the sheer pleasure of holding him, her first born. He started to pull away and she released him.

"What are you going to do?"

She saw her opportunity and she clutched at it. "Ralph, I need you now. Josephine and Michael and Pasquale need you. Even your father needs you. You have to be strong for us. You must take on some responsibilities, more than you should at your age. I want you to go to school. After school you must go to the store. I will be working there when you arrive. Then I will come home to care for the children. You will have to lock up every night. Antonio is helping all he can." She held up her hand as a gesture for him to say nothing. "Oh yes, I know you don't like him, but he is our friend. He is my friend and I need him, we need him. He is going to help at the ovens during the morning baking time but he has his own business and can't spend too much time helping us."

"You must be one of the grownups now. Between the three of us we will have to manage the bakery somehow, for a while. Will you do it? Will you help me and the younger children?" She was very deliberate to not include him among the younger children. If she was going to rely on him as a man then she was going to treat him like a man.

For a moment Ralph just looked at her and then suddenly embraced her, "You can depend on me, Mama, I'll do whatever you want."

"Ralph, I love you as my first son. Always remember that."

"I love you too, Mama." He called her Mama for the first time since Youngstown. It was a sweet pain that shot through her.

*****

With a few minor variations, everything went according to plan. After another week of Giovanni's absence, it was decided that Maria should go to the police since they apparently were not involving themselves. They also made sure the news that the police had been informed was circulated throughout the ward. Still no one came forward and soon it was generally assumed that Giovanni had been killed and buried somewhere by 'them'. It happened from time to time. Everyone knew that it was the way the mob handled its internal problems. As long as it did not affect them, the great majority of the neighborhood just shrugged their shoulders and went on with their lives. Little did they know that even the organization wondered what had become of Giovanni. Eventually the mystery of Giovanni's disappearance became old hat and talk about it subsided. People had their own affairs to contend with and new gossip replaced the old. As far as Mario was concerned he had the good sense to say nothing and in time he left Newark to go only God knew where. No one ever missed him.

The police did nothing other than file the paperwork. Ultimately the entire incident was buried in the history of the ward.

*****

Both Maria and Antonio knew that they could not manage the bakery indefinitely. Some permanent plan would have to be worked out, and soon. They talked about it each day as she came to the store and he was getting ready to leave. One day, about a month after Giovanni disappeared, and after Antonio had left for the day, a man entered the store and introduced himself to Maria. He said his name was Aldo and that he came from Kearny, across the Passaic River from Newark. He said he heard that the bakery was for sale.

"How did you get that idea?" Maria wanted to know.

"I just heard that your husband passed away and that you might be interested in selling the business. I have some friends downtown in Newark and they know that I am employed as a baker in Kearny and that I am looking to have my own shop somewhere. One of them mentioned your shop. Is it true, is it for sale?"

Maria was intrigued. For some reason in her discussions with Antonio the idea of a sale had not come up. They were thinking more in the vein of hiring a manager. She ran the idea through her head quickly.

"It is possible that we are considering selling but there is someone else who might be interested too." She was thinking of Antonio. "Would you be so kind as to return late tomorrow afternoon so that I might have time to think about your proposal?"

He agreed and left just as Ralph arrived from school. On her way home she was so preoccupied with the idea of selling that before she realized it she was entering her apartment. She released the baby sitter, kissed Josephine and Michael, and spoke with them as she went into the bedroom to fetch Pasquale. She sat down on the floor and started to play with him all the while thinking of what a sale would mean to her and her family. For the first time in a long time she was thinking something through without advice from Antonio.

It struck her as being very odd that she would do such a thing. She had only done that with Giovanni. She thought of him now and realized that he was just someone she had known once. She had no feelings; he was someone she had once loved. The old Italian saying flashed through her mind, *L'amore fa passare il tempo; Il tempo fa passare l'amore,* love makes time pass; time makes love pass. She was sorry that he was dead but life was for the living and she had responsibilities.

Her thoughts turned to Antonio. How did she feel toward him? She knew that she still loved him very much. Their love had not been diminished by their troubles. What's more, she admired him, respected him, and marveled at his intelligence. None of that had changed either. What had changed was the possibility of ever being with him again. In her heart she knew that she wanted to be with him and would go to him if ever she could. That old Italian saying did not apply to them. But for now, being together was impossible. She would have to plan her life without him and that was the deepest hurt of all.

The more she thought of it the more she felt that a sale was the best possible solution to her present dilemma. Would Antonio want to buy the bakery? In the end she resolved to tell Antonio that she was thinking about selling out and about Aldo's visit. Maria wanted to offer it to Antonio first. If she sold the business, she decided it would have to be with the building. She could accept a down payment and take back a mortgage. That would give her an income and maybe enough to buy a small house somewhere so she could move out of the neighborhood. It suddenly dawned on her that the bakery's bank account was still in her name as well as Giovanni's. He had never changed it. She smiled as she realized that he probably never thought about it either. That's how much business sense he had. Thank God he had been such a marvelous baker.

Maria didn't know how much money was in the bank. She made a mental note to check Giovanni's papers the next day. She knew that the bakery and the building on Eighth Avenue were free and clear thanks to Gia's legacy. The more she thought of the whole idea, the more appealing it became. If she moved out of the neighborhood she could enroll the children in a different school and solve the problems that she knew they were having with their classmates. It would also lessen the tension between

Antonio and his wife if she were gone. Of course he would have to agree that she could see Tony from time to time and that he must be told that she was his mother when the time came. Yes, the idea was becoming very attractive to her.

She felt like her old self again, in control of her fate. She continued to run through the details and possibilities all through dinner and while getting the children ready for bed.

When the apartment was quiet, she sat alone in the parlor going over and over in her mind what she would say to Antonio. Finally she made the decision. *'Yes, a sale is what I will do, either to Antonio or to Aldo or to someone else if need be.'* She went to bed, and for the first time since Giovanni had disappeared, she fell into a deep untroubled sleep.

Chapter XXVIII

A DREAM GONE 1907

The next day, when Maria arrived at the store, she told Antonio about Aldo's unexpected visit. She was surprised when Antonio told her that he too had come to the conclusion that she should sell. She was surprised because he had never mentioned it.

"Maria, I considered offering to buy the bakery myself. But I don't want that responsibility. I couldn't get up at four every morning to supervise the baking in addition to my delivery business. I just want to expand what I have. I have been saving as much as I can to buy a truck and I don't have any extra cash."

"I understand, Antonio. There is no need to explain. So what do you think, should I sell to this man?"

"If he is qualified and capable I think you should. My one concern is that he maintains the quality for which the bakery is noted. We must be sure that everything stays up to old Luigi's standards. Not just for myself, but if you take back a mortgage we want the business to remain successful. I think a buyer would be foolish to change a successful business."

They decided she should sell to Aldo if a deal could be worked out.

"Antonio, would you handle the negotiations for me and make the arrangement for the sale?"

"Of course I will, you know I will do anything for you." There in the back room of the store he took her in his arms and they kissed those passionate kisses as before. Reluctantly she pushed him away.

"No, Antonio, no. I still love you but no, at least not now, and not here."

He seized the opportunity to tell her that all this time he had continued to rent the room on Ogden Street. She was neither surprised nor indignant. He decided to bring the matter to a head right then and there.

"Should I cancel the room? Yes or no?" he demanded, but his eyes, those beautiful blue eyes, were begging her to say 'no'.

She whispered to him, "No my love, keep it, but for now we will not use it."

He sighed in relief and kissed her on the cheek. "I'll return later this afternoon. It would be best if you stayed until Aldo gets here. You'll have to tell him I have the authority to negotiate for you. Then you can go home and leave us to talk." She agreed and Antonio left waving good-bye.

"*Ciao*," they said to each other.

When Ralph came to the bakery from school she told him that Antonio was going to meet with someone and that it was all right for them to use the back room. He was a little annoyed about it but said nothing. She sensed his reaction and said, "It will be all right. Please do this for me."

She had no sooner finished speaking with Ralph when Aldo and Antonio arrived almost simultaneously. Ralph remained in the store and Maria, Antonio, and Aldo went into the back room. She told Aldo that she was willing to sell if the price and conditions were right.

"This is my friend, Antonio. I have every confidence in him. He is going to handle the sale for me. I hope that we can get together on an agreement." She smiled at him. She looked at Antonio and with a nod of her head she left the two of them in the back room and she walked into the store. She gave Ralph a reassuring kiss on the cheek and said, "I'll see you at dinner."

*****

Aldo proved to be an intelligent businessman even though this would be his first venture. He had been a baker for many years in Kearny and Antonio was impressed with his knowledge of the trade. Antonio took an instant liking to him and hoped that they could reach an agreement.

"I don't want to change anything. The sale would have to include all the recipes and the names of all the suppliers." Antonio felt relieved and any doubts he had over a sale to Aldo disappeared.

"I'm glad to hear you say that. As I told you, I will be your largest customer and I don't want anything to change either. If we can agree on the price I promise to spend some time with you helping you get the hang of things."

The deal was struck. Antonio was able to obtain a good price for Maria especially since she was willing to accept a reasonable down payment and take back a mortgage. Aldo said he would make the necessary arrangements with his lawyer and if all went well the sale could be consummated within one or two weeks.

The next day Antonio told Maria that an agreement had been reached. He suggested that she should continue with the present schedule for staffing the store.

"You can depend on me to help down at the ovens until Aldo takes over."

He wanted to take her in his arms once more but decided against it. He would wait until a time when she agreed to meet him at Ogden Street.

After Antonio left, it came to her that she must tell Ralph what she was going to do. After all, the business belonged to his father and Ralph worked at the store faithfully after school and on Saturdays. She didn't know if he expected the bakery to be his one day. She decided to tell him that night after dinner. She would have to use all of her tact and handle the explanation just right. It would be awful if he found out from neighborhood talk or even worse for her to tell him after the sale was completed.

After dinner she and Ralph had a long talk. He had never shared his aspirations and dreams with her and she didn't know what to expect. She blamed herself for that and wondered if he ever spoke with his father about what he wanted to do with his life. It upset her that in spite of all her troubles she had never taken the time to talk with him. She was being very hard on herself. After all, Ralph had shut her out of his life after she had told him about Antonio. Nonetheless, she suddenly felt a strong sense of remorse.

"Ralph, I'm going to sell the bakery. I can't manage it and neither can you. Besides you must finish school. I am so sorry if you thought it would be yours someday."

"Mama, why do you say that? I don't want to be working in the store all my life. I only went to work there because I liked to be with Papa."

"Oh Ralph, I'm so relieved. Tell me what you want to do when you finish school."

"I want to get into the automobile business. There's going to be a place for good mechanics and that is what I want to do. Maybe I will even have my own garage someday. The car industry is really growing. If you sell the store I'm going to try to get a job in a garage on Saturdays."

She was amazed at his ability to think so far into the future. She had not shared anything with him since she had told him about Josephine and she realized how much she had missed. *'My God, he's not quite seventeen and he's thought it all out!'* She vowed that she would take an interest in his future and support him in any way she could. It was evident that he had accepted the fact that his father was probably dead. He was coping with the loss very well. He had been closer to Giovanni than any of them in the past few years.

*****

The contract was signed and Aldo purchased the bakery and the building just before Christmas of 1907. Giovanni's dream was gone forever, just like he was. Maria just shrugged it off. Neither the bakery nor Giovanni had meant anything to her for a long time. She deposited the down payment in her bank account downtown and also transferred the cash from the bakery account. Her cash reserve would be more than sufficient for her to buy a small house somewhere. Her living expenses would be covered for the term of the mortgage that she took back from Aldo. In fact there would be a small surplus that she would be able to save.

'We won't live in grand style but we will be comfortable and secure.'

Maria planned to rebuild her clientele as *La Scrittore* after she relocated. She was also thinking of starting a seamstress business on her own or working part-time in the garment industry. The future was beginning to look bright.

*****

One day soon after the 1908 New Year's Day Holiday, Antonio waited for Maria as she left her house with Pasquale to go food shopping. Since she no longer needed to go to the bakery anymore, they had not seen each other for a while. He called to her in a casual way from across the street and walked over to her. He commented on how big Pasquale was getting. He told her that young Tony was growing just as fast and that looking at Pasquale was almost the same as looking at Tony. They exchanged pleasantries there on the street; passersby did not even notice them. As he tipped his hat goodbye and said, *"Ciao,"* he whispered a time and date.

She said nothing and began fussing over Pasquale as if looking for an excuse to delay a reply. She was embarrassed and her face showed it with a mild blush. He remained silent, not taking his eyes off her. They made eye contact and, looking into those deep blue eyes, she nodded a silent, 'Yes'. She took Pasquale by the hand and walked away without saying good-bye.

The tryst was as passionate and intimate as before. Nothing had diminished. Afterward, lying side by side in bed, their conversation was centered on the twins. She wanted to know all about Tony and he wanted to know about Pasquale. The twins would be three years old in April. They traded stories about the boys almost as if they were separate parents bragging about their children. They decided to meet in the park with the twins from time to time.

"But we will have to be careful," he said. "Ever since Tony was weaned from the wet nurse, Joanna has been grudgingly taking care of him and I'm afraid that if she knew I was bringing him to see you, she might refuse to do it any longer. That was why I haven't been pressing you for meetings in the park before."

"Then be very careful. Don't do anything to jeopardize how things are."

"I will. I'll try to take Tony for a walk on Sunday in the park while everyone is at mass. If neither of us can make it, it will be all right, we'll just make it another time."

She agreed but made it very clear that meetings that way must be very infrequent and for just a short time. She did not want to establish a pattern that might be noticed.

Once more they made love. Then she got up and began to dress. He could not take his eyes off her.

"My God," he exclaimed, "The mother of six children and you still look like a virgin."

It pleased her that he got such pleasure just looking at her body. She smiled but said nothing as she finished dressing. It was amazing that she still did not wear any makeup. Then she blew him a kiss and with a cheerful, "*Ciao*," was out the door. He waited a while. Then he dressed, made the bed and left.

That Sunday, as promised, they both took the boys to the park. It was the first time since their baptism that the twins were together.

"Maria, it is not good for them to grow up not knowing each other."

"Yes, Antonio, you are right. We must make sure that we find a way to let them become friends."

"Maria, we must do more than that. When they are old enough we should tell them that they are brothers."

"I agree. We will have to wait for the proper time. It will be difficult but we must do it"

Until that time came they agreed to meet with the boys somehow, somewhere, even if on a very limited basis. They each loved the twin they were raising but had a strong desire to see the other. The twins bore a remarkable resemblance to each other. They were also very much alike in temperament and behavior. Seeing one was almost like seeing the other. As time passed the boys seemed to recognize each other as playmates.

Sporadically, Antonio and Maria met at Ogden Street. As usual, whenever they were together they never set a date to meet again. They always relied on chance meetings on the street to prearrange another rendezvous. They passed each other often because they practically lived across the street from each other. They did not mention Ogden Street every time they encountered each other but when they did, it was a spontaneity that only added to the passion they shared. They were content with the arrangement and resigned themselves that this would be their life, clutching at what little time they could manage for themselves. It was a marvel that their love remained as strong as ever under these circumstances. Even apart they shared a life together.

*****

Antonio was doing everything he could to reestablish a relationship with his children. He often wrote to Emmanuella in Italy and after a while she began writing back to him. She had grown to be a young lady and now, in 1908, she was twenty-four and married. Antonio and Joanna were grandparents.

Frank was twenty, Theresa was eighteen, Grace was eight, and Tony was three.

Antonio spent as much time as he could with all of them. He tried to get Joanna to join them but she would not join in if Tony were included. She refused to lend any legitimacy between her children and the boy. Tony's presence was a constant reminder of her husband's infidelity. It only reinforced her self-image as a martyr. She cared for the child but in a loveless way, like a hired nanny. Tony reacted in kind. He loved Antonio and tolerated Joanna. He called Antonio 'Papa' but never referred to her by any name.

Frank was still upset that he was not his father's namesake, that this interloper had stolen his birthright. Grace was less antagonistic toward Tony but nonetheless there was no sibling bond between them either. Theresa hated Tony and her father; she was like her mother in that regard, only more so.

It was a stressful environment that Antonio was not able to smooth over. They were walking on eggs all the time. But he loved all his children and refused to give up on any of them.

Antonio tried to cater to Joanna as much as he could but there was no response from her at all. She didn't even argue with him anymore. She treated him like a boarder.

*****

Another Christmas passed and 1909 had almost arrived. Ralph was eighteen and would be graduated from Barringer High School in June. Josephine was twelve, and showed signs of growing into a beautiful woman, just like her mother. Michael was eight and still a joy to the family. He had a special personality that lit up a room when he walked in. Everyone loved Michael. Pasquale was three going on four. Josephine doted on him constantly. The family had grown closer after Giovanni's death and the children idolized Maria. She was content. Things were going well for them.

The only cloud in their lives was that occasionally the neighborhood bullies called the children names. Maria's solution to this problem was to redouble her efforts to find a house and move from the area. She had the means to do it and so she resumed her house hunting in her spare time.

Antonio had advised her to buy a multiple family house, preferably a four family house; the income would help her. But she did not want that responsibility. Maria had known too many years of trouble being a landlord.

*****

The day after Christmas, after the children were asleep, she bathed and put on her nightclothes and then sat in the parlor reading a book. She dozed off with the book still in her lap. Suddenly she felt someone shaking her arm and tugging at her nightgown.

"What is it?" she had no idea what time it was, "What's wrong?"

It was Michael. "Mama, I don't feel good, and my throat hurts."

Chapter XXIX

FEVER 1908

Maria felt Michael's forehead with the back of her hand. '*My god, he's burning.*' He was sweating and his pajamas were soaked. She brought him into the kitchen and wiped his face with a wet cloth. She took his pajama top off and began to wipe down his back and chest with cool water. She tried to give him some water to drink but he could not swallow it. He began to cry. She carried him back to his bed and got him to lie down. She had been through many childhood illnesses with fevers but this time Michael's appearance frightened her.

She checked on Ralph; he was cool and sleeping normally. She woke him and told him to dress and run for the doctor. She went into Josephine and Pasquale's room. Josephine was cool and she was breathing normally also. She went over to Pasquale; he was burning with fever. Josephine woke up and wanted to know what was happening. Maria told her that everything was all right and for her to go back to sleep. But that was impossible. She watched her mother go back and forth between Pasquale and Michael.

"Josephine, go wet some towels with cold water and bring them to me." Pasquale was awake now and was crying very hard. Michael was still crying. Again she tried to get him to drink some water but he could not swallow.

Ralph came running back into the bedroom. "I got the doctor, he's coming right away." 'Right away' seemed an eternity instead of the half hour that it was.

Maria was holding Pasquale trying to comfort him when the doctor arrived. Ralph let the doctor in and Maria brought him into Michael. He started to examine Michael.

"Where does it hurt?"

"My head hurts and I feel like I'm going to vomit. The light hurts my eyes and my neck is sore."

"Try to touch your chest with your chin," the doctor told him but Michael could not do it. He said his neck hurt too much. The doctor examined the rest of his body and noticed a reddish, purple rash beginning to appear. He went on with his questions, which were accompanied by all the usual medical scrutinizing of the mouth, the eyes, the pulse, and the feet. Then he took Pasquale from Maria's arms. The baby was crying and flailing his arms and legs. It was difficult for the doctor to make an examination but he continued, ignoring the child's cries and squirming. The doctor noticed the same symptoms on the baby that he did with Michael. Next he called Josephine and began to examine her and then Ralph.

'Why is he examining them?' Maria wondered, *'They aren't sick.'*

He told Josephine to get dressed and to wait in the hall with Ralph. They looked at Maria for guidance and she told them to do as the doctor said. The doctor resumed his examination, first Michael, then Pasquale, then Michael again. When Ralph and Josephine were out the door the doctor turned to Maria.

"*Signora,* I think the boys have meningitis. This is the fifth case I have seen in the neighborhood. Your two older children seem to be fine. The disease is very contagious so it is best for them not to be here. I will treat the sick children. We must watch them very closely and try to keep them as cool as possible. I will have to notify the Board Of Health. They will quarantine the apartment, maybe the entire building, so it's best that your two oldest children are not here. It is for their protection. Do you have a place where they can spend the night?"

She thought of Giustina and went to the door to open it. The doctor stopped her, "No," he said," Talk to them through the door."

"Ralph," she hollered, "Take Josephine and go to Giustina's. Tell her what has happened and ask her if you can spend the night there. I will come for you tomorrow."

The doctor was packing his bag. "There is nothing more I can do for them now. Continue to keep them as cool as possible and get some liquid into them as soon as you can. I will have some medicine sent to you and some rubbing alcohol too. Keep the room darkened, pull down the shades and cover the sides and keep the door closed. Their eyes will be very sensitive to light. The Board of Health will be here tomorrow." The doctor went to the sink and scrubbed his hands with yellow laundry soap and then rinsed them with some alcohol before he left.

Maria spent the rest of the night doing her best to comfort the boys. The fever raged on and with each passing hour she became more and more frightened. They showed no sign of improvement. They cried incessantly. She had done as the doctor had ordered and darkened the room. Without any light, she lost all sense of time and she was startled to hear a knock on the door. When she went into the kitchen she realized that it was daylight.

She went to the door and called out, "Who is it?" She muttered, "Thank God," as she heard Giustina,s voice, say, "What has happened? Are you all right?"

Maria would not let her into the apartment and instead told her through the door all that had happened. Maria told her that there was nothing else

240

that she could do except care for Ralph and Josephine. Giustina promised to stop by during the day to check on her. While they were talking the delivery boy arrived with the medicine.

"I'll pay the delivery boy."

"Thank you, leave the medicine on the floor by the door. When you are gone I will get it."

"OK, it's by the door. I'll wait down the hall for a few minutes. Let me know when you have given the medicine to them."

After getting the medicine she went back into the bedroom. Michael was still whimpering but Pasquale was quiet. *'Thank God he went to sleep.'* She went back into the kitchen and got a spoon to give the medicine to Michael but she had difficulty getting him to swallow it.

"Michael, just wet your lips with the medicine and then lick it off."

It took a while but she felt confident that he swallowed some of it although he still complained that his throat hurt. She decided that she would have to wake Pasquale and use the same tactic with him. She bent over him and gently shook him. He did not respond so she shook again. Still no response and it was then that she realized that he was dead.

Her scream was near hysteria and alerted Giustina who ran back towards the door. Maria picked up Pasquale and cradled him in her arms and without thinking ran out of the apartment almost colliding with Giustina in the hallway.

"He's dead, he's dead! No! No, he's dead!"

Giustina pushed Maria back into the apartment and without any regard for herself went right in behind her. Maria was still hysterical and screaming. Giustina tried to take Pasquale from her but she would not let go of him. It was all she could do to quiet Maria. By now some of the neighbors had come to the door. Giustina told one of them what happened and asked if she would summon the doctor. This time the doctor was there in a few minutes.

Maria let him take Pasquale from her arms, expecting a miracle. There was no miracle. The doctor confirmed that the boy had died. When death comes it comes quickly. Maria was beside herself. The doctor carried the baby's body into the parlor and placed it on the sofa. Then he came back into the bedroom and removed the sheet from Pasquale's bed. He walked back to the parlor and covered the body. Giustina remained with Maria, half consoling her, half restraining her. Michael was still whimpering in his bedroom, almost delirious with fever.

"Stay with her," the doctor instructed Giustina, "I will make the arrangements." He left and went to Michele's funeral parlor on Garside Street. Giustina was holding Maria to her breast. They were both crying inconsolably, rocking back and forth together.

In Maria's hysteria she cried to Giustina, "First Augusta and now Pasquale. God hates me for what I have done! He hates me, I know it!"

Giustina said nothing; she just held her dear friend tightly. Maria was exhausted. Giustina tried to guide her into her bedroom to lie down but Maria resisted. She took Maria by the shoulders and looked straight into her eyes.

"Maria! Maria! We have to be strong to take care of Michael. Come lie down. I will stay with you, I promise. Think of Michael."

She shook Maria to get her back to her senses. Giustina guided her into her bedroom and helped her lie down on the bed. She took Maria's shoes off and put a light coverlet over her and sat on the edge of the bed holding her friend's hand. Nothing was said.

In about an hour they heard the apartment door open and footsteps in the kitchen and parlor. The doctor had returned with Michele. The doctor signed the death certificate and handed it to the funeral director. Michele picked up the lifeless body and said to the doctor, "Oh that poor woman. This is the second child I have had to take away from her."

He carried Pasquale's body down the stairs to the waiting hearse parked in front of the building. By now some of the neighbors had congregated in the street near the front door. They were shaking their heads and making the sign of the cross, forehead to chest, left shoulder to right. Death came often to the ward but when it was a child they all mourned the loss.

Maria and Giustina heard the footsteps from the parlor and the sound of the apartment door opening and closing. More footsteps as the doctor came into Maria's bedroom to check on her.

She screamed at him, "Oh my God, you're taking my baby away from me."

He sat on the edge of the bed. "I'm so sorry, dear Maria, but we have to move him as soon as possible due to the nature of the illness. There's no other option. I'm so sorry."

He patted Maria's hand and said he was going to check on Michael. When he was finished with his examination he went back to them.

"There's no change with your other son but I don't think he is any worse either. Keep up with the medicine and keep the room dark. Try to get as much liquid into him as possible. There is the danger of dehydration"

He looked at Giustina, "You know you should not be here. It's not safe." He knew even before he finished his sentence that she would remain anyway.

"As long as you are here, probably it would be best to stay. No sense in exposing your own children. Lock the door behind me and don't let anyone in. I'll get word to your husband and then I'll return later tonight."

242

Late in the morning the Board of Health inspector arrived. He was dressed in a black suit and wore a round, black cap with a visor. He had a silver badge over his left breast pocket. He looked more like a train conductor than a city official. He tacked the dreaded red quarantine poster on the front door of the apartment building. Then he signed it and dated it. It served to forbid anyone except the doctor from entering or leaving the building.

Antonio was unaware of what was going on. He went to work as usual and was on his way home when he saw a small gathering of people in front of Maria' apartment building. Out of curiosity he walked over to see what was going on. He nudged the person next to him.

"What's going on?"

"Haven't you heard yet? Maria's house is infected with the meningitis and the building is quarantined. One child is very ill and the youngest boy is dead. The undertaker's already been here. Hey, where are you going?"

Antonio was pushing his way through the small crowd. Someone who knew him stopped him.

"Antonio, you can't go in there. It's the meningitis. It's quarantined! You'll bring the germs back to your own house."

He stopped in his tracks. He turned and walked across the street toward his house, tears rolling down his cheeks. He was about to enter the front door when he hesitated. Instead, he turned around and walked up to Garside Street to Michele's Funeral Parlor. He thought, '*He was my son and I am the one who should make the arrangements.*'

*****

"Antonio, the burial should take place immediately with no viewing since the disease is so contagious."

"All right, Michele, you have my permission to do whatever you must do. I'll tell Maria what we have done."

Michele shook his head, "Oh that poor woman, *che peccato*, what a shame! She has lost two children and could not go to the funeral and burial of either one."

Antonio went back to Maria's house. As he approached the building he saw one of the neighbors at a window on the third floor. He motioned to her to open the window. He asked her if she would call for Maria. In a few minutes Giustina called to him from the window of Maria's parlor.

"Antonio, what a tragedy. I can't believe it."

"How is Maria doing, is she all right? Is there anything I can do?"

"She's sleeping just now, the doctor gave her something and I don't want to wake her. She has been through so much. I'm taking care of her and helping with Michael. He is very sick too but he seems to be holding his own. The doctor thinks he will be OK in a few days."

"I made arrangements with Michele. We have to bury Pasquale right away. I gave my permission. Tell her I'm having him put next to Augusta."

She asked if he would stop by her house to tell her husband that she was confined to Maria's house. "Please come back and tell me how the children are."

"I'll go over right now," he called back to her. It was about all they could say to each other in that public forum.

It fell to Giustina to tell her dear friend that Antonio had already made the burial arrangements and that she would not see Pasquale ever again. Strong as she was, it was almost too much for her to bear as she went into the bedroom to inflict more pain on her friend. She didn't want to do it. But she felt that Maria was her friend and who else was there who could tell her. Maria had awakened and wanted to know to whom she was talking from the window. With loving tenderness and compassion she told Maria what Antonio had done and why he had to do it that way. Again they held each other tightly and cried together.

The doctor returned that evening. He examined Michael and said that he was stable and thought that the fever would break in a day or two. "He is a strong boy. Just continue with the medicine and continue as you have been doing. I'll stop by tomorrow when I make my rounds." Both Michael and Maria fell asleep soon after the doctor left.

Giustina walked into the parlor, sat near the window, and stared out into space. She reviewed in her mind the troubles her friend had endured. First it was her father's death, then her mother's, then Augusta and the trouble with Giovanni. Then Antonio came into her life and the two of them managed to put a death curse on their respective marriages. Now Pasquale was dead and Antonio had Tony. She could not understand why one life was so filled with adversity and another life seemed to be so trouble free. Not only could she not understand it but her own good fortune frightened her.

'Strange,' she thought. 'My life has been so orderly and without any difficulties and Maria has had nothing but trouble. Who makes these decisions that one must suffer and not another?'

While these thoughts were racing through her mind she fell asleep, sitting up in the chair.

*****

Giustina had been born in 1865, the same year as Maria. She was born in Calabritto, in the province of Avellino in the region of Campania. She

244

emigrated from her hometown with her mother and father during the turmoil of the fight for the unification of Italy. Her father, like Maria's, was a supporter of the Vatican. But he was not so much opposed to the unification, as he was opposed to stripping the Pope of the Papal Territories. He did not mind that the Pope's temporal authority would be lost but he felt that the Vatican should still retain ownership of the land. Realizing that his political values were being destroyed he decided to take his wife and only daughter to the New World where men were free. They left for America in late 1869 just before the unification became a *fait accompli* for Italy. They settled in Newark, in the small Italian part of the first ward, surrounded by Irish immigrants. Giustina was only four years old when they arrived.

Because she was so young when her parents immigrated she grew up thoroughly americanized. In fact she acted as interpreter for her parents as they assimilated into the American culture. She was educated in American schools and was graduated from high school in 1879.

She married an Italian immigrant when she was twenty and by the time she met Maria, she was already the mother of two boys. Her husband started out as a day laborer in the construction industry and over the years worked his way up to a foreman's job. They were comfortable and lived a quiet life. Although his education did not match hers, that difference between them was never an obstacle to their good marriage. In her case opposites did attract. He respected her mental capacity and she admired him as a husband and provider. It was a true love match.

Soon after Maria arrived from Italy the two met and became fast friends and it wasn't long before they became inseparable. But throughout their friendship it was always Maria who needed help, never Giustina. Giustina never knew any trouble, but Maria seemed stalked by tribulation.

Giustina always felt guilty about her lot in life whenever she compared it to Maria's. And now her friend was in trouble again and Giustina was by her side as always.

When Maria first told Giustina about her affair with Antonio, she was appalled. Everything she had been taught as a Catholic and in her upbringing demanded that she conduct herself with the highest morality. But Maria was her best friend. She had other friends but Maria was different. She was smart, confident, and independent even when she was devoted to Giovanni. She always kept her sense of self. She admired Maria and saw a lot of similarities to her own personality. That was why she remained so loyal to her friend. Also, deep down inside she knew that their situations could have easily been reversed. With a feeling of gratitude she thought, *'There but for the grace of God go I.'*

*****

For three more days the two of them cared for Michael as the doctor had instructed. Little by little they were able to get him to take some liquids and get more medicine into his body. They constantly applied rubbing alcohol over his body to keep him cool. On the morning of the fifth day of his illness Maria woke and went into Michaels darkened room. She felt his forehead with the back of her hand. Still a fever but there was no doubt that he was cooler. "Thank God," she muttered to herself.

She shuffled out through the kitchen and into the parlor. Her moving about woke Giustina who was sleeping on the sofa. They looked at one another and their eyes said all that was needed. One son was dead and the other alive. Why? Neither of them could find the answer.

They went into the kitchen and washed and Maria started to prepare something for them to eat. Coffee and a little bread was all that either of them wanted. Maria sat in stony silence sipping the hot coffee.

"What's wrong with me, Giustina? I can't cry anymore. There are no tears left. Thank God Tony was not here and was spared the sickness. Six children and only four of them left and I only have three of them. And you, dear friend, you always stood by me. Giustina, I tell it to you now, if it had not been for you for all these years I don't think I could have survived."

They went in to Michael and this time they managed to get some soup into him although it was still difficult for him to swallow. But at least he kept it down. That was a good sign. Giustina's husband came by and they talked, he on the street and she from the window. Antonio had been stopping by every day on his way home from work to talk to Maria a little in the same way. Later that evening the doctor paid a visit. He examined Michael and breathed a sigh of relief.

"His temperature is almost normal. I think he will sleep well. If he is cool tomorrow you can get him up for a little while but be careful, he is going to be weak so don't let him overdo it. Try to let him sit up in the parlor so he can look out the window, it will cheer him up and keep him still and quiet. Feed him whatever he will take but nothing too heavy. I will notify the Board of Health so they can take the quarantine poster down."

Later when they looked in on Michael he was sleeping and his breathing was normal. His forehead was cool to the touch.

Maria was the first one up the next morning and she looked in on Michael. He was cool and still sleeping peacefully. Giustina awoke and they made breakfast and decided to have coffee in the parlor. It was a clear sunny day and the room was bright and cheerful. They talked a while and were interrupted by Michael calling. Maria went in to ask him how he was feeling.

246

"I'm hungry," he said. She breathed a deep sigh of thanksgiving. She knew that he was well again.

Giustina came into the room and said, "How would you like to have breakfast in the parlor and look out the window, it's a beautiful day?" She picked Michael up and carried him into the parlor. Maria followed with a pillow and some blankets to keep him warm. They settled him in the big chair by the window and wrapped the blankets around him being sure to cover up his feet.

"You just sit here and Mama will get something for you to eat, maybe some hot oatmeal and a cup of hot chocolate. You'll like that, won't you?"

Maria and Giustina started for the kitchen but then they stopped, as if frozen, when Michael said, "Mama, why is it so dark in here?"

Chapter XXX

DARKNESS 1909

Maria and Michael were sitting side by side on a bench in the eye doctor's office. Her family doctor had recommended him to her. He was a German ophthalmologist and was highly regarded in his profession. She had no knowledge of German so the framed testimonials hanging on the walls were unintelligible to her. However, one she recognized as probably being a university diploma indicated that he was educated in Hamburg. She felt a little more at ease because German doctors had very good reputations, if you could afford them. His office was on Bank Street in downtown Newark between Broad Street and Halsey Street, easily reached by trolley. But they did not take the trolley, they road in a taxi and now they were sitting in the waiting room.

The doctor's nurse, who also substituted as his secretary, began to open a case file for Michael. Maria explained to the nurse that they had been referred by their family physician and she handed her a note that he had written. The nurse asked them to wait while she read it. Maria was very impressed with her professionalism especially when she asked for personal statistics on both Maria and Michael. Usually doctors took care of everything themselves or when necessary their wives did some of the paper work. But for the most part, the only records they had of patients were those that they kept in their heads.

Doctors were usually neighbors of their patients and in many cases close friends or relatives. They conducted their practice out of their homes using the front room as an office and examination room. If the doctor was busy with a patient others would have to wait in the hall or foyer until they were called. Mostly they had a limited, neighborhood practice and never hesitated to make house calls, day or night, good or bad weather, whenever the situation warranted it. An office visit cost fifty cents and a house call fetched seventy-five cents. If you could, you paid cash on the spot, if not, then the charge was put on account. Many of the credit accounts were never paid.

But this doctor had a large waiting room and a private office with a separate examination room. It was obvious that his residence was located somewhere else, '*Probably up in the Forest Hill section of Newark,*' she imagined. Maria wondered how much the fee would be. '*C'entra, it did not matter.'* She would pay everything she had as long as Michael was able to see.

'*Oh please let him see!'* she prayed, over and over as she waited. As Maria prayed she thought of the terrible events of the past week and of this morning when they first suspected that Michael might be blind. She made a special prayer to St. Lucy, the patron saint for people with eye afflictions.

*****

'*Mama, why is it so dark in here.'* Those words still rang in her ears. She could not forget the fear and anxiety that overwhelmed her when she heard them. Giustina had been by her side in the kitchen doorway and had clutched her arm so tightly that it hurt. Simultaneously they had rushed to Michael's side.

Maria knelt on the floor in front of him and looked at his eyes, Giustina, standing next to her, was bending over to look at him. They saw an expressionless stare on his face. His eyes were pointed straight ahead with large, round dilated pupils. He did not focus his eyes on either of them. He just appeared to be looking, wide eyed, at the window.

It was Giustina who first waved her open hand back and forth in front of his face. There was no reaction, just that expressionless stare.

"Oh no," moaned Maria. She was still kneeling in front of Michael and she sank back on her heels.

"Mama. Where are you?" he asked. There was no reply from either of them. Giustina was the first to regain her composure.

"I'll go for the doctor," she exclaimed and she ran out the door, down the steps, and out into the street.

Maria remained kneeling on the floor, staring incredulously at her son. She could not believe what was happening.

'*It's all a temporary condition, it will pass, just like the fever.'*

In her mind she went over and over all of the possibilities her layman's knowledge of medicine permitted in order to explain what was happening.

The family's doctor rushed into the parlor followed by Giustina. Without a word to Maria he moved her out of the way and looked down at Michael. He began to examine the underside of his eyelids. He asked for a candle. He lit the candle and held it in front of Michael, slowly moving it closer to his face, then back again, then side to side. He did it several times. Michael's pupils did not change in size nor did his eyes move. There was no reaction to the intensity or direction of the light. The boy was not focusing.

There was no doubt. Michael could not see anything. The doctor straightened upright and shook his head from side to side. All this time Michael kept asking to have the gaslight turned up so he could see. The doctor took Maria by the arm and led her into the kitchen. Giustina stood in the doorway watching Michael and listening to what the doctor was saying to Maria.

"*Signora*, right now your son can't see. I have heard of this condition after meningitis but I have never seen it myself. I have no experience with this complication. As far as the fever is concerned, it is gone. There is nothing else I can do. You must take the boy to an eye specialist as soon as possible, today, now! I know of an excellent doctor. I will write a note to him explaining what has happened. His office is not far from here. I suggest that you dress the boy and take him there immediately."

Maria handed the doctor some stationery that she used for her letter writing. He sat down at the kitchen table and began to write. She quickly dressed Michael as Giustina ran down the stairs to look for someone to drive them downtown. She knew that there was usually a taxi waiting in front of Rocco's old restaurant a few blocks away. Thankfully it was there and she directed the driver to Maria's apartment. The taxi pulled up just as Maria came out the front door carrying Michael. Maria put her son in the car with help from the driver. She gave Giustina a look of gratitude. The doctor handed the note to Maria and he gave the driver directions to the eye doctor's office.

The taxi sped away down Seventh Avenue towards Broad Street. The doctor and Giustina, both shocked and stunned, watched the taxi until it was out of sight.

It took only about fifteen minutes to reach Bank Street and now Maria and Michael were waiting for their turn to see the doctor. Michael was sitting on her lap and she had her arms around him. Since they had left the apartment Michael had not uttered a word. Maria looked at him intently.

'*What can be going through his mind?*' she was thinking to herself, '*By now he must realize he can't see.*'

She was afraid to talk to him for fear of saying the wrong thing. She sat there holding him tightly, and they waited. When the nurse called to her she tried to pick Michael up but he would not let her. He stood up, clung to her arm, and walked where she walked. '*Oh St. Lucy. Help us!*'

The nurse handed the note to the doctor and he read it very carefully. He was a stout man, impeccably dressed, with a white smock covering his upper body. He looked almost comical with a reflecting mirror mounted on his head. He had a goatee which he stroked as he read. His manner was very calculating and his speech was deliberate, almost abrupt, with a thick, heavy, German accent. Yet he was very gentle with Maria and especially so with Michael.

The examination took some time. Maria was close by sitting on a stool off to one side. She watched the doctor's every move, looking for a smile, anything to give her hope, but it never came. The doctor said nothing nor did his demeanor reveal what he was thinking.

When he was finished he took Maria by the arm and guided her into his private office adjoining the examination room. The nurse stayed with Michael who was unaware that his mother had left the room. The doctor motioned Maria into a chair in front of his desk as he sat down behind it. His facial expression was very somber. He looked at her and she began to flood him with questions. He was amazed at her almost complete lack of accent. Her vocabulary was such that he quickly determined that he was dealing with an educated and highly intelligent woman.

'*Good,*' he thought to himself, '*I will be able to talk with her.*' Maria waited for him to speak and she steeled herself for the worst.

"Madam," he began. "Sometimes when there is a high and prolonged fever such as meningitis, the central nervous system can be affected adversely. We don't know why this is so or even if it will happen in a given case. We do know that with meningitis there is a swelling of the meninges, the lining between the skull and the brain, and sometimes the brain itself becomes swollen. The skull is not pliable so sometimes the pressure causes damage to parts of the brain. Unfortunately this is what has occurred with your son. The part of the brain that has become damaged is the part that controls the sense of sight. The damage can be slight or total. There is no regeneration of destroyed brain tissue and the damage cannot be corrected and is irreversible. Madam, I am sorry to have to tell you that your son is blind and will be for the rest of his life. There is nothing that can be done." The ophthalmologist waited to observe her reaction, ready to render aid if it was needed.

Maria sat motionless as the information sunk into her consciousness. Suddenly she felt numb. The doctor waited patiently, saying nothing. When she began to speak he knew that she had not quite accepted the bad news. He anticipated what she was going to ask and he spoke before she did.

"Madam, in your pain I know you are grasping at any straw but believe me there are none to grasp. The condition is permanent. I am so sorry."

Again he waited until he felt that the full impact of what he had told her had run its course. She slumped in the chair as her face gave away her complete resignation to Michael's condition. She shuddered at her total helplessness and lack of control. Her pain increased as she came to the realization that it was Michael who would be the one to suffer the most. That beautiful, intelligent, cheerful boy who was loved by everyone; what would become of him now? He had only turned seven last March, he hadn't even started to live and already his life was over.

'*Why didn't he die with Pasquale?*' She hated herself for having that thought. She fought back tears brought on by guilt, remorse, and anger.

The doctor was watching her very closely. It was not the first time he had given such terrible news to a loving parent. When he thought she had run the gamut of emotions he started to speak once more, slowly and deliberately.

"Madam, there is something else you must think of now that you have accepted the awful truth of your son's blindness. It is the extreme change that will take place in his personality. He is going to have to accept his condition, young as he is. He will become angry and his anger will erupt into violent behavior, to you and to the world. He will not find any answer to why this tragedy happened to him, mainly because there is no answer."

"You will have to watch him carefully so that he does not harm himself. You will have to be prepared for him to take his anger out on you and tell you that he hates you. You are the closest to him and you will be the object of the anger and hatred born out of his frustration. It will be so because you are the one who will have to tell him that he will never see again. I would tell him but in the long run it will be better if it came from you. You will be the proverbial messenger bearing the bad news and for a while he will hate you for it."

She attempted to speak but he held up his hand and said, "No. No. Don't say anything just yet. Just listen to what I am telling you. The terrible anger will happen, be assured of that. And it is worse when blindness comes to people who were able to see at one time. Being forewarned of the traumatic change will help in some way for you to cope, not only for yourself, but also for your son. Do you have other family?"

She nodded, "Yes. I have another son and a daughter, I am a widow." She was going to add that there was another son but she did not; what purpose would it serve? It would not help Michael.

"Then," he continued, "They must be warned. They must be prepared to see a marked change in Michael's attitude toward them. You must explain to them that when they are abused by Michael it is the blindness talking, not him. Be sure that they completely understand the situation. They must not fight back. They must suppress any feelings of sibling rivalry. Anything else will only make matters worse. It will not be easy, I assure you, but you must all cooperate."

"It is not necessary to bring Michael back to see me. If you should want to come back to talk with me please feel free to do so and bring Michael if you wish."

"One other most important matter. Michael's normal education will now be interrupted. But that need not be. In fact, it must not be. Along with the usual education he will be in desperate need of special education. Take this business card. It is for an organization that specializes in caring and teaching juveniles who are blind, even babies. It is called The International Sunshine Society. The society has its headquarters in New York

252

City, but they have recently opened a boarding school here in Summit, New Jersey. I strongly urge you to contact them. The sooner Michael comes under their supervision the easier it will be to help him, not that it will ever be easy. Do it, Madame. It is the best help you can give your son even though it will mean sending him away, but it is not far from Newark. If you cannot afford it then I think there is a New Jersey State program that will aid you. The school will be able to help you out in that regard. Here, take the card, and don't let a day pass until you contact them. Will you do it?'

She said that she would and he rose to his feet indicating that he was finished. As he escorted her to the door and out to the waiting room he thought, *'What a remarkable woman. It is a shame that she must suffer through this heartache.'*

*****

It was Antonio who made the arrangements for Michael to be enrolled in the Arthur Home of the International Sunshine Society in Summit, about fifteen miles away from Newark.

Antonio had recently purchased his first delivery truck. He had only been using it for two weeks and it had already helped him in his business. He was able to make his deliveries much faster and as it turned out it was less expensive to operate than renting a horse and wagon, especially since he was able to park in front of his apartment building for free. He still needed to rent one horse and wagon, but only for half a day. He wanted a second truck but he could not afford it just yet. He was very proud of his accomplishment and wanted to drive the truck himself although he insisted that both of his deliverymen learn how to drive. Because of this more efficient delivery system, Antonio found he had more free time in the afternoon.

The day after Maria's visit to the eye doctor, Antonio drove alone out to Summit and made the arrangements for Michael. There were only three other students in the school. They were young girls. The facility was small but Antonio was impressed, especially with the staff.

After returning to Newark, he advised Maria to do as the eye doctor had suggested and send Michael to the school immediately. Reluctantly, she agreed. So, on the next Sunday morning, Maria found herself riding in the front seat of the new truck, with Antonio driving, and Michael sitting on her lap. All of Michael's clothes and belongings were in the back of the truck.

Maria was quiet during the drive. She was thinking of her situation. *'Now,'* she thought, *'I am going to lose my third child. Now I will be the one who will be alone.'*

Ralph had been graduated from high school and was working as an apprentice mechanic in a garage on High Street near Summer Avenue. He worked six days a week and came home to wash, change his clothes, and eat dinner. Then, very often, he was off, out into the night with his friends.

Josephine was a joy to be with but she was growing up too and soon would follow Ralph into the world. The young girls nowadays did not stay home for long. They got married very young and some of them even went off to live on their own. For better or for worse times were changing. The old generation was giving way to the new. The changes were an irresistible force and there was no immovable object to stop them. The thought of being alone weighed heavily on Maria's mind.

Then suddenly, like a flash of light, an idea took hold of her mind. She wanted Tony back.

Chapter XXXI

TONY 1909

Saying good-bye to Michael was a heart wrenching memory that remained with Maria for the rest of her life. Antonio parked the truck in the driveway of the school and they each took one of Michael's hands. They guided him up the path, then up the steps to the porch. In the little time since he had become blind he rarely allowed anyone to carry him. They had to guide him with verbal instructions.

"Michael, there are three steps...Michael, there is a doorway ...Michael, there is a chair in front of you."

He refused to allow Maria to be indulgent with him. He would not let his mother carry him or try to comfort him. She cringed at every rebuff but at the same time was heartened by his show of independence. He was going to need it, and early on she did all she could to encourage him. Every time he tried to do something on his own her instinct was to rush to help him. It was very difficult for her to restrain herself. She would watch him and clasp her head in her hands to help keep her from interfering. It could have gone the other way; he could have become dependent on her for everything.

After Antonio's first visit to The Arthur Home she told Michael that he was going to a special school where the teachers could help him. She was very careful not to give him any hope of ever seeing again. She tried to have him understand that they could teach him things that she could not.

He had been very quiet all during the drive to the school but as they went through the double front doors he became unwilling to cooperate and started to create a disturbance. She was having difficulty calming him down. One moment he was screaming that he would not stay at the school. Then he yelled that he hated her. Then he begged her to take him home. He started kicking and flailing his arms. Antonio had to help restrain him. He finally quieted down and allowed Maria to put her arms around him and hold him tight. She almost changed her mind about letting him stay. It was only Antonio's support that enabled her to resist the temptation to bring him back home.

*****

The International Sunshine Society was founded in 1903. Its mission statement was to provide education and training for blind babies. Its first facility was at Dyker Heights at 48th Street and 13th Avenue in Brooklyn, New York. Although it was a privately owned entity, the school was partially funded by the State of New York and tuition was free to New York State residents. In January 1909 the society opened a facility in Summit, New Jersey on Pine Grove Avenue not far from the railroad station. It was called The Arthur Home and it was situated on four and a half acres. The property had previously been a farm and contained a cottage as well as some outbuildings. The land was a private gift to the society. The school had been in operation for a short time when a large stone and brick building had been erected. The school had a capacity to handle forty students.

*****

Antonio had been informed that the tuition was not free as it was in New York. He was told that Maria could make application to the State Commissioner of Charities for financial assistance. He took the papers for Maria to apply for aid. He informed the school staff that in the interim he would meet any expenses.

He explained Michael's history to the staff. They said that they would accept him immediately and the sooner the better. They wanted to have a strong hand in helping Michael develop positive attitudes before he had a chance to develop negative ones on his own. Antonio agreed and he took it upon himself to enroll Michael right then and there. He knew that Maria would concur as soon as he described the school to her and recommended that Michael be enrolled there.

The eye doctor had been correct in predicting Michael's personality change. When Maria told Michael that he could never see again he flew into a rage. He began to call her names that she did not even know he knew. He told her that he hated her and was glad that he was blind so that he would never have to see her again. Through it all she stood erect with her hands over her ears trying to block out his bitter and cutting ravings. She said nothing. She felt as though she was tied to a post and being flailed by a stinging lash at his every word. She bore it as a penance. With each invective he hurled at her she whispered, "God forgive me."

He had become aggressive and abusive and began to have temper tantrums. Ralph and Josephine, forewarned as they were, would leave the room or the apartment whenever he started. It was incredulous that such behavior could come from her happy, mild-mannered and loving son. She did not think he would ever be able to cope with his affliction.

'*Pray God they can help him at The Arthur Home.*'

In addition to all of her other emotions, guilt feelings had been added whenever she thought that it would have been better if God had taken him along with Pasquale. She hated herself for thinking that he would have suffered less, but the thought was invasive and came to her of its own accord.

Her heart told her not to bring him to the school, to keep him home where she could smother him with love and affection. Her mind told her that in the long run that would be a mistake. Michael needed the kind of help she was not trained to give. Being a motherly teacher came as naturally as giving birth but this was different.

*****

The time for the dreaded separation had come. Michael was quiet now. While they waited in the foyer she looked at Antonio for reassurance. Maria promised Michael that she would come to see him every Sunday. As she made the promise, Antonio nodded yes. Then realizing that the boy could not see him he said, "Yes, Michael, I will bring Mama to see you every Sunday, I promise."

Their promises seemed to help a little but not much and not for long. When the staff came in, Maria had to force herself to let them take him from her arms. They reassured her that it was the best thing she could do for her son.

"In time you will be amazed at what we can do for Michael. For now it will be better if you just leave immediately and not prolong the parting."

Maria and Antonio turned to leave while the staff led Michael down the hall. Michael started screaming again, "Mama, don't leave me here. Mama! Mama! I'm sorry, I didn't mean it." She would have run after him but Antonio restrained her and when they could no longer hear him they left.

Maria was silent all the way home. Antonio let her be and said nothing. When they got to her building she got out of the truck but Antonio did not. She looked at him and thanked him profusely for all that he had done.

There was an awkward moment and she whispered, "Antonio, I need to see you at Ogden Street." They decided on a day and time and he drove off.

It was so strange because all he did was drive across the street turn the corner onto Wood Street and park the truck in front of his tenement building. She stood in front of her building and could just about see him get out of the truck. She knew that Ralph and Josephine were playing up at the park. It was almost ludicrous that now she was going to go up to her empty flat and Antonio was going up to his to be with her son. The absurdity of the moment only served to reinforce her resolve to get Tony back. She made up her mind that when they met at Ogden Street they would do nothing else except talk about it. But that is not what happened.

Maria was waiting for him. As soon as he entered the room they were in each other's arms and their passionate lovemaking was as always. Afterward, lying close to each other, her head on his chest, she asked him how things were at his house. He told her the truth. They never kept anything from each other. Joanna was the same, brooding and reproachful. There were times when he thought she might be able to forgive and forget but they were few and far between and nothing ever came of them.

Frank was tolerant of Tony but winced every time he heard his father call the boy by name. Long ago Antonio had admitted to himself that he should never have named the boy after himself. It was a mistake and it made Frank feel that he had taken second place in his father's affections. Theresa was very bitter toward her father and Tony. She barely acknowledged their presence. While she was never disrespectful toward her father her aloofness made him aware that he had completely lost her. Grace was too young to fully understand but he feared that as she grew older, she would follow her siblings.

"It is not a happy household," he confessed to Maria. "The tension and stress are always present and coping is not easy for any of us. But I will not give up trying."

Neither of them had been in a happy household for a long time and they had longed for this quiet time together. They didn't recognize what should have been obvious to them. They were deeply in love, it was true, but their time together was quality time without the naggings of running a home and taking care of a family. While they were together they had only themselves. Among the mainstays of their relationship were these short times together when they could shut out the world and its troubles. But that was not reality and they deluded themselves without realizing it.

Even before he told her she knew that there was trouble in his house. She was sure that Tony was the focal point of much of the problem Antonio was having with his other children and Joanna. She disliked setting him up this way, but she was obsessed with wanting Tony back. She let Antonio go on about his family problems. It was part of her strategy and she hated herself for the subterfuge.

Antonio was giving to her and to himself the very reasons why he should let go of Tony. She never knew that he had used the same strategy on her when he first asked her to give Tony to him. It was amazing how alike they were in their thought processes.

She remained silent as Antonio recited the litany of his concerns. When he was finished she broached the subject that she had thought was the reason she had wanted to meet with him. Now she knew that was not the only reason. She had wanted him; she needed him.

258

"Antonio, once before, just after the twins were born you asked me not to speak while you told me something. Now, my dear love, I ask the same of you. Please say nothing while I speak." He lay silent, his arms around her, knowing her well enough to expect something very serious.

"Antonio, how our lives have changed. Sometimes I want to blame God for all of our troubles but I realize that God is incapable of doing evil, let alone of sending it to us. No, my love, we have only ourselves to blame for all that has happened. I don't think I could have saved my marriage with Giovanni; his desires were elsewhere, not with me. But you are more to blame for the intolerable situation in your home. Joanna never did any wrong to you. When she came to America she had every right to have high expectations, just as I did. She and I were both disillusioned. Now there is trouble in your house and in mine too. We can remedy both. My arms ache for Pasquale but he is dead just like my Augusta. My arms ache for Michael but he is gone also. Your family needs peace. We can solve all of the problems with one stroke."

She held him tightly against her, she could feel his naked body pressing on hers, and then slowly she whispered to him, "Antonio, I want Tony back."

It was the one thing he did not expect. He was dumbfounded at the request. He said nothing for a long time and then he too held her as tightly as he could. She knew him. He was running all the reasons and options, pro and con, through his mind at lightning speed. It was Antonio's way. Even so, it took a while. She waited. Finally he lifted her face up to his and gave her a long tender kiss.

"Maria," he began, "Please don't take what I say to you as retaliation, you know me better than that. In all love and sincerity, all I can say to you is the same thing you said to me when I asked you to give Tony to me."

She shuttered remembering what she had said to him just after the twins were born. He felt her body shaking next to his but that did not stop him.

"Maria, how can I say yes to such a request? How can I say no? The truth is I cannot say either. You know what you are asking. So now, dear Maria, it is I who do a terrible thing to you." Then she heard her own words echoing back to her.

"I love Tony. He is my own son and he is something from you that I have with me all the time. He is only four and we are just coming to know each other as his personality develops. I love him and he loves me. He hardly knows you, only the little time you have spent with him in the park. To lose him now would be like losing part of myself. I cannot keep Tony from you and I cannot give him to you. You will have to make the decision for both of us and I will abide by it." She looked deeply into his beautiful blue eyes that she loved so much and then softly echoed the words he had spoken four years ago to her.

"Then I want him."

*****

Early in the evening a few days later, Antonio, carrying a small bundle of all of Tony's clothes in one hand and holding Tony's hand with his other, walked the short distance from his apartment house to Maria's. He carried Tony up the stairs and knocked on the door. When she opened the door she looked at Antonio standing there, framed by the doorway, and a flash of memory brought back the image of him standing just like that the first time she ever saw him. This time he was holding their son in his arms.

Ralph and Josephine were sitting at the kitchen table watching the entire scene unfold. Maria had prepared both of them so that they knew their brother Tony was coming back home to live with them. To them it was like getting Pasquale back. Ralph was a little apprehensive about the move; Josephine had cried tears of joy when Maria told them.

Antonio did not speak. He handed Tony to Maria. He put the bundle down on the floor just inside the doorway. He did not enter the apartment. For a moment their eyes met and then he turned and walked down the hall and then down the stairs. She wondered if she would ever see him again.

It was only after she heard the front door close that she closed her door and brought Tony into the kitchen to Ralph and to Josephine's open arms. Like all mothers, Maria never ceased to be amazed at what children thought and said.

Josephine held Tony tightly and said, "He's just like me, isn't he?"

Ralph said, "Wow, he's just like Pasquale!"

From that time on Tony was given Giovanni's surname just like Josephine and he was raised as a brother to her and Ralph and Michael.

260

Chapter XXXII

MARIA'S HOUSE 1909

Tony came back to live with Maria in late February 1909 just before he was four years old. His birthday was coming up in April. She was determined to be in a new school district by the time he was eligible for school the following year. So she resumed her house hunting. It was a while before she found a house that was suitable. It was closer to Seventh Avenue than she wanted to be, but far enough away so that she would be out of the central part of the ward. Ralph would still be able to walk to work.

There were two great advantages that helped her to decide to buy the house. The first was the school problem. The second was that she would be moving away from St. Lucy's and could register in a different parish even though it was adjacent to St. Lucy's. All she could think of was a new beginning for all of them.

The house was at 142 Garside Street between Park Avenue and Bloomfield Avenue. The single family, three-story house on a thirty-foot wide lot was about a mile away from Antonio's tenement. There were three bedrooms on the second floor and a very large bedroom on the third. And, luxury of all luxuries, on the second floor there was a bathroom with a bathtub! In the bathroom there was a hot water heater and attached to it was a gas meter. The meter required a twenty-five cent coin to operate the heater for an hour. The hot water was stored in a large galvanized tank next to the tub. In order to be as economical as possible they would have to work out a schedule for bathing. The gas company sent a collector around once a month to empty the coin box.

The house had been electrified. On the first floor, in the rear of the house, there was a very large kitchen with a coal stove. In the front, a large parlor with a bay window overlooked the street. In between there was a large formal dining room. The house had a full basement with a coal-burning furnace that heated the house with steam radiators. It was a common sight to see teakettles and pots of water on the radiator covers. In the winter, the warm water was used for washing and the process also helped to keep the humidity at a comfortable level. A further economy was the practice of sifting ashes from the furnace to salvage any unburned pieces of coal. Of course, the ashes were stored and spread on sidewalks and steps during the winter when they were covered with ice. Everything was completely used; waste was kept to a bare minimum.

In the back of the house, off the kitchen, there was a small porch overlooking a yard. Maria planned a small vegetable garden just like Papa had in Pietramelara. The house was ideal for their needs and she had enough money to buy it outright, without a mortgage. She had worked out a budget and she was convinced that the move was financially feasible.

The mortgage payments she received from the sale of the bakery were enough to live on and she still expected to work as *La Scrittore*. She thought too that she might be able to earn additional income as a seamstress and she planned to use the third floor as a fitting and sewing room.

The next time that Antonio drove Maria to see Michael, she told him about the house. She went over the details of the budget she had prepared. He concurred with her estimates and agreed that she could carry the house.

"Do you want me to handle the arrangements?"

"No, Antonio, from now on I must make my own way. I'll do it. I'm glad that you agree, because I'm going to buy it."

"Well. Now you will be a land owner"

"Antonio, now I will not have to pay rent. You can see that I will be able to manage very well with the mortgage payments from Aldo. I think you should stop giving money to me."

"But I have an obligation to Josephine and Tony. The money is not for you; it's for them. Please don't cut me off from that."

"Oh Antonio, I don't want you to feel that way. But your family obligations come first. Please don't put me in the position of taking anything away from Joanna and your children. Also, I need to feel independent, not from you, but of you. Do you understand? I must make my own way."

"All right, but at the slightest need you must promise to come to me, do you understand that?"

"Yes, especially if the need is for Josephine or Tony, that I promise."

"Now I have some exciting news to tell you! I bought a tenement building. It has six apartments and it is located in the ward. Joanna and I are going to take one of the flats. I needed a large mortgage but the rent income from the five tenants will more than take care of the payments. It has a large backyard and the children will love it. It's a big step for me."

"Oh, Antonio, I'm so happy for you. You always wanted to invest in real estate and now you've done it. I'm proud of you. I'm sure your family will be happy there. Where is it?"

"It's at 9 John Street between Eighth Avenue and State Street only four blocks from where you live now. It is about three miles from the house you plan to buy, so we won't be too far away from each other. I will still take you to see Michael."

"Oh, that's wonderful. I will always try to bring Tony and Josephine along so that you can see them."

"I am very grateful to you for doing that."

By now, Josephine knew who Antonio was. She was always very respectful to him but she never spoke to him on her own initiative. She just answered him whenever he spoke directly to her. As she matured she was becoming more and more uncomfortable with knowing that he was her father. Nonetheless, it gave Josephine a warm feeling knowing that she and Tony shared the same heritage. She loved her brother, Tony, and they became very close. As for Tony, he was always happy to see his father and Antonio made a great fuss over his son. Maria promised Antonio that he could come to her new house to see the children whenever he wanted.

"Now that I will have my own house you will be able to come and visit me whenever you like. It would be best during the day when Ralph is working. I am sorry that he doesn't like you. But when you come, maybe Josephine will be home and Tony will always be home until he goes to school next year."

"Maria, do you think I should give up the room on Ogden Street?" As soon as he asked he was sorry he brought the matter up.

"I think it would be best if you did. However, we cannot substitute my new house for Ogden Street. But always remember I love you now and always."

Having set the limits and at the same time extending the invitation, the thought of what would happen if he did come to visit and she was alone passed through her mind. She shook her head to drive the thought away. She still loved him and it hurt not to have him for her own. The same thought crossed his mind and he decided not to give up Ogden Street. He did not tell her. He decided to wait and see what happened.

*****

The closing on the new house took longer than Maria expected. Josephine had to continue at Seventh Avenue school for a few months before being transferred. Maria moved into her new house on December 1st of 1909. She had turned forty-four that past July and now she was a property owner once more, just as she was back in Pietramelara. It gave her a sense of security that she hadn't felt for a long while.

She had ambivalent feelings about the spirit of the coming holiday season. Two of her children were dead and one was blind and living away at school. But she planned to make the holidays a happy family affair and she dreamed of restarting her life anew.

Ralph was almost nineteen and doing well at his job as an automobile mechanic. He dreamed of owning his own garage one day. After paying

263

his mother for room and board, he saved every penny he could in order to make that happen. Josephine had turned twelve in September and was growing into a beauty, just like her mother. Michael, at eight was a cross she would bear for the rest of her life. Tony had turned four in April and was a delightful child. His personality was very much like Michael's. Josephine doted on both of them to a fault.

Maria tried to count her blessings but whenever she did, her trials were always included in the tally. Nonetheless, she maintained her strong spirit and that got her through. She would persevere and not allow herself to become vanquished. However, she often regretted that she told Antonio to give up Ogden Street. She coped with the problem, reasoning that it was the better choice for all of them.

Although she had moved some blocks away, Maria continued to see Giustina. Josephine was old enough to baby sit for Tony and the two friends would spend an entire Saturday together going downtown to do some shopping. They also met at the park during the week whenever she brought Tony there to play on the swings near the reservoir. Often, Maria could not help but reminisce about that night during the San Gerardo Feast when Antonio literally dragged her around to the back of the boathouse. She could not shake the memories of Antonio nor did she want to. But in spite of her longings for him, her new life was bringing with it peace and contentment.

*****

Michael had been at the Arthur Home for only a few months when the school staff recommended that her weekly visits be changed to once a month. They explained that it would help Michael to become more independent. Antonio continued to drive her out to Summit for the visits. Maria always brought Josephine and Tony with her so that they too could visit with Michael. Also it allowed Antonio to spend some time with his children. Ralph refused to go with them. He made his own arrangements to see Michael from time to time.

The school made a large room available for the visits so that the family could have some privacy. Michael always walked to the room alone. He had been taught how to walk through the halls running the fingertips of one hand along the wall. As he walked, he counted his steps so that he always knew where he was. He had memorized the floor plan of the entire building. Maria and the children would be waiting for him and suddenly he would throw open the door.

"*Ciao*, Mama," he would yell as he proudly walked into the room unaided. Before anyone else had a chance to say anything, Josephine would run to him with her arms outstretched.

264

"Michael," she would scream. Tony would be close behind her shouting and the three children would be kissing and hugging each other.

When they calmed down a little, Maria would come to Michael and put her arms around him and kiss him. Uncontrollably, tears would fall from her eyes, tears that he could not see, but he could feel. It was always a difficult and emotional moment for her.

"Michael, *mio bambino, come stai*, how are you?

Antonio discretely remained in the background. He felt that anything he did or said would be an intrusion. He would wait for a while before he greeted Michael.

The staff thought that it would be very good for Michael to have a pet. Maria thought so too and on one visit she brought a kitten and gave it to Michael.

"Here Michael, I brought a present for you," Maria said as she handed the kitten to him. "It's a little kitten, just for you."

Michael took the kitten in his hands and said, "What color is it?" A sharp pain ripped through Maria's body. She didn't have a chance to answer.

"It's white, all white," squealed Josephine.

"It doesn't matter," said Michael. "It feels all furry to me so I will call him Fluffy. Come on, let's bring Fluffy up to my room so he can see where he will sleep."

He took them all to his room holding the kitten in one hand and running the fingers of his other along the wall. He showed them his toys and his closet. All of his clothes were hung up in a precise, predetermined order and his dresser drawers were laid out in an unchanging pattern. It was how they taught him to dress himself without any help.

The school had suggested that he learn to play a musical instrument and Maria had purchased an inexpensive violin for him. He was beginning to make progress with it and he liked to play for them. It was good therapy for him. Michael came to adore Fluffy. The kitten followed him everywhere and would jump up on his lap at every opportunity.

The teachers were training Michael how to read Braille. He was very proud that he could read and he showed off this accomplishment to his mother whenever she visited.

"Listen, Mama," he would say as he opened a book. Then he would read to her. She listened to every word and complimented him on his progress as tears streamed down her cheeks, tears of love that he could not see.

The staff looked upon their profession as a vocation, not merely employment, and they dedicated their lives to caring for their charges. Their efforts showed in Michael's progress. He was beginning to adapt to his handicap, not only physically but also psychologically. Maria still had guilt feelings whenever she saw him; she could never stop blaming herself. Sometimes it would take days for her to snap out of her depression after a visit. It was a bittersweet time for her; happy to see her son yet saddened that he could not see her.

The staff allowed her to take Michael home for the holidays. She was determined that Michael should have a share in the family celebration in her new house. She felt strongly that he should retain his sense of identity within the family. He was her son and he had brothers and a sister. She was determined that he should feel that, not just know it.

Ralph had brought a large Christmas tree home and they all helped in decorating it. Josephine would hand a decoration to Michael.

"Here, Michael, take this red ball and hook it on the tree, right here," and she guided his hand to one of the branches.

The visit home worked out very well and they were all astounded by how quickly Michael memorized the floor plan of the entire house. By the time it came for him to return to school he was navigating from room to room without any help.

Just after New Years Day of 1910, Antonio and Maria drove Michael back to The Arthur Home. There was no trouble; he seemed to be very comfortable with going back. A welcome peacefulness settled into her household but it was disrupted because of two unexpected visitors soon after the holidays were over.

CHAPTER XXXIII

THE CHURCH 1910

The first visitor was the pastor of the First Italian Baptist Church of Newark. The church was originally known as the Garside Street Mission. The first services were held in the Old Soldiers and Sailors Home on Seventh Avenue and Garside Street in 1887. In 1894 a site was purchased at the corner of Mt. Prospect Avenue and Park Avenue. The first church building was constructed there and dedicated in 1894. The location was only a short walk from Maria's new house. The pastor lived at 134 Garside Street just four houses away from Maria's new home.

As he introduced himself, he sensed her caution. He guessed that she was probably a Catholic and was uncomfortable with his visit. She was making an assessment of him as she wondered why he was calling on her. He was slightly built, not much taller than she was. He was balding and wore eyeglasses. His tone was soft and had a slight lilt to it. Maria guessed that he was in his early sixties. He spoke in classical Italian, and beautifully.

"Signora, I am Reverend Pietro from the Italian Baptist Church. I am also your neighbor. I live only a few houses down the street. If you have a few moments I would like to welcome you to our neighborhood."

"Well, thank you Reverend, won't you please come in?"

She ushered him into the parlor and pointed to the sofa.

"Please, sit down. I'll make some coffee and we can visit together. I'll be back in a moment."

While she was gone he looked around the parlor. There were two red velvet wing chairs on either side of the bay window. The sofa he was sitting on was along the wall opposite from the entrance to the room from the vestibule. There was a coffee table in front of him. A large rectangular mirror was hanging over the sofa. There were a few simple oil paintings on the papered walls. The room was simply decorated which lent a touch of elegance to it. He thought, *'What else could one expect from a woman of such obvious class?'*

Maria returned carrying a tray with cups, saucers, and a coffee urn. There was also a dish of pastries. She still asked Ralph to stop by at the old bakery and bring some home. She placed the tray on the table and poured coffee for each of them.

"Where did you live before you moved here?"

"Not far, only from Seventh Avenue."

"And do you have children, signora?"

"Yes, I do. Unfortunately, I lost one just recently in a terrible sickness that left another of my children blind. He is away at a special school, but I have three more at home with me."

"And your husband?"

"I am a widow."

It was obvious to Maria that he was unaware of the scandal surrounding her. She breathed a sigh of relief. *'They don't know about me here. Thank God.'* He was visibly upset to hear of her troubles.

"Signora, please, do not hesitate to call on me if I can be of any assistance to you."

Even though he was a Protestant, Maria took an immediate liking to him and admired his obvious intelligence and education. It was a pleasure to hear someone speak Dante's language. After about an hour he took his leave. Maria was grateful to him for his kindness and sensitivity. He had made her feel very welcome and secure in her new surroundings.

But that euphoria lasted only until her second visitor arrived about two weeks later. Maria was alone in the house except for Tony who was napping. These were the quiet times when she could think things through. Her meditation was interrupted by an unexpected knock on the front door and when she answered it she was surprised to see the priest who was the pastor of her new parish standing on the porch. Her new parish was Sacred Heart and the church building was up on Park Avenue between Clifton Avenue and Ridge Street, just behind the partially completed Cathedral. She thought that it was very considerate of the priest to pay a visit. She felt very flattered. *'My goodness, visits from two clergymen in as many weeks!'*

'Maybe he came to bless the house,' she thought as she ushered him into the parlor.

Maria had never met him although she had seen him as celebrant of mass on Sundays. He was tall and muscular. He had black curly hair and bushy eyebrows. His manor was stern. He had a deep resonant voice and he was an excellent homilist. She liked his sermons and was very pleased at this opportunity for them to become acquainted.

"Please, come in and make yourself comfortable."

She pointed to a chair by the window. As he sat down she offered him some coffee, but he declined.

"Maria, this is not a social call. I am here to speak to you about a very grave matter. I will be very brief and to the point. Maria, your relationship with Antonio has got to stop. The two of you are a scandal to the church."

"Just a minute."

"No," he said in a raised voice with his hand held up. "I must say what I came to say. You let him come to your house and drive you and your children out to Summit on Sundays. Don't you realize how that looks?"

"I don't care about how it looks."

Maria was becoming agitated. She was incredulous, dumbfounded, and speechless at his callous remarks. He went on and on in this vein and slowly Maria regained her composure and began to fight back.

"You have unmitigated gall to come into my house and criticize my life!"

"Your life is a scandal!" he yelled at her, pointing his finger in her face. "I know all about you and your children"

"What do you know about my life? My life has been ruined by authority figures like you. You set yourself up to be judge and jury, you go too far!"

He stood up, towering over her.

"I can see that you will not listen to me. So I tell you this, unless you amend your ways you are not welcome in my church."

"Your church!" She jumped to her feet and looked at him up and down with contempt. "It's not your church. You are only the pastor. I have every right to come to mass. I'm a baptized member of the church and you can't stop me."

"Maria, if you come to the altar rail I will refuse you the Eucharist. I will do it publicly so that everyone will see that the church and I do not condone your public sinfulness. I will do it! If you don't change your ways then don't come to mass!"

Defiantly, Maria stomped over to the front door and opened it. She stood silently holding onto the doorknob glaring at him with contempt, signifying that the conversation was ended and that he should leave. But as he stepped through the doorway, her anger got the better of her.

She blurted out, "If your church doesn't want me then I don't want your church."

He walked out onto the porch and she slammed the door after him. It took a while for her to calm down. The argument was so unlike her. She hated confrontation. But the entire incident had caught her off guard and she had reacted badly.

"Well, what has been done has been done," she exclaimed out loud," I'm not going to move again. I will just find another church that will accept me for who I am! I will join the Italian Baptist Church!"

And that is what she did.

*****

The next Sunday, Antonio came to drive her to see Michael. This time she asked Ralph to stay at home to watch the children. She wanted to be alone with Antonio when she told him about what had happened with the priest. All during the drive to Summit she recounted her argument with him. She compared his diatribe with the warmth and concern of the Baptist minister. As she related the incident, she became very agitated and could hardly contain her herself. She was shaking with anger. Antonio remained quiet throughout the ride, aghast at what he was hearing. Maria slowly calmed down and became pensive.

"What would make the priest act the way he did? He seemed to know everything about us, about Josephine, and about Pasquale and Tony too. He knew so many details. Even about separating the twins. It was awful. How did he know all about us? I thought I was making a new start."

"I know!" exclaimed Antonio. "The pastor at St. Lucy's and that priest are very good friends. They probably talked about us." Antonio became angry and in a threatening tone he said, "Well, I'll take care of him, don't you worry."

"Let it be, Antonio. Don't make matters worse. I only told you because I have decided to join a different church and I feel comfortable with the decision. I can't endure the finger pointing any longer and I am not going to subject my children to it any longer either."

At this point in the conversation they had reached the Arthur Home. It was time to see Michael. On the way home after the visit, they talked only about Michael and how pleased they were with his progress. Her altercation with the priest was not mentioned. When they arrived at her house, Maria invited him in for some coffee but he declined saying he had to attend to some business. They said good-bye. Antonio drove directly to St. Lucy's rectory.

When the priest opened the door Antonio stormed right past him and demanded, "Have you been talking to the pastor of Sacred Heart about Maria and me?"

"Yes, I have. I did it to try to get Maria to end her relationship with you. Antonio, what you are doing is wrong and it must stop! It is against the laws of the church"

"Don't you tell me what to do. You have no idea what my life is all about. You only know about your laws!"

"The laws are there to protect the family. Nothing can replace the family. You have made a mockery of the laws and hurt your family. You have ruined your life and Maria has ruined hers. And the families have suffered."

Antonio exploded into a rage. "You have it backwards, the families suffer because of your laws! I will never set foot in St. Lucy's again."

270

It was an ugly scene. Antonio stomped out of the rectory and slammed the door behind him.

It all happened so quickly that Antonio did not allow himself time to calm down. He drove straight back to see Maria. He did not go in. Standing on the porch he related to Maria what had just happened. He left saying he would pick her up again the next Sunday and they would go to the Baptist Church together.

"Are you sure Antonio? It would be wrong of you to make the change just because I decided to change. Please don't do it for me."

"Yes, I'm sure, and I am not doing it just because of you. I have not been happy at St. Lucy's for a long time. The pastor is a dictator and I just don't like being an onlooker. I know I never mentioned it to you before. I did not want to upset you. But now I feel relieved that it is out in the open. I am going to go where my heart leads me. If the Baptist Church doesn't pan out for me then I will go somewhere else. I need to feel a part of the church, not just an idle spectator! It is not a dogmatic problem. I still have my faith. It is a clerical problem."

As a result of the double altercation, Maria and Antonio joined the First Italian Baptist Church of Newark. On the Sundays that they did not drive to see Michael, they attended services at the Baptist Church up on Mt. Prospect Avenue, but they walked there separately.

Maria insisted that Ralph and Josephine join her in becoming Baptists. At first they objected but eventually bowed to her will; they were tired of the finger pointing also. Tony was too young to object. Thereafter, Maria and her family attended the Baptist Church.

Joanna refused to leave St. Lucy's and so did her children. Antonio's decision to join that woman in a heretical church was just one more reason for her to alienate herself from her husband.

When Sunday services were over Maria's children were eager to get home. Ralph escorted them. It wasn't far, less than two blocks away. Most of the children in the congregation went back to their homes without their parents. The adults usually remained behind and socialized. The practice allowed time for Maria and Antonio to be together for an hour or so with their newly found friends. On occasion, they would go for a walk in the park. Sometimes they would encounter people on the street that knew them. Their snickering made her very uncomfortable but she just shrugged it off.

*****

Ralph was opposed to his mother's continued friendship with Antonio. His demeanor when Antonio was present made that obvious. Ralph wanted to put a stop to it. He thought he found a way. One day Ralph announced to Maria that he would be able to borrow a car from his employer.

"I will take you and the children to see Michael. You don't need a ride from anyone else."

Maria was amazed at his tone of voice. It was as though he had become head of the family and he was making family decisions. She also resented that Ralph would not even use Antonio's name. He referred to Antonio as 'anyone else'. She wondered how long Ralph had been working on the arrangement. Maria was boxed in; she could not refuse.

"Ralph, I am happy that you can do this for me, but I don't want any misunderstanding between us. I know that you don't like Antonio, but he is the father of Josephine and Tony. As long as he wants to see them, I will not stop him. The next time Antonio comes to take me to see Michael, I will tell him it is the last time and thank him for all the help he has been to the family."

Ralph did not like his mother's comment but he felt that he was making progress in getting the family more independent from Antonio. The next time Antonio came to drive Maria to see Michael, she did not take Josephine and Tony along. They stayed at home with Ralph.

Maria was quiet for most of the ride. She was trying to put words together in her mind. She was grateful to Antonio for faithfully driving her out to see Michael every month. She found it hard to frame the words to tell him that she didn't need him anymore. She did not want to hurt him. She concluded that there weren't any right words so during the ride back from seeing Michael, she just spoke plainly and told him what Ralph had done.

"Antonio, this is the last time you can drive me out to see Michael. I am so sorry, but I must do what I must do. I have to keep peace in my family. Please try to understand."

She studied his face trying to read his reaction. She saw nothing. When they arrived at Maria's house, Antonio parked his truck and turned the motor off.

"Maria, may I come in for a few minutes?"

"Yes, of course, come in. Go into the parlor and make yourself comfortable. I'll make some coffee for us. It will only take a few minutes."

He walked into the parlor and sat on the sofa and waited for her. In a few minutes she came into the parlor carrying a tray. He watched her as she set the small table in front of the sofa with dishes and a coffee urn. There was a small plate with pastries on it. She performed the ritual with such grace and class that he could not help taking her hand as she sat down next to him. She smiled at him but withdrew her hand from his. She was telling him that he must not show any affection for her in her house.

272

"Maria, I must talk with you about us. We are slowly pulling apart. This almost casual friendship is not enough for me. We need to be alone more often. I need to be alone with you. I have no one to talk with, to communicate with. The truth is I need to see you like we used to on Ogden Street."

"Oh Antonio, I feel the same way. But think for a minute. That is how we got into all of this mess that we are in. We are just now beginning to work things out. Our lives are just settling down for us and for our families too. Our friendship is strong and our love will never end. I feel that. And oh, Antonio, the children are getting older now, yours, mine, and ours. We cannot fail them again. Think about it."

"I have thought about it, it's all I think about. That is why I bring the matter up. What you say is true, but you and I also need some happiness together. I need you Maria, and I want you. The emotions just do not go away."

Her heart ached for him. It was difficult enough for her not to be with him and she could only imagine how much more difficult it was for him.

"Antonio, let's not talk about it for now. Let a little more time go by and if we both still feel the same then we will work something out."

He decided for the present he would still not tell her that he never gave up the room at Ogden Street.

Chapter XXXIV

A FAMILY 1910

In the fall of 1910 Tony entered the first grade at the Franklin School located on Park Avenue. The school had been named after Benjamin Franklin and built on a piece of privately owned property that had been donated for that purpose. The gift carried a stipulation that the name of the school could never be changed. Josephine was transferred to Franklin and was in the eighth grade. Michael was still at the Arthur Home.

Ralph was slowly beginning to consider himself to be the head of the family now that he was not only paying room and board to his mother but was also driving the family to see Michael every month. Ralph was confident that he had put an end to his mother's relationship with Antonio. But it also put an end to the time Antonio could spend with Tony and Josephine during the drive out to Summit.

Antonio missed Tony very much and would stop by Maria's house to see him very often. Ralph would be working and if Josephine was at home she went upstairs to her room. She would not see her father. Maria and Antonio did not make an issue of it. They let her do as she pleased and he spent the time with Tony and Maria.

Antonio continued to pressure Maria for a return to their previous relationship. On rare occasions he stopped by when the children were at school. It was then that they could make love.

"Maria," he whispered on one occasion as he took her in his arms. She did not resist. He undressed her in the parlor and stared at her naked body. "Maria, I love you and I need you."

"Me too, Antonio. Hold me and love me. Make me feel good and block out the world for me."

They made love on the sofa and afterward clung to each other. He continued to caress her body as she kissed him over and over. Then she pushed him away and started to dress.

"Antonio, get dressed. The children will be home soon."

He got up from the sofa and dressed, watching her all the time.

"Maria, this is not the same. We are hurrying and it feels like we are doing something wrong. We should be talking with each other but instead we are rushing because we don't want to get caught. It is no good this way."

"I know, Antonio. I know. I want more than just this too. But let's be content with what we have."

"Maria, don't be upset, but I never gave up the room on Ogden Street. I just couldn't do it. I want what we had there again, no rushing, just having each other and sharing our lives. I tried to tell you before but I was afraid you would become angry. Are you angry?"

"Oh, Antonio. Don't you know that I love you? Being together is as important to me as it is to you. I could never be angry with you for wanting to be with me."

They agreed to rendezvous on Ogden Street again. Sometimes, when the children were at school all day they also managed to take trips downtown and take in a vaudeville show.

*****

Michael was graduated from the Arthur Home in 1912. After his graduation he returned home to live with the family. He was twelve and that fall Maria enrolled him in the Robert Treat School for handicapped children in Newark. Tony was in third grade and Josephine was a junior at Barringer High School.

With Michael living at home Maria's responsibilities to him demanded more and more of her time. She had to take Michael to school in the morning and pick him up in the afternoon. It was a tight schedule for her to get home with Michael by the time Tony got home. By late afternoon Josephine would come home from high school and help her prepare dinner so that by the time Ralph came home they were able to sit down as a family at the dining room table. Maria was determined that they would have this time together and she succeeded.

While at dinner they often played the old language game. Her strategy for helping them grow intellectually was to steer the conversation to topics that were a little above the normal interests of children their ages. It forced them to expand their minds and horizons. Michael also enjoyed the time they all spent together. The children came to adore their mother more and more as they matured.

Josephine would always prepare Michael's plate for him with the precision that he had learned at the Arthur Home; meat or fish on the part of the plate closest to him, potatoes on the right and vegetables on the left and bread at the far side of the plate. As Michael sat down she would hand a napkin to him and he would tuck it under his chin. They all marveled at his ability to eat properly. He used to joke that the only reason he liked macaroni so much was because everything was all in one dish.

Michael often joked about his handicap, it was one of the ways that helped him cope with his blindness. Maria was always upset when he did

275

it but she never berated him for it. It made her sad and at times made her cry. Tears would roll down her cheeks, tears that Michael could not see but her other children could.

*****

Caring for Michael prevented Maria from starting her own seamstress business. Instead she took a part-time job as a seamstress in the garment industry at the Weingarten Corset Factory on High Street. It was the era of the hourglass figure and the demand for corsets was high. Experienced sewing machine operators were able to find a job easily. Of course the factory employment did not begin to compare with making elegant dresses. She worked on a piecework basis and was able to arrange a schedule around her responsibility to Michael. She started work after she dropped him off at school and ended her workday in time to pick him up when his school day was over.

One afternoon when Antonio stopped by to visit with Tony, Maria decided to tell Antonio that they could no longer see each other as often as they had been doing.

"Antonio, we will have to stop seeing each other so often. I can't make the time for us. I have to work as much as I can."

"I know. I wish you would let me help, not for us, but for Tony and Josephine."

"No, Antonio. I can't let you do that. I must make it on my own. I will see you as often as I can, I promise. Maybe at night once in a while and on a Saturday when I can."

'Well,' he thought, 'Her independence is one of the traits I admire in her.' He did not want to change her, as if he could. So he lived with it. It was Antonio's way.

*****

Maria and Antonio always met at church early on Sunday mornings. When circumstance permitted they would take a short stroll through the park and then to her house. He would tip his hat to her and with a slight bow they would say "Ciao" to each other. Then he walked down Garside Street toward his home. She still felt uncomfortable walking with him. The church and the park were so near to the heart of the ward that it was impossible to avoid seeing people who knew them both.

In 1914 another Italian Baptist Church was founded in the Silver Lake section of Bellville, about five miles north of where Maria lived. Called the First Italian Baptist Church of Silver Lake, it was in the center of Bellville's Italian community and easily accessible from Maria's house by simply walking a half block to Bloomfield Avenue and catching the #27 trolley. From his house, Antonio could walk down to Broad Street and catch the same trolley as it came up from downtown. It was very convenient for them to coordinate riding on the same trolley. They both joined the church in Silver Lake.

Once she boarded the trolley and met Antonio, they would ride along Mt. Prospect Avenue to Heller Parkway and disembark. They walked up the steep hill and through the northern end of Branch Brook Park and over the wooden bridge crossing the Morris Canal. At that point the canal was the city line between Newark and Belleville, and Heller Parkway became Franklin Street. The church was located a few blocks up Franklin. Usually Maria had Josephine, Michael, and Tony with her. When Ralph went to church, he had the borrowed car and he drove the family to church. After the services he drove the children home and Maria returned with Antonio by trolley. She got off at her stop and he remained aboard and continued down to his.

The arrangement was a sore spot with Ralph and Josephine. They became more and more vocal in expressing their objections to Maria.

"I've told both of you before. My friendship with Antonio means a lot to me. Now please stop harping on the matter. Let it be."

Ralph and Josephine were forced to accept the situation. But finally they convinced each other that it wasn't too bad. They thought, '*After all, Mama was only with Antonio in church and on a public trolley.*'

A bible study group formed and it met in the basement of the church on Wednesday nights. Maria and Antonio joined the group. The study of the scriptures ranged from religion to philosophy and included discussions of history and related contemporary problems. They both thoroughly enjoyed the challenge. The meetings were also in public and the children knew where their mother was going so they did not make any issue of her going with Antonio.

Maria and Antonio did not use the trolley for transportation to the bible study meetings. Antonio would pick her up in his truck after dinner and often other parishioners rode with them. Church on Sundays and the weekly bible class studies satisfied their religious, social, and intellectual needs. When they could arrange it, Ogden Street satisfied their conjugal needs.

Josephine and Ralph were convinced that Maria's affair with Antonio had ended even though they met twice a week. No one ever suspected Ogden Street.

"After all," Josephine said to Ralph. "Mama is forty-nine and he's fifty-four. They're too old. Let's leave them alone."

"I guess you're right. It's over between them and if they just want to be friends then it's all right with me."

"Good and if he wants to come here to see Tony once in a while let him. I will be here."

As far as Antonio's family was concerned, they were all convinced that his affair with 'that woman' had ended even though they too knew that he saw her at his 'church' on Sunday mornings and Wednesday nights. Even Joanna stopped her nagging and on occasion she and Antonio would socialize with their relatives and friends. A certain calm settled over his household too. That is except for Theresa. When she married she resigned herself from the family and made no effort to be with any of them. Grace and Frank seemed to put the past behind them and he came often to see his parents after he was married.

Life continued this way without any incidents and for the most part they were all content. Antonio continued to stop by to visit Tony and they developed a father-son relationship.

The downside for Antonio was that Josephine just ignored him. That constant rebuff was a hurt to Antonio that he could never shrug off. Ralph never stopped hating him and Michael just accepted the situation and did not comment one way or the other. Things settled down for both families and they enjoyed a welcome stress-free life. Then one day in 1916 Josephine asked her mother if she could bring a boy home to meet her.

*****

"Mama, I have met a boy that I like very much and I want you to meet him."

"Who is he? You never said anything to me. What does he do? Is he Italian? Is he educated? Why didn't you say anything? Where did you meet him?"

"Mama, please. I'll tell you all about him but I want you to see him for yourself."

Maria didn't know why she was surprised; it was time. Maybe it was because she had been so concerned with Michael and the duties of being a single parent that she did not realize that Josephine had matured into a lovely person who needed to get on with her life. After her graduation from high school she took a position with the Prudential Life Insurance Company; the national headquarters was located downtown on Washington Street. Everyone called it the Pru.

"I met him at the office. He is a law clerk and he was working on an insurance matter. His name is Ferdinand. We have been having lunch together and he walks me home for part of the way. He lives over near South Orange Avenue. Can I invite him over for dinner?"

"Of course you can. I didn't mean to sound like I don't want you to meet someone, it's just that you took me by surprise."

278

Josephine invited him home for dinner one Saturday and Maria took an instant liking to him and so did the other children. He was not very tall. He had a pleasant way about him but still he manifested a professional bearing. And, to Maria's delight he spoke Dante's language. He and Maria talked so much that Josephine could hardly get a word in.

Maria thought, *'Well, maybe we will have a lawyer in the family.'*

After that he came calling on Josephine very often and sometimes they would go downtown to a show. Maria was comfortable with Ferdinand and encouraged the relationship. As the courtship progressed Maria found she could no longer depend on her daughter to look after Michael. Therefore she had even less time to spend with Antonio at Ogden Street but still they managed.

Another surprise came when Ralph told her that he had an opportunity to purchase a garage further up Garside Street near Second Avenue.

"Mama, the garage caters to the rich clientele in the Forest Hill neighborhood. A lot of them rent garage space, so there is a steady rental income. And they depend on the garage to wash the cars and keep them clean. It's named the Forest Garage."

Ralph had been saving every penny he could, even working in his spare time and on Sundays, repairing cars on his own. However he did not have enough money to make the purchase.

"Mama, I don't have enough money for the down payment. Can you help me out? The owner says he will take back a mortgage. I know I can meet the payments. A lot of my friends will come to me for repairs plus the present customers. I know I can do it."

Maria thought back to the night she told Ralph that she was going to sell Giovanni's bakery. That was the night her son had first told her about his dream to own a garage. She could not refuse him now.

"Of course I will help you. I will take out a loan on this house to make up what you need. Ralph, I want you to have your dream. And Ferdinand can take care of all the legal matters."

*****

By now, Ferdinand was treated as part of the family. Maria became furious when she found out that his mother did not know about him courting Josephine. It turned out that his mother, Flora, knew of the scandal concerning Maria and Antonio even though she lived over near South Orange Avenue, far away from the ward. Flora considered Maria to be a *putana* and a heretical *putana* at that because she had joined a Protestant church.

"Ferdinand, I am sorry that my private life is effecting yours, but your mother has no right to condemn Josephine. It is true that Antonio is her father. I don't know why she tries to deny it. Antonio is a fine man."

"I know, but I can't control what my mother feels. Josephine and I have decided that to tell her just now would create a bad situation for me. We have decided to wait until I pass the bar and become established. Then I will tell my mother that I am going to marry Josephine, and that's that."

Maria said, "Josephine, do you agree to that? I will support your decision whatever it is. But I must tell you that I am very angry. You are a wonderful girl and Ferdinand is a wonderful man. Neither of you should have to keep your relationship a secret."

"Yes, Mama. I think it is the best thing to do right now. We can make our plans after Ferdinand passes the bar."

But before any plans could be finalized, fate stepped in. America went to war in 1917. Ferdinand was called up to serve in the army. Maria did not want to see him go into the service but she thought that it might delay any plans that he and Josephine might be making. She did not want to see her daughter become entangled in a bad relationship with Ferdinand's mother. Maria hoped that time would somehow solve the problem. What she did not know was that because of the war the couple decided not to wait as they had promised. They were secretly married, downtown, at the City Hall, by a judge, of all people!

Soon after their marriage, Ferdinand received orders to leave for army service. Ralph, almost twenty-seven, was not called up, and besides, he had never become a naturalized citizen, not for any particular reason, it was just that he never gave the matter any thought. Tony at twelve was too young and of course Michael could never be called.

*****

Josephine kept her marriage a secret from everyone except her mother. Just before Ferdinand left, she decided to tell Maria.

"I think it is better this way, Mama. I want to do it right. We can make the announcement after Ferdinand comes back home."

"I am very angry with you Josephine. My only daughter gets married and I am not there, and by a judge. It's a sacrilege!"

"Mama, it's not only Ferdinand's mother that I am concerned with, it's also the Prudential. They will not allow married women to work there. If they find out I will be fired. I need the job. I have to support myself while Ferdinand is away."

"Hah, the Pru. What a joke that is. I can name twenty married women who work there and the Pru doesn't know about them. It's a stupid policy. I hope their other policies are better."

"Oh, Mama. Please don't make jokes. This is very serious for me."

"I'm sorry, Josephine. I guess that as I grow older I am becoming less flexible, and that is not a good thing. Please forgive me. All right, you can

280

tell your mother-in-law when Ferdinand comes back home. But before he goes you must get married in church. On this I insist. I will work it out with our pastor so that your mother-in-law doesn't find out about it. Oh my God your father won't even be there to give you away!"

"I don't want to talk about that. However, I will agree that we should be married again in the Baptist Church."

And so, Josephine and Ferdinand were married for a second time in July of 1917 by the pastor of the Italian Baptist Church. Almost immediately afterward Ferdinand was sent away to an army camp in the south.

Josephine's only contact with her husband was through the mail. He was never able to get home on leave for all the time he was in the service. In the meantime she lived at home with Maria. Josephine and Ralph both paid room and board and it was a great help in managing the household expenses. As a result Maria had to work fewer hours and she was able to see Antonio a little more often. There were even times when Josephine would stay home to take care of Michael on Saturday. Tony liked to go up and work with Ralph in the garage and sometimes he would take Michael with him.

Now with these new arrangements Maria and Antonio were frequently able to spend an entire Saturday together. Sometimes they even managed to go into New York City to the museums or to a vaudeville show or the opera, and there was always Ogden Street. Sundays they met briefly after church and during the week there was the bible study group meeting.

They were getting on in years. Maria had turned fifty-two in July and Antonio was fifty-eight in June. Their relationship had started over twenty years ago and remained strong throughout their trials and tragedies.

Chapter XXXV

NEW HOUSE 1918

In April of 1923 Maria purchased a one family house at 292 Garside Street adjacent to the Forest Garage that Ralph had bought back in 1917. The house was very similar to her old house with a back porch overlooking a large back yard where she planted a vegetable garden. She tended to the garden almost every day. The work was not as easy as it used to be and she noticed that she was getting tired earlier in the day. She bought a couple of rocking chairs that she put on the porch and in the afternoon she relaxed there as often as possible.

Maria and Antonio were still in love and they met at church on Sundays and the bible study group on Wednesday nights. They were together often on Saturdays and they still met at Ogden Street. Maria and Giustina maintained their close friendship through the years and visited each other's homes whenever they could manage it. On occasion they went downtown together to shop and they also met in the park. Maria had long since settled into a quiet acceptance of her lot in life.

One day, a few months after she moved, she was relaxing on a rocking chair when Giustina paid a visit. The two friends sat on the back porch and talked.

"Well, Maria, are you all settled in your new house?"

"Yes, it is very comfortable. It's good for Michael too. He works for Ralph as much as possible. He needs no help. I am thankful for how independent he is. He leaves and goes down the steps and then runs his fingertips along the garage wall and counts his steps. Just the way they taught him at the Arthur Home. He is gone almost all day and the work is such good therapy for him. It's such a load off my mind now that he has found something he can do."

"How are things between you and Ralph? He acted very strangely toward me the last time I saw him. Is anything wrong?"

"We have had a falling out and it hurt me very deeply. You remember, after he bought the garage he wanted to buy the house across the street from the garage. That's when I sold my old house and I lent him the money to buy his house. He wanted to be near the garage and I thought it would be good for Michael. So he bought it and the five of us moved in."

"Yes I remember. I was wondering how long Josephine would be with you when the war ended and Ferdinand came home."

"Well, that was a minor problem too. After Ferdinand came home, it wasn't long afterward that Josephine became pregnant. When they told Ferdinand's mother, she was furious and made them get married again in the Catholic Church. Poor Josephine, she had to marry her husband three times just to satisfy the families. I should never have forced her to marry in the Baptist Church. It was interference on my part. I was wrong."

"Yes, you were. We shouldn't interfere like that. The children should be left alone to lead their own lives."

"Yes, and that is why I wanted to move out of Ralph's house. When he married Florence last year and she became pregnant I thought that they should be alone to raise their family without a mother-in-law hovering over them. Besides, I did not want to burden Florence with Michael's handicap. And that's when the trouble between Ralph and me started. When I asked him for the money that I had loaned him to buy the garage and his house he refused to pay me back. He said that all the time that Michael and Tony and I lived with him he paid all the bills and never asked for anything."

"Well, Maria, to a certain extent he was right."

"I know, but remember, I kept house for him. He didn't have to do a thing. Well, we had an argument and we haven't talked with each other since. Oh, Giustina, for the first time I had to go to Antonio for help. You don't know how I dreaded doing that."

A flash of memory raced through Maria's mind as she recalled the first time that she ever asked Antonio for money. When they were together at Ogden Street one night she asked him for help.

"Antonio, it pains me very much to ask you, but I cannot live in Ralph's house any longer. There are a lot of reasons, but the most important is that we are not speaking to each other and I don't see a way out because the problem between us will not go away. He owes me the money and he won't pay me."

"Don't worry about it, Maria. Sometimes money causes a rift in a family and it is very hard to overcome. You mustn't let it ruin your life. I'll give you whatever you need. Maria, I don't do it only for you. I do it for Tony too. Just walk away from it. You were always strong enough to walk away from problems that couldn't be solved. Do it now."

"Thank you, Antonio. But remember, it is only a loan, I will repay you someday."

"All right, let it be a loan if you insist. Just buy the house and move out as soon as possible otherwise the problem will fester and ruin the entire family."

Giustina interrupted her thoughts. "Maria, are you all right? You seem to be off into another world?"

"Oh, I'm fine, I'm sorry, I was just thinking back to when I asked Antonio for help so I could buy this house."

After Giustina left, Maria recalled Antonio's words again, "I do it for Tony." She knew that Antonio loved Tony very much. She wondered how things would have turned out if she had not taken Tony back after Pasquale died. But that was only idle speculation. She knew that Tony met his father from time to time. Although he really could not remember back that far, he had convinced himself that he was able to recall the time he had lived with Antonio until he was about four years old.

Tony would say, "Mama, I met my father today and we had a nice talk."

"Tony, why don't you call him Papa? That's who he is. Why do you always say 'my father'? You should call him Papa. He loves you very much, you know."

"I know, Mama, I know." But Tony would just let the matter drop and Maria would shake her head and feel sad.

When Tony was graduated from Barringer High School in June of 1923 he took a job as a bond clerk in a brokerage firm named Eisle and King downtown on Bank Street. Maria found a job as a seamstress close to home. She enjoyed making elegant dresses again. She tried to reestablish herself as *La Scrittore* but there was not much of a need in her new neighborhood, so she gave up the effort. With Tony's room and board and her income she was able to manage household finances. Ralph paid Michael for whatever work he could do. Maria, Michael, and Tony lived comfortably and peacefully.

Ralph lived across the street from them with his wife Florence and they were the parents of a baby girl. Josephine and Ferdinand lived on the other side of Newark on Littleton Avenue near South Orange Avenue. They had a son. Maria's family was growing.

Antonio was still living in the ward on John Street with Joanna and Grace. Theresa and Frank had married and were starting their families. The ill feeling between Antonio and his daughter Theresa never healed. As far as both families were concerned, the affair between Antonio and Maria had ended even though they still met at church. No one ever knew nor even suspected about Ogden Street, not even Giustina.

*****

One Saturday morning while Maria and Giustina were relaxing on Maria's porch Tony walked out to them and greeted Giustina as he walked over and kissed her on the cheek.

284

"How are you Tony?" Giustina said. When she saw him she often thought back to that day when she assisted the midwife and Tony and Pasquale were born.

"I'm fine." Turning to Maria he said, "Mama, I'm going to a concert in the park this afternoon with someone and I have invited her to come for lunch. Is that all right?"

As soon as he said 'her', all ears perked up. There had not been a hint of any girl in Tony's life, at least not about one that he considered inviting home. Giustina and Maria threw a knowing glance at each other. Before anything further could be said, the considerate Giustina stood up.

"Well, I have to be going. I still have a little shopping to do and I need to get supper ready. Maria, don't get up. I'll let myself out. *Ciao.*"

Maria thought, *'I'm not going to say a word. Let him tell me when he wants to.'* However, when he said nothing for a few minutes she could not restrain herself and with a mother's authority she said, "So, who is this girl?"

*****

Tony had met Edith at a church dance at the social hall of St. Michael's Catholic Church on Belleville Avenue. All of Tony's friends were Catholic and he attended a lot of the social functions that the church had for young people. Edith worked as a librarian at the Newark Public Library downtown on Washington Street. They each packed their own lunch and, weather permitting, they would meet in Washington Park just across the street from the library and have their private picnic. They liked to watch the comings and goings at the huge Ballantine Mansion that had been built on the fortune made in the brewery business. The mansion was almost next to the library.

"Isn't it a beautiful home, Tony?"

"It sure is. They must have more money than God."

"Well, a lot of people say that. But it doesn't bother me any. They do a lot for Newark. Did you know that they donated almost all of the land for the northern section of Branch Brook Park? And that big French Renaissance Gate at the north entrance to the park, they donated that too. That's why they call that street Ballantine Parkway. I think it is beautiful."

Tony and Edith met very often after work and they would walk hand in hand up Broad Street to the intersection with Bloomfield Avenue. There they parted company and each walked up Bloomfield Avenue but on different sides of the street because one block up at the corner of Rowland Street, Edith's father had a shoe store. Edith did not want to be seen by her father walking hand in hand with a man in public. Her father would never stand for that.

In time Edith told her parents about Tony and asked if she could invite him to meet them. To her surprise they seemed deeply disturbed when she told them about Tony. She did not understand their reaction. After all, she was of the age when boys would come courting, albeit in a supervised manner. She shrugged off their obvious lack of enthusiasm for her having met a man that they did not know. But Edith's parents did not protest and they agreed to meet Tony. Still Edith did not quite understand their rather cool attitude until one day when she and Tony were walking home from work and Tony said that he had to meet someone.

As they continued up the street she noticed a very well dressed, distinguished looking man standing on the corner looking at them. As they approached him, Tony went over to him and kissed the man first on one cheek and then the other, as Italians do. Tony introduced Edith to the man. Tony and the man began to speak in Italian. She felt that the conversation was private so she walked a little farther on and waited. After a while Tony said good-bye to the man who turned toward her and with a slight bow, tipped his hat good-bye, a perfect gentleman. She smiled back at him and then the man walked up Seventh Avenue and out of sight.

"Who was that?"

"Edith, I have to tell you something. He's my father and he's Josephine's father too. He and my mother had an affair for many years but it's over now. I wasn't sure if you knew about it. It was an open scandal for a long time."

Tony took her hand and they continued up Broad Street to Bloomfield Avenue. She could see that the meeting pained him very much. Now she understood why her parents reacted the way they did when she first told them about Tony.

"Tony, it doesn't make any difference to me so don't worry about it. I think my mother and father probably know about it. That's why they were a little apprehensive when I first told them about you."

"I was a little afraid about that."

"Well, don't worry about that either. They like you very much and so do I."

*****

Edith and Tony were married in February of 1926 and they lived in Maria's house. She had taken an instant liking to her mother-in-law and to Michael. The four of them were very compatible. Edith admired Maria for her patience and care of Michael. All the time Edith lived with her mother-in-law she never saw Tony's father come to the house. However, she was well aware that they went to church together at the Italian Baptist Church in Belleville and that Maria attended the bible discussion group meetings with him every Wednesday evening. As long as Tony never brought the matter up neither did Edith. She also knew that on occasion Maria would go downtown shopping alone. She would have liked to go with her but since she was never asked, she never requested it. She noticed that more often than not, her mother-in-law came back from these trips without any purchases. But Edith never commented on it.

In June of 1927 Edith gave birth to a boy. Tony wanted to name him Anthony. By now Edith had come to know Tony's father's name and she wondered if Tony wanted to name their son after himself or after the baby's grandfather. It did not matter to Edith, but Maria was overjoyed.

There was some mild tension when the baby was baptized in St. Michael's Church. Edith and Tony had been married there and Tony had promised to raise any children as Catholics. Maria had long realized that she had made a grave error by insisting that Josephine marry in the Baptist Church. Her insistence and interference had only added to their stress. She vowed never again to repeat the mistake of interfering in her children's lives. So the boy was baptized Catholic and lived in a Baptist home with his Catholic mother and Baptist father. Ralph and Florence had two more children, a boy and another girl. Josephine also gave birth to another son. Maria had six grandchildren now and she loved them all. But little Anthony lived with her and she held him every day so the bond was stronger. She doted on the child shamelessly. His name was Anthony but she called him *piccolo* Antonio.

Now Maria could hold the grandson that was hers and Antonio's.

After supper she would sit there on the porch rocking back and forth with *piccolo* Antonio in her lap. It was almost like holding Pasquale again. So many memories, the good and the bad, would flood into her mind. *L'amore fa passare il tempo. Il tempo fa passare l'amore.*

*****

Of course Maria had told Antonio about Tony's baby being his name-sake. Antonio was pleased and asked her to arrange for him to see the baby. It was easy for Maria to accommodate his request because she often walked the baby in his carriage. When she could, she would walk the baby all the way down Garside Street to Bloomfield Avenue and Antonio would meet them. Although the secrecy of these meetings pained him very much, Antonio was always very happy to see Maria and their grandson.

On one such prearranged meeting Maria did not show up. The following Sunday she did not show up for church services either. Antonio was very concerned and on Monday he stopped in to see Tony at the office where he worked. That was how Antonio found out that Maria was ill.

Chapter XXXVI

"PLEASE, TONY" 1928

Maria began to notice her feelings of fatigue around the time that little Anthony turned one year old. She had decided to have a birthday party for him and she invited Josephine and Ferdinand along with their two boys and Giustina and her family. She also invited Ralph but only Florence and their three children came. She also asked Edith's parents and her brother and sisters and their families. She decided to celebrate the birthday on a Sunday so that everyone could come. She outdid herself with dinner and with Edith's help, spent almost all of Saturday in preparation. Maria had some of Giovanni's cake and pastry recipes and they baked one of his famous birthday cakes. On Sunday Maria felt too tired to go to church. There was no way to get word to Antonio.

In the morning she worked with Edith preparing the antipasti. Tony walked all the way down to Aldo's for fresh Italian bread. Edith's father brought wine that he made in his own press. It was a great effort and Maria attributed her unusual fatigue to the hard work over the last day and a half. The dinner party was a huge success. Everyone left by eight o'clock. It was early for Maria but all she could think of was to get to bed as quickly as she could so she retired immediately after everyone was gone. She did not sleep well that night.

She was still employed part time as a seamstress and on Monday she had to force herself to go to work. As the day progressed she began to feel a little better. On Tuesday Antonio stopped by at Tony's office to inquire about Maria.

"Tony, where was your mother on Sunday. Is she all right?"

"Mama hasn't been feeling well for a few days but she seemed to be fine this morning. I know she is planning to go to the meeting tomorrow night."

"I'm glad to hear it was not serious. I am going to the meeting also. Please tell her that I will meet her at the usual time."

The other church members who used to ride to the bible study meeting in Antonio's truck had long since provided their own transportation so rather than have Antonio pick her up alone, they decided to use the trolley. After supper on Wednesdays Maria walked to Second Avenue and then up the hill to Mt. Prospect Avenue to catch the trolley to Heller Parkway. It was a little inconvenient but they thought it was the prudent thing to do. They timed it so that Antonio would board the six o'clock trolley at Seventh Avenue and Maria would board the same one as it stopped at Second Avenue.

This Wednesday it was no different. As the trolley came to a stop she could see him waving to her. She smiled and waved back at him. It was summertime and the open-air trolleys were in use. Antonio stepped into the street and helped her up the step to the seat he was holding for her and they settled down for the ride to Heller Parkway.

"I was concerned when you didn't show up for services on Sunday."

"I wasn't feeling well and I would have had to rush back for the party anyway so I decided not to go. I am sorry but there was no way to get word to you. Oh Antonio, it pained me not to have you there. Your name-sake grandson was a year old and everyone was there except his grandfather."

She knew that Antonio felt the pain too so she said no more about the party. They began to enjoy each other's company. It was still daylight when they got off the trolley. It was a beautiful summer evening. They strolled leisurely, hand in hand, through the park toward the church. As they were crossing over the canal bridge, she stopped and clutched the right side of her abdomen.

"What is it Maria?"

"I don't know, just a sudden pain but it has passed."

"Do you want to go home?"

"No, it's all right, let's go on." During the meeting Maria was unusually quiet. Antonio noticed her lack of participation in the discussions.

"Maria, you're not feeling well, I think we should leave now."

When she did not protest, he became even more concerned and said that they would take a taxi home. She agreed and soon the taxi was letting her off in front of her house.

"I'll help you inside."

"No, I'm all right."

"Promise me you'll see a doctor tomorrow. If you don't I will come and take you myself."

"I promise."

On impulse she leaned over and kissed him gently on the mouth, her hands on both his cheeks. She got out of the taxi. He waited until she was safely through the front door before he told the driver to pull away.

On Friday morning Maria was in the waiting room of a gynecologist that had been recommended by her family doctor. Normally she would not have gone to see her doctor. After all, you just don't run to see the doctor with every little ache and pain. Besides, she was getting older, sixty-three now. But this time she didn't feel like she was having one of the normal aches and pains of aging. She sensed that something was wrong with her body and so she reluctantly went to see her family doctor. After his examination and listening to her complaints he suggested that she see a specialist and recommended the one whom she was waiting to see.

The examination was very thorough. She didn't like anyone touching her down there, that is anyone except Antonio, and she smiled slightly at the thought. But it was part of the examination so she subjected herself to it. After she dressed the doctor told her that he wanted her to undergo further tests.

"What's the problem?"

"I'm not sure, Madam, that is why I want more tests. I want x-rays taken and I also want some blood work done. I'll give you a prescription to see a radiologist but right now I want the blood samples. We will have the results in about a week."

After Maria dressed, the doctor gave her the prescription and told her to come back in a week and by then he would have the results of all the tests. She left knowing as little as she did when she first went to see her family doctor. While she waited for the week to pass she was still feeling fatigued. The pain in her side would come and go and every now and then she also felt it in her back on her right.

On Sunday she felt well enough to go to church so she dressed and walked up to the trolley stop. As the trolley slowed, she saw Antonio waving to her. He stepped into the street to help her aboard, but she motioned for him to come to her.

"Antonio, I've changed my mind, I don't feel well enough to go. I want to go back home."

"I'll walk you to your house."

"No, Antonio, I'll be all right." She kissed him gently on the lips. "*Ciao*," she said and turned away from him.

He watched her as she walked down the Second Avenue hill. When she got to Garside Street she turned and looked up at him standing there watching her. She waved to him and he waved back and she was gone. He waited a minute or two and then hurried down the hill. When he got to the corner he looked down Garside Street past the Forest Garage and he could see her climbing the steps to her house. Once he knew she was safely inside he continued down Second Avenue to Summer Avenue and turned right. He decided to walk home instead of going to church alone.

On the next Friday Maria went to the gynecologist's office. This time Josephine drove her. Instead of being ushered into the examination room, the nurse led them into the doctor's private office. Maria introduced her daughter to him.

"Madam," he began. "The test results have come back and I must tell you that I don't feel they are conclusive. However, I have a strong suspicion that you have a cyst on your right ovary or possibly a tumor. I cannot tell for sure but I cannot rule out either possibility. I have discussed your case with some of my associates and in light of the test results we are all of the opinion that we must perform exploratory surgery to see what it is that is causing you this problem. We cannot force you to take this step but we strongly urge you to agree as soon as possible."

Maria was stunned. "Are you trying to tell me that I have cancer?"

"Not at all. There is of course that possibility. If it is a tumor it can either be malignant or benign. We will not know until we see it; that is, if it is a tumor. In short, Madam, we can do nothing for you until we know what we are dealing with."

He turned to Josephine and said, "We urge your mother to have this procedure performed. If you want, I can make the arrangement and let you know when it will be done. If you do not agree now then you will have to let me know when you do make your decision. Right now there is nothing more I can do for your mother. Do you understand?"

"Mama, I think we should follow the doctor's advice. After all, why are we here if we don't do as he says?"

Maria nodded, "Yes, make the arrangements."

The doctor told her he would advise her soon. She could expect that the surgery would be in about a week.

The operation was to be performed at the Columbus Hospital. As it turned out it was the following Friday. And so, in early August, Maria underwent exploratory surgery and that is when their worst fears were confirmed. It was discovered that she had a cancerous tumor of the right ovary and that it had metastasized. They could do nothing for her and the doctor advised the waiting family that she would probably die within six months, a year at the outside.

Antonio had been stopping by at Tony's office every day to inquire about Maria and he knew about the impending surgery. He felt it would be imprudent for him to go see Maria at the hospital during regular visiting hours so he waited until that night, after visiting hours were over. He managed to slip by the front desk and locate her room. He went into the dimly lit room. She was sound asleep. It was obvious that she had been sedated for the night. He looked down at her lying motionless in the bed. She looked drawn and tired even in her sleep. Fearing his presence might awaken her he slipped out of the room. He was unaware of the terrible diagnosis that had been given to the family only a few hours before. He would not be able to see Tony until Monday so that it was three days later that he found out that she was terminally ill. Maria had been told immediately, she had demanded to know.

In a week she was discharged from the hospital. She was in a wheel chair, protesting that she could walk but the family would hear none of it.

Josephine and Edith had converted the dining room into a bedroom for Maria so that she would not have to climb the stairs to her bedroom. Maria mildly protested the arrangement but realized it was for the best. She would be able to walk into the living room and there was a small bathroom in the back, off the kitchen. They tried to get her into bed but she wanted to sit in the living room near the window but that did not last very long. All of the activity was tiring for her and she decided that she should go to bed. She remained there until the following day.

In a few days she was able to care for herself and she settled into her new sleeping quarters. During the day she spent her time sitting in a chair in the living room looking out the window. The children did everything they could to make her comfortable.

Ralph, in light of his mother's condition, reconciled with her. He stopped in frequently during the day to see her. Edith was there to care for her and little Anthony was a joy to watch. He was walking now and he was getting into everything. Edith tried to restrain him but Maria protested.

"*Lascialo*, leave him alone. I like to watch him and besides he always comes to me when I call him."

"*Vieni qui, piccolo* Antonio," she would call to him in Italian, just like Papa used to call her. "Come here." And he would run to her. It was never too soon to teach the young ones the language. The boy helped pass the time for her.

During the day, only Maria and Edith were in the house. Tony was working and when Michael was not at the garage, he was up in his third floor bedroom. He had built himself a wireless radio and had become a ham radio operator. It was something he could do in his dark world and he spent most of his hours with his new hobby, talking with people he had never met. He was so preoccupied when he was on the radio that sometimes he wouldn't even come downstairs for dinner. Edith would bring something up to him. By now she had assumed the responsibility of caring for Michael.

Josephine stopped by almost daily. Giustina came to visit very often and Ralph came and went many times during the day. The family tried to keep Maria occupied as much as possible. She read a great deal. When she did rest, she thought of Antonio.

As soon as Antonio was told the tragic news he wanted to see Maria. Tony told him that it was not possible; it would cause a great problem. Josephine and Ralph would not permit it. So it was Tony who kept his father advised of Maria's condition. Antonio had to resign himself to the situation. He couldn't break into the house.

For months there was no noticeable change in Maria's appearance other than her fatigue. Although her pain was not yet severe, the doctor had given her a medication to manage it. Her condition remained stable through the holidays.

When it was possible, Tony arranged for his father to see Anthony. Maria was very grateful to him for his compassion and understanding. On a Saturday or Sunday, Tony would take Anthony out for a stroll in his carriage and push it up Second Avenue to Mt. Prospect Avenue and they would meet with Antonio for a little while. Antonio gave a Christmas present to Tony to give to Anthony. It wasn't much, only a little toy. It struck Antonio that all the time that he and Maria had been together they had never exchanged gifts, not even on birthdays. It didn't seem necessary, they had each other, and that was all they wanted.

After the holidays, Maria began to take a turn for the worse. She was losing weight very rapidly, her appetite was almost gone and she refused most food. The pain was becoming more severe and she was taking sedatives more frequently. Through it all she remained alert and, surprisingly, her voice was still strong. By the middle of February it was obvious that she could not last much longer. Maria knew that her end was near and she had made her last good-byes with the family and Giustina.

Maria cried to herself. '*Oh, I can't say good-bye to piccolo Antonio, he doesn't understand. I love him so and I will not be able to see him grow up. Oh God, that is the worst pain!*'

*****

One evening, after Michael was in his room and Edith was putting Anthony in his crib for the night, Maria beckoned to Tony to come near. He bent over her and asked, "What do you want Mama?"

She whispered, "Tony, I want to see your father, please, just this once, do this for me."

He stood up and looked down at her. He wanted to say no but he could not bring himself to deny her and with tears in his eyes he nodded, "Yes."

The next time Antonio came to Tony's office the arrangement was made. It was the Monday in the last week in February 1929.

Chapter XXXVII

THE LAST VISIT 1929

Promptly at 10 PM Antonio walked up the steps of Maria's house. Tony had made the arrangements with him the day before. Tony wanted to be sure that Michael was in his bedroom and would not hear Antonio arrive. He had to tell Edith and had asked her to stay in their second floor bedroom. Anthony would be asleep. Tony was sure that none of the family would come to visit at that hour of the night.

Antonio had planned to drive his truck to Maria's house and park it nearby but changed his mind at the last minute because it looked and felt like it was going to snow. But he knew that the real reason was he did not want to take the chance that anyone might see it. He shook his head at the irony of it. *'Why should such a thing matter at this time?'*

Spring was only three weeks away but winter would not let go of its icy grip. He had bundled up in his winter coat, hat, and scarf and put on a pair of gloves and rubber overshoes and set out for Maria's house. He hated being forced to see his beloved Maria in secret. It made him feel like he was doing something wrong.

From his house, he walked down Seventh Avenue to Broad Street and boarded the #27 trolley as he had done for so many years. Up Broad Street it went, then up Bloomfield Avenue then over Mt. Prospect Avenue to Second Avenue. The ride lasted twenty minutes and in that time memories of meeting Maria every Wednesday flashed through his mind. He half expected to see her standing on the corner waving to him, ready to board the trolley. He was brought back to reality when the trolley screeched to a stop. He actually looked for her but she was not there.

As he expected, it had started to snow and the cold ground was already covered in a white blanket. No one was on the street as he walked down the Second Avenue hill to Garside Street. He turned and walked past the Forest Garage to Maria's house. There was an eerie silence, the snow muffling all sound. At the appointed time he walked up the steps to the porch and before he could knock on the door Tony opened it.

They embraced and kissed each other on the cheek. Tony never knew what to call his father. When he lived with Antonio until he was four years old, he used to say Papa but he stopped that when he went back to live with Maria. Thereafter, out of respect, Tony refused to call him Antonio and he could never quite bring himself to call him Papa. Through the years he just talked with his father without addressing him by any name. But this night was different and as he held his father he said, "Papa, I'm so glad to see you. Come in. Mama is waiting for you."

The change was not lost on Antonio. He had to fight back the tears as he embraced Tony all the more. All Antonio could manage was to nod his head.

Maria had owned the house for six years but Antonio had never been inside before. The front door opened into a small foyer directly in front of a long staircase on the left that led to the second floor. A darkened hallway along the right side of the stairs led to the kitchen. Immediately to the right of the front door was a pair of glass French doors. Tony directed his father to go through the doors into the living room and then to the left, into the dining room that had been converted into a bedroom for his mother.

"Papa, I'm going upstairs. When you are ready to leave just let yourself out."

They embraced once more and Tony went upstairs. Antonio's emotions prevented him from saying anything. He took off his coat, scarf, and hat and hung them on a mirrored valet stand in the hallway. He took off his rubbers and opened one of the doors and walked into a dimly lit living room.

"In here, Antonio." He looked to his left into the darkened dining room and could barely make out the bed. "In here," he heard her say again and he just followed her voice. She was lying in bed with her head propped up on some pillows. He walked toward her voice. There was a chair that Tony had thoughtfully placed next to the bed.

"Sit here, my love, sit here and talk with me."

His eyes were adjusting to the dim light coming from the living room and he was able to make out her face. She looked so drawn and exhausted. It broke his heart to see his beautiful Maria reduced to this. Her hair was straw-like with no shine to it. Her eyes were sunken into her skull. Her fleshless cheekbones were almost protruding through her taut skin. Her full red lips were thin and colorless. He took her hand in both of his and bent over her and gently kissed her on the mouth and sat down.

"Maria, how are you feeling?"

"I'm holding up, I just feel so weak and frustrated. When I am sedated the pain is not too bad but then I don't think very clearly. I haven't taken my medication today because I wanted to talk with you this last time."

He started to speak but she interrupted, "No, dear Antonio, it is true, don't let us waste time by pretending that it is not. My time has come."

"Oh Maria, your pain is mine. You belong to me and I don't know how I will be able to let go of you."

"Antonio, we had our love and we still have it, never forget that, never forget what we have been to each other. It is a rare thing that we have. I know of no one else who has experienced a love like ours and to make it perfect we are also best friends. The only fault is that it is illicit in the eyes of society and the church."

He was quick to interject, "I don't look at it that way. I am only concerned with how God looks at it and He knows that what we have is honest and without malice. We intended to hurt no one, although I know we have. There was no lust, neither of us pursued the other, it just happened. We could not deny our emotions. It would have been like denying our very selves."

"I know, my love, I know. It was as though life played a dirty trick on us. Bringing us together too late, when we each belonged to someone else."

"Maria, you know how I married Joanna. It was something we drifted into; our families and friends always expected marriage of us. We never explored any other life. I tell you now, as I have before, the only reason I never left her was because she is a good woman and never did me any harm. She was the bride of my youth and the mother of my children. What we had aside from that was a long acquaintance, nothing more. I cannot even say that we were friends. Certainly we were never intellectual friends and yes, I must say it, we were never equals. So don't ever feel guilty about it. You never took me away from her. We lived together and did what we were supposed to do. I am sorry that she did not have some kind of love in her life that would be a personal satisfaction for her. When the children came, she buried herself in their lives and there was no room for me, and I did the same thing. It was the family that mattered. That kept us together and that is why I never left her. Neither of us knew any other way until I met you. Please believe me when I tell you that you never had anything to do with our failed marriage. It was not a strong bond even before I met you. Don't torture yourself on that account."

"Antonio, I am sorry for all of the people in the whole world who did not have what we had, including Joanna. I thought I had it with Giovanni. Oh yes, I loved him with a strong love but it was a different kind of love than the one he had for me. His was a shallow, physical love and that kind does not last. Believe me when I say that when he became a different Giovanni, when he was no longer the person I had loved and married, I was devastated. It was as if he died and another man took his place. Once my Giovanni was no more, my love for him was no more, and that was long before he was killed. I lost him before we moved to Youngstown but I thought that I found him again there. We should have never moved back to Newark; it was a mistake because I lost him again. But through it all I always loved you. Antonio, is it possible for a woman to love two men at

296

the same time? I was in such turmoil then. But when Giovanni left me for the second time that solved the problem. I didn't care anymore and when he was killed I was sorry for him, as I am sorry for anyone who dies, but it was a little different because he was the father of Ralph and Michael. They lost a father and that was a tragedy. Even Josephine suffered because she looked on him as a father. With you it was never something that I had lost. Even when we parted and I moved away my love for you never diminished. I took it with me. And that last night we had together before I moved to Youngstown, I thought it would be our last. I resigned myself to never seeing you again. I was determined that I would do what I was supposed to do but life brought us back together again, we did not plan it. Do you think God is angry with me? I will see Him soon and I am afraid of Him."

"Don't be afraid, my love. God made us all and knows what our problems are better than we do. If He is angry, it is like a father being angry with a child."

"Antonio, do you really think there is a hell? I don't know. How could God put someone in hell? That is an evil thing and God can't do anything evil."

"Yes. God can't do anything evil but that is not the issue. I believe that anyone who wants to be with God will be with God because that is what God wants. If people do not want to be with God then even God cannot force them to accept Him. We are free to do whatever we want. If God could force us to do something we don't want to do then we were never free to start with and if we are not free then we can't choose. No, God chooses everyone with His free will. We either accept or reject Him with our free will. For those who reject God, eternity will be without God and that's what hell is. We make the choice; God has already made His. So don't be afraid Maria, I know that you have made your choice and so have I. If in our lives we have made God angry, then we will have to be held accountable. What that accountability will be I don't know. But whatever it is, we will not be separated from Him because he has chosen us and we have chosen Him. I believe it and I know that you believe it too."

He saw her wince with pain and asked if there was anything he could do. "Do you want me to leave?"

"No, not just yet, stay with me a little while longer and when you leave I will take a pill that will put me to sleep."

They were quiet for a while, both lost in their own thoughts. She could barely see his face but she was able to make out those deep blue eyes she loved so much. She was hoping that he could not see her very well. She did not want his last memory of her to be the way she looked now. She thought of the beautiful body she once had. Antonio liked to stare at her naked body; he could not take his eyes off her, especially when she was standing in front of him.

She remembered the warm feeling that would engulf her knowing that she was giving him such pleasure; that she was the object of his desire. But that was all gone now. She tried to shake her head to drive those thoughts away like she used to do but she did not have the strength to move her head. *'My God, how can I think of those things now. I'm sixty-four and I'm dying.'*

She had lost so much weight. Her firm breasts were no more, lying flat against her chest. Her hands were devoid of any flesh. She could only imagine what her face looked like. She had not seen herself in a mirror in months. She did not want to remember herself as she was now. She wanted the memory of how she had been. Thankfully she had still retained her youthful appearance the last time they were together at Ogden Street. *'Good, that's the way he will remember me.'* A sharp pain jolted her back to reality.

"Antonio, there is something I want you to do for me."

"Anything," he replied.

"I want you to promise that you will stay in contact with Tony. He loves you, I know he does, but he has such mixed emotions about you. He wants you as his father but he is so hurt that you cannot be his father. He does not remember those few years he lived with you. He thinks he does but that's only because I have told him about it. He only remembers living with me and he never knew Giovanni at all. I don't think you will ever be able to win over Josephine. She has gotten to the point where she just denies that you exist. In that way she can think that you never happened, that we never happened. Well, if that is what she needs in order to cope with it, then let her be. I have tried so many times to explain to her that there are no illegitimate children only illegitimate parents. But she cannot accept you and me together. So when you see Tony, try not to involve Josephine in any way. Do you promise me?"

"Yes, dear Maria, I promise you but not just for you but for me also. I love him. He is our son together. It hurts not to have Josephine too but I promise never to make trouble over it. And I promise also to see little Anthony. He is our grandson. I will never tell him who I am; why burden him? If Tony wants to tell him when he is old enough to understand, then I leave it to him to do so. These things I promise you."

She smiled and said, "I never paid you back for the loan you made to me for the house."

"Don't think of such things."

"Antonio, I have signed the house over to Ferdinand and Josephine. I did it when I was still angry with Ralph and I know that Tony is not ready to carry the house. He and Edith are just starting out. I did it because Ferdinand promised to let Michael live here always and Tony too. Ferdinand is an honorable man and I know he will keep his promise and care for Michael. I am so grateful to Edith for the care she gives to him. Even Florence comes over to help with him. My affairs are in order now and that is a great relief for me."

For hours they alternated between conversation and silence. They smiled when they could and unseen tears rolled down their faces. He never let go of her hand. Finally she whispered, "What time is it?"

He looked at his watch and was amazed at how the time had passed. "It is almost six; it will be dawn soon."

She breathed a deep sigh. "I love you with all my very being, Antonio. But I think you should go now. Soon the baby will wake up and Edith and Tony will get up too. You should not be here when they come downstairs. Please dear Antonio, go. I am so tired. I want to go to sleep now."

He sat motionless for a minute. He bent over her and kissed her gently on the mouth with all the love he could communicate and he felt her love return to him. She felt the tears falling from his eyes mingling with hers and rolling down her cheeks. He pulled slightly away from her and whispered.

"Good-bye, Maria."

"Good-bye, Antonio."

He let go of her hand and stood up. His shadow crossed her face and he could not see her. He turned away from her and walked back into the living room and into the foyer. He put on his coat, scarf, and hat. He reached down and put on his rubber overshoes then walked out the front door closing it silently behind him. He stood on the porch for a moment while he put on his gloves. It had stopped snowing and the sky had cleared revealing a magnificent view of the heavens, and a bright, crescent moon. The ground was covered with about two inches of pure white snow with a bluish tint to it. The reflection of the moonlight on the snow made it seem almost as day although dawn was still an hour away. He decided to walk home.

He was alone on the street. Only the crunching of the snow beneath his feet broke the silence. He walked down Garside Street, crossed Third Avenue, then Fourth and then across Bloomfield Avenue. He walked past the house that Maria had bought back in 1909. *'God, that was twenty years ago.'* He used to visit her there to see Tony and sometimes Josephine. He recalled when he would pick her up to drive her to see Michael when he was away at the Arthur Home. Once more he felt the pain that Josephine was never friendly. He smiled as he recalled the few times that he and Maria made love in that house.

A little farther on he crossed Park Avenue and then Sixth. Looking up Sixth Avenue toward the park he could see the huge, uncompleted Sacred

Heart Cathedral. *'My God, will they ever finish it, it's been almost thirty years since they started!'* He continued along Garside Street until it ended at Seventh Avenue and he crossed over to the other side. On his left was Wood Street where Tony had lived with him just after he and Pasquale were born. That had been a very difficult and stressful time. He passed Maria's old house on Seventh Avenue where she had lived after she returned from Youngstown, twenty-eight years ago. That house was where the twins had been born and Michael had become blind and Pasquale had died. His heart was heavy with sad memories.

Antonio wondered what would have happened if he and Maria had not separated the twins. Would Tony have died in the terrible epidemic too? He had taken Tony away from Maria only to bring him back to her a few years after Giovanni was murdered. There were no good times in that house either.

He passed Boyden Street where Grace was born back in 1900. Finally he got to his house on John Street just as the eastern sky began to light up. It had been a long walk; he was oblivious of the time.

As he climbed the steps to his porch he thought, *'Oh, dear God, I will never see her again.'*

Two days later, on Saturday, March 2nd, Maria died. It was Giustina who told him, dear, trusted, friend Giustina, loyal to the very end.

*****

It hurt that he could not go to Maria's house for the wake but Antonio was determined to go to the interment. On Monday she was going to be buried at the East Ridgelawn Cemetery in an area that was called Delawanna, a section of the town of Clifton. He drove his truck out to Delawanna, past the main entrance driveway to the cemetery and parked up the street where it would not be seen.

There was a small gate leading to a footpath that led directly into the burial area. He had no trouble finding the gravesite; it was the only one that was open with the dirt piled high to one side and some chairs opposite facing the grave. He positioned himself a short distance away at the edge of a small clump of trees on a slight knoll so that he had an unobstructed view looking down onto the grave. He took off his hat and waited.

It was a beautiful sunny day and there were only slight traces of snow left on the ground. Soon it would all be gone. The temperature still had winter in it but was mixed with the promise of the coming spring. He saw the funeral cortege enter the cemetery and the cars park in the lane just beyond the grave. The hearse was the first to park and immediately the pallbearers carried the casket from the car to the gravesite and rested it on straps over the open hole.

300

The family began to leave their cars and wend their way among the gravestones toward the casket. He was annoyed at how few people attended. None of those for whom she had been *La Scrittore* were there. Dear Giustina with her husband came to make their last farewell. Also the pastor of their Italian Baptist Church and a few people that were in the bible study group had come.

Josephine and Ferdinand led the way with their two sons. Next came Ralph and Florence with their daughters and son. Ralph was beside himself with grief. Then Edith followed holding little Anthony in her arms followed by Tony with Michael clutching his arm for guidance. Michele, the undertaker, was there. It was he who had buried Augusta and Pasquale and now he was burying their mother. In death their bodies would be apart. The children were buried in the Catholic Holy Sepulcher Cemetery over on Central Avenue in Newark. And only God knew where Giovanni was buried.

Everyone gathered around the grave, the women sitting on the chairs with their youngest children in their laps, the men standing behind them. Antonio looked down at Edith holding Anthony, his grandson whom Maria loved so much.

The pastor started the ritual with readings and prayers. Antonio could not hear what was said but he could see the entire ceremony. When the pastor was finished, the family members each placed a flower on the casket, one by one, and then started to walk back to the cars. The last to leave was Tony still guiding Michael. As Tony turned he faced the trees where Antonio was standing and their eyes met. Tony knew that his father would be watching from somewhere. The eye contact did not last long but in it they exchanged their feelings for each other and the loss they both shared. For the first time Tony felt a deep sorrow for his father. He turned away and led Michael to a waiting car.

When they were all gone and the cars had driven off out of sight, Antonio walked down to the grave. The casket was still resting on the straps above the grave. He picked up some flowers and placed them on the casket as the gravediggers began lowering the coffin into the open hole. He did not want to see them shovel dirt onto his beloved Maria. He turned away as they started. He put his hat back on and slowly walked down the path toward his truck.

As he walked out of the cemetery he sighed and thought aloud, '*Well, I guess this afternoon I should go down and cancel the room at Ogden Street.*'

THE END